W9-CEQ-590

Chelsea Quinn Yarbro

BLOOD GAMES

a novel of historical horror

Third in the

Count de Saint-Germain series

ST. MARTIN'S PRESS
NEW YORK

this one is for

Michael Moorcock

with love and music

Library of Congress Cataloging in Publication Data

Yarbro, Chelsea Quinn, 1942-
Blood games.

I. Title.
PZ4.Y25B [PS3575.A7] 813'.5'4 79-22853
ISBN 0-312-08441-2

 For information, write:
St. Martin's Press, Inc. 175 Fifth Ave., New York, N.Y. 10010
Manufactured in the United States of America

This is a work of fiction. Its setting is historical and some of the characters are based upon actual persons living in the time of this novel. All reasonable effort has been made to re-create the conditions and attitudes of first-century Imperial Rome with as few distortions as possible.

The historical events described in the course of the book are reconstructed from various sources, whenever possible from contemporary accounts and eyewitness reports. When such documentation is not available, or reports conflict, the description resulting has been arrived at through exigencies of plot rather than to grind any philosophical or academic ax.

At first, such technological devices as metered chariots and sedan chairs, central radiant heat, indoor plumbing, eyeglasses, assembly-line factories and fast-food stores may seem highly anachronistic, yet such things did indeed exist at the time depicted.

The interpretation of the characters of actual persons, along with those of the fictional ones, is wholly that of the writer, and should not be construed as representing or intended to represent any person or persons living or dead.

PART I

Atta Olivia Clemens, Domita Silius

Text of a letter from an Egyptian apothecary and spice merchant to Ragoczy Sanct' Germain Franciscus in Rome.

To the man now calling himself Ragoczy Sanct' Germain Franciscus, the servant of Imhotep sends his greetings.

I have your requests for spices and medicines and will do my utmost to fulfill your commands to me. There may be some trouble getting a few of the rarer items, as it is not easy to move about the land now that the Romans are here. Be patient with me, my master, and I will see that you have all that you require of me. Two of the items you specify must come along the Silk Road and it may take more than a year to bring them. You have said that you will wait any reasonable length of time, yet I feel I must warn you of these circumstances. I feel sure you would want me to be confidential in regards to your order, and so I will not mention by name the things you have asked me to get for you.

Earth from Dacia is another matter. We may provide that amply, although I am surprised to find you are without it. Nine large barrels of it come with this letter to you. You say that you are building a villa outside of the walls of Rome and some distance from the Praetorian camp, and I have assumed you need the earth for that. We are also, as partial filling of your order, sending the fine tiles you specified, and dyed cotton and linen in the colors you have stated. By the end of harvest time we should have the cinnabar, turquoise, carnelian, jasper, agate, sardonyx and alabaster in the quantities you wish, and will send them to you as quickly as possible. The selenite might take longer, for moonstones of the quality you wish are not easily found. I will send agents into

Parthia and Hind to search. Do not, I beg you, be disappointed if they do not find your gems at once. You say that you can obtain rubies and diamonds, and so I will not search for those. Should you change your mind, you need only send me a message and I will procure the jewels you desire.

You indicate in your letter that you do not anticipate visiting this land for some years. It saddened me to learn of this, for your return is much hoped for among those few of our brothers that are left. You would be welcomed heartily by all that remain here. Our school, of course, now must meet clandestinely, and there is little we can do to change this. Not only do the Romans distrust us, but our own people, seduced by Greeks and Romans alike, think that our ways are outmoded. The priests of Imhotep are become merchants because they fear to heal! Should you come back to us, it might be otherwise.

Forgive this outburst, my master. It comes from my despair, not from your absence. It is well that you are in Rome and not here. Alexandria is a shame to us, and Luxor is forgotten. You told me once that if I should walk into the desert, I would not find a peaceful death, but ravening madness. So I will not walk into the desert, though I think that I have lived too far beyond my years.

Whatever you ask of me, and the rest of us, it shall be done. Yet do not condemn me if I am disheartened.

Farewell, to you and my brother Aumtehoutep
Sennistis, High Priest

1

DUSK HAD FALLEN, turning the very air of Rome an intense blue in the last struggle of day with night. The evening was warm and the breath of the city pungent, but the air in the Greek-style atrium smelled of cinnamon, scented by the dozen little braziers where incense burned. Now the slaves were busy lighting the hanging lanterns and setting out the low tables beside the couches where the guests would recline for the banquet.

Petronius strolled through the atrium, half-smiling as he watched the slaves work. He was tall for a Roman, with fashionably cut brown hair that was touched with gray now. At thirty-four his attractive face had a curiously unfinished look and his dark blue eyes were tired and old under straight brows. Rather than a toga, he wore a charioteer's tunica, but instead of rough linen, his was made of fine white silk. He stopped beside the fountain and sniffed at the water as he caught it in one hand. A faint scent of jasmine perfumed the fountain. Satisfied with the fragrance, Petronius stepped back. Near him, hanging on the bow of a blooming peach tree, a tintinnabulum sounded its little phallic chimes as the evening breeze touched it. Petronius reached out and negligently tweaked the branch so that the tiny silver bells jangled together. He was about to go to the kitchens at the back of the house when his houseman, an old Greek slave called Artemidorus, stopped him.

"Master, a visitor," said Artemidorus as he hurried into the atrium.

"A visitor? Not a guest?" The banquet would not begin for almost an hour, and it was more usual for the guests to arrive late than early. "Who is it?"

The houseman bowed slightly. "A Senator."

Petronius sighed. "What does he want?" For he undoubtedly wanted something, which was part of the price exacted of those who stood high in the young Emperor's esteem.

"He did not say, master. Shall I refuse him?" The old Greek was eager to do so, and he smiled as he asked.

"No, better not. He'll only come back later and be more insistent. Show him . . . where? . . . into the receiving room, I guess, and tell him I'll be with him shortly. It would be a pleasure to keep him waiting, but with guests coming . . ." He felt resigned to the company of the Senator. "Artemidorus, do you know which Senator this is?"

The houseman paused. "Yes. I know him." He said it with distaste, and the faintest sign of fear.

"Aaaaah." Petronius drew the word out. "Tell me."

"It is Cornelius Justus Silius." There was more disgust in his voice.

"What can that old ferret want with me?" he wondered aloud. "Bring him here, then. And make no attempt to hide our activities. He will want me to include him, and it will be a great pleasure to decline." He motioned Artemidorus away and signaled one of the slaves to bring a chair from the house.

"Just the one?" the slave asked, leaving off rubbing the tables with lemon rind.

"For the Senator," Petronius said sweetly, then chose the nearest couch and sank down upon it.

He did not have long to wait for his inopportune visitor. Very shortly Artemidorus returned, escorting the Senator Cornelius Justus Silius. "Good evening, Justus," Petronius said, indicating the chair the slave had brought.

Justus eyed the chair, fuming at this minor, casual insult.

The Senator was an expert in such matters, having over the years learned how to dash hopes with the lift of his brows. He was close to fifty now, and had weathered three severe political storms since he had come to the Senate twenty-three years before. With a slight shrug of his heavy shoulders he took the chair, concealing his dislike of Petronius with a condescending smile. "I heard you were expecting guests, and so I won't stay."

Petronius leaned back on the couch and watched Justus through narrowed eyes.

"I have a minor problem, and ordinarily I wouldn't trouble you with it, but I haven't been much in the imperial presence of late, and you're more familiar with the latest . . ."

"Gossip? Quirks? Outrages?" Petronius suggested.

"Imperial tastes!" Justus snapped. "I'm planning on sponsoring a few days of Great Games, and as editor, I would want to present those encounters that would most please the Emperor, particularly if you can suggest some novelty that would satisfy Nero. I'd be much appreciative, Petronius. And while I'm not a rich man—"

"What would you call rich?" Petronius interrupted with a disarming smile. "You have eight estates and your family has always been wealthy, hasn't it? I had not heard that you had suffered any misfortune of late."

Justus moved uncomfortably and adjusted his toga. "It's true that I have some substance, but my lamentable cousin did much to compromise our name when he made that ill-considered alliance with Messalina . . . Claudius ruined that woman, and Gaius should have realized it." He watched Petronius closely.

"That was years ago," his reluctant host said, sounding bored. "Nero is not overly attentive to the glorification of Divus Claudius. Surely a man of your rank and substance does not need a kind word from me."

"Not a kind word, no," Justus said heavily. "But the Great Games must be spectacular and original enough to bring me recognition once more."

"Why? Are you plotting again?" He asked it lightly, with elegant mockery, but the question was serious.

"I?" Justus shook his head, an expression of gentle sagacity on his rough-hewn features. "No. I should think the family has learned its lesson by now. We know what plots lead to."

"But you seek to return to Nero's notice," Petronius pointed out politely.

"That's a different matter." Justus gave Petronius a measuring look. He had heard that Titus Petronius Niger was more subtle than he seemed and more intelligent than was thought. There were those verses, of course, and strange, sarcastic tales he was said to have written. He decided on another tack. "It does me no good at all to sit back, tend my estates and go to the Senate upon occasion if I don't have a sensible relationship with Nero. Think a moment. He could seize my lands, imprison me or my wife, or both of us, he could decide that he must have all my revenues, leaving me not precisely a beggar, but close enough. If he is well-inclined on my behalf, then I need have no worries. It would be a great weight off my mind. I confess, since I've married again, I've felt a growing need to make my position secure, not for myself, of course, but for Olivia, who is certainly destined to outlive me."

"Your first two wives didn't," Petronius observed.

"Corinna is still alive. It may appear cruel to divorce a madwoman, but there, what could I do? I had no heirs and was not likely to get them with her. She is well-tended and I have reports from those set to care for her." He did not want to talk about his first two wives, but it would be unwise to avoid the subject. He knew Roman opinion came out of gossip and rumors, and he could not afford any more hints that Corinna's insanity and Valentina's death were his fault. "Valentina, well, nothing but good of the dead, naturally. An unfortunate young woman."

"All your friends must hope that Olivia will not be similarly unfortunate." Petronius decided that he did not like

Cornelius Justus Silius. He had long considered the old Senator an unpleasant and self-serving man, but this latest hypocrisy for his wives was ugly. Only the most cynical Roman would feel anything but pity for Atta Olivia Clemens, who at age twenty had been all but sold to Justus by her high-bred but ruined family.

"The welfare of my wife is my concern," Justus said tightly.

"Yes, it is," Petronius agreed. "But about these Games you mentioned . . . ?"

"I would want to have them in June, before it is too hot to enjoy them. It may be a little late to start, but with your assistance I'm certain that a creditable number of contests can be arranged. I've already spoken to the masters at the Great School and the Dacian School and they tell me that my fighters are ready to appear in the arena. I watched a retiarius work out with a secutor, and was quite pleased. The retiarius handled his net like a veteran and when the secutor pulled the trident out of his hands, he was still able to immobilize him with the net. They train well at the Dacian School, just as well as the Great School. The secutor . . . I saw him out of his armor. A great beast of a man, some sort of bastard German, and itching for a real fight. I may want to have a closer look at that one. They call him Arnax, but I gather it's a nickname: his native one is probably unpronounceable." His eyes were distant, lingering on the hard muscles and brutish face of his German secutor.

Petronius' soft, lazy voice interrupted his thoughts. "You can't have an entire course of Games depending on your fighters alone." He had seen the expression change on Justus' face and it confirmed his suspicions. "You'll have to arrange for others, as well. The masters of the Schools should be able to tell you who has fighters ready to go. The Bestiarii School will have new talents just now, too. I know of a Lusitanian who works with trained bears. He hasn't been seen too much. I think that Marcus Sextus Marco owns him, but I may be wrong." He knew for a fact that the Lusitanian bear trainer had been sold a few days before to an unnamed buyer, but it pleased him to think he could send Justus on a fool's errand.

"Bears? That's a start, I suppose." Justus shifted in the chair and wished that Petronius would send for wine.

"That foreigner, Ragoczy Sanct' Germain Franciscus, surely you've met him?" Petronius said with sly condescension. "He has a very special charioteer, an Armenian woman with her own team of horses. I've only seen her once. You might find out if he'll let you have her for your Games. He's got access to animals, too, if you're planning to have a venation. Ordinary wild beasts are no longer interesting, unless you have a tribe of pygmies to hunt them. See if Franciscus can find you a few unusual animals for the hunt."

Justus nodded slowly. He had considered opening his Games with something other than a hunt, even though it was traditional, but might reconsider. "No, I don't know this fellow. A foreigner, you say?"

"Apparently from Dacia, but not a Daci himself. His body slave is the most arrogant Egyptian in Rome. Where have you been, Senator? Franciscus has been in Rome almost a year, and you say you haven't met him?" Petronius was enjoying his unwelcome guest's discomfort. He decided to make it worse. "He has been asked by the Emperor himself to teach him to play the Egyptian harp."

"Nero and music!" Justus scoffed, doing his best to ignore an unpleasant twinge of anxiety. "He will tire of it, and then this foreigner will look elsewhere for society."

"Perhaps." As he propped himself on his elbow, Petronius caught sight of Artemidorus gesturing impatiently from the other side of the garden. Time was getting short, he knew, and his guests would arrive soon.

Justus would have liked to object knowledgeably, yet could not. To any other man he would have shown an angry face and a rude departure, but he could not afford to alienate this infuriating man who lounged so insolently before him. "He has access to animals, you say?"

"Bacchus alone knows where he gets them. Tiger horses, white bears, tigers of all sorts, thick-coated leopards from beyond Hind, camels, Sythian hounds, broad-antlered deer from the far north, great elk from Britannia, he can get them all, and more besides. He claims to have blood relatives everywhere to do his bidding." Petronius laughed low in his throat.

The list was astonishing. Justus listened greedily, wondering how he might approach this foreigner. "It would be a splendid venation, with such animals," he said reflectively.

"Certainly one of your Blue friends will give you the introduction you wish. Not that the Blues are doing so well," he added sweetly. "Green, however . . ."

"Nero belongs to the Greens," Justus snapped. "No one

dares award too many prizes to the other racing companies. The Blue faction did well enough when Claudius was alive." For a moment he dwelt on the pettiness of the young Emperor and his blatant favor for his racing corporation. The factions were quite old, he reminded himself, and had survived longer than the Emperors.

"Of course," Petronius said soothingly. "I merely thought you might heed a gentle warning." He waited for Justus to interrupt, and when this did not happen, he went on, "If you must remain with the Blues, be a little circumspect with Nero. His devotion to the Greens is real, you know."

Justus all but snorted. "A foolish desire left over from his childhood."

"He still wears his hair like a charioteer," Petronius said. "His interest, believe me, is not idle. If you cannot respect that, think twice about trying to win his favor." He toyed with the silk tassel that hung from the knotted cord around his waist. "Was there anything else, Senator?"

While Claudius had been Caesar, no one would have dared to speak to Justus in that tone, but the world had changed. Justus tried to swallow his wrath. "Not of immediate importance, no. I am, naturally, grateful for the time you've given me."

Petronius doubted it, but nodded an offhanded acknowledgment. He waited for Justus to rise so he could bring this annoying interview to an end.

"There *is* one thing . . ." Justus said with a deliberately casual wave of his hand.

"I thought there might be." Petronius swallowed a sigh. "What is it, Senator? I regret that I haven't much more time to spare."

As if in response to a cue, Artemidorus hurried into the atrium. "Master, forgive my interruption, but the Greek pantomimes are here."

"Take them to my reception room, will you, Artemidorus? I won't be much longer. If they want to prepare themselves, they may use the solarium." He looked back at Justus. "What else was it you wanted?"

"By the Balls of Mars! . . ." Justus forced himself to stop this outburst. "Forgive me. I was impetuous." He grabbed at his spread knees through the folds of his toga. "The matter is, well, somewhat delicate."

"I would hardly have thought myself worthy of your confidence," Petronius remarked, anticipating the request that was to come.

"I'm not a young man," Justus said heavily. "No, not any longer. Yet I have a young wife." He paused portentously. "She is a creature of . . . appetites. The young so often are. I find that my energy is not what it was . . ."

Petronius felt an unaccustomed disgust as he recalled all the whispers he had heard about Cornelius Justus Silius. "If you mean that you like to watch hired men rape your wife so that you can satisfy yourself with her"—he ignored the sputtered objection that Justus began—"you must ask others to help you."

Justus was now too angry to guard his tongue. "A man with your reputation! Telling me that you will not pander to my—"

"I am the official arbiter of elegance, Senator. Elegance. Paying your gladiators to brutalize Atta Olivia Clemens hardly comes under my jurisdiction. Speak to that secutor of yours, that German you were telling me about, Arnax or whatever his name is. He should suit your purposes." This upsurge of indignation was as startling to Petronius as it was to Justus. With an effort of will he maintained his languid pose. "Believe me, Senator, I have no wish to interfere between man and wife. You must excuse me." He rose in one quick, graceful motion.

Justus remained seated a bit longer. "What you said of me is not true," he muttered.

"Isn't it? The rumors of Rome are always full of scandal. No doubt you've been maligned." There was very little conviction in his words. He looked down at the Senator. "I really must leave you now, Justus. The pantomimes are waiting."

"Effeminate Greeks, with their paints and postures! They might as well be priests of Attis!" He crossed his large, hard arms over his chest.

"I feel I should remind you that Nero admires Greek pantomimes almost as much as he admires charioteers." The words were soft, almost caressing.

"A passing fancy," Justus said firmly. "He is not yet thirty. Give him a few years and he will put such things behind him."

"And if he does not?" Petronius expected no answer and started away across the atrium, pausing only to add, "When you know more of your plans for the Games, come again and I will find some of the pantomimes you despise for entertainments between contests. Many of the Roman people share the Emperor's enthusiasm for them. There was a riot the last time this troupe performed."

Reluctantly Justus stood, displeased at the way the conversation had gone. "It will not be necessary."

"If you are determined to return to Nero's favor, you will learn otherwise." He picked one of the flowering branches from the peach tree in a wooden tub by the fountain, and the tintinnabulum shook its little phallic chimes at him.

"Are there other Games planned for the summer?" Justus hated to ask the question, particularly of this soft-spoken man. He had to know what competition he would have.

"Not in the Circus Maximus, in July. Four days of Games should be a welcome diversion, and you might be able to overshadow the Games of Italicus Fulcinius Gracchus." His smile was snide. "However, I doubt you will. With your permission, Senator." In the next moment he was gone from the atrium.

Justus glared after Petronius, wishing he could pursue the man and lash him as he would lash an insolent slave. The thought of that satisfaction brought a wolfish light to his curiously light brown eyes. There would be time for such revenge after he had gained the good wishes of Nero. A pity that the Emperor was so greatly influenced by Petronius. Perhaps, he thought, in time Nero would allow himself to be guided by wiser, more experienced men. He glanced scathingly at the slaves who had come into the atrium bearing bowls of spice-scented water. He rose slowly and walked toward the far end of the atrium, where Artemidorus waited to escort him from the house. At the fountain he paused, thinking what satisfaction it would give him to spit into the perfumed water. There would be time enough for that later, he promised himself, after the summer, after his Games, when the Emperor would seek him out and do him honor.

With this thought to cheer him he strode through the peach trees toward Artemidorus.

Text of a letter from the Greek stonemason Mnastydos to the Emperor Nero.

To my glorious Emperor on the twentieth day of October in the 816th Year of the City, hail!

Too much honor have you given me in allowing me to address you directly, O Nero, but as you have charged me to inform you of my thoughts and observations concerning the damage of the terrible fire that swept through the city at the height of summer, I will do all that is in my power to obey you.

The destruction, as anyone who has walked through the rubble in the streets knows, is calamitous. Many of the shops near the Circus Maximus cannot be replaced in any way, for the fire burned there too fiercely and too long. Their loss, however, is minor compared to the catastrophe that has been visited upon so many of our noblest and oldest buildings. The treasures you specifically asked about, in the old Temple of Minerva, are wholly lost. It grieves me to tell you this, for I know in what esteem you held those fine trophies. The building itself is no longer safe to enter, like so many others. It is true that its columns still stand, but they are no longer sound. A hard winter, long rains or a heavy storm might be all that is needed to topple the whole. Since you have asked that I give you my opinion, it is this: take down the Temple of Minerva while the marble may yet be salvaged, and use it for your own splendid new palace. We cannot restore the temple to its full glory, but the marble, while it is intact, may be used again. It is fortunate that the Temple was not in the heart of the fire, or the marble would have been ruined as well as the treasures of the Temple.

The war prizes you mentioned have melted down into bits of twisted metal. One or two of these have been recovered, but they have been cracked and blackened by the fire. As you requested, I have taken those that are intact to the foreigner Ragoczy Sanct' Germain Franciscus at his villa outside the walls of the city. I have his assurances that if there is anything that may be done to save them, he will do it. He has already repaired the three alabaster urns that were taken to him, and with such skill that it is difficult to see where the fire touched them.

The extra rows of benches installed in the Circus Maximus for the Games of Cornelius Justus Silius have fallen. Without them the seats will accommodate no more than sixty thousand. It might be wise to build them up again, since the crowds were so great at his Games that every seat was filled and we heard that all the aisles were packed. The gigantic elk from Britannia that were not killed in the venation died in the fire. It was a shame to lose those magnificent animals. Silius was fortunate indeed to be able to show them in the arena, and would have realized a great price for them if the fire had not claimed them as its own.

With your permission, I will instruct my fellow stonemasons to remove any usable stone from the buildings damaged by the fire so that your architects may inspect it and select that which is suitable for your palace. The rest may go to repairs of the Circus Maximus, so that the Great Games may continue. Should you require more speed, I know of two groups of stonemasons, slaves of your esteemed Senator Marcellus Sixtus Tredis and of your great general Cneaus Domitius Corbulo. These stonemasons are most highly skilled in their work, and would undoubtedly exert themselves most mightily on your behalf. Certainly neither the Senator nor the general would begrudge you the use of their stonemasons.

The Jewish prisoners who have been set to this task are useless, as they have no experience with fine marbles. Set them elsewhere, O Emperor, where their skills and strength may be of use, and find us more Greek stonemasons, or you will lose even more of your beautiful marbles through their ignorance.

A few of the insulae that were thought lost may be rebuilt, should their owners deem it worthwhile, but I have already reported to them on that business, and await their answers. Should it be your desire that we turn our attention to those buildings, we will do it at once with all our hearts. If you do not give us orders to the contrary, we will set to work rebuilding the insulae upon the request of the owners.

Most humbly I thank you for hearing my report. It is an undeserved honor to address you, O my Emperor. When you gave the order that freed me, you made me the more your slave. Now that you have asked for this report, when you have so many around you of greater skill and higher station than I, my devotion is rekindled in an already ardent breast. Any task you require, great or small, you have only to ask it of me and I will surely do it, in gratitude of the deference you have been pleased to show me.

Unto death I am your man
Mnastydos
Stonemason of Rhodes
(by the hand of Eugenius, the scribe at the Temple of Mercury)

2

HERE UNDER the stands the stink was worse, hanging miasmically on the hot, unmoving air. The sounds from the stand above were muted by the thick stones, though it was occasionally difficult to determine if the loud, mindless shout came from the throats of men or animals. In their wall brackets torches flickered, turning the underground twilight to a dull, ruddy glare.

Necredes, Master of the Bestiarii for this day's Games, stood beside the burly executioner from Dalmatia as he fingered the thongs that held the wrists of a dense-muscled young woman to an iron ring.

"Tighter, I think," Necredes said, ignoring the cries of

outrage that came from his prisoner. "Stretch her high before you lay her back open."

The executioner nodded as he obeyed, cursing when the young woman tried to force her knee into his groin. "The Twins save me from Armenians," he grunted as he bent to secure her feet.

"Free me!" the young woman panted, fury in her eyes as she fought her restraints. "You have no right! Only my master can do this!" She was able to land one hard kick in the executioner's ribs before he finished knotting the thin ropes around her ankles.

"You disobeyed," Necredes said in an oddly satisfied tone. "You have defied an express order."

The young woman glared at him. "I spent eight years training my horses. I will not put them into the arena with lions." Her dark hair was cut short and fell in disheveled tangles around her young vixen's face. She was strong and her short tunica revealed the well-defined sinew of her arms and legs. There was no fear in her.

Necredes clicked his tongue in disapproval. "You will do what I tell you to do, slave." He motioned to his executioner as he stood back. "Twelve lashes."

The executioner stepped to a low table where his instruments lay. There were mallets, scrapers, knives and hooks on one side, and his various whips on the other; plumbatae with long lashes twined through heavy rings of lead, flagelli with knots of bone tied to the ends of broad hide strips; and rods with long tails of leather braided with wire. It was one of these last the executioner selected, slicing the air with it once or twice to get the feel of it. The muted scream of the lash seemed louder than the din of the crowd above them. Satisfied, the executioner took up his position.

At the first fall of the rod, the woman stifled a scream. There was a line of pain across her shoulders that burned with the intensity of acid. She braced herself for the second blow, her arms tightened to take the impact as she had been trained to do so many years ago when her father had taught her to dive off the back of a galloping horse. This was not the same. The second stripe fell across the first, and she gasped as a hot, hideous weakness loosened her taut body. She felt blood on her back, and looked quickly down at her torn tunica, aghast at the rusty stain that spread rapidly through the fabric. There were ten more blows to endure, and for the only time in her life she doubted her courage.

"Again," Necredes said, not quite able to disguise the pleasure of this command.

The executioner raised his arm, his shoulders bunching for the hard downward swing.

"Stop that." The voice, though low and pleasant, carried a quality of indisputable authority. Necredes and the executioner turned toward the sound.

The man who stepped into the unsteady torchlight was somewhat taller than the average Roman, but that was the least obvious element of his foreignness. He was dressed in a black knee-length Persian gown embroidered at the neck and cuffs of elbow-length sleeves with red and silver thread. Tight black Persian trousers clung to his legs and were tucked into heeled Scythian boots of red leather. Dark, loose curls framed his aristocratic face. His mirthless half-smile was fixed and his compelling eyes glowed.

Necredes stiffened. "Franciscus."

The stranger nodded, motioning to another man who now stepped into the light. He was younger than his master, and though he wore an amber slave's collar, his bearing was noble. Tall and slight, but with the massive shoulders and arms of a charioteer, he wore a racing tunica of the Reds and carried a cloak over one arm.

"The punishment!" Necredes snapped, hating the sight of the elegant foreigner.

This time the executioner hesitated.

"I said, stop that." Ragoczy Sanct' Germain Franciscus reached out and caught the lash as it came down. The sound of the strike was sharply loud and the executioner paled as the foreigner's small, beautiful hand closed on the rod and pulled it away. The executioner was a slave and he had struck a free man, an uncondemned man.

The black-clad intruder seemed to sense his thoughts. "On whose orders?" he asked.

"A-a-ah . . ." The executioner waved his hands toward Necredes, too frightened to speak. He had flogged too many men to death to be willing to face such a sentence. If the stranger brought complaint against him for the inadvertent blow he had received, that would be his fate—flogging with the murderous plumbatae.

Sanct' Germain turned toward the Master of the Bestiarii.

"Who gave you permission to beat one of my slaves?" He spoke pleasantly enough, with greater cordiality than Necredes would have expected under the best of circumstances, and the cool courtesy terrified him more than open hostility would have.

"She . . ." Necredes stopped to clear his throat so that he would sound less frightened. "She disobeyed a specific order from the editor himself."

"What order?" Sanct' Germain had favored the woman with nothing more than one quick look, but he stood near her now, and touched her side once. "Who gave you the right?" In a sudden wrathful movement, he flung the leather-braided rod away from him. "Well?"

"She disobeyed . . ." Necredes began again and his throat was quite dry.

"A specific order," Sanct' Germain finished for him. "On whose authority did you command my slave *anything*!" He came across the evil-smelling room. "Answer me."

"It is my right, as Master of the Bestiarii, when the editor requests . . ." The words sounded ludicrous to Necredes now, and involuntarily he stepped back.

Sanct' Germain pursued him. "The woman is mine, Necredes. She belongs to me. What I tell her, she will do. No one else has that right. No one." He had forced the Master of the Bestiarii to retreat to the far wall, and he stood over him, the force of his gaze as potent as Greek fire.

Necredes cringed away from the hated, melodic voice. "As Master of the Bestiarii—"

"Master? The vilest rat is more worthy of that title than you." He turned away, disgusted. "Cut her down," he ordered the executioner, and as that frightened man hurried with clumsy hands to obey, Ragoczy Sanct' Germain Franciscus returned to his slave and looked down at her with compassion in his penetrating eyes. "Tishtry?" he said gently.

"I am . . ." Absurdly, since the worst of her danger was past, she felt tears well in her eyes. A moment later the thongs that bound her to the iron ring were cut, and to her horror, she almost collapsed at her master's feet.

His strong arm caught and held her until she could stand again, and although he did not look at her, there was comfort in that sustaining touch.

"Franciscus," Necredes spoke up from the far side of the room, the name deliberately loud.

Not by so much as the flicker of an eyelid did Sanct' Germain give any indication that he had heard Necredes call his name. He turned to the charioteer. "Kosrozd, my body slave is waiting. Give Tishtry your cloak."

The charioteer opened the garment he had been carrying, holding it for Tishtry, who was now trembling violently.

"Gently," Sanct' Germain admonished him. "She's bleeding. Aumtehoutep will have to take great care of her." He helped Kosrozd place the cloak around Tishtry's shoulders, paying no attention to Necredes' muttering.

Tishtry looked up when she had once more got control of herself. The light from the torches caught on the collar she wore, made of amber and embossed with her master's name. "My horses . . . ?"

"Kosrozd will see to them. They are safe," he assured her as he touched her tangled hair. "They will be taken to my villa tonight, when I leave the Circus."

She could not rid herself of worry and she gripped his arm tightly as she looked around the little stone room one last time. "Must I go? He"—she gave a scornful glance to Necredes—"might order someone else to drive them through the lions."

"I doubt he would be foolish enough to do that," was Sanct' Germain's soft, sinister reply.

"But he wants them in the arena." Her voice had risen, and she looked beseechingly from Sanct' Germain to Kosrozd.

"I give you my word, Tishtry, that no one but yourself will drive those horses. Will that satisfy you?" There was still sympathy in his voice but his eyes had hardened.

Both slaves knew that tone, and neither of them would ever question it. Tishtry lowered her eyes and nodded mutely.

"Go, then. Aumtehoutep is waiting." He stood aside for her, watching as she reluctantly allowed herself to be supported by Kosrozd. "When she is safe, Kosrozd, come back to me."

The executioner moved farther out of the light.

With the slaves gone, Necredes felt braver. He straightened up and strode the few necessary steps across the room to confront the foreigner. "Franciscus, you aren't Roman . . ."

"All the gods be thanked for that," he interpolated quietly.

"And it may be that you don't realize," Necredes went on through clenched teeth, "that it is the Masters who give the orders for the editors of the Great Games. I was not told by the editor to spare your Armenian slave and her horses. You cannot interfere in this way."

As Necredes faltered, Sanct' Germain regarded him with the air of someone finding a pustulant beggar in the kitchen. "How many others have you deceived with that explanation?" he asked. "Do you pretend that you are unaware of the law? Must I remind you of it?" His finely drawn brows lifted. "Had you forced Tishtry to enter the arena for a contest that would destroy her animals, since she has not been so condemned, she could accuse you in any open court, and you would have to pay not only the price of the horses that were destroyed at your order, but compensate her for the years it would take her to replace them. In addition to any damages I would require of you. *That*, Necredes, is Roman law, and has been since the time of Divus Julius."

It would not do to give ground now, Necredes thought. He raised his stubbled chin. "Do you also know the penalties for slave rebellion? That woman of yours tried to stab a Roman citizen. If she had succeeded in the attempt, she, and every slave you own, every one, Franciscus, would have been executed, probably in the arena." He managed to meet the foreigner's hot stare without obviously flinching.

"No," Sanct' Germain corrected him gently. "That would only happen if she had killed *me*." Strangely, he chuckled. "Necredes, little man, leave my slaves alone."

Necredes was silent as anger seethed in him. As he watched the foreigner turn away, he vowed that one day he would exact a price for this humiliation—it would be pleasant to plan his revenge slowly and meticulously. His eyes went to the table with the executioner's tools, and then to the executioner himself, who stood in the deepest shadow of the room, watching Necredes uncertainly. "You!" Necredes burst out. "If one word, if so much as a breath of this, is spread, you will die by the beasts!"

The executioner nodded his understanding, but stayed in the protecting corner, out of the light.

Ragoczy Sanct' Germain Franciscus walked quickly away from the tiny, fetid room where he had left Necredes. His controlled fury had not yet dissipated, and he did not trust himself to speak to those who greeted him casually. It was at such moments that his foreignness was a benefit to him, for he might behave in many odd ways and neither give offense nor attract undue attention to himself.

Down at the far end of the corridor he saw three Libyan armentarii walking a number of caracals on leashes. The Libyans sang softly to their trained cats, calming them in preparation for the next venation.

Sanct' Germain moved closer and hailed the nearest of the armentarii in his own language. "What is it you hunt this afternoon?"

The Libyan looked up, startled to hear his native tongue from this foreigner. He glanced at his fellow grooms before he answered. "Small wild pigs, they tell us, from Germania and Gaul." He shook his head, frowning now. "I don't like it. Our cats are not heavy enough for boars. My cousins and I"—he cocked his head toward the other two armentarii—"fear that our little brothers might be killed. They are trained to bring down birds and small antelope, not pigs."

One of the other armentarii smiled nervously. "We tried to argue, but . . ." His shrug was fatalistic. He reached down and patted the nearest tawny head, and the hunting cat pushed upward, eyes closing, short tail curling against his flank, a deep purr in his throat.

"They are beautiful animals," Sanct' Germain said, dropping to one knee, not heeding the quick warning from the Libyan armentari who held the leash. "Splendid cat, magnificent cat," he said softly, and reached to touch the tufted ears. The caracal lowered his head for those expert fingers that found the very spot that wanted scratching. As Sanct' Germain stroked the rich fur, he felt his anger fading at last.

"He won't often let strangers approach him," his Libyan trainer said, new respect and curiosity in his voice.

"Perhaps I am not a stranger," Sanct' Germain suggested as he got reluctantly to his feet.

The armentarii exchanged quick looks, and one of them made a sign with his fingers.

"That won't be necessary," Sanct' Germain said as he stepped back, feeling profoundly alien.

The nearest Libyan armentari tried to smile. "Excellency, we meant no offense, but we live so much with our cats that . . ." He broke off nervously. "Truly, they do not like strangers."

Sanct' Germain had no answer for them. He stood silent while the Libyans tugged their elegant caracals away.

"I do not think they know," said a voice behind him. Sanct' Germain turned quickly to face Kosrozd. "The cats like you, my master, and their trainers are jealous."

"I wonder." His expression was enigmatic as he studied his slave.

In the next moment they were forced to move aside as a squad of Greek hoplites marched down the narrow corridor, their spears up and shields held uniformly at their sides. At their head, their captain called out crisp marching orders.

"They are to fight Armenian charioteers with archers," Kosrozd said expressionlessly as the Greek troops went by.

"Who do you think will win?" Sanct' Germain studied the Persian youth as he answered.

"It will go hard for the hoplites," Kosrozd said when he had given the matter his consideration. "But if the Armenians can't break their formation, in the end they will lose. If they keep their distance and let the archers pick off the back rows first, then the Armenians might win."

Sanct' Germain nodded his agreement. "The Armenians aren't often so circumspect in their fighting, not as I recall."

A sudden increase of noise from the stands above distracted both men, and they looked quickly toward one of the narrow windows that gave onto the arena. There was nothing to see in the little slice of light that was colored red from the great awning that sheltered the crowd from the relentless Roman sun.

"What event?" Sanct' Germain asked.

Kosrozd could not entirely disguise his revulsion. "Asses trained to violate condemned women."

The noise grew louder, and then one terrible shriek rose above the crowd, a cry born of acutest agony. It hung on the stinking air, then stopped abruptly.

"Well," Sanct' Germain said as he turned away from the window, "it's over." He put one hand on Kosrozd's shoulder and drew him away. "Do you race again today?"

"Yes. And once tomorrow. The Reds haven't done well in this set of Games and they are pressing me to win." He was relieved to be speaking of racing again. In his seven years as a slave in Rome he had not learned to accept the Roman mob.

"Would you rather not race for them? Since I'm not a citizen, I cannot join a racing faction, and there is no reason for you to race for the Reds if you'd prefer Blue or Green or White."

"Or Purple or Gold," Kosrozd added fatalistically, adding the two recently created factions. "No, it makes no difference what color I wear—the race is the same."

"You could race for the Emperor's Greens. He gives lavish rewards to his charioteers." They were walking through the maze of halls and stairways toward the portion of the Circus Maximus that was set aside for charioteers.

"When they win. When they lose, he is equally free with his punishments. He had Cegellion of Gades dragged to death behind his own team." Kosrozd paused a moment and looked at his master. "We do not live long, who race here."

"The cruelty is new," Sanct' Germain said reflectively. "There was a time, only a few years ago, when Nero forbade the wanton killing of animals and contestants in the arena, and only made an exception of political criminals. Now . . ." His face grew somber and he walked in silence, Kosrozd beside him.

They had almost reached the charioteers' rooms when Kosrozd grabbed his master's arm. Sanct' Germain stopped and looked unspeaking at the wide, long-fingered hand that crushed the cloth just above his elbow.

"I . . . I must talk with you." The words were desperate, spoken in an urgent whisper.

At last Sanct' Germain met his eyes. "Yes?"

"Do you . . . will you take Tishtry to your bed again?" He blurted out the question and waited for his answer.

Sanct' Germain had been a slave himself and was not surprised at how much they knew. He pulled his arm away. "Not immediately, no. She's badly hurt."

"Will you sleep alone?" He knew that he had no right to ask such a question, and half-expected a curt dismissal or a blow.

"Sleep?" There was an ironic tinge to the word.

"Is there anyone else you desire more?" He was risking too much, he thought, but could not stop himself now.

A strange, remote look of anguish crossed Sanct' Germain's face, and for one suspended instant his penetrating eyes were fixed on a great distance. "No. No, I no longer desire anyone else more."

Kosrozd felt a chill as he stood beside Sanct' Germain, and

he almost faltered in his purpose. "Then . . . will you . . . would you . . . want me?" He knew that he might be sold for this impertinence, or sent to Treviri or Divodurum or Poetovio to race in the provinces, far away from Sanct' Germain in Rome.

"I am very old, Kosrozd, far older than you think," Sanct' Germain said kindly. "The price of caring is the pain of loss, and I have lost . . . much."

"You are alone," Kosrozd murmured. "And I am alone."

There was mockery in Sanct' Germain's expression now. "More alone than you, though we are both sons of princes whose kingdoms are lost to us. Kosrozd Kaivan," he said, using his slave's full name and seeing the young man start. "Oh, yes, I know who you are. It is a pity your uncles could not find more trustworthy conspirators. You're fortunate to have been sold into slavery. Another king might have dealt more harshly."

"He roasted my father on a spit!" Kosrozd burst out.

"But spared his children. And left you a whole man. Remember that. Persia is growing gentler with age."

An aurigatore spotted Kosrozd and came into the hallway. "It is almost time. I've got your chariot ready."

"A moment, Bricus." He watched his master with intent young eyes. "Will you sell me? Or send me away?"

Sanct' Germain considered this. "I suppose I should, but I won't. I'm . . . touched by your . . . interest." Then abruptly his tone changed. "Come, you must prepare for the race."

Kosrozd made one last attempt. "Tishtry told me once that you did not behave as she expected."

"Very likely," he said dryly.

"It would not matter," Kosrozd insisted.

"Wouldn't it?" He was interrupted by another prolonged shout from sixty thousand voices. When the sound had subsided, he said, "For some there is death in what I do." The coldness of this statement was directed inward, filled with old bitterness.

Kosrozd laughed bleakly as his glance turned toward his waiting chariot. "Death. There is death in what *I* do." Without looking at Sanct' Germain again, he went through the door, walking quickly to his aurigatore, who had just begun to lead four high-strung horses from the stable on the far side of the Gate of Life.

Text of a letter to the Emperor Nero.

To Nero, who is Caesar, lord of the world, hail!

As a citizen of Rome, no matter how lowly, I approach your august presence on behalf of those who are my brothers and who are unjustly condemned to vile and glorious deaths for their religion.

You have said that Rome will tolerate all forms of worship, and surely there are temples enough in Rome to give an outward sign of that tolerance, but that is illusion. You have shown yourself to be utterly opposed to those who have chosen to worship the only true manifestation of God on earth, and have set the might of the Roman state against us.

Perhaps you still confuse us with the rebellious Jews who have risen in revolt against your rule in their land. It is true enough that we follow the teachings of a man who was a Jew, but it is wrong to condemn us along with them, for we do not question political rule, and we do not share their objections to Roman presence. We who follow the teachings of Jesu-bar-Joseph and his disciples are not in agreement with other Jews. There are, it is true, a great many Jewish sects, and often there is little accord between them, but in one critical issue we differentiate ourselves from all Jews: most Jews, in reading the prophesies of the great teachers of the past, believe that there is one coming to free them from the bonds of this world, an anointed master who will be the path to all liberty. We who call ourselves Christians believe that this prophecy was fulfilled with the birth of Jesu-bar-Joseph sixty-five years ago. We do not reject his salvation, as do the rest of the Jews, but accept him as our redeemer, and worship him as the living presence of God.

If you are determined to persecute us, there is little we can do to oppose you, but I beg for myself and my brothers that you do not continue to identify us as Jews, since we are not Jews. Many of us languish in prisons and at the oars of triremes because you and your deputies have not taken the time to learn the difference between us and Jews.

I beseech you to examine your heart and take heed of your own laws, O Caesar, so that those innocent of rebellion may not continue to suffer for your ignorance and the ignorance of other Romans. You have accepted without prejudice all the false gods of the world, all the evil worship done anywhere that Roman troops have trodden. Why, then, do you forbid us, who have the promise of true salvation to offer you, and the one path to God, to practice our faith with the same openness and freedom as you allow to the misguided women who frequent the Temple of Isis? Certainly Egyptian Isis is no more foreign than we are. Why is it impossible for you to extend her protection to us? If you continue to deny us, then all will know that Roman justice is a lie, and you will be hated in this life and cast into darkness when you die, for your abuse of those who willingly follow the rule of the True God.

Though you kill my body in this world, still I will pray for you, here and before the Throne of God.

Most humbly, and in the Name of Christ,
Philip, freeman of Rome

3

On the far side of the luxurious room Arnax lay snoring, his discarded clothing tucked under his head for a pillow.

The room was softly perfumed, and hanging lamps gave it a soft glow, showing the rumpled bed and the two figures who faced each other there.

Atta Olivia Clemens watched her husband, dismay on her bruised face. "Justus . . ." she said cautiously. Her hands were unsteady, and had Cornelius Justus Silius not chosen that moment to cover her with his now-urgent body, she would have clenched them. As it was, her fingers hooked into the silken sheets. Her flesh was newly marked by Arnax's lust, and it took more of an effort than usual for her to keep from crying out as her husband pushed into her.

"Lie still!" he commanded thickly as she flinched.

She was pitifully glad to obey. She stared past his shoulder toward the ceiling, and wished, as she had almost every night for the past two years, that she would die and at last be free of this hated marriage.

A little while later, Justus moved off her, grunting his displeasure. "You weren't doing it right," he muttered as he looked down at his flaccid organ.

Torn between relief and apprehension, Olivia drew the sheet around her for protection. "I submitted," she protested. "Even when he beat me. Do you want me to die? Will that be enough?"

Her question brought to Justus' mind all the unpleasant rumors that had persisted about his third marriage. "No, of course I don't want you to die. But I think it ought to be possible for you to find someone who can do what is needed."

"But I thought he"—she flung out a hand to point at Arnax—"was what you wanted. You said he would have to be more forceful. You saw him! How much force do you require now, Justus?" She drew her hand back and held it over her mouth. She wanted terribly to be calm.

"Brute force is one thing," Justus said slowly as he regarded the sleeping secutor, "but there are other sorts of fear. I think that perhaps you should look elsewhere. Find a man who is different from the others, whose tastes are . . . devious." He permitted himself a half-smile of anticipation. "I know of men who take their enjoyments . . . strangely. Surely you can seek out one such."

Olivia shrank back in the bed. "How strange?" she asked in a thread of a voice.

"I leave that to you, Olivia. But I warn you, choose well. I don't want to have another night as disappointing as this one." He started to rise as he reached for the Parthian night robe that had fallen to the floor some time before.

She tried to nod, but found she could not move. Her body seemed to belong to someone else now, some malformed child. "Justus," she said, fixing him with her stare, "no more. I beg of you. Send me away, anywhere. I'll go meekly, without complaint, no matter where you send me. I'll live simply.

I won't ask you to help me in any way. Let me go. Please, please let me go."

He opened his small eyes very wide at her plea. In this light they appeared almost sand-colored, and their very lightness was frightening. "If that is what you want, Olivia, of course I will send you away." He was drawing on his robe as he spoke, catching the loose garment around his waist with a brightly dyed cord.

"Oh, thank you." She gripped her hands together over the sheet. "When may I go?"

"Why, as soon as you wish," he said rather abstractedly. "I'm certain your family will understand, however, when I have your father imprisoned." He looked back toward her, drinking in the horror in her eyes.

"But . . ." She could find no words to say. Her eyes filled with tears that slid down her face, unnoticed by her.

"I've explained it to you before," Justus was saying with patient indulgence. "So long as you are with me, and obedient, your father, indeed, your whole family, is safe from me. My quarrel with him, after all, is financial. Your brothers will have their debts paid, your father may maintain his house and keep his estates, and indulge in a few harmless extravagances with my goodwill. But the day you leave me, my cherished wife, on that day your father will find all his obligations spelled out, your brothers will lose their rank and they will be fortunate to find a home with your sisters' husbands." His laughter was unpleasant, as he intended.

"No!" she cried out, and gasped in fear as Arnax stirred in the corner.

The secutor did not awaken.

"Do be more careful," Justus said as he raised an admonishing finger. "I want no rumors among the slaves. Let them all think that you are wanton. Otherwise they might not be so willing to come to you, and that would be a severe disappointment to me." He reached out and raised her chin with his fingers. "Do you know what it is to need to watch you rut, wife? Can you imagine how humiliated I would be if it were known?"

"Divus Claudius was like you," she said, with every bit of defiance she could find in her fear.

"Divus Claudius was Caesar!" His hand cracked against her jaw. "He made his wife a whore until my cousin found her. He made her drug herself with men. Gaius was a fool to change her." He was breathing quickly, his eyes slightly unfocused. Olivia recognized the signs and steeled herself for another onslaught. "That Gallic soldier," Justus whispered. "You wanted him. You helped him mount you."

This accusation was not new, and it was with weariness that Olivia reminded him, "You told me to help him, Justus. You thought that he might not want a woman. You said I should urge him." She was not horrified at this memory now, with almost a year of other, increasingly degrading nights.

"You remember him." Justus moved closer to her, leaning over her as he grabbed for her arms.

"I remember all of it, Justus," she said, her shadowed eyes bright with loathing.

He pushed her back against the pillows. "Thinking of vengeance, Olivia?" He tugged his robe open. "Don't forget your father and brothers. And your sisters. So long as you please me, they are safe." Brutally he forced her knees open.

Outrage rose afresh in Olivia's heart, and though she knew it would anger her husband even more, she struggled against him, striking out with her tightened fists and twisting as his weight came down on her.

When he had finished, he did not at once move away from her. "Do you want me to bring the Tingitanian in from the stables again?"

Of everything she had endured, the Tingitanian had been the worst. The thought of that relentless, cruel body that smelled of rancid oil, dung, and something more, something gaggingly sweet, almost made Olivia choke.

"Reluctant, wife?" Justus asked as he got off her. "A stable slave is not to your taste? If I sent you to the lupanar, you'd have doings with worse than stable slaves." He read the revulsion in her face, though she tried to mask it. "It could come to that. Unless you can find someone who will do as I require. Think of that while you make your selection." He was tightening his robe once more. "I wonder how you would look in a yellow wig?" he added wickedly.

"Only whores wear them," she objected. "I am a wife, not a whore." Her anger increased, shutting out her fear. "You have used me intolerably, Justus. If you did not hold such power over my family, I would denounce you in court, and obtain maintenance and a divorce. You may coerce me and threaten me, but I am still your wife, and I will not be made a harlot to the world. Bring any filth you want into this house, but I tell you now, that if you force me to submit anywhere but here, I will kill myself, and I will say why I kill myself." She spoke softly, so as not to disturb the secutor, but there was an earnestness in her words that made them a vow.

"I'm sure your father will applaud such heroism from his prison. If he ever learns about it." Justus was on his feet, looming over Olivia once more. "I'll have Sibinus remove the secutor," he said in a different voice. "What a brute he is."

"You'll allow that?" Olivia said, almost laughing in disbelief.

"Certainly. I'm growing tired of such men. You must find another sort of lover." He folded his thick arms over his chest. "I want to see you overcome, not beaten."

Olivia had taken one of the pillows and held it now close to her body, finding comfort in having it between her and her husband. "I will keep your wishes in mind, my husband." There was just enough sarcasm in her tone to make Justus turn to her one last time.

"See that you do, Olivia. I admit that it amuses me to have you defy me, provided that you do not make the mistake of thinking that it will give you any power whatever." He touched the fine linen hanging that could be pulled around the bed. "What becomes of your family is entirely in your hands. It would be most unwise of you to have me for your enemy."

"You are already," she responded hotly.

"You think so? How innocent you are." Justus chuckled. "One day you will see how I deal with my enemies, and then you will understand how fortunate you are." He bent down and kissed her forehead. "Come, then, it isn't so terrible, is it? You have all my wealth at your disposal, and an honorable name. If I hadn't offered for you, your father would have been lucky to find you a line officer to marry. Can you honestly tell me that you would rather broil or freeze in some distant outpost with a rough soldier as a mate, half a dozen hungry children, whose only hope was getting a farm before your husband was cut down in battle?"

"Yes, Justus." She saw his brows twitch in disbelief. "If that soldier treated me with honor, then I would know myself a fortunate woman."

"What absurd notions you have of honor," Justus said as he turned away. "Tomorrow, wife, I will be leaving for a few days. I expect that when I return you will have found someone more likely to do as I require." As he crossed the marble floor, the long Parthian robe brushed against the stone. When he got to the door, he clapped his hands briskly. "Sibinus," he ordered, "the secutor is finished here. See that he leaves shortly, and is suitably rewarded."

Sibinus slipped into the room. He was more like a ferret than any man Olivia had ever seen, and she had never felt comfortable in his presence. Now his long, lean hands moved furtively over his long tunica and his narrow eyes darted from Justus to Arnax to her. "Suitably rewarded," he repeated.

"Do not, of course, tell him that the money comes from me. If you can, contrive to make it seem that my wife has sent it." Justus had given these instructions many times before, and Sibinus knew them as well as his master did, but it always distressed Olivia to hear these plans, and so they were repeated.

"I will wrap the coins in her new veil." An expression that might have been a smile stretched his mouth.

"Excellent. I trust you to finish the business." He put a coin in his slave's hand, then went out the door.

Sibinus came into the room, crossing the floor in a curious, sideways walk, as if he feared apprehension at every step. He paused to look once at Olivia, then scurried to the naked secutor. There he bent over the recumbent form, and shook Arnax gently, saying a few soft words that Olivia could not hear.

Arnax stirred and opened his eyes with an oath. He thrashed wildly, grabbing his clothes and hunting for a weapon.

"No, good secutor," Sibinus murmured. "Do not make such sound, or someone may tell my master of what you have done here tonight with his wife."

This warning had an immediate effect. Arnax became quiet, almost docile, immediately. He looked toward the bed once, favoring Olivia with a lewd, frightened smile.

"My mistress will reward your prowess and your silence when you have left her." Sibinus was already helping the big man to his feet, holding his tunica and cloak while Arnax struggled to lace his sandals.

At last he was dressed, and with a last show of obsequious deference, Sibinus bowed him toward the door, following him after covertly pulling one of Olivia's veils from the chest by the bed.

Olivia looked at the closed door, filled with shame. She had tried to do as Justus wished in order to protect her family, but after every such night, her doubts grew. She had once told her mother of Justus' needs, and her mother had listened with strained sympathy, advising Olivia to think of something else, and to offer at the Temple of Venus for her husband's tastes to change. The unbidden question then had plagued Olivia—would her mother have said the same thing if her family's safety were not dependent on Olivia's docility? She had wondered that every time since then when she had seen her mother, and for that reason had learned to give inconsequent answers to her mother's occasional questions.

There was no one she could trust. Not her mother, her father, her brothers or sisters. The loneliness of that admission brought tears to her eyes, and impatiently she wiped them away. Tears would not help her. She rose and pinched out the perfumed lamps, then drew one of the sheets around her as she went to the window.

The new year was only seven weeks old, and the last storm of winter was blowing itself out. The clouds had gone earlier and only a frozen wind was left to scour the sky. A moon just past full hung over the city, lighting the world gently, deceptively, so that even the incompletely repaired buildings that had been gutted by the fire the summer before now had a grace and majesty. Beyond them there was a flash of silver where the Tiber made a sinuous, caressing curve around the city.

How many people slept out there? she asked herself. With so much humanity around her, there had to be an ally for her. She turned away from the window. Her husband had ordered her to find a lover, not an ally, someone who was . . . unusual. Her skin was touched with gooseflesh, and she told herself it was the cold. She returned to the bed, pale under her bruises, a sudden weakness possessing her. It reminded her of when she had miscarried, a year after her marriage. Until that moment she had consoled herself with the thought that Justus would not subject the mother of his heir to the degradation he had required. After the pain and the blood, her hopes were dashed. Her Greek physician had given it as his opinion that she would not bear any child to term. At the time, Justus had claimed to be disappointed, but thinking back, Olivia now wondered if, in fact, he had been pleased.

She pulled the blanket up under her chin and lay back. The oil of jasmine could not quite cover the pungent scent of Arnax's sweat. In vexation, Olivia got out of the bed and padded toward the door. Nestulia, her body slave, was supposed to sleep in the alcove across the way, though tonight Justus might have sent her away, as he often did.

The alcove was empty. Olivia stepped back into her room and closed the door, leaning upon it in her hopelessness. Then, there being nothing else she could do, she went to her bed and stripped the sheets and blankets from it, then climbed onto the bed to pull down the linen hangings, which smelled only of the perfumed lamps.

A handbill for the Theatre of Marcellus, for performances the first week in March, the 817th Year of the City.

The Theatre of Marcellus announces
in anticipation of the
glorious
Neronian Games
the Emperor has consented
to perform the epic
NIOBE
accompanying himself upon the Greek lyre

Six Greek pantomimes
will interpret the epic in dance

A note appended to the handbill adds:

The Emperor hasn't favored Rome with an epic since he went out on the walls to serenade the fire of last summer, to praise its might as greater than his. Then he sang of the Fall of Troy.

4

A WARM BREEZE carried the fragrance of blossoms across the training ring at Villa Ragoczy. The spring was pleasant, mild and promising, and from the vineyards that rose in neat lines up the hills to the fruit trees behind the extensive stables, the new villa seemed alive with its touch.

Only Tishtry occupied the training ring with her big Syrian gelding. The horse wore a special bridle and half-saddle that was little more than girths with a thick horn. As the horse cantered around the mid-portion of the ring, Tishtry used the horn to vault from one side to the other of the horse. She shouted encouragement as she rode and leaped.

When at last she was satisfied, she pulled the gelding to a slow walk, guiding him with her knees toward the gate.

Sanct' Germain was waiting for her, one neatly booted foot on the lowest fence rail. He was dressed for riding in black Dacian tunic and leggings. He smiled as she came nearer. "You are better?"

"Almost myself again," she answered, grinning. "Shirdas here is out of practice."

"He looked fine just now," Sanct' Germain assured her. He spoke educated and courtly Armenian with the same slight accent that colored his Latin, giving his speech a quality that was oddly archaic to Tishtry's ears.

"That's because I was forcing him." She swung expertly off the gelding's back. "You see, I am strong enough. When do I return to the arena? The Neronian Games begin soon, and there are great prizes to be won."

"In payment for great risks," he warned, reaching over the fence to put one fine small hand on her shoulder.

"There is risk in anything," she said lightly. "Riding is my life. I was born to it, like my father and his father." She reached to open the gate. "I've got to rub down Shirdas."

"One of the other slaves will do it," he said as he held the gate open for her and the big horse.

"I care for my own horses," she answered briskly. Then she looked toward the far side of the courtyard where her master's mount waited. "You care for your own, don't you?"

He admitted it, and started across the courtyard beside her. "What do you think of him?" he asked, indicating the black stallion that waited at the hitching rail.

This was a splendid animal, heavy-bodied and well-muscled with an erect neck, a broad, intelligent head and steady eyes. Mane and tail were full and long and there was thick feathering around each hoof. The small ears pricked as Sanct' Germain approached.

"Do you like him?" Sanct' Germain put one hand on the glossy flank. "I had him sent from Gallia Belgica."

"He's beautiful. How are his hooves?" The arena was known to be very bad for hooves.

"Better than the Iberians, but not quite so tough as the Libyans. I was thinking that he could compare well with the Sicilians, though he's not quite so fast. He comes from a marshy area, so his hooves are hard enough." He stood aside so that she could examine the stallion more closely. "He's steady-tempered, with excellent stamina."

"He looks it." She ran expert hands over the stallion, who stood quietly for this inspection. "You should be proud of him. I'd be willing to give a great deal for such an animal." Neither of them considered it odd for a slave to say such things. Often slaves who appeared in the Great Games amassed large personal fortunes. Tishtry herself, while not rich, had some prize money and owned ten horses, which would have been a considerable amount for many Roman freeman.

"You need not give a thing. He's yours." Sanct' Germain untied the lead rope and handed it to her. "Two of your mares are ready to be bred."

Tishtry looked from her master to the fine black horse. "You don't mean that."

Sanct' Germain smiled. "Of course I do. I wanted to give you a present to mark your recovery. I couldn't think of anything you would like more. If there is something else, tell me."

She held the lead uncertainly. "Mine? Truly?" This time when she touched the stallion her hand was almost reverent. "It is a princely gift, master."

He said nothing. His pleasure at her delight was genuine but remote. It was such a little thing to give a horse to a slave, yet her gratitude disturbed him. He nodded toward Shirdas. "Rub him down, and then take the stallion to the end of the compound. You'll want to check his hooves and teeth at your leisure."

"They're fine; I know they're fine," she said happily.

"I hope so," he said, though he had already inspected the stallion and knew he would not disappoint Tishtry.

She turned to him, smiling. "I would like to try him in the ring, my master, to see how he goes."

"He's yours. Do as you wish. The ring is open for a while longer. I'm going to ride out after the charioteers. They're on the practice road and I want to see how Glynnth, this new Briton, does." Since his villa was occupied, he had made it a habit to follow his charioteers on their course through the vineyards and orchards, particularly when, as now, he had a new slave whose skill he wanted to assess.

"Glynnth is clumsy," Tishtry said offhandedly. "I watched him this morning. His aurigatore was angry with him because he would not stand properly in the chariot."

"Hardly surprising," Sanct' Germain remarked. "Have you ever seen Britannic chariots? They're more like carts."

"He was good with the horses," Tishtry allowed. "He handled the reins well, for a barbarian."

"For a barbarian," Sanct' Germain repeated, looking down at the stocky woman in ragged leather breeches, loose linen vest, with copper bracelets on her arms and three protective amulets on thongs around her neck.

"Britannia is a mad place," she said seriously. "I heard a tribune say that they paint themselves blue."

"So I understand." He touched her hand briefly. "When I return, I would like to talk to you."

This time she looked squarely at him. "Why? Have I offended you?" It would be like her master, she thought, to give her this horse by way of farewell. "I haven't been well enough to come to you, but if you—"

"You are better now. That is one of the things we must discuss, but not the only one." He looked down at her open face. "Would it trouble you to come back to my bed?"

"You are my master," she said with a shrug. "It is good to sleep in the master's bed."

"I see." It was what he had expected her to say, and he told himself that it was the most sensible attitude, yet he was strangely disappointed. "Would you rather go to someone else?"

"In time," she said when she had given the matter her

thoughtful consideration. "I enjoy what you do to me." She stopped abruptly.

His smile was sad. "Later, then. I will be in my library, I think. I will tell Aumtehoutep that you're expected. He'll admit you promptly."

Tishtry frowned at the mention of the somber Egyptian who was Sanct' Germain's body slave, but though she found him haughty and distant, she knew it was only through his skill that her strength had been saved. The salves he had applied had ended the pain, and after that, Sanct' Germain had set the Egyptian to nurse her. She liked him no more now than she had then, but her respect for him bordered on awe.

"Is something the matter?" Sanct' Germain studied her face closely. "Tell me."

"It's nothing. I was remembering what Aumtehoutep did after Necredes had me beaten." She moved her hands as if pushing an ugly thing away. "That is behind me." It was not entirely true. There were two crossed scars on her back that would be with her all her life.

Sanct' Germain touched her face. There was hardly any weight to his fingers but they seemed to her to be penetrating as sunlight. "Tishtry, do you ever wonder what will become of you?"

"You told me about that when you took me to your bed. It doesn't seem real, though. Perhaps I will believe it when it happens." She put her hand on the flank of the black horse. "This is real. The other . . ." With a shrug she dismissed it.

He accepted this. "I'll expect you later, then."

"Certainly." She was more interested in the horse than in him. He was faintly amused by this, finding her honesty as delightful as it was blighting. Giving her a casual wave, he turned on his heel and went to get his horse.

The charioteers had pleased him, he decided when he had returned to Villa Ragoczy. Tishtry had been right about the Britannic charioteer Glynnth—he was clumsy, but showed promise. He had handled the four nervous horses with more wisdom than artistry, and Sanct' Germain had decided to speed up his training. The twenty-two other charioteers were familiar to him and all but one attracted only moderate attention. The exception was Kosrozd. As always, he had driven the best of the lot, keeping the lead easily over the long, difficult practice route. The beautiful young Persian handled his light chariot with a singleness of purpose that showed, more than his erect bearing, his warrior training.

Dusk was beginning to soften the warm golden light when Sanct' Germain dismounted in the courtyard of Villa Ragoczy. He was dusty from the long ride, and anxious to wash away the grime of the day. He tugged the saddle from his gray stallion's back and summoned a slave to take it away. While he rubbed the gray down, he sent another slave into the house with orders to prepare his bath. He worked on the horse with familiar economy, so that it was only a little later that he crossed the courtyard toward the rear entrance to his villa.

Aumtehoutep met him at the door. "The bath is ready, my master," he said in his native tongue.

Sanct' Germain answered him in the same language. "Excellent. I need it tonight, old friend." He had already begun to undress, pulling the Dacian tunic over his head and handing it to the lean Egyptian at his side.

"Two more crates arrived from Ostia today," Aumtehoutep said as he gathered up his master's clothes.

"Stones?" Sanct' Germain reached for the robe Aumtehoutep held out to him. As always when naked, he stood with his back to the Egyptian, and did not turn until the robe was tied around him.

"That, and more earth from Dacia." Aumtehoutep's voice was light and curiously neutral, as if nothing could touch him or move him on this earth.

"From Sennistis?" It had been almost a year since he had heard from the high priest of Imhotep.

"Yes." He gave Sanct' Germain a steady look. "He is not well, my master. He thinks he is near death."

Sanct' Germain put a hand to his eyes. Poor, faithful Sennistis, who had been so loyal and devoted, he thought. "I feared that."

"And I." Aumtehoutep betrayed little of his feelings with his face, but he had been with Sanct' Germain for centuries and his master could read the finest nuance of his expression.

"Do you want to go to him?" He stood in the doorway between his bedchamber and the bath now, his dark eyes full on his slave. "You have only to ask. I would not deny you. If it is your will, you may return to Egypt a free man, with one of my old estates to keep you."

Aumtehoutep looked away. "What good would it do? If he

is minded to die, there is nothing more to say. Egypt is foreign to me now, more foreign, perhaps, than Rome."

There was no answer to that. Sanct' Germain knew that sense of foreignness in every fiber of his being. He closed his eyes a moment in private acknowledgment of that loneliness.

"Will you want anything else, my master?" Aumtehoutep said in his usual polite manner.

Sanct' Germain was always grateful for the Egyptian's tact. "I doubt . . . No, wait. When Tishtry comes, send her in to me here." He indicated the quiet room where scented steam rose from the waiting water.

"As you wish." With the slightest of bows Aumtehoutep slipped from the room.

Left to himself, Sanct' Germain strolled into the bath, his Scythian boots clicking against the mosaic of semiprecious stones. Lamps burning perfumed oils hung around the shallow pool, lighting it with a ruddy glow. Sanct' Germain pinched out all but two of the lamps, so that the room was sunk in its own twilight.

Near the tall, narrow windows there was an elaborately carved wooden bench, and here he sat to draw off his boots. The sun was down and night was taking hold of the world. Sanct' Germain flexed his toes, feeling stiff from the long ride of the afternoon. He rose, slipping out of his robe. Warm water rose above his waist as he entered the bath, and he sighed with pleasure. There had been a time, long ago, when he would have faced even so little water as this with dread, but he had learned to build his baths with linings of his native earth, and to fill the soles of his shoes with it, so that water lost its threat to him.

He leaned back, half-floating, his eyes almost closed. The tension eased out of his body, leaving him drifting, languid, subtly aroused.

Behind him a door opened and uncertain steps entered the tiled bath.

Sanct' Germain set his feet on the floor of the pool. "Tishtry?" he said quietly.

"My master?" came the answer from the scented gloom.

He smiled. "Come. Bathe with me." He raised one arm in invitation and the water ran and splashed around him.

She stepped out of the shadows. On the edge of the pool she hesitated. "You wanted to talk to me?"

"Yes." He moved nearer to where she stood, reaching up

at last to pull at the hem of her rough woolen cloak. "Don't be afraid, Tishtry."

"You don't frighten me," she said almost gruffly. "I haven't bathed with a man before." There was no seductive pretense in her. She loosened the girdle at her waist and pulled the full-cut robe over her head. Each movement was utilitarian and clean. Carefully she folded the robe, placing it near the door, away from the pool.

"Tishtry." He came to meet her as she stepped carefully into the water. Taking her hands as he would a child's, he drew her away from the side of the bath, toward the center, where the shadows were deepest and the air was still.

"It's big," she said rather apprehensively.

"Three times my height on each side." He released her hands. "There. Lie back. The water will support you."

"I don't know how to swim," she confessed, but attempted to do as he had instructed her. She was nervous, and started to thrash as she felt her feet lift from the bottom of the pool.

Immediately Sanct' Germain was beside her, reassuring her, one arm lightly under her shoulder. "As if you were sleeping, Tishtry. Lie back." He moved away from her again, and let her try once more.

This time she fared better. At first she was uncertain, but the warm water soothed her, and the dim light saved her from embarrassment. Gradually her anxiety left her. She spread her arms to the side and felt herself carried by the still water. It was so pleasant, so dreamlike to drift there, that she hardly felt it when Sanct' Germain moved nearer. His hands moved with the water to caress her, slowly, lightly, never forcing, yet always finding the ways to summon her to joy.

When he drew her softly into his arms, her need for him had begun to build from a sweet titillation to a demanding thirst. His hands were more insistent now, exploring each awakening delight. She sighed, her body as entirely alive, as entirely sensitive as the finest Aeolian harp. His lips sought out her passion, filling her with a splendid delirium.

At various places around the pool, water had splashed out. In the pool the tempest of the two bodies continued. Tishtry felt something within her gather, but the release eluded her. She braced her hands against Sanct' Germain's shoulders. "Do as you wish," she whispered breathlessly. "I'm well-served."

With more force than he had shown before, he pulled her

back into his close embrace. "By all the lost gods," he murmured, his mouth just below her ear, "take pleasure of me, woman."

The intensity of his demand evoked an unknown hunger within her. Responding with an urgency that she had never known before, she abandoned herself to her desire.

When, sometime later, he carried her from the pool, she was deeply satisfied. There was no more reluctance in her. She stood quietly while he wrapped her in a new robe of fine silk that matched the one he wore.

Taking her hand, he led her from the bath to his bed, and tenderly lifted her onto it. She smiled up at him. "You did not do that before," she whispered.

"You didn't want it before." He sank down beside her. "You are learning to have fulfillment."

"But you?" she asked, a slight pang of guilt coloring her contentment.

"There is time enough for that," he said as he parted her robe.

This time she warmed quickly, eagerly, her appetite sharpened by her earlier enjoyment. She moved into his hands, meeting his lips, hoping to call him from his essential remoteness. When she was certain that she could endure no more pleasure, she heard his soft voice. "Come to me." There was one keen instant as his mouth touched her throat, and then the surge of his ardor carried her to satiety and wonderful languor.

Text of a letter to the Senator Cornelius Justus Silius from Subrius Flavus.

To the Senator Silius, greetings;

I and my associates have reason to believe that you are as unhappy about the state of rule in this empire as we are, and for that reason, we ask that you consider well what follows. Should you decide to stand with us, we welcome you. If not, we charge you upon your honor not to reveal what is set down here, as more than our lives are at stake.

What Julius and Augustus built, Lucius Domitius Ahenobarbus, who now wears the purple and calls himself Nero, has done his best to destroy. You may argue that he promised well at first, and there is no one who will deny that he was a charming lad when he was twenty. Those abuses which seemed to be the product of youth have grown since that time, and his judgment and good sense are no longer in evidence. When he was young, I loved him, as did all worthy soldiers. As long as he was deserving esteem as Emperor, I was the most loyal of his men, and my oath to him was doubly sacred. Yet how can any Roman, from the highest noble to the lowest slave, feel he merits anything but odium. His stepfather, his mother and his wife have died at his orders. For that alone I have learned to hate him. My hatred grows with each new atrocity. I have seen my Emperor change from an intelligent, respectful youth into a greedy and debauched tyrant, an actor, a singer of Greek nonsense, a charioteer and a burner of cities.

This man must be removed from power if the empire is to continue. Rome is without virtue while Nero rules us. The philosopher Seneca, who was Nero's tutor, is with us. He knows more profoundly than any other man how far Nero has turned from the path the Emperor should tread. If Seneca opposes Nero, who loved him once as a son, it is sign enough that his Emperor is no longer deserving of the loyal love of his people.

We have others with us, men of judgment and rectitude who have given unstintingly of their minds and fortunes that we may bring about the changes that are so desperately needed.

In place of Nero, we have proposed to elevate Gaius Calpurnius Piso. There are those who claim that he is a trivial young man, given too much to light pursuits. It would be useless to deny that he gambles, and fancies himself something of a singer, but were it not imperial fashion, he would comport himself with more dignity. He has assured us that he will seek our guidance and be attendant to our advice. The people like him, as much for his winning ways as for his handsome appearance. There are those, of course, who admire him for little more than his beauty, but this has ever been a problem with the lower ranks, who are more easily swayed by appearances than the more intelligent nobility. Be certain that Calpurnius is an acceptable candidate for the purple, more modest and less headstrong than Nero.

In less than a month the ill-advised Neronian Games will begin, and that will give us the opportunity we need to strike out at the Emperor who so greatly abuses us. There will be great confusion, and we may take advantage of it. It will be appropriate to bring Nero down at his own Games, as it will show our intentions to be rid not only of him but of everything he has come to represent.

Say you will help us to restore honor and order to the purple. We place our faith in you, Justus. Join with us and be rid of Nero. It is true that the undertaking is dangerous, but think of the reward, not only in dignity, but of the opportunity once again to be near the seat of power. You have suffered much at imperial hands. Take your destiny now, and help us to triumph over Nero. There is nothing more honorable than service to the empire, and there can be no greater service than aiding in the end of the Neronian reign.

In the hope that you are with us,

In faithful confidence,
Subrius Flavus

5

THERE WOULD BE twenty-seven guests tonight, and Petronius was determined that nothing would be lacking for them. The dining couches had been set up in his arbor and six specially built fountains cooled the warm May evening.

Artemidorus, dressed in the Greek fashion as a compliment to the Emperor, made one last check of the three U-shaped dining areas, each with the proper nine couches. He frowned, not wanting to forget any detail.

"Have the chickens been drowned yet?" Petronius asked after sneezing violently. "I thought I told you to remove all the roses."

"They were removed. There are four bushes of them in the adjoining garden, in full flower," he reported sadly. "I went to speak with Corrastus, but he wasn't willing to cut the blooms off, not even for money."

Petronius sighed. "I may sneeze most of the night. Hardly proper for the Emperor's host, but I can't change my plans now. Tigellinus would never let me forget it. I wonder if I have time to send a message to Sanct' Germain? He made me a concoction once that stopped my sneezing awhile."

"I'll send a messenger to him," Artemidorus offered.

"It might be wise." He took one end of his toga and wiped his eyes. "Yes. Do that. He is staying in the city for a few days, at the house of that Greek physician. Now, about the chickens?"

"Triges drowned them half an hour ago. He used a red Lusitanian wine. And I have made him promise not to use one drop of liquamen."

"Good." He managed to stop another sneeze. "Roses are the curse of the gods! Let me see: tarts with honeyed wine, asparagus, kid cooked in milk, Gallic ham dressed with Mauretanian pomegranates, oysters from Britannia, pickled vegetables from Baetica, wines from Jura and Pannonia, the chickens, lamprey in a sauce of herbs, salmon roe in cream"—he ticked off the menu on his fingers—"dormice in cheese bread, calves' livers with mushroom, geese with garlic and snails, pears, apples, grapes, berries . . . Will it be adequate? Nero has sworn that he has given up elaborate dining, but I don't know." Petronius' face tightened about the eyes. It was difficult to know what Nero would want from day to day. He had taken him at his word and arranged for a simple dinner, yet now he was unsure if it had been the wisest course. He had invited those guests Nero had wanted, including Cornelius Justus Silius and his wife. Thinking about it, he anticipated a miserable evening. If only the dancers from Hind were all that Sanct' Germain had promised they would be. Without unique entertainment, Petronius had a ghastly fear that his banquet, charming though the concept might be, would certainly be a failure, and that, coming now, would be disastrous. Petronius had been losing influence with the Emperor, who was now showing increasing favor to the Praetorian captain Tigellinus. For Petronius, an unsuccessful party could set the seal on his influence and lead to ruin.

"Master?" Artemidorus interrupted these disheartening thoughts. "Shall I send the messenger?"

"Yes. Yes, of course. I'm going into the house for a bit. It may help. Send word to my wife that I would like to speak to her before the guests arrive." He gave one last apprehensive look to the couches and the specially created arbor, then hastened through the garden to the rear entrance to his home.

He was at his desk, stylus in hand, when his wife tapped at the open door. Petronius put his writing aside as he smiled. "Come in, Myrtale."

"You wished to speak to me?" She was a tall woman, almost as tall as her husband, and was attractive without being pretty. Her most arresting feature was her dark auburn hair, which she wore simply dressed. There was a serenity in her face that found no reflection in her husband's expression.

"I'm worried." As always, he was direct with her. "I'm afraid I've made a serious error with this banquet."

"Why?" She sat in a chair not far from him. "Do you think there will be trouble?"

"I hope not, but I'll admit I'm preparing for it." He rubbed his chin. "I wanted you to be warned. I know the slaves will gossip, no matter what happens. I wanted you to be prepared."

"That's kind of you." They regarded each other affectionately but without passion. Theirs had been an arranged marriage, and though each respected the other, their interests were almost in diametric opposition, Myrtale being as drawn to religion and scholarship as Petronius was drawn to entertainments and pleasures.

"Nero is coming. I had planned an outdoor supper, nothing too fancy. There will be dancers to perform later, not Greeks, but new slaves from Hind." He reached for his stylus, but only held it, and he made no move to pick up his tablet.

"There is novelty there," she said. "It would be to your credit."

"So I've told myself," he responded, not quite laughing. "If the festivities seem to end early, you will know that it did not go well."

Myrtale studied her long, tapering hands. "Husband, I know you will do as you think best, and I am certain that you have not acted foolishly. However, if you are inclined, we may retire to my estate in Dalmatia, and give it out that I have been ill. I am not seen enough to have any doubt this." She smiled, and her sober expression was transformed. "It might be best. You have wanted more time for writing."

"I'll consider it," he said, knowing he would refuse to leave. "I thought you ought to be prepared for unpleasantness, however."

"It is kind of you," she said agan.

"Since that revolt of Subrius Flavus has been stopped, Nero sees enemies in the branches of trees." He put the stylus aside once more. "I can't blame him. They came very close. If he hadn't been warned . . ."

His wife watched him. "Would that have been so terrible, to lose Nero? You have said yourself that he is not the man he was five years ago."

"Oh, that's true enough. It saddens me. But I can't think we'd be better off with Gaius Calpurnius Piso wearing the purple. He's nothing more than a puppet." He rose suddenly. "I must go. I can't imagine any god would favor me, but you might give an offering for me."

Myrtale wanted to make light of his concern. "The Greek Dionysus might be appropriate. He is fond of ceremonies and performances and wine."

"And madness," Petronius said, looking away. "Don't be anxious, Myrtale. No doubt I'm allowing myself to magnify the situation. Forgive me for burdening you with my foolishness." He stepped out of the room, unable to face her. What would become of her and their two children if he did indeed lose Nero's favor? He could not bring himself to think of it.

He was almost at the garden gate when Artemidorus hastened up to him, a little flushed and out of breath. "Master. The slave has returned from Sanct' Germain."

Petronius paused. "And?"

Artemidorus held out a little alabaster jar. "He says that half the contents mixed with wine should get you through the banquet."

With a sense of relief far greater than such a minor consideration warranted, Petronius took the flask. At least he would not sneeze the evening away.

"I've taken the liberty of sending for wine," Artemidorus said, glancing toward the kitchen area at the back of the house.

"Excellent." For the first time in several days, Titus Petronius Niger dared to hope that the evening would not be a catastrophe.

Most of the guests arrived late, but that was to be expected. Secundus Marcellus was the first to arrive, and he was annoyed to find only his host waiting. Within half an hour, most of the others had assembled, but no one dared suggest that the meal should begin, for the Emperor had not arrived.

Sanct' Germain came a little later than most of the guests, and he brought with him the three slaves from Hind, as he had promised.

"A thousand thanks," Petronius said.

"For what? You knew I would bring the dancers." He was magnificently dressed in a long robe of Persian design. The black silk of which it was made had been brought from the fabled lands to the east, and had taken more than a year to make its journey along the trade route that bore the name of the precious fabric, the Silk Road. Sumptuary laws limited the jewelry any foreigner could wear, even a wealthy and noble foreigner, and so Sanct' Germain had limited himself to a large pectoral of onyx and electrum in representation of his signet, the eclipse.

"For the flask. Not one sneeze for more than an hour." Petronius was chagrined. "What an absurd complaint."

Sanct' Germain dismissed this with an idle gesture. "There are many such antipathies. Look about you. Hadrianus Tullian, there, cannot endure the taste of anything from the sea. With you, it is the scent of roses." He walked beside Petronius into the garden. "It's really quite beautiful here. The night, the fountains, so many lanterns . . ."

This was precisely what Petronius wished to hear. "I wanted to get away from the elaborate. These banquets are becoming nothing more than competitions in excesses."

"Which is hardly elegant. I agree." Sanct' Germain looked across the grass to the artificial arbor. "Positively arcadian."

Petronius caught the slight sarcasm in his guest's cultured voice, and stiffened. "It disgusts you?"

"No." Sanct' Germain laughed outright, which was rare. "I was thinking of Arcadia. A more desolate, bleak bit of land would be hard to imagine, but because shepherds graze their flocks there and pipe to relieve their unutterable boredom, the region has got a reputation which, believe me, it does not deserve."

This was an intriguing beginning, and Petronius was eager to pursue it, but a blare of trumpets announced the arrival of the Emperor, and he excused himself to greet his august guest.

Nero apparently approved of Petronius' new simplicity. He had discarded his lavish clothes for an ostentatiously simple Ionic chiton and chlamys whose only extravagance was that the cloth was shot with gold thread.

Three of the Praetorian Guard accompanied the Emperor, each in formal and elaborate armor, their red soldier's cloaks thrown back from their shoulders. They were silent, careful men, who quickly stationed themselves about the garden.

"I'm sorry I had to take this precaution," Nero said with a negligent wave of his hand. His voice, though rigorously trained, had never lost its slightly muffled quality, as if he were speaking into a barrel.

"A lamentable necessity," Petronius agreed, inwardly cursing his canny rival, Tigellinus, for surely these men would report the entire evening in detail to their captain.

The Emperor glanced around the garden. "I see you have done me the favor of inviting Justus Silius. A gracious gesture. He did me a great service recently."

"Indeed." Petronius fell into step beside his illustrious guest. Covertly he signaled Artemidorus to alert the musicians.

"And there is the foreigner from Dacia, who is not a Daci," Nero went on, studying Sanct' Germain. "He showed me designs for a new sort of hydraulic organ, which is exactly what is needed in the Circus Maximus. You must remind me to discuss it with him." The arrogant young head lifted.

Petronius murmured his assent. It was painful to look at the twenty-seven-year-old Nero. Ten years before, when he had risen to the purple, he had been a handsome, cherubic youth, with skin like roses and cerulean, sly, knowing eyes. Now those eyes were hard, the skin was marked by dissipation, and his early enthusiasm had turned to rapacity. When, Petronius asked himself, had he begun to hate this Emperor who had been so full of promise?

"A bower!" Nero cried out in delight as he saw the couches set for dining. "You never fail to create novelty," he said to Petronius. "Just when luxury was threatening to make me completely jaded, you do this."

That was one remark that Petronius devoutly hoped the Praetorians would report to their captain. He responded with graceful thanks, and concealed his satisfaction as the hidden musicians began to play. Perhaps he had worried in vain.

All but one of the guests moved quickly toward the couches as Nero sank down on the one set on a dais.

"Sanct' Germain?" Petronius said, surprised to see that the foreigner did not join the others in hurrying to recline.

"I had thought to see to the dancers. You will excuse me, I'm certain. Since this is their first appearance in Rome, and it is before the Emperor himself, I want to be certain they are fully prepared." His smile was quite bland, but Petronius sensed that it would be unwise to question him.

"Shall I have food sent to you?" He felt that he owed Sanct' Germain this consideration.

"I'll . . . dine later."

Petronius wished he could fathom the ironic light in those commanding dark eyes. "Some wine, then?"

"I do not drink wine."

There was nothing more Petronius could say. "As you wish. Your couch will await you, when you are ready to join us."

"I thank you," was the distantly courteous response.

As he turned to join the others, Petronius gave one last speculative look to Sanct' Germain. What was it about the man that so perplexed him? He put the matter from his mind, and focused his whole attention on the Emperor.

The meal was almost over when Sanct' Germain came back into the garden. More than an hour had passed, and the gathering had become more raucous as the unwatered wine was unstintingly poured by the most beautiful cupbearers money could buy. He took his place on the one empty couch and waved away the slave who approached him.

On the dais, Nero lay back, his usually petulant face now lit with a singularly attractive smile. Propped against his belly he held a small lyre, and this he plucked in uncertain accompaniment to the music of the pipes that came from the shrubbery. The other guests were somewhat weary of applauding his efforts, but did not have the courage to stop.

The ponderous figure of Cornelius Justus Silius rose from his couch, and the Senator approached the Emperor. "Very like the god Apollo," he effused.

"Apollo?" Nero said, stopping in the middle of his aimless tune.

"God of light and music," Justus went on, determined to make the most of this opportunity.

"And medicine," Nero said thoughtfully. "I cannot help but think that he must cure by singing. Music is the rarest, the highest art." His thick fingers plucked at the lyre again.

From her couch, Olivia motioned to her husband to withdraw, not trusting the caprice of the Emperor. She was ignored. Justus had spent the afternoon berating her for the lack of success she had had in finding a more stimulating lover. The Syrian merchant had been a bore, Justus told her, the magician from Britannia was a sham, and the last, a freeman from Raetia, had been demented enough to imagine himself in love with Olivia. Looking around the select gathering, Olivia bit her lower lip. Justus had renewed his threat of the Tingitanian from the stables, and the memory of that was enough to make her food turn to rocks inside her. Her eyes wandered over the gathering, searching and desperate. Would Justus tolerate a high-bred man as her lover, she asked herself, or must it be a freeman or soldier or slave? The sound of Petronius' voice turned her thoughts away from her predicament.

"It is fitting that in this gentle setting, evocative of all that is best is nature, we be entertained in a manner appropriate to our condition." He stood beside his couch, urbane, ineffably elegant, deeply weary. "So it is that I have procured through the good offices of Ragoczy Sanct' Germain Franciscus"—he indicated the foreigner with a gesture—"an entertainment that is truly new to Rome."

Nero had propped himself on his elbow, a greedy fascination in his alert blue eyes. "New?"

"Completely," Petronius assured him. "These are not the fine Greek pantomimes that Rome has come to love, but dancers of entirely different skills." He remembered how apprehensively he had approached Sanct' Germain about new entertainments at the end of autumn. He recalled that Sanct' Germain had been amused by his request and had promised to find him something that would astound every Roman who saw it. "These are religious dancers," he said, and faced the resultant groan with good humor. "Not in the manner you might expect. They come from Hind, where much of the worship is carried out in a manner that would please the most demanding Roman."

"How do they worship?" Nero asked, piqued beyond patience.

"They worship with their bodies. They have made a ceremony of the act of coition, and devote sacred texts to these matters. These dancers train from earliest youth to express every refinement of lust." Petronius heard Nero chuckle. "At the end of the arbor, where the extra lamps are hung, they will dance for you."

As Petronius spoke, Sanct' Germain had risen and gone for the three slaves from Hind. He addressed them in their native language. "You are to dance now. The man on the dais is the ruler of many lands. If you please him, it will be well for you."

The small, slender man turned his huge, liquid eyes to Sanct' Germain. "It is not the same as when we dance in the temple."

"Perhaps not," Sanct' Germain said. "Nonetheless, dance to satisfy him and you will be rewarded. He does not like to be disappointed."

The two small voluptuous women exchanged frightened glances. "He is a big man," one of them breathed.

"Yes," Sanct' Germain agreed. "Take your places." He stepped back into the shadows, and made his way to his couch as the sinuous notes of the flutes began to slide through the night.

Under the soft lights, the three dancers began to move. Their tawny skins took on the look of polished metal, and their slow, chastely sensual display completely absorbed the Romans. As the lithe bodies twined, embraced, moved apart and combined again in ever-more-convoluted variations on coupling, the guests watched, silent now, their faces lit with increasing avidity.

Cornelius Justus Silius leaned toward his wife. "Olivia, that is what I want, but faster, and harder."

Olivia swallowed against the sudden obstruction in her throat. It was difficult for her to watch the dancers before Justus spoke, and now she wanted to avert her eyes. That the dancers should make that terrible ugliness into such beauty distressed her. Worst of all was her fleeting suspicion that there could be beauty in the act and it had been denied, would always be denied her.

From his vantage point on the dais, Nero devoured the dancers with his eyes. They were enticing, their movements the essence of temptation. If he had been a little more drunk, he would have joined them, so that their supple bodies would fasten on his. He wished now that Poppaea were not pregnant, so that he could possess her in all the various ways the dancers implied. It maddened him to be refused the delight of her body while his child grew within her. He felt jealousy gnaw at him. He set his teeth. To be jealous of his own unborn child! It was the greatest folly, and yet it burned in his heart.

As he watched the dancers, Petronius was pleased. They were as remarkable as Sanct' Germain had promised they would be. He had feared they would be nothing more than the usual demonstrations of exotic and uncomfortable coital positions, and his fears had proved groundless. This was much more than the sexual display he had asked for—this was a worship that was art. He leaned back on his couch and let the fluid movements of the dancers enthrall him.

The dancers were almost to the end of their performance. Sanct' Germain, who had watched them with an odd, remote smile on his lips, rose and slipped away from the arbor. He knew that there would be requests made of him for the use of the dancers' skills, and he had to prepare the dancers for those demands. As he started to cross the grass, he noticed the large, haunted eyes of one of the women guests upon him. The intensity of the look startled him momentarily, for it was filled not with passion, but despair. It took him a moment to recall who she was—Atta Olivia Clemens, the young wife of Cornelius Justus Silius.

When the dance ended and the last sound of the flute faded on the warm breeze, the guests were loud in their approval. Petronius gracefully disclaimed all credit, but made sure that they would all remember that the dancers first appeared at his banquet.

"How intensely moving!" Nero cried over the babble of voices. "There is nothing like it in all my experience." There was no need for him to mention that his experience was vast—his varied sexual exploits had provided Rome with gossip for years.

The guests were quick to agree with him, and for once their enthusiasm was genuine. They spoke quickly, their voices brightly loud, and their movements showed their awakened concupiscence. They were eager to touch each other, to show their bodies, to invite new attention.

Olivia felt some of this, too, and wished she could be swallowed up by the darkness. For Justus to see her now, with this strange longing in her, would be worse shame than anything he had subjected her to so far.

"I am inspired!" the Emperor announced as he got to his feet. In the pale light his blond hair was silvery, his face young. He reached uncertainly for his lyre. "Let me sing my tribute to those incredible dancers, so that art will reward art."

Response this time was forced, and one or two of the guests exchanged quick, telling looks. It was dangerous not to show themselves delighted to hear whatever Nero wanted to sing, for music was one of the genuine loves of his life.

Petronius had followed Sanct' Germain to the area in the shrubbery that had been set aside for the dancers. He glanced over his shoulder toward the arbor, where he could hear a lyre being tuned. "It's unfortunate," he said softly.

Sanct' Germain's voice was dry. "What? That? You're probably right."

"I didn't mean it the way it sounded. You see, he does have some talent, and when it suits him, his discipline is enormous. But he has been given a small gift and great power, and so . . ." He stopped.

"The power is more important, then?" Sanct' Germain had seen the ravages of power before, had once known it himself. The price he had paid because of it was immense, and the memory of it still had a sting.

Petronius looked away. "Agrippina—she was his mother . . ."

"Yes, I know."

"She taught him to live without limits. She controlled him for years by denying him nothing, and for a while, her power exceeded his. He changed, after a while, when he learned that no one could refuse him. He is still, I believe, looking for the limits of his power. Sometimes I think," he went on, meeting Sanct' Germain's penetrating look, "that the reason he loves music as he does is because it is the only thing in his life that will not surrender to his power, but makes demands of him, instead."

"And does he realize this?" Sanct' Germain inquired, his fine brows lifting.

"He used to, perhaps. Now, I don't know." He felt suddenly very helpless and forced himself to assume the same confident stance he had achieved a little while before. "You've given me a great success."

Sanct' Germain said nothing, but a wry smile pulled at his lips. It had been so little a thing. "Shall I send the dancers to the arbor? Or do you think that would be unwise?"

"It's probably most unwise, but I'll undoubtedly ask you to send them shortly."

The beginning of a song sung by an unsteady baritone in quiet acceptable Greek echoed from the arbor.

"He's begun. I must return and show my pleasure," Petronius whispered hastily, as if at this distance he might still offend the Emperor by speaking while he sang. "When he is through, then bring the dancers. They will be most welcome."

"As you wish." Sanct' Germain watched Petronius make his way back across the dark garden. His thoughts were bleak now, but all that his face revealed was a remoteness that nothing seemed to touch.

Text of one of several identical letters from the architects Severus and Celer, dated August 24, the 817th Year of the City.

> Esteemed and noble citizen of Rome:
>
> You, along with all Rome, must be watching with awe the building of the Emperor Nero's Golden House. This glorious structure, when complete, will be the largest, most splendid building anywhere and will be the rule by which all other magnificent buildings are measured. The gardens alone have already attracted the admiration of the world.
>
> Many of you have had the opportunity to inspect the

domus transitoria and we feel it would be only just to say that no building has ever had a more beautiful, more spacious vestibule.

As architects for this grand venture, we are eager to have your assistance and advice on how best to ornament this palace, which will stand for all time as a monument to all that is finest in Rome. Do you know of any noble works of art that might suitably adorn these august walls? Perhaps there is, in your own home, some particular object that you feel would enhance the beauty of the building. Let us encourage you to bring it forth, and not be ashamed to make an offer because you feel that it would not be worthy of so great a place in the world. It is in the little items, the finishing touches that magnificent buildings become complete works of art.

The Emperor has assured us that any citizen offering such additions to his palace will earn his gratitude and praise. Those who have reason to show their love of the Emperor will find it now quite reciprocated. To have the favor of the Emperor as well as the honor of being represented in the splendor of his palace is the highest good to which any Roman may aspire.

We are certain that you will show your sincere devotion and help us make the Golden House the most remarkable testament to the glory, might and scope of the empire that has ever risen beside the beloved Tiber.

For ourselves and the thousands who labor in the tireless realization of the Emperor's dream, we send you our appreciative thanks. Your generous response will please all of us.

Severus and Celer
Architects to the Emperor Nero

6

FOR THE LAST three hours the stands of the Circus Maximus had been filling. Sailors had run up the high masts above the seats to unfurl the huge multicolored awning that would protect the thousands of spectators from the intense Roman sun. Vendors of food and drink forced their way through the tightly packed mob, crying their wares over the oceanlike roar of conversation.

In the lower seats, the nobility were beginning to gather, entering their marble boxes with cushions and little awnings that could be stretched over individual seats to lend extra shading from the sweltering morning. Most of them carried pomanders and bags of sweet-smelling herbs and spices which they held to their noses to block out the overpowering odor of the more than sixty thousand Romans crammed into the stands above them.

The crowd cheered as the nobility arrived, for that meant that at last the Games were about to begin. Occasionally insults were shouted to particular Senators and lesser nobles, but these jeers were haughtily ignored, being beneath the notice of highbred Romans.

A sudden blare of trumpets, two for cadence and one for the low drone, announced the arrival of the Emperor, and for a moment the huge stadium was relatively silent, the roar of voices dimmed to the drone of bees. The fanfare was long, and the instruments were played more for volume than quality of sound, and it served well enough. As the trumpets fell silent, Nero, dressed today in a full robe like an actor's, of shimmering green silk, strode into the imperial box.

From every point in the arena, the infectious cries came. "Ave! Ave! Ave!" The sound was an intense physical presence in the Circus Maximus.

Nero grinned and raised his hand in acknowledgment.

Immediately the shout grew louder, coming faster. Nero stood alone in the imperial box, a flush of pride on his still-boyish face. When he lifted both hands in the same gesture of an actor accepting applause, the response was deafening.

Finally the tremendous sound subsided and Nero motioned to the rest of his party to join him. Four slaves carried in green cushions to place on the large marble chair where he would sit, and one of his Greek attendants handed him the wire-framed eyeglasses of fine green crystal that Nero habitually wore to protect his eyes from the glare of the sun.

Once he was comfortably disposed, Nero gestured to those in his company to be seated. Tigellinus, with a tribune and two centurions of the Praetorian Guard, framed the imperial seat. To Nero's left, Vibius Crispus shared a plate of cold grouse with Aulus Vitellius, who had recently furthered his political career through his triumphant management of the

Neronian Games on behalf of his Emperor. On Nero's right, the young Marcus Cocceius Nerva, who had helped contain the most recent conspiracy, was in deep conversation with the distinguished general Cnaeus Domitius Corbulo. As the crowd renewed its cheers, Corbulo's long, sensitive face took on a cynical smile, and he turned away from the young Nerva to make some remark to the Emperor. Apparently it was successful, for Nero threw back his head with extravagant laughter.

Since he had Nero's attention, Corbulo asked, "Where's Petronius. I see Tigellinus, but the Arbiter is absent."

Nero made a face. "Petronius won't attend the Games since I've lifted the ban on killing of gladiators and animals."

Tigellinus smiled his malice. "Petronius is not in sympathy with true Romans."

This was overreaching, and Nero reprimanded him gently. "My good Praetorian captain, it was I who ordered the ban on slaughter. For a time it seemed so wasteful, all that death."

The rebuke struck home. Tigellinus straightened up, his color heightened, and was silent.

Another bray of trumpets announced the arrival of the Vestal Virgins, and once again the crowd became quiet as these venerable women entered their box. The reaction of the mob in the many tiers of seats was less vociferously enthusiastic, but still genuine and respectful.

There was one last brazen shout from the trumpets, then the hydraulic organ that was mounted in the spina which ran down the center of the Circus Maximus gave a peremptory belch, then launched into a spirited march tune as the Gates of Life opened and the great parade began.

The editor of this series of Games was Vivianus Septimus Corvino, a newly created Senator of twenty-nine who had just recently acceded to his father's dignity and estates, and was determined to make a stir in society. The mob was generally unimpressed with such social-climbing minor nobles, and their reaction to Corvino was typical. When the young Senator appeared in his fantastically ornamented chariot to make the first pass around the spina, there were catcalls from the upper seats. Corvino, noticeably nervous of the two lions that drew the chariot, led by slaves in silver armor, started to sweat as he heard the sound. The hoots and applause grew more raucous, and by the time he had made his way all around the spina and was prepared to mount the steps to the podium where he was entitled to sit, his face was set with fury because of the derision the crowd had heaped upon him. He climbed to his seat on the podium and glared at the Emperor.

With a loud, discordant blast, the trumpets joined the wheezy bellowing of the hydraulic organ, announcing the parade of the various combatants and contestants who would be appearing through the next three days of Games. Knowing the temper of the Roman populace, the editor had kept to tradition and put the charioteers first, though their races would not come until later that day. There were three ranks of chariots, four chariots to each rank, and the crowd shrieked out its pleasure, since it meant that there would not be the usual two, but three races during the Games.

In the second rank of chariots, Kosrozd held his team with steady, experienced hands. As always, the horses were nervous, but he had long since become used to the problem and was no longer flustered by the noise that swelled around him. He glanced toward the Blues' charioteer in the next vehicle, already searching, studying to find any little flaw or lack of skill that would give him the advantage when he raced later that afternoon. The Blues' charioteer returned the careful, measured look with hard eyes.

Behind the charioteers came all the trained fighters: gladiators, retiarii with their nets and tridents, marching with the armored secutori who would try to kill them before sunset; bestiarii and venatori came next, many of the bestiarii with their specially trained animals. Two gigantic Nubians led ostriches somewhat apart from the others, as the huge birds were known to have unsteady tempers.

So far the crowd approved of what they saw, and the reaction became more favorable as the parade continued. It would be a worthwhile three days for all of them. There was much to see, and a promise of real fighting.

In the imperial box, Corbulo leaned forward as a troop of essedarii passed beneath in their high-fronted chariots.

"They interest you, General?" Nero asked politely.

"I wish we'd had them in Armenia," was Corbulo's thoughtful answer. "We could have used their lassos to break up the infantry. A few units like that, and we might have been able to take on the Persians." He leaned back and folded his arms over his chest. "Well, it's over now."

"Would you like to go back to Armenia?" was Nero's next, too-innocent question.

"I am a warrior, my Emperor. I want to be with my soldiers, but thanks to the folly of my son-in-law, I would not blame you for keeping me here. It's good strategy, even though in this case it isn't necessary." It was a clever answer, stealing the march on Nero's interrogation.

"Your son-in-law should have stayed away from conspiracies. Why didn't you warn him?" Nero was growing petulant as he thought of the recently failed attempt on his life. "If Justus Silius had not had the courage to warn me, you would cry 'Ave' to Piso now, and perhaps fight with those wretches who face the wild beasts for the amusement of Rome."

"Would you call Silius courageous?" Corbulo returned, but without any enjoyment in the game. "The people love you too much, my Emperor, to trade you for another." It was true enough that Corbulo spoke without flattery.

The parade was almost through; most of the participants had already left the arena through the Gates of Life. Only a last few bull riders and dwarfs cavorted on the fine white sand as the trumpets and hydraulic organ blasted out the last of their march.

Sanct' Germain stood near the stables as Kosrozd approached in his chariot. "How are they?" he asked when the young Persian was near enough.

"They'll do. Titanius"—he nodded toward the largest horse on the leftmost side of the team which would have to hold the other horses steady on the sharp turns around the ends of the spina—"is very strong. I've had him out on the practice trails and it should make a difference." He handed the reins to one of the stable slaves as he came out of the chariot.

"When do you race?" Sanct' Germain inquired, coming up to Kosrozd.

"We're the fourth or fifth event, just before the break at midday. Not a bad time, really. The heat won't be too great. Jeost is the unfortunate one—he's scheduled to do his exhibition race the hour before sunset. By that time, the heat will be unbearable." He had fallen into step beside his master as Sanct' Germain led him a little apart.

When they were sufficiently removed from the other charioteers, Sanct' Germain turned to Kosrozd. "I've had a talk with Drusus Stelida. He's heard a rumor that the Blues have instructed their charioteers to win today at any cost."

Kosrozd recalled the expression on the Blues' driver during the parade. and nodded once. "I'll remember that."

"The Whites might give support to the Blues for that. They both want to run the Greens off the track." Sanct' Germain stopped walking. "You're in an odd position, Kosrozd. I don't belong to any of the four factions, and that means they can attack you with impunity. The Reds are staying out of this particular confrontation."

A unit of Gallic cavalry clattered by, and Kosrozd watched them. "They're fighting Parthian cavalry. It looks like a good match."

Sanct' Germain followed Kosrozd's gaze. "I'd give the edge to the Parthians—they've got the better horses and their armor is lighter. I doubt those Gauls will get close enough to use their spears and axes." He returned his attention to Kosrozd. "I realize that this is not quite within the official rules, but so long as you carry this strapped to your leg"—he bent and pulled a long, thin-bladed knife from his high-topped boot—"you can say it's for the traces. Remember that the Blues are giving their drivers flails. Don't let him get close to your side, or he'll go for your shoulders with it."

Kosrozd took the knife, his expression very serious. "I don't know how to thank you."

"Thanks?" Sanct' Germain asked sardonically. "I paid a great deal of money for you, and I won't allow political caprice to interfere—"

A loud blare of trumpets cut through the rest of what he said, and saved Kosrozd from having to make a reply. Around them activity increased dramatically, and there was the sound of straining ropes as massive cages were lifted into position.

"The first event is a venation, isn't it?" Sanct' Germain asked as the sounds of distressed animals became louder.

"Yes. White bears, wolves and wild oxen at first. Senator Silius has bought half a dozen Hyperborean venatori for this hunt. They're good fighters."

Sanct' Germain could not quite conceal his disgust. "Now that Cornelius Justus Silius is back in the Emperor's favor, he's fully determined to make the most of it."

"You have bestiarii scheduled here today?" Kosrozd asked, thinking that he had not seen any of them when he had come to the Circus the night before.

"They fight tomorrow. Most of them are lion handlers, and

one of them works with the big Asian bulls. They'll be sent in tonight." Sanct' Germain now owned more than fifty bestiarii, a great number for a foreigner, but insignificant to a Roman noble.

Kosrozd accepted this. "I must prepare, my master. The venation is almost started. There will be a race after that, then forty pairs of gladiators will fight, and then I race." Like all charioteers, Kosrozd spent a considerable amount of time exercising and strengthening his arms and shoulders.

"Good fortune on the sands," Sanct' Germain said as he turned away from the Persian charioteer. He made his way through the warren of halls under the stands toward one of the stairs that would take him into the stands. He did not hurry. The venation promised to be a long one and Sanct' Germain had discovered that he was sickened by the carnage of these hunts.

When at last he entered the box of tribune Donatus Egnatius Balbo, all but a few of the animals lay in heaps on the sand. The venatori had not fared much better—there were only seven of them still capable of facing the two huge white bears and one wild ox that remained.

"Sanct' Germain," the tribune said as he waved his guest to one of the marble seats. "You should have got here sooner. There was real sport for a while. The wolves got three men between them and tore them to pieces." As he spoke, he kept his eyes on the white bears that stood on their hind legs, long claws curved to rip open the vitals of any venator foolish enough to get too close.

"I was detained with my charioteer," Sanct' Germain said shortly as he dropped onto the hard stone.

The Circus Maximus was heating up, and the smell of slaughter mixed with the effluvium of the crowd. It was worse than any battlefield Sanct' Germain had known, for battlefields had not been sheltered with the enormous awning that flapped gently overhead.

Only one white bear was left, the ox and the second bear having fallen to the venatori. Already the Gates of Death had opened and teams of slaves with ropes and hooks were coming to drag away bodies of animals and men impartially.

With a terrible coughing bellow, the last white bear collapsed, transfixed by two javelins.

"Excellently done!" Egnatius cried out, though Sanct' Germain could hardly hear his words through the howl of the crowd.

As the last of the animals were dragged away, sand wagons circled the spina, spreading a thick layer of new white sand over the blood. The slaves spreading the sand worked carefully, for if the scent of blood lingered at any one location too strongly, the racing horses would balk, refusing to run where death was too apparent.

"There's going to be an aquatic venation later on, after the midday meal. Crocodiles and hippopotami; Egyptians and Numidians will hunt them from rafts. That's always worth watching, particularly when one of the venatori falls into the water." Egnatius' face was flushed, partly from the terrible heat of the Circus and partly from pleasure.

"Indeed," Sanct' Germain murmured, and wondered how he might excuse himself without seeming impolite.

Egnatius' young wife was pouting, and complained to her husband, "They say that Telcordes won't fight today. He isn't recovered from the wound in his shoulder."

The tribune laughed as he patted his wife's thigh, and said to Sanct' Germain, "Celia adores gladiators, and that brute from Cyprus has caught her fancy. I don't understand it, myself, how a well-bred lady decides that she would swoon for the dubious pleasure of taking a professional killer to her bed."

Celia stared moodily at the long, thin wall of the spina. "I heard from my body slave that Mocantor says that Olivia, Domita Silius, has bedded Telcordes."

Her husband scoffed at this. "If half of what slaves said were true, the rest of Rome would never have time to get out of the sheets."

Below them the sand was almost ready for the first race. The tribune's box was on the return side of the spina, away from the starting line, so the beginning of the race would not be visible. They watched as the four chariots came from the Gates of Life to the edge of the spina to line up.

"The Whites have a good team, there," Egnatius said. "What do you think, Sanct' Germain? You breed horses."

"Showy," Sanct' Germain said after a cursory glance. "They're handsome enough, but they won't last the course."

His predictions proved accurate. By the time the erectores had removed five dolphins and four eggs from the high columns at the end of the spina, indicating that four and a half laps had been run, the Whites' team was lagging, although the charioteer lashed them with the light whip that was more for directing the team than spurring them on. The Blues' team was in the lead with the Greens' immediately behind. Hoping for an advantage, the Reds' chariot swung close in around the spina, and the left wheel caught on the nearest meta, those tall marble cones that acted as bumpers at either end of the spina.

The crowd shouted as the Reds' chariot was dragged forward and sideways by the force of the impact, and for a moment it seemed that the charioteer would be thrown from his vehicle into the wheels of the Whites' chariot.

At the last possible instant, the charioteer rocked his chariot free of the meta and continued on the course. The sound of applause was colored by moans of disappointment from the upper stands.

Nero, who had been watching the race intently, was openly delighted when the Green team made the winner's solitary circle of the spina, to the noisy acclaim of the crowd. At the end of this last, glorious lap, the charioteer pulled up before the imperial box.

"Hyacinthos," the Emperor called out, and waited while the mob became quieter. "Hyacinthos, this is your fiftieth win for the Greens." The reaction to Nero's words was mixed. Some cheered and called the charioteer's name, others booed. Nero held up his hand for silence. "In acknowledgment of that, today you are a free man, and a citizen of Rome!"

An eruption of noise followed this proclamation, and the sound did not lessen until the overjoyed Hyacinthos had left the arena through the Gates of Life.

"Nero knows what the people love," Egnatius observed. "By tonight, they'll be singing songs about this in the taverns, and every whore in the lupanar will swear that she slept with Hyacinthos on the night he was freed."

"I thought Crispus owned Hyacinthos," Celia said, puzzled.

Egnatius dismissed the question. "He'll be compensated. If they didn't arrange this in advance."

Once again the procuratori dormi were smoothing the sand, eliminating the deep grooves left by the chariots' wheels.

The trumpets gave the call of the gladiators as the Gates of Life opened, and eighty armed men marched to the podium to salute the Emperor and the editor of the Games.

"You don't have any gladiators, do you, Sanct' Germain?" Egnatius asked as the fights began.

"Gladiators are very expensive. It takes years to train them, and they need more attention than bestiarii. And a bad afternoon can bankrupt you." He turned so that he would not be watching the two men below who fought with the traditional wide-bladed swords with only their smallest shield to protect them. By decree of the editor, they were provided Corinthian helmets, which were considerably less protection than their usual headgear. "Also," Sanct' Germain added, "I am a foreigner. Roman officials are suspicious of foreigners with too many highly trained fighters in their possession."

"How cynical," Egnatius said distantly as he leaned forward for a better view of the arena.

"Look!" Celia said as she pinched her husband's arm. "That one! That's Plaudes, the one who killed Murens last month."

Before the gladiatorial combats were through that morning, Plaudes, like Murens before him, had left the arena through the Gates of Death.

When the sand was once again clean and smooth, the second group of charioteers came through the Gates of Life. Kosrozd had drawn the starting position one place over from the spina, with the Blues in the favored position. He had already tied the ends of the reins around his waist and was feeling for the best hold for each horse's mouth.

"Keep behind, Persian," said the charioteer in the Greens' colors to his right.

"Only if my horses aren't swift enough," he snapped.

There was a last flurry of activity at the starting gate and then the race was on. Kosrozd held his position the first two times around the spina, pacing his horses for a last, demanding sprint. They were to race seven full laps, and he did not want to tire his team too quickly.

Sanct' Germain watched closely as Kosrozd's chariot passed beneath his box. The Persian was doing very well, his nerves were steady, and he drove as if in battle.

Over the next two laps Kosrozd began creeping ahead of the inside chariot, not enough to take the lead on the inner track, but sufficient to strengthen his position and to press the Blues' driver.

"Your charioteer is very good," Egnatius said as Kosrozd finally began to pull ahead of the Blues on the inner track. "I give him one more lap before he's got the lead on the spina."

"Perhaps," Sanct' Germain allowed as another dolphin came off the high crossbar on the lap counter.

The chariots were on the far side of the spina, out of Sanct' Germain's sight when a sudden distressed, greedy cry went up from the specators, and whole tiers of people leaned forward, shouting. Those on the same side as Sanct' Germain craned their necks, trying in vain to see what had happened.

They did not have long to wait. The chariots rounded the metae at the end of the spina, and now there were only three of them. The Blues' chariot was no longer in the race, and Kosrozd was trying to hold his chariot on course in spite of wheel that was nearly off its axle. He was almost around the turn when the wheel broke free and the chariot lurched heavily onto its side.

A terrible hush fell over the stands, and for the time it would take to count five there was as much silence as there ever was in the Circus Maximus, and the muffled thunder of hooves on sand could be heard to the top row of the stands. Then the incredible welter of thousands of voices broke out again as Kosrozd, still tied to the reins of his horses, was dragged behind them over the white sand.

At first sight of Kosrozd, Sanct' Germain had moved forward, intent. His face had gone white as he watched Kosrozd twist, trying to grab the knife in his high sandals that would cut him free.

For a little time it looked as though he might succeed, for he had pulled himself around so that he could grab the reins in one hand. Then the end of the spina loomed and the horses, long used to the course, cut in close to the three tall metae. There was too much noise from the crowd for Kosrozd's shriek of agony to be heard, but Sanct' Germain saw the terrible impact before the horses dragged him on.

Sanct' Germain was out of his seat on the instant, and with a terse word to Egnatius, left the box, running down the stairs to the stable area, pushing his way past bestiarii and various fighters in his rush.

Two moratori were already moving through the Gates of Life to grab Kosrozd's maddened team as Sanct' Germain dashed into the area by the stables. A surgeon was waiting, and he looked up laconically as Sanct' Germain approached.

"You're the owner?" he asked as he dropped his well-used tools into a pot of water hung over a brazier.

"Of the charioteer for the Reds, yes." As he spoke, his foreign accent was stronger, which was the only indication of the degree of his worry.

The surgeon nodded. "The Blues' charioteer will go out through the Gates of Death." He was a man of grizzled middle age, the veteran of many military campaigns, and now resigned to his degrading work of tending to those wounded in the arena.

The moratori had caught the horses at last, and were dragging the team by main force toward the Gates of Life.

"Those lads," the surgeon said, indicating the moratori, "they've got a rough job. Catching a team of racing horses isn't my idea of soft work."

Sanct' Germain was not listening. He hastened to the open doors where the moratori stood calming the team. Ignoring the horses and the shocked exclamations of the moratori, Sanct' Germain went to Kosrozd's side.

The Persian charioteer was, mercifully, no longer conscious. His left shoulder was broken and a white shard of bone pushed through the mangled skin. Bruises and abrasions marked the rest of his body, and a deep gash in his leg was steadily pumping blood.

Angry with worry, Sanct' Germain took the knife from Kosrozd's ruined sandal and cut the reins at last. He motioned away the medico who came to drag Kosrozd to the surgeon, and instead took Kosrozd in his arms as easily as he might have lifted a child. Holding the charioteer with care, he took him across the stableyard to where the surgeon waited.

"You've a deal of strength, to carry him that way," the surgeon remarked as Sanct' Germain lowered Kosrozd onto the low pallet by the stable wall.

Sanct' Germain had no response to make to that. "He's badly hurt."

"I can see that," was the testy rejoinder. "I'll have to get the saw if I'm going to take that arm off."

"*No!*" Sanct' Germain grabbed the surgeon by the shoulder. "I forbid it!"

The surgeon gave a patient sigh. "Look, foreigner, it's not that I want to do it. But take a look for yourself. There are three bones broken around the shoulder. If I leave the arm on, he won't be able to use it, and the wound will fester and kill him. This way, he's got a chance to live. That's all you can hope for."

"I said no." He did not relax his grip on the surgeon's shoulder.

"There isn't any choice." The surgeon wasn't annoyed, but he disliked the attitude of the foreigner. "If you think you can do better . . ."

Sanct' Germain released the surgeon, who cleared his throat in preparation of ordering him to leave, but he was startled to see the foreigner kneel once again and lift the charioteer as he had before. "Stand aside, Surgeon."

A new voice interrupted them. "Franciscus, if you take that slave from here, no one will be responsible for what happens to him." It was the Master of the Bestiarii, Necredes, who stood to one side, an unpleasant expression on his hard features.

"That is quite acceptable to me." Plainly, Sanct' Germain did not want to be kept waiting any longer than necessary. "I will sign a document to that effect as soon as I have Kosrozd in a sedan chair bound for my villa."

"How do I know that you will not change your mind? You must give me that document first." He was close to smiling, and waved the surgeon away.

"You have my word on it," Sanct' Germain said, and started away toward the arches that led to the street.

Necredes hurried after him. "I won't be cheated by you as I was once. You'll say that I harmed your slave, or that no one cared for him."

Sanct' Germain's dark eyes took on a steely glitter. *"I gave you my word.* Stand aside!"

What might have occurred next was never known, for one of the bestiarii came running up. "Necredes, the big crocodile has gotten loose from his cage. We've got to have help with him!"

"Where?" Necredes demanded.

"Second level down. The door of the cage opened. We can't drive him back." The words were lost to Sanct' Germain as he hurried through the arches toward the street.

There were a number of chairmen standing about waiting for the Games to reach their midday break. Sanct' Germain chose four men who lounged beside a palanquin with several luxurious cushions and curtains to close it. "You, chairmen!" he shouted.

The largest individual turned. "Me?"

"Your palanquin. Get it ready." He had come up beside it and was carefully setting Kosrozd down in it.

"Hey! He's bleeding. You can't ruin our cushions."

"I'll pay for them." When he was certain that Kosrozd was well-supported, he reached and bound the smallest of the cushions tightly against the deep cut in his leg. The bleeding had lessened, but not enough to reassure Sanct' Germain.

"Get him out of there!" ordered the chairman.

Sanct' Germain straightened up. "I'm hiring you. You can't refuse legitimate hire."

The chairman gave him one caustic glance. "How do I know that?"

Sanct' Germain had endured more interference than he was willing to tolerate. "You know because I wear jewels in my rings, good citizens, and because that man's slave collar bears my name. The cost of your services outside the walls of Rome—"

"Outside the walls? Are you insane?" the chairman demanded.

"—is two sesterci per thousand paces. If you will carry this man to my villa, which is three thousand paces beyond the Praetorian camp, my body slave will give you three times that. All you must say is that it is because of the eclipse." Sanct' Germain reached into the bag that hung from his belt and extracted four gold coins. "This is your first payment. You must hurry."

The chairman grumbled even as he motioned to the other three to take up their positions. "Right, boys," he said like the old soldier he so obviously was.

When the palanquin had disappeared down the dusty street, Sanct' Germain stepped back through the arches of the stableyard, then turned toward the long hallway that would lead him back to the stairs to Egnatius' box. He had just come in from the sunlight when a voice spoke to him in the darkness.

"Sanct' Germain Franciscus." The voice was low, distinctly feminine, with the hint of a tremor.

He stopped, his eyes still dazzled by the brightness outside. "Yes?"

"I want to talk to you." She moved closer, keeping to the shadows. "I want to know you better."

"Better?" Sanct' Germain waited as his vision at last adjusted. He recognized the woman with a start as Olivia, Justus Silius' wife. He recalled the strange, frightened way she had looked at him in Petronius' garden.

"I want . . . I want you to . . . come to me. At night. Soon." Her face was flushed, her eyes still wide and frightened.

Sanct' Germain's thoughts were still on Kosrozd and the hideous injuries the Persian had sustained, and so he found it quite difficult to deal with Olivia. Ordinarily he had a deft and flattering reply for such offers, but now he stepped back. "I am sorry to disappoint you, Domita. It isn't wise for one so . . . foreign as I am to accept such invitations as yours." He set his jaw. "Let me pass, Domita."

"No. No." She stepped in front of him. "You mustn't deny me. You can't." There was a curious desperation in her pleas, and her hands lifted toward him as if seeking help. The lascivious charm most women displayed in these moments was entirely lacking in Olivia's manner. Sanct' Germain frowned at this strange supplication. He remembered the gossip he had heard among the gladiators and other arena combatants about this woman, about her constant seeking for new and violent lovers, and suddenly the gossip seemed at odds with the fearful eyes of the woman before him.

"When, Domita?" he heard himself ask in a harsh voice.

She sighed, actually sighed. "In three days. Two hours after sunset. Come to the door by the garden. A slave will admit you." Her mouth turned down at the corners, almost in distaste. "I will be in my bedchamber to receive you." She turned abruptly, making a gesture as if to push something away from her.

There were bellows and squeals and shouts from the arena as the aquatic venation at last began, but Sanct' Germain hardly heard the sounds. He stared after Olivia, his mind in new turmoil. Far down the passage, she passed through two pools of light, and it seemed to Sanct' Germain that she was fleeing from the dark and violent world below the stands. If that were so, why had she sought him and the others out? He could not fathom what had made him weaken toward her, but the more he considered it, the less he desired to find out. She was a dangerous woman to know. She was the wife of a powerful Senator, and Sanct' Germain a foreigner. Then he realized one other thing about her: she was terrified; and against his will, that understanding woke the sympathy within him.

Text of a letter from Nymphidius Sabinus, with Tigellinus, the commander of the Praetorian Guard, to the general Cnaeus Domitius Corbulo.

To the honorable general, Cnaeus Domitius Corbulo, greetings:

Since the hand of the Emperor and fortune have elevated me to share jointly with Ofonius Tigellinus the command of the Praetorians, I believe that with this honor go certain responsibilities, which I must exercise if I am to discharge the duties of my office with merit.

The Emperor, as I am certain you are aware, has suffered much this year. It is not only the conspiracy of Gaius Calpurnius Piso that has wounded him deeply, but some of those involved in the conspiracy were those he most loved. Seneca and Lucan accepted their fates and killed themselves for their role in that plot. It is some comfort to reflect that although they betrayed the Emperor, still they recalled that they were Romans, and died with dignity.

More recently, the tragic death of Poppaea, when she was so near to giving Nero a child, has been a severe blow to the Emperor, and he deeply grieves for her, blaming himself for her untimely death.

You have expressed yourself willing, even anxious to return to your legions, and we have made note of these wishes. Until now we have striven to be circumspect in your case because of your son-in-law's part in the late conspiracy. However, much has changed in the last few months, and we feel it might be advisable, even beneficial, to have you once again defending the honor of Rome in the field, where you desire to be.

At this time, the Emperor would find a victory noteworthy. You have often shown yourself to be the most capable of generals, well-loved by your men and devoted to the cause of the Emperor, the Senate and the people of Rome. For that reason, we are requesting that you reserve some time for us to speak, so that we may reach a more thorough understanding of the wishes of the Emperor and the Senate. It is senseless to let so capable a general as yourself fritter away his time in Rome when the empire is so much in need of your skills.

Conquest and triumph are certainly the highest reward to which any commander can aspire, but in addition, there is official recognition and honor to be given those who best serve the Emperor. Let me assure you that should you be willing to lead your men into battle once more, Nero would be much inclined to advance you and your family here at home, removing forever the stigma of disloyalty that now touches your house.

Let me have your reply by the messenger that brings this, and we will meet at your earliest convenience. I am confident that you will be eager to undertake the venture we will propose to you.

In anticipation of your interest, I salute you, Corbulo.

Nymphidius Sabinus
Commander, with C. O. Tigellinus
The Praetorian Guard

7

IN THE NORTH atrium of Villa Rogoczy lights burned although it was well past midnight. This untypical feature of the villa held not only its owner's personal quarters, but rooms where none but the somber Egyptian Aumtehoutep was allowed to enter. The slaves who lived in the apartmented barracks between the villa and the stables spent many hours in exciting and wildly inaccurate speculation on what those private rooms might contain.

Sanct' Germain stood in one of those chambers now, bending over the pallid form of Kosrozd. His face was grave as he inspected the inflamed wounds that gaped on the Persian's body. "Are you certain that all the splinters of bone were removed?" he asked in a low voice.

"All that I could find," Aumtehoutep said stiffly.

"I'm not accusing you, Aumtehoutep. Considering the damage done here, I'm surprised you were able to do so much." He had not looked up from Kosrozd. "His breathing is shallow, his pulse is fast and weak. And though the bleeding is stopped . . ." His gesture was one of helplessness.

"There is a limit to what art and skill can accomplish," the Egyptian agreed. "You know that better than I."

"If I had Sennistis and all the priests of Imhotep here, I doubt we could save him. Not after two days like this." There was a remote anguish in his dark eyes. "How old is he, do you suppose?"

"Seventeen, eighteen, certainly no more than twenty." Aumtehoutep went to an inlaid chest in the corner. "Do you want your tools?"

"So young," Sanct' Germain mused. "I can't remember being seventeen, or eighteen, or twenty. Or ten times those ages." He put one small hand on Kosrozd's forehead. "The fever is worse."

"How much longer, do you think?" Aumtehoutep held the chest open. "We have cordials for the pain."

"If he regains consciousness, I suppose we must use them." At last he stood up and rubbed his eyes. "A pity."

"Yes." Aumtehoutep's voice was colorless and he did not meet his master's eyes.

"You think I should save him?" Sanct' Germain asked, a cold smile on his lips. "Aumtehoutep?"

There was uneasy silence between them; then the Egyptian answered, as he stared at the chest. "I think it would be well to set his bones. If you do choose to . . . heal him, he would be able to race."

"Ah, yes. And precisely how do we explain his recovery?" He shook his head with annoyance. "Why won't you look at me?"

Aumtehoutep did not answer the second question. "There would be scars, and that's expected, but men have lived through worse than this and returned to the arena."

"Not as charioteers," Sanct' Germain snapped.

"Perhaps not. But you said that the surgeon never inspected his wounds. They don't know how badly he was hurt, and occasionally superficial hurts look worse than mortal ones." He closed the lid of the chest and turned to face Sanct' Germain at last. "He isn't ready to die."

"Neither am I," Sanct' Germain responded, but his face was troubled. "Do you think he could accept . . . changing?"

Aumtehoutep took an impulsive step toward Sanct' Germain. "Set his bones. Wake him. Deliver him. He'll acquiesce to the conditions of his change, because you gave it to him. You granted as much to that Assyrian captain . . ."

The anguish in Sanct' Germain's eyes contradicted the smooth sarcasm of his smile. "That was centuries ago. This isn't the same."

"Perhaps this isn't as necessary as that was, but with his adoration"—Sanct' Germain winced as Aumtehoutep said the word—"can't you reconsider?"

Sanct' Germain studied his somber companion. "You don't usually ask this of me. Why now, old friend?"

"You've been alone for too long." He said it slowly, and the etched lines of his face seemed to deepen in the light from the oil lamps.

"Alone?" Sanct' Germain tried to laugh, and failed. "Very well. I'm alone. What alternative is there?"

Aumtehoutep answered with difficulty. "There is the affection of others."

"Affection?" Sanct' Germain echoed. "Do you imagine, my kind good friend, that I could reveal my true nature and be treated with anything other than repugnance and detestation?" His voice held more suffering than anger. "That unfortunate young man"—he indicated Kosrozd's still form—"offered himself to me, in ignorance, oh, sincerely, I don't doubt that, but without any comprehension of what I am. Do you think his . . . adoration would survive learning the truth?"

"When there was plague in Luxor, you took me from the Temple of Thoth, and the plague spared me. Why do you refuse now to spare Kosrozd?" He put his hand on Sanct' Germain's shoulder. "You have been a good master to me for more years than I can count, you have treated me with . . . humanity . . ."

"Aumtehoutep . . ."

"Why do you hold yourself aloof?" He was careful not to raise his voice, but the intensity of his feeling made his words seem loud.

"Because," Sanct' Germain said slowly and distinctly, "I am afraid. Those good lusty Romans tolerate my foreignness because they don't understand the full extent of it. And while they may wallow in blood for sport in the Great Games, they would not regard my . . . tastes with the same approbation."

"But you have admitted many times that for you to be truly nourished, there must be emotion as well." He crossed his arms, determined to have an answer from Sanct' Germain.

"Of course, but any strong emotion will do. Terror is as strong, though not as durable as love. Gratified desire is as potent as intimacy, and more easily available. Tishtry serves me very well for that, and she has no complaints of me." Under his gentle self-mockery there was abiding pain, but he spoke lightly enough. "Tomorrow night I'm supposed to visit a Roman noblewoman. In her case, I think it must be terror I evoke. She didn't approach me with any apparent fervor."

The compassion Aumtehoutep felt for his master pulled at his body with physical force. "And is it enough?"

Sanct' Germain closed his eyes, and answered very softly. "I think I would be willing to give half my years for someone who would know me for what I am—for all I am—and would accept it all without reservation. In almost two thousand years, I haven't found that. I admit," he said in a different tone, "for some of that time I wasn't searching for such a person." He stopped and studied Aumtehoutep's face. "Do we have Persian earth here?"

It was not in Aumtehoutep's nature to smile, but there was a creasing about his eyes. "There is some in your laboratory. You wanted to process certain elements out of it."

"I can order more for that." Now that he had made up his mind, he gave his instructions quickly. "Take that earth and line the couch in my library with it, then make up a bed for Kosrozd. I'll need a soporific cordial for him when I'm through, salts to restore him to his senses, clean linen to bind his shoulder when it's set, the herb paste that dries up infections, tincture of poppies to relieve his pain while I set the bones, and my tools must be boiled with astringent leaves. I will need two changes of robe—make it my priest's robes. I don't want to wake him with his blood all over me." He moved quickly to the door. "I'm going to wash. Expect me back within the hour. For the first, make it the short robe, without sleeves, and be sure there is a pail of water and soap near me."

Aumtehoutep nodded at these familiar requests. He felt a profound relief that his master had agreed to save the young Persian. He set about his tasks quickly, familiarly, stopping occasionally to look at Kosrozd, to touch his brow, to listen to his breathing.

By the time Sanct' Germain returned, everything was ready. A brazier was set up near the bed where Kosrozd lay, and a pan of water boiled there. Beside it a small table was placed for easy access, and on it all of his tools were laid out with long strips of clean linen above them.

"My robes?" Sanct' Germain inquired after he had given an approving nod to these arrangements.

"In the side room. The short robe without sleeves is white, the other, black. He will feel more comfortable if he sees you in black." Aumtehoutep bent to scrub his own hands in the pail of water he had just brought.

"Of course," Sanct' Germain said as he went into the small adjoining room. The garments were set out exactly as Aumtehoutep had indicated. Sanct' Germain cast his Persian tunic aside and drew the white Egyptian robe over his head. He secured it at the waist with a wide belt, then turned and returned to the room where Aumtehoutep waited by Kosrozd's couch.

"Should he be secured?" Aumtehoutep asked.

"It's probably a good idea. He's got a great deal of strength in his arms, even now. I don't want to fight him." While Aumtehoutep bound Kosrozd to the couch with leather straps, Sanct' Germain made a last check of his instruments. "Where's the cauterizing iron?"

"I thought you were going to bind the wound with linen."

Sanct' Germain gave his Egyptian slave an exasperated frown. "If there is more bleeding than I anticipate, I'll need hot irons to stop it. He's lost too much blood already."

Chastened, Aumtehoutep went back to the chest and drew out three thin irons. "I'll set these in the coals of the brazier. Will they be enough?"

"If they aren't, I won't be able to save him anyway." Sanct' Germain made a circle of the couch, studying Kosrozd intensely. "I'll need better light. Bring four or five more lamps. Did you give him any herbs for sleeping yet?"

"The compound is in the jar on the nearest shelf. So are the other preparations you requested." He left the room then to get the lamps.

When at last all was ready, Sanct' Germain took a moment to withdraw into himself. No matter how many times he worked on battered and maimed bodies, and over the centuries he had done it hundreds more times than he could remember, it was never something he got used to. There was always the realization that the damaged bones and flesh were part of a human being, mortal, unique. He let his breath out slowly. "Very well. I'm ready."

It was more than an hour before he had bound Kosrozd's shoulder and thigh in the meticulous, layered strips of linen as he had been taught to do more than a thousand years before. When at last he was satisfied, he stood back. "It will do, I think. If he accepts his . . . change, he should have no trouble with the shoulder."

Aumtehoutep had bent to wash his hands in the pail beside the couch. The water was tinged now with blood, and the rough soap that frothed into harsh suds took on the color. "How long do I let him rest?"

"Ideally, for several hours, but it's too late for that. In three hours it will be dawn, and he must have taken my blood by then, or we'll have to wait until nightfall again." He was already untying the knot of his belt. "I must wash before I put on the other robe. Let him have an hour, and then wake him. Be certain he's not in too much pain. Don't use the poppy—that will make him fatigued and disoriented. There's a strong solution of willow bark and pansy that's an effective anodyne. Make sure he has that now, so it will have taken effect when he wakes."

"As you wish, my master." Aumtehoutep had gathered up the bloodied instruments and put them in the pail. "I'll set these to boil with astringent herbs first."

"Fine." He stopped in the door to the side chamber. "I won't be long, but if there is trouble, call me from the bath. He could still begin massive bleeding."

Aumtehoutep nodded and continued his work. The efficiency with which he did his tasks showed the economy of long practice. No movement was wasted, nothing was done abruptly. When he had gathered together all the things that were to be removed from the room, he stopped by the shelves and took down the bottle of anodyne solution. He unstoppered it, wrinkling his nose at the scent, and poured some of it into a cup no larger than the last joint of his thumb. He went back to the couch and stared down at Kosrozd. The charioteer was lividly pale, his breathing unsteady. Aumtehoutep bent and lifted his head with care. The Persian's mouth was slack, and it was with difficulty that Aumtehoutep tipped the anodyne liquid down his throat. Kosrozd coughed once, but neither gagged nor choked.

Before he left the room, the Egyptian loosened the straps that had held Kosrozd to the bed.

Somewhat later, Kosrozd woke, a sharp stinging odor in his nostrils. He tried to shake his head, but found he was too weak. He tried to push the vial that was held to his nose away from his face, but his hands were heavy and light at once, and would not do the bidding of his will. In a distant part of his mind, he knew he was badly hurt, and in terrible pain, but the knowledge was strangely muffled, like screams heard through a pillow. He blinked, and his vision swam.

"Kosrozd." It was Sanct' Germain's voice, more compassionate than he had ever heard it before. Kosrozd tried to answer, but his tongue was thick in his mouth, and his voice was barely a whisper. At last he managed to say, "The race?"

"Yes. You were hurt." Now that Kosrozd was responsive, he closed the vial of pungent salts.

"How?" It seemed so strange to him. His weakness must be a part of someone else, someone he stood two or three paces behind and controlled like a puppet. His right shoulder felt huge, as if it had been inflated. He looked at his master, and his bewilderment grew. Sanct' Germain was dressed in a black garment of fluted linen. One arm and shoulder were bared, but the rest of him was enveloped in the crisp material. He wore a peculiar, stiff headdress over his dark hair and there were wide bracelets on his uncovered arm.

"The wheel came off your chariot. You were dragged by your horses." He said this gently, without embellishment.

"Dragged." He tried to remember, but found his mind refused to penetrate the blankness surrounding the accident. "I started the race . . ." he said uncertainly. "The first lap, the Blues' driver . . ." What had the Blues' driver done? It eluded him.

Sanct' Germain read the distress in Kosrozd's face. "No, don't pursue it now. It's not important." He had seen this many times, this closing of the mind that shut away the most dreadful moments and hid them.

"Where am I?" He did not recognize the room, and Sanct' Germain appeared to be so different.

"At my villa. This is one of those rooms that the entire household speculates about. As you see, no torture chambers, no debauched maidens, no religious paraphernalia, no cache of arms." These were the most prevalent theories in the slaves' quarters about the closed wing, and Kosrozd was slightly startled that Sanct' Germain knew of them. "This is where I study, where I . . . live. In the room next to this, there is a good deal of equipment that I use in compounding medicines and other things. I also have quite an extensive library, a large bath, my bedchamber, and rooms where I keep various items that are of value to me." He did not add that many of those items would be of value to others, as well, as he numbered large jewels, rare art and experimental alloys among them.

Kosrozd nodded, wondering now why Sanct' Germain was telling him so much.

"I want you to understand more before . . ." He broke off and resumed in a sharper tone, "Because of your father's folly, you are a slave instead of a prince, you are in Rome instead of Persia, and you are an arena charioteer instead of the leader of an army. You have excellent reason to be suspicious of everyone, including me. Yet, Kosrozd, consider very carefully what I tell you."

Though he tried to sort out what his master was saying to him, Kosrozd was increasingly baffled. "My master . . ."

"When you were dragged around the arena, you were very badly injured. Your right shoulder is broken in three places. You have two serious lacerations in your left thigh. Your skin was badly abraded by the sand. You were bruised all over your body. I've done everything I know to save you, except one. You will have to decide if you want . . ."

"If you don't do this one thing, will I die?" The possibility of death was not frightening, and he thought that perhaps the fear, like his pain, was hidden deep within him.

"It's likely." He had never found that question easy to answer, but Kosrozd's acceptance bothered him.

"What is it you do?" He had tried to move, but his body once again did not respond, and what little effort he had mustered had almost exhausted him.

"I do very little." Sanct' Germain fingered one of the wide bracelets. "I am not quite what you think me."

"You are my master," Kosrozd said, his brown eyes softening.

Sanct' Germain made an impatient gesture. "I told you once that there is death for some in what I do. Occasionally there is life, as well."

"Would it harm you?" Kosrozd asked quickly.

"No. It will not harm me." His smile was both sad and

wry. From one of the bracelets he pulled a tiny knife. "My blood, and the blood of those like me, has certain . . . virtues. Those who drink of it acquire those virtues. You will be proof against all but the most ruinous death. You will age very little. You will gain strength and endurance. You will also be shunned if you let this be known. You will find that the sun is harsh and burning. You will have to sleep, though you will sleep very little, on a layer of your native earth. You will not be able to cross running water unless you line your shoes with that earth. Most water will make you uncomfortable unless it is contained in your native earth. You will no longer live as other men. You will be nourished only by blood. You may take it from animals or from humans, but you will come to need . . . humanity. You will lose the ability to take pleasure as most men do unless you are glutted with blood. You will be very, very lonely." He waited, the little knife glinting in his hand. "Well?"

"Do you regret being what you are?" His dying eyes were luminous with adoration.

"At times. We all do." Memories rushed in on him as he spoke, and he forced them away.

"You offer me this because the alternative is death?" He saw Sanct' Germain nod. "If the alternative were life and freedom, I would still take the gift that comes from you."

Sanct' Germain looked away. Kosrozd was so touching and so foolish. Then he turned back and lifted the little knife. It was only a small nick. His blood welled up as he bent over the young Persian. Kosrozd's head rested close against his master's shoulder, held there by Sanct' Germain's strong, sustaining arm.

Text of a letter from Ofonius Tigellinus to the Emperor Nero.

To the august Emperor Nero, hail:

In accordance with the powers you have been

gracious enough to invest in me, I have followed my intended course of investigation of those who have sought to betray you and bring dishonor to the title of Caesar.

I have heard it said that in my vigilance I have turned Rome into a city of eyes and ears, and if by this they mean to say that villainy may no longer be hidden from official scrutiny, then I gladly accept that designation and regard as beneath contempt the hostility of those men whose duplicity I have discovered.

Great Nero, you are a man of too generous, too forgiving a heart. You refuse to believe ill of those around you. I have many times remarked on the tolerance and leniency of your nature, which stems from laudable traits of loyalty and affection. In this case, it is the more difficult, as my suspicions of a certain man have been confirmed, and the man is one who enjoys your kindness as much as he has earned my enmity. Naturally, you will be reluctant to think anything but good of this man, and it is known that I am too much his rival in social matters to be disposed to regard him with beneficence. In matters of conspiracy, binding proof is often difficult to obtain, particularly when, like this man, imperial favor protects them.

It distresses me much to have to displease you, to be the messenger that brings you word of ingratitude and betrayal. Yet it must be thus, or you will be exposed to more danger. I cannot endure the thought that you might, in your magnanimity, overlook the perfidious conduct of those close to you.

For many years you have shown favor to Titus Petronius Niger, and you have given him the full glory of your patronage. He has often been your companion, and you showed him great distinction by making him the Arbiter of Elegance for your court. His heart should be filled with profound satisfaction and gratitude to you for your recognition. Instead he has allied himself with those who oppose you. First he gave his sympathy to the cause of Gaius Calpurnius Piso, and not content with this treachery, he looks about for new conspirators with whom to plot your ruin.

Not for my personal vengeance, but for your safety, and the safety of the imperial purple, I entreat you to authorize me to arrest and punish this man. How much must he do before you realize the enormity of his malice? Behind the smiles, the pleasures, the grace of the man there is evil lurking. You, in your honor, do not perceive it.

Knowing how cautious you are apt to be, I will await your response as long as is necessary. You may want to ask others of their opinion of this man, or you may wish to find another solution to the problem. I would urge you not to banish him, for who can tell what schemes he may undertake away from the careful observation of Rome? In the provinces, he might find like-minded men who would lend their support and fortunes to just such another plot as Piso spearheaded.

When you have given the matter your thoughtful consideration, send for me, and we will make those arrangements which seem most appropriate to you. It might be wise to leave the Senate out of this conference, for this man has too many friends there who would warn him of your intent, and give him time to gain power and protection elsewhere.

I assure you, O Emperor, that at all times, your interests are foremost in my mind, and that nothing shall keep me from defending you from any threat whatever. It is always an honor to serve you in all things.

With obedient respect,
C. Ofonius Tigellinus,
with Nymphidius Sabinus, commander
The Praetorian Guard
the tenth day of November in the
817th Year of the City

8

SANCT' GERMAIN approached the house of Cornelius Justus Silius reluctantly. The angry and anxious note he had had two weeks ago from Olivia, berating him for not keeping their assignation, had named this night as a time she must see him. He had almost decided to send his regrets once more, but something in the reprimand disturbed him, and in the end he had donned his most impressive robe of black Persian silk, had two horses harnessed to his best chariot, and had driven into the city, to this impressive house on the Aventine Hill.

The door by the garden was, as had been promised, half-open, and a slave waited for him, a rail-thin, rat-faced man of late middle age, who bowed obsequiously. "The Domita expects you. One of the grooms will see to your chariot. If you will keep silent and follow me . . . ?"

Sanct' Germain disliked the slave, and was not anxious to entrust his horses to any groom of Justus Silius, but he held his peace. If he caused a scene now, he knew he could expect public embarrassment later. "Very well. Go quietly."

The slave bowed again, and lifted a lamp to light their way through the darkened hall.

The Domita's room was on the northwest side of the house, in what was obviously a fairly recent addition. The door was of carved and painted pearwood, the floors of green marble. The slave knocked once, then opened the door for Sanct' Germain.

Olivia sat up from where she had reclined on the pillows of her bed, one hand to her breast, her eyes bright with what Sanct' Germain was startled to realize were tears. "You did come."

"I don't recall that you left me much choice," he said coolly.

She drew back from those quelling dark eyes, and to cover this retreat, she busied herself with pulling back the hangings around her bed and securing them to the tall bed-posts that were carved-and-gilt satyrs. "No, of course I didn't," she said in a failing tone.

He gave the room one swift, comprehensive glance. The murals were elegantly done, showing every refinement of seduction. Here Mars and Venus coupled beside his discarded armor, there Helen was carried off by a jubilant Paris, and on the far wall, Jupiter in all his glory ravished Semele.

Olivia was speaking again. "Since you wouldn't come before, I had to insist . . . It was necessary." She glanced swiftly to the hidden door where Justus waited. "It was necessary," she repeated, then tried once again to overcome his forbidding reserve. "Attractive men, you know, are not too common." This was meant to be flirtatious, but was more like a cry for help.

"If you wish to command, there are slaves who must obey

you," Sanct' Germain said quietly, dangerously. "I do not like to be threatened, Domita."

She reached for one of the pillows to stop her hands from shaking. He would be worse than she feared. His menace was almost stronger than that of her husband. That black-clad, sinister foreigner on the far side of the room appalled her now that he was actually in the room. "Come nearer," she suggested timorously.

"Is that what you want?" He could sense her fear of him, and was perturbed by her determination to take him to her bed.

"You wouldn't refuse me again?" she asked with a certain amount of wistfulness in the words.

What was it about that woman? Sanct' Germain asked himself as he stood with arms folded while she lay back and beckoned to him. He could see tension in her body, and she would not look at him directly. He had known more women than lived in Rome, many of them lovely and seductive, but they never had the effect on him that this awkward, inept young woman did. "Precisely what do you want of me, Domita Silius?"

"Isn't that apparent?" she pleaded. She had to make him respond. Justus had told her that if she did not succeed with Sanct' Germain this time, he would bring not only the Tingitanian in from the stable, but the huge Boetian bodyguard he employed, and let them both take their pleasure of her. She wished her hands did not tremble so much as she lifted her silken robe to show her body.

"Gladiators and foreigners," Sanct' Germain said as contemptuously as he could. "Are we safer because we won't approach your husband?" His robe whispered on the marble as he moved nearer, and his black Scythian boots were sharply loud at each step. "Why do you want me?" he challenged her as he walked. "Why? Aren't there gladiators enough in the arena for you?"

She flinched at the question. "I . . . I'm not interested in them just now." It was impossible to meet his intense, enigmatic eyes. How much she wanted to dismiss him. Her hands were icy, her heart battered at her ribs, her head began to ache insistently. She caught her lower lip between her teeth, wishing she had the courage to send Sanct' Germain away and face whatever indignity Justus would mete out to her.

"I do not like being used, Domita," Sanct' Germain said in

a soft voice that cut like a blade. He knew she was afraid of him, and that was good. If he could frighten her badly enough, she would not demand he see her again. She might not object when he denied her his body.

"Used?" she laughed unhappily. "You?"

This time when he moved, he moved swiftly, covering her naked body with his own clothed one. He forced his mouth on hers, felt her tighten against him. He sank one hand in her hair and pulled her head back so he could kiss her again. His other hand he forced between them and ripped the open robe away from her. She lay beneath him, curiously passive. There was none of the crazed ardor he had been expecting, neither for pleasure or pain. Puzzled, he pushed himself onto his elbow and looked at her. Was she waiting for him to rape her? he asked himself. To cover his confusion, he reached to pinch out the lamps that hung around the bed.

Her hand on his arm stopped him. "No."

"You have no choice, Domita." His fingers closed on one wick, and then another.

She had never felt so helpless. No other man had insisted on darkness, and if Justus could not see what transpired, he would be furious. So softly that there was almost no sound to her voice, she whispered, "My husband . . ."

"Is coming?" He also whispered, dreading her husband's arrival. Justus Silius was known to be a cruel man, and he was gaining power. It would please him to make Sanct' Germain's life in Rome difficult.

She shook her head, her face pinched and flushed.

Sanct' Germain's hand hovered near another lamp. "What, then?" As he saw her expression clearly, he understood. Her fear, her humiliation no longer puzzled him. "Watches?"

Her hand went to his mouth to stop the word, though it was almost too quiet for her to hear. She nodded rapidly and turned her face away from him, wishing that the night would close over her like the sea. This was much worse than her earlier embarrassment. Sternly she tried to master herself as she had so many times before, but even as she fought herself, she felt tears on her face.

"Olivia?" He touched her cheek with one small, gentle hand. He hated now to think of what she had endured. He knew gladiators, whose pleasures were as brutal as their profession. For this woman to be subject to her husband's desires and the lust of men who killed each other for the amusement of Rome—it was obscene. How had she found the courage to resist for so long? "Olivia."

At that she turned to him, and saw the compelling tenderness in his dark eyes. She had long since despaired of finding such solace and compassion, and her terror, her sense of degradation and shame, almost shattered her. She pushed at him, squirmed under his weight as he held her, choked back sobs. The fright she had had for him before was only for his strangeness and the violence she felt lay coiled within him. Now she was nearly crushed by his understanding. Beatings, abuse, she knew she could survive as she had in the past. But if she once experienced concern for herself, and pity, it would be devastating to have to return to what she had known at the hands of others.

He held her until she knew it was useless to fight. Then he bent his head close to her ear. "Let him watch," he murmured. This time his kiss was leisurely and thorough. His lips lingered on hers as he drew her close to him.

"No. I can't," she breathed. "Don't."

"Yes." He kissed her eyelids, which were wet, the line of her brow, her ear. "Yes, Olivia." He was gently persistent, never forcing his way. He let her lie in the circle of his arms, protected, unmoving. He traced the line of her vertebrae. Her skin was soft and fragrant under his fingers. He could sense her weariness, and beneath that, her long-denied yearning. "Rest, Olivia."

She made a last, halfhearted struggle to break away from him, but sighed and was still. She did not want to resist. She wanted to lie here forever. If she had to resign herself to her husband's demands, she would take what little succor she could find. The silk of Sanct' Germain's robe was pleasant to her skin, his small hands touched her surely, holding her, exploring her. His caress was like his kisses, lingering and kind. Her arms went around him before she realized she wanted to hold him, and she turned her head to meet his mouth with hers.

Knowledge and acceptance flickered between them, as if each had opened the soul to the other. Neither had anticipated the moment, and both were shaken. It had been centuries since Sanct' Germain had experienced such intense intimacy. It was not Olivia's pleasure that gave him his satisfaction, that called to him so persuasively, but Olivia herself. This alarmed him, for it made him more vulnerable than he had ever been. He stopped stroking the line of her hip to look at her.

Now her eyes met his without trouble. "What?" she asked as she touched his mouth with one finger. She liked his face, she decided. She liked the large, dark, arresting eyes, the wide forehead and fine brows, the high, sculptured cheekbones and the classic nose that was not quite straight, the ironic mouth, the well-defined jaw. It was a good face, she decided, a friend's face.

He waited while she studied him, feeling his reserve giving way to her. From the depth of his being he wanted to confide in her, and because he could not bear the thought of her repugnance, he kept silent about that, only saying, "Let me love you."

Olivia could not speak to answer. She guided his small hands to her body, suddenly weak with desire. As he touched her with ever-increasing ardor, she felt her body waken to him, made pliant by his caresses.

It was a joy to see her discover passion at last, Sanct' Germain reflected as Olivia began to breathe more deeply. His satisfaction as she achieved her consummation was almost as complete as her own. She lay back, her face flushed, her mouth open, every line of her body replete with gratification. She would not deny him his own need.

Something of this seemed to communicate itself to her. "But you? You haven't . . ."

"No. I am not like that." He stroked her thigh, feeling her quiver. "But I don't want to give you pain."

She looked at him, her expression serene. "You cannot do worse than has been done to me already." What did her husband think of this? she wondered, mildly shocked that she had so competely forgotten he was watching.

Her words stung him. "It's not my intention to be someone else you endure." His newly roused sensitivity was quite delicate, not entirely welcome.

Olivia blinked, surprised by his reaction. "I didn't mean . . ." Some of her delight faded, blighted by the tone of his voice.

He determined to recapture their intimacy. "I know. Olivia, listen a moment. I don't want to hurt you, but what I want may . . . upset you. I would rather not indulge myself if it would give you a disgust of me." It would always be possible to call Tishtry to his bed, but the thought seemed strangely empty.

Her face softened, and she held out her arms to him. "Whatever it is you want, I am willing."

This time he inflamed her more quickly, and at the height of her fulfillment, he bent his head to her throat.

He left her more than an hour later. She had followed him to the door of her chamber, her hand in his. "I won't forget you," she had whispered.

"I won't give you the chance to do that." His dark eyes smiled down at her.

She shook her head in sudden despair. "My husband won't allow it." As it was, she was already anticipating his anger, and his vengeance. The very thought of the Tingitanian stablehand revolted her.

"What is it, Olivia?" He had seen the disgust in her face, and his concern made him anxious for her.

"Nothing. My husband . . ." What could she tell this foreign man now? She leaned her head against his chest.

"Your husband has no right to use you as he does." It had been a useless thing to say. He had begun to hate Cornelius Justus Silius.

Olivia had nodded. "He doesn't like . . . pleasure. He isn't stimulated by it." How she had wanted to weep, but she was too proud for tears. "He will try to keep you away."

"He won't succeed. I promise you that, Olivia." He had kissed her then, one last time, his arms enfolding her, holding her close to him.

When Sanct' Germain was gone, Olivia turned to face her husband. She crossed the room slowly, her naked body glistening in the soft lamplight.

A moment later the hidden door opened and Justus burst into her room. His heavy face was set and there was heightened color in his cheeks. "What in the name of Priapus was that?" he demanded as he lifted his hand to strike her.

She staggered under the blow, but met his ire with her own. "That was my satisfaction, Justus."

"'Why did you permit it?" He reached for her shoulders in order to drag her back to the bed.

"Don't!" she screamed. It was too much to stand, going from Sanct' Germain's ecstatic embraces to the malevolent hands that bruised her now.

"You don't defy me!" Justus roared at her. "One more evening like tonight and your father and brothers will suffer for it, I promise you!" He had almost decided to make her pay for her treachery this very night, with his Boetian bodyguard.

"I didn't know he'd be like that," she protested as he flung her toward the bed.

He glanced down once, and the beginning of a smile curled his mouth. There was blood on the pillows. Perhaps the foreigner had been rougher than he thought.

Olivia saw the blood, and said, "The brooch on his robe cut me." It was a convincing lie.

"Is that all? Why didn't you provoke him?" He stood over her, his large hands bunched into fists at his sides.

"How?" She knew he would have no answer to that question. "I didn't know what he was like. How could I?" She was breathing rapidly, and she grabbed for one of the sheets to pull around her.

Justus tugged it away. "You should have dismissed him, then."

"You mean I should have summoned slaves to throw him out bodily? Perhaps I should have said you were expected. I didn't know what he was like, Justus. I didn't!" Her protestation had the ring of truth, she knew. "You suggested I approach him."

"Liar!" The back of his hand lashed her, then the front.

"You did!" she yelled as she raised her arms to protect herself. "That night at Petronius' home, after the dancers came back. Petronius told you that Sanct' Germain had supplied the dancers, and you told me to try for him. You told me!" She knew she would be heard by the slaves, but it didn't matter.

He did remember, as he remembered the terror in her eyes as she saw the Emperor circle the waist of the smaller of the two women dancers. Olivia had felt sorry for the woman, and refused to believe that Nero's favor was a signal honor. "That was months ago."

"He didn't come the first time I asked, Justus. You were angry then, too. No, don't hit me again," she said as she put out her hand to him. "You tell me that I've disappointed you, but how could I know? How could I know?"

"His reputation is . . . odd." He put one knee on the bed and began methodically to slap Olivia, now on the shoulders and face, now on the stomach and breasts. "Lie back," he grunted as he dragged his robe open.

Without meaning to, Olivia drew back from her husband, one arm thrusting out to push him away. It was too soon, she thought desperately. She had not had enough time to put her rapture behind her. She was still touched with pleasure and fulfillment, and to be violated by Justus was loathsome.

"Your brothers, Olivia." Justus smiled as he inexorably pushed her back under his massive body. Perhaps Sanct' Germain had not been quite as unsuccessful as he had thought. Certainly Olivia had never been so revolted by him before. He chuckled. He could not recall a time when she had fought him so much. It was a welcome novelty, and for that reason, if no other, contributed to his enjoyment.

Olivia willed herself to be still, to be silent as her husband moved on top of her. His presence was vile. She was afraid that if she opened her mouth to protest, she would vomit. It had been so little time, hardly more than an hour, since she lay beside Sanct' Germain, ready to dissolve with satisfaction. Now this. Her body was slick with sweat; her arms felt leaden. Good Mother Isis, she begged, let him be quick.

A letter from Ragoczy Sanct' Germain Franciscus written in his native language to his body slave Aumtehoutep.

Aumtehoutep, old friend:

I am going to Cumae after all. Petronius is much troubled, and has renewed his request that I visit. I did not want to leave you just now, with all the recent changes around us.

Your idea of making small houses for the arena slaves is an excellent one. I should have thought of it myself. By all means, see that two-room cabins are built for all the bestiarii, and assign Tishtry and Kosrozd private ones. It will arouse little suspicion if you do the same for a few of the others. You should have the first of these built in a month, and I should be back well before then.

The larger cages that were ordered for the tigers are ready, and should be delivered in the next two or three days. Be certain that these are not put near the stables, or there will be panic. I have promised Tishtry the pick of the tiger cubs. The animal must be given to her within half a day of its birth, otherwise it will never be close to her.

On my way to Cumae, I will stop in Ostia and arrange for the new shipments from Sennistis to be brought to you. The designs for the mosaic in the transitoria are in my library, and as soon as the stones arrive, put Protuos and his crew to work on it.

There is a note enclosed with this that must be delivered to Olivia, Domita Silius. You must be very careful, for her husband has forbidden her, on pain of beating and worse, to have anything to do with me. Do not trust her slaves, but see if perhaps she may be approached at the Games. You might be able to speak to her when Justus sends her under the stands to approach gladiators.

Look for me in three weeks. I doubt that I can make my visit much shorter than that. There are rumors everywhere that Nero is going to banish Petronius, and he is preparing himself to leave for whatever distant and hostile outpost the Emperor selects. There is little I can do but bid him farewell, and that I must do.

Your loyalty and courage, as always, fill me with gratitude.

R. Sanct' Germain Franciscus
(his seal, the eclipse)

9

PETRONIUS' VILLA stood high on the cliffs overlooking the sea. It was a magnificent setting: a little promontory with wind-bowed cypresses on one side, and easy access to the beach below on the other. The garden flanked the long colonnaded transitoria and opened onto the unusual three-sided atrium.

The building was painted a soft coral and in the evening sun it glowed like red gold.

From his study, Petronius could look out at the indigo ocean. His desk faced a large, unscreened window, and he sat there now, staring out into the smoldering sunset. In one hand he held an iron stylus; and in the other, an official document, the seal broken, dangled from his negligent fingers.

He was roused by a tap at the door. "Yes?"

"Sanct' Germain. Your house slave said you wanted to speak to me."

"Come in." He tore his eyes away from the window and rose to greet his guest. "Sit down. I suppose you've heard?"

There was no point in denying it. "About the soldiers? Yes, I saw them leave. The tribune has left six men at the foot of the hill, and one by the cliff." He had gone out to check this not long ago.

Petronius sighed. "I have the order." He held up the document. "Prison, and then death. For all my family. Tigellinus is determined." He put the stylus aside and rubbed his face. "These are my instructions. I've made a copy for you, in case there are any questions later."

Sanct' Germain glanced down at the neatly written lines. "It isn't necessary, Petronius."

"But it is. Someone, preferably someone who is disinterested, must have this. Otherwise I leave everything at the mercy of the August Emperor, and Nero, I find," he went on lightly, bitterly, "is not well-disposed toward me."

There was nothing Sanct' Germain could say. He held out his hand for the closely written sheets. "What shall I do with them?"

Petronius looked at them, then back out at the sea. The sun was down and a band of tarnished silver lay along the horizon. "Keep them for the moment. They are dated and have my seal. Three of the sheets are grants of freedom for some of my slaves. I want you, if you will, to be certain that the grants are honored. It would not be the first time that Nero seized all the household of such a dangerous criminal as I am." He reached for the stylus again. "I've also prepared a few words for the Emperor. I will send it with the tribune outside. It would please me if you will find out if Nero sees it."

"Your tribute?" Sanct' Germain asked, knowing it was proper for a man in Petronius' position to send laudatory verses to the Emperor, exonerating him of blame and praising his rule.

"My tribute, yes." Petronius' smile was more of a sneer. "I want to do one honest thing in my life, Sanct' Germain. I fear that Nero will find more bees than honey there, but as that has been my experience of him . . ." As if he were suddenly tired, Petronius sank into the chair at his desk once more, and motioned Sanct' Germain to the long padded couch by the wall. "I am sorry that I have to ask anything of you, but there is no one else here who is as safe as you are. They are Romans, and for that reason, they are at the command of Nero. None of them is free to help me, and so, it must fall to you. I can't ask it of anyone else here, Sanct' Germain."

"Yes." He nodded slowly. "Very well. If there is anything else, let me have it before morning. I will want to be away before the soldiers return, or they may ask that I give up your effects, and I would have to." He rolled the documents together and secured them with a ribbon that Petronius held out to him. "What time do you leave?"

"I'm not leaving," Petronius said rather distantly when he was satisfied the roll was properly tied. "Keep that hidden, or there might be difficulties."

"Not leaving?" Sanct' Germain looked across the darkening room.

"The Emperor wants to see me beaten to death with the plumbatae. I am going to disappoint him." He rose to strike flint and steel to start the nearest lamp. "I've always loved solitude, but I never found the time for it. I kept thinking that there would be years for it, sometime later. Then I could write something worthwhile. It was so important to take advantage of imperial favor." He lit a second lamp. "How I deceived myself!"

"What about your guests?" Sanct' Germain asked softly.

"They are still my guests. I promised them entertainment tonight, and they shall have it. I will enjoy it, too. There are Greek musicians to play for us, and you have brought that enormous Egyptian harp. I've hired some dancers from Sicilia, and that new poet from Mons Veridium to read his verses. A very pleasant evening, really." All six lamps were burning now, and he reached to slide the shutters closed. "You *will* play for me, won't you?"

Sanct' Germain sat very still. "Yes," he said after a moment. "I will play for you."

"Thank you." Petronius turned away to open a box on his desk. "This is my seal." He held out the ring to Sanct' Germain. "I want you to compare it to the impression on the things I gave you, and if you are satisfied it's genuine, I want you to break it."

"Break it?" Sanct' Germain had seen the seal before, and a quick look assured him that the impressions on the documents he held were correct. They were rolled loosely so that the impression would not be distorted. "It's authentic. Why do you want it broken?"

Petronius looked down at his hands. "Shall we say that I am anxious to avoid imperial caprice? If Nero or his soldiers had the seal, they might use it to do mischief. My freed slaves might find themselves condemned to the galleys. Friends might discover that I had sent them messages implicating them in criminal acts. All my land might be found to be owed for gambling debts. It's happened before, Sanct' Germain. I've seen it." Though he spoke easily, his face was serious. His dark blue eyes were oddly clouded. He had been blinded by his own confidence, he thought. He had catered to Nero's pleasures and thought that the affection the Emperor professed for him was genuine. "It may have been, once," he said aloud.

"It may have been once?" Sanct' Germain echoed, his fine brows raised.

"It's nothing," Petronius said impatiently. "Well, break that, won't you?"

Sanct' Germain held up the carved jewel and studied it. The stone was sardonyx, and the figure in it was of Diana with her stag and bow holding a tower in one hand. The workmanship was excellent. "A pity," Sanct' Germain said as he dropped the ring to the floor and brought his heeled boot down on it.

"Good," Petronius said when he had picked up the ring again. The stone was broken and the ring itself cracked and bent. "That much is safe. There are only a few more things to do."

"I'll leave you, then," Sanct' Germain said, and started toward the door.

"No." Petronius caught his arm. "No, I must have a witness to all this. Stay. I need your help." When he got no immediate response, he said, "I don't ask you lightly. I trust you to honor your word. I haven't much more to complete. Stay." Much of his courtly polish deserted him, and he stumbled over his words, so great was his urgency.

"All right." Sanct' Germain regarded him evenly, trying to imagine what Petronius might have been like in ten years, or twenty. The time was lost now, but if it had turned out otherwise . . . He shut the thought away. He had learned long ago how useless such speculation was. "Do as you must."

Petronius let his breath out slowly. "I am grateful, Sanct' Germain." He went to the door and clapped twice, and waited in silence until his secretary appeared. "Tell my wife that I am ready for her and the children now."

His secretary was one of the slaves who was to be given a grant of freedom. He bowed slightly, sorrow in his eyes. "At once, my master."

"What now?" Sanct' Germain asked, feeling deeply weary.

Petronius had gone to a red-and-gilt chest by the wall, and as he opened it, he said, "A necessary precaution. I will leave nothing to chance." He lifted out a chalcedony cup which was carved in the likeness of Atlas holding up the world. For a moment his eyes glowed with pleasure as he looked at the cup. "Do you remember when you gave this to me, Sanct' Germain?"

"Yes." It had been shortly after he came to Rome, when Petronius had brought him a copy of a book of verses he had just written. They were not like his other work, which was facile and cynical. These verses were deeply personal, as compelling as some of the poems of Catullus and the Greek Sappho. Sanct' Germain had been moved, both by the poems and by the gesture of confidence. In one of his private rooms he had made the cup for Petronius. "I read the poems occasionally. They're quite remarkable."

"So I tell myself," he said sardonically. He had put the cup on his desk, where it caught the lamplight. "Nero covets this, you know. He almost commanded me to give it to him."

Sanct' Germain nodded. "Did you tell him who made it?"

"No. He would have insisted you make them for him, as well, and that would have made this one seem . . . cheapened. I trust you understand." He stared down at the cup. "It's exquisite. It's wholly unique, and I have wanted to keep it that way."

"I'm highly complimented." He said it honestly, and knew that Petronius understood.

"Then I trust you'll forgive the use I make of it?" From a little box on the desk he took a small glass bottle that was heavily stoppered and filled with a thick, dark fluid. He opened the bottle carefully and poured out the contents into the chalcedony cup. To this he added wine from an old Greek amphora that he took from his red-and-gilt chest. As he swirled the mixture in the cup, he said rather slowly, "There was a time, you know, when Nero would have refused to give this order. He wouldn't have been capable of it. Not for love of me"—here he gave one mirthless bark of laughter—"but for dislike of killing. It wasn't that long ago."

"You were expecting banishment, then," Sanct' Germain said to fill the silence that followed.

"It seemed likely." Satisfied with the contents of the cup, he set it down on his desk. "He's banished people before, quite irresponsibly. Banishment is so convenient. Killing, this official killing, is new." He ran one hand through his soft brown hair. "He had his mother killed, of course, but that was different. You didn't know Agrippina. I think I might have strangled her myself."

"Why aren't you being banished?" It was a question that had been bothering Sanct' Germain since he had learned of the soldiers' arrival that afternoon. "Falling from favor is hardly crime enough to die for."

"That isn't the accusation, oh, no," Petronius said bitterly. "Tigellinus isn't so careless. His spies have claimed to have discovered the amazing extent of my involvement with the Pisoan conspiracy, and my intent to be part of another one. Certainly I'm far too dangerous a man to be kept alive. The proof they've concocted is, I understand, most convincing. With such evidence, I stand utterly condemned. That was one of the reasons I had you break my seal. They might use it for . . . anything. I can't allow that. No one should have to suffer because of me. Though many will."

Sanct' Germain said nothing. He looked around the pleasant room with its tasteful furniture and appointments, and the unfinished pages that lay on the desk, an old metal figure of a dancing grotesque weighting them down. "The little statue . . ."

"This?" Petronius held up the small figure.

"Yes. It's Etruscan, isn't it?" He liked it, that strange squat little figure that bent as if twirling, an archaic smirk on its outsized lips.

"I believe so. When the Stormwind Legion was camped on the Padus for a month several years ago, one of the centurions found this and I bought it from him the year after. A very elegant bit of art, don't you think?"

"Certainly." He took the dancer from Petronius and held it in his hand. It most surely was Etruscan, from five or six hundred years before, not long after the Etruscans had settled in Italy.

"If you like it so much," Petronius said, cutting into Sanct' Germain's contemplation of the statue, "take it with you. There is little enough I can do to thank you."

Sanct' Germain held his hand so that the dancer seemed to spin on his palm.

"You love art; you collect it. Keep that to remember me." He gestured in a way that included the whole villa. "Nero's apt to seize all this. It's his right, and he's wanted it for years, and he can claim it now without impediment."

There was a knock at the door, and both Petronius and Sanct' Germain were startled.

"It's Myrtale and our children," Petronius said, as if to reassure himself. "Enter!"

Myrtale was subtly and magnificently dressed, her stola of costly luminous green fabric from Hind. Her institia indicated her rank and honors, and over this, a palla of almost invisible linen from Cos was fastened with a fibula of intricately worked gold. Her steady eyes were tranquil as they rested on her husband.

The children were another matter. The older, a girl of about nine, was doing her best to emulate her mother, but she was pale and graceless, looking about her in quick, darting glances. She had been dressed in her finest clothes, which made her even more apprehensive. When Petronius held his hand out to her, she clung to it with both of hers. Her younger brother stood by the door, his small arms folded belligerently over his chest. His silk tunica was askew and its belt almost undone. There were tears in his eyes. When his father gestured to him, he turned away, sobbing.

Without relinquishing his daughter's hands, Petronius crossed the room. "Marcellus " he said as he turned the six-year-old toward him. "It won't last long. It will be over, and you won't have to be frightened. The soldiers won't take you, or Fausta, or your mother or me. We're going to trick them." He stopped; a moment later he had cleared his throat and was able to speak again. "I have something for you to drink. It will make you very sleepy, so you'll have to go to your room and lie down for . . . a while." He felt Fausta's hands tighten on his and he pulled her closer to him. "Six isn't very old to be grown up, Marcellus, but I want you to do the best you can."

Marcellus turned, crying in earnest, and buried his face against his father's waist. Fausta was determined to do better than her brother, but tears slid down her face, and her lower lip trembled.

At that, Sanct' Germain wished fervently he could leave. This was too private for an interloper to see. He turned away as Petronius embraced his family, and put his attention on the little Etruscan statue.

It was Myrtale who broke away first, her face still serene, though her eyes were wet. When she spoke, her voice was slightly thickened, but there was no fear in her. "Where is the drink, my husband? It's useless to delay any longer."

Petronius felt as if a hot fist had closed deep inside him. Numbly he turned toward the desk. "I have it here," he said in a voice that could not possibly have been his own. He took up the chalcedony cup. "A little for each of you."

Myrtale took the cup. "Is it unpleasant?"

"The taste?" Petronius asked, pretending not to understand her. "A little bitter, I'm told, but not undrinkable."

"Petronius," she said solemnly. "Answer my question."

His jaw felt suddenly tight. "I am told that it is not painful. I specified that. You've had pain enough from me without . . ." He watched as she raised the cup to her lips and drank. There were so many things he had wanted to say to her, and would never have the chance to, now. "Myrtale, we are not the same. You've never been as restless as I am. But I have always valued you, and I regret that my folly has brought you to . . . this." It was not what he wanted to tell her, but she seemed to understand. She gave him the cup and leaned against him, kissing his cheek.

"It's not important, my husband. Soon or late, death comes for us all. I rejoice that you did not abandon us to the whims of the Emperor."

"Did you think I would ever do that?" Petronius demanded, his face hardening. Her condemnation now filled him with grief.

"No, I did not think that." She looked down at their children. "Come, Fausta, Marcellus, taste the wine your father has prepared for you."

The boy took the cup first and drank quickly. "It's sour," he said as he wiped his lips with the back of his hand.

"That isn't important," Myrtale said gently. "It is good wine." She put her hand on her son's shoulder. "I will take you to your room shortly, and if you like, we will talk awhile, until you are sleepy."

Fausta had taken the cup and looked down into it. "There's not much left, Father."

Petronius touched her fair hair that was just starting to darken. "Don't worry. I'll take care of myself later. You drink that now." He was very calm now, and looking at his family, he felt a distance opening between them that would never again be bridged by their closeness. "I have loved you all," he said as he touched each of them in turn, taking the chalcedony cup from Fausta at last. He dropped on one knee and embraced his son and daughter. By the time his veins were empty, they would be still and cold. There was no going back. He wanted to ask them to understand one day, and realized that was foolish. There would be no more days for understanding. He rose slowly and kissed his wife. Their lips met without passion, their bodies touched without need. Now they were comrades, and Petronius realized that was what they had always been.

"I will leave you, my husband. You have a great deal to do, still, and our remaining can serve no purpose." She gave him a brief courageous smile, then held out her hands to their children. "Come, Fausta, Marcellus. We will walk in the garden and I will tell you a story until it's time to lie down." She went out of the door without looking at her husband again.

When the door closed behind them, Petronius put his hand to his eyes and took a long, shuddering breath. Then he mastered himself and picked up the cup. "Sanct' Germain," he said as he looked at the cup. "Forgive me for this." In the next instant he had raised his arm and hurled the cup to the floor where it fragmented.

Sanct' Germain remained seated, unmoving, while Petronius made one last inspection of his red-and-gilt chest. His heart ached for this man, but he could say nothing. Petronius wanted his reserve, not his affection and friendship, and though Sanct' Germain had been content to stay aloof for centuries, it was now one of the most difficult tasks he had ever set himself.

"My wife and children will die tonight," Petronius said quite conversationally as he went to the door again. Already the event was unreal, as if it were something that had happened long ago, to someone else. "That will spare them much." He clapped his hands, and when his houseman appeared, said, "Send Xenophon to me."

Sanct' Germain had risen from the couch. "Do you still need me? If you want me to sing tonight, I must tune the harp." This was true enough, but it was something he could do quickly. When he had changed, so long ago, he had ceased, among other things, to be able to weep. For him, all pain, all anguish, was inward, and there was no release in tears.

"Not quite yet, Sanct' Germain. There is one more thing, and then I'll release you." He managed a sardonic smile. "There was a time not so long ago when Senators and generals came to me to ask favors. You would think that one of them might remember that and intercede, wouldn't you?"

"Perhaps they, too, are suspect," Sanct' Germain suggested without conviction.

"I'm not a fool, Sanct' Germain, and neither are you. I am like a leper whom no one dares to touch for fear of infection. It is unfair of me to demand so much of you, but it must be done." He sank onto his chair again. "In another month, the garden will be in full flower. I'm sorry to have to miss it."

"Yes." Sanct' Germain picked up the dancing figure. "I will keep this, Petronius. I will keep it in an honored place."

Petronius was no longer interested. "As you like."

There was a discreet tap at the door. "It is Xenophon, master," said the old voice in a strong Greek accent.

Petronius did not turn. "Enter, Xenophon."

The old slave carried a small wooden box, a basin and long strips of linen. He walked to Petronius' side and stood quite still. "I will do as you wish, my master."

There was a moment's hesitation; then Petronius turned in his chair and held out his arms. "Do it, then, and be quick. Make the bindings tight. I want to enjoy myself."

Sanct' Germain watched as the old Greek physician set the

box and basin on the desk and lay the bandages beside them.

"It's an honored tradition," Petronius said as Xenophon selected a long, thin knife. "Women are fond of doing this in the bath, so that the blood isn't so noticeable." He winced and his jaw tightened as Xenophon's knife slipped under the tendons of his left wrist. When the knife was withdrawn, blood spurted out. Petronius waited impassively as the wide linen bandages were wrapped over the wound. The pain moved up his arm, aching, giving him a curious weakness, which he accepted for the moment. He could resist it later. "I'm told two of my ancestors died this way. And for similar reasons." Again the little knife moved, this time in his right wrist, and the blood rushed and spattered on the floor, still hot. Petronius shivered as Xenophon wrapped the wrist. "How long, do you think?"

"If you keep the bandages on, most of the night, perhaps. If you loosen the knots, it will be faster. Remove the bandages and it will be fairly fast." The Greek's face revealed little, but his eyes were large and mournful. He dropped the knife into the basin. "One of the slaves will clean the floor."

"Don't bother," Petronius said as he got unsteadily to his feet. He felt active now that the first pain was past, strangely elevated and clear-minded. With one hand he steadied himself; then he extended his arm to Sanct' Germain. "I needn't keep you any longer. You've been kind, and for that I am grateful. I won't have the opportunity later to thank you for all you've done." As Sanct' Germain held out his hand to clasp Petronius' arm above the bandages, Petronius gave him a swift embrace. "My approbation isn't worth much anymore, but you have it, nonetheless."

Sanct' Germain still held one of his host's arms. "It means a great deal to me. I won't mock that gift." He could feel Petronius slip away from him on the first tug of that dark tide that would claim him before morning. There was nothing left to say now but the meaningless phrases that he could not bring himself to utter.

Petronius stepped back, freeing himself from Sanct' Germain's grasp. "No, you won't." He made a curt nod of dismissal to Xenophon, and when the Greek had gone, he turned again to Sanct' Germain. "It's a foolish waste, all of it."

Inwardly Sanct' Germain was stung, but he recognized the intent of the comment and adapted his manner to it. "Indeed.

But wise men have been saying that for centuries, and even they have been ignored."

An appreciative flash lit Petronius' dark blue eyes. "And who am I to contradict wise men?" His voice caught, and then he went on with the same smooth manner he had always used. "I will not trouble you with farewells, since they always degenerate into unbecoming pathos. Take the statue, deliver my papers, and do not forget me for a little while."

"And my harp? What would it please you to hear?" He found the pretense difficult to maintain now, and he could not make his tone as light as Petronius'.

"I leave that up to you. By that time, I'll probably be too drunk to care." Abruptly his mood changed. "Dis consume your harp. Take what I've given you and go. Leave tonight. Leave now. If I have to watch you, I'll untie my bandages at once. Let them think what they want of me—that I am a cynical lover of pleasure. I don't want the other known. So go. Go." He almost thrust Sanct' Germain from the room.

"If that is your wish," Sanct' Germain said from the door.

"Yes. Your things will be sent later. Go. In the name of whatever god protects you, go." His voice had become harsh and his face pale.

Sanct' Germain nodded. "I'll be gone within the hour. May it be as you wish it to be." He turned away down the short corridor that led to the guestrooms on the south side of the house.

Only when he had heard Sanct' Germain's footsteps fade did Petronius let himself say, "Farewell, my truest friend," before he turned his attention to greeting his guests at dinner.

Text of letter from the tribune Donatus Egnatius Balbo to his fellow-officer Lucinius Ursus Statile, stationed at Ariminum.

Ursus, you old bear:

Rumor has it that the Cat's Paw Legion is going to

Greece in the autumn. Our general has been hearing palace talk, and he is convinced that Nero is intending to participate in the Olympic Games there. The Emperor has long said that he would like to see such a competition, but hasn't indicated that he thought he could take part. That, it seems, has changed.

You've probably heard about Petronius' suicide last month. They say that the banquet was the best he's ever given. One of my cousins was there, and toward the end, Petronius gave him ten silver goblets. He gave gifts to everyone there, and joked with them until he was gone. I know that he's supposed to have plotted against Nero, and Tigellinus condemns him at every turn, but Tigellinus was always envious of Petronius, and I wouldn't trust his motives for a moment.

Suspicion is still on Corbulo, though it has lessened of late. That is why he thinks we may go with the Emperor, after all. And imperial attention is better for advancement than a war or a plague any day, and much less trying. I look forward to those Games. I think that the Emperor may want to acknowledge Corbulo's service at last, and Greece would be an excellent place to do it. The general is less optimistic, but that is to be expected. After the foolish things his son-in-law has done, and the trouble he caused, I can well understand the attitude of caution the general has adopted.

Another rumor making the rounds at the moment concerns the Emperor and Statilia Messalina, who was Vestinus' wife. Of course, with Vestinus dead because of his foolish alliance to Seneca and Piso, Statilia Messalina is free to marry again. I can't recall whether this will be the fourth or fifth time. Though why she should bother to marry the Emperor confounds me. They've been in and out of each other's beds for months. She may want power, and marriage to Caesar is one way to have it, though it's often a little uncertain with Nero.

Zaducchur, the Cappadocian gladiator that Almericus Hilarius Arval owns, has bought his freedom and has become a partner in the Great School. You remember him, don't you? He was the one who killed ninety-seven men in one hour last year. He's a real loss to the Games, but I suppose it was wise. He's not so young anymore, almost twenty-five, and it was to be expected he would retire soon. Upon his purchasing his freedom, the Vestals presented him with an oak wreath. Nero was furious, but that's hardly surprising.

Work on the Golden House continues, and it is quite amazing to see. The main building is simply gigantic, and the gardens grow more fantastic from year to year. There are woodlands and fields, as if you were deep in the country instead of within the walls of Rome. The largest of the lakes, near the Via Sacra, has stopped traffic and new roads have had to be built to get around the latest extension. Three blocks of insulae have been torn down to make way for another branch of the palace. You would be astounded to see all the things that have been gathered into that building, incomplete though it is. The Emperor has commissioned the muralist Fabullus to do the walls and ceilings. I admire his work, but find that man's behavior insufferable. He refuses to work more than two hours a day—and demands a full day's payment for those two hours—and he always wears a toga when he works. Such affectation!

Expect to see me at the end of May. I have promised my father that I would visit his estate outside of Mutina before returning to duty, but that should not take too long. It will be good to see you again. I've missed your lies about the women you've had.

Until the end of May, then, good fortune to you.

Donatus Egnatius Balbo
Tribune, XIV Legion, the Cat's Paw
the nineteenth day of April in the
818th Year of the City

10

IN THE CALDARIUM of the Claudian Baths, the steam rose in clouds through the softly lit room. There was a gentle murmur of conversation from the largest of the pools, where a number of men relaxed in the hot water.

There was another, smaller, shallower pool off to the side, and it was here that Caius Ofonius Tigellinus sat, resting his painful limbs. Standing beside him were two procurators attached to the Praetorian Guard. If the heat made them uncomfortable in their paludamenti, metal loricae and high-laced caligulae, they made no complaint and only their reddened faces revealed their discomfort.

Beside Tigellinus sat Cornelius Justus Silius, the hot water making him sweat as he listened to the Guard's commander speak.

"It is unfortunate about Petronius, for it circumvented justice, but it can't be helped now. There are other problems I must talk to you about, and this is an excellent time, wouldn't you agree?"

Actually, Justus thought that it was unbearable, but he said, "There is a certain privacy here, it's true."

"All Rome takes the baths, and who is to say what is done here? Also, as my physician insists that I bathe in hot water twice a day, I feel I must use my time to advantage." He sighed and moved slightly in the hot water. His skin was noticeably pink even in the muted light of the caldarium.

"Have you noticed any relief?" Justus asked, immediately at his most solicitous.

"At times. At others, nothing seems to help me. Well, the outcome is with Apollo and Jupiter, and there is no sense for me to be worried." His next words were brisker. "You said you had some information to impart to me. What is it?"

Justus looked uneasily at the two Praetorians, and lowered his voice. "I have cause to worry, Commander."

"So have we all." Tigellinus sighed.

"No, truly, Ofonius, this is not of that nature." He leaned forward and the water sloshed around his chest. It was impossible to represent properly the suspicions he had in this setting. He determined to overcome this disadvantage, and tried to overlook the steam, the heat and his undignified position. "I have heard certain things that disquiet me. You know that the equestrian classes are unhappy with the Emperor, and it is inevitable that another conspiracy be directed against him. It will happen. It must. And when it occurs, there will be greater unrest and confusion than already plagues us."

"I'm aware of this," Ofonius Tigellinus said, sounding bored.

"I have twice been approached, in the most circuitous way, by discontented Senators who look only to find the right leader before they rise again in open revolt."

This was rather more interesting. "Go on."

"I have found nothing certain yet, but before I proceed, I

want to be sure I am safe from official wrath if I take the time to learn more from these men. I am willing to do everything I can to protect the Emperor, but I must, myself, be protected. Should the men be discovered and my name be among those they mention, then I would find myself in desperate straits. But if you are aware of my intention, and if you can make yourself available to me covertly, I believe that I can do you a great deal of good. I have served that way once already."

"I know that." Tigellinus had the largest network of spies that had ever existed in Rome, and there was almost nothing that escaped the vigilance of his men. Yet one of Justus Silius' rank and station might be very useful. He sighed as he moved. The hot water was not doing much to alleviate his pain today. "Let me consider your offer. No matter what is finally decided, I know I may depend on your loyalty. However, if it appears that you can gain access to the traitors, I will be more than willing to give you full authorization to proceed with your infiltration without the possibility of later recrimination."

"Thank you, Commander," Justus said enthusiastically. "You are helping me tremendously. To have the privilege of aiding the Emperor, no matter how menial that service is, must be the greatest honor to any true Roman."

This effusive remark disgusted Tigellinus. The more he had to deal with Cornelius Justus Silius, the less he liked or trusted him, but he could not afford to lose so useful a tool, so he kept his face set in severe lines and said, "The virtues, as ever, are in short supply."

Justus was not fooled by Tigellinus, and it angered him. It was demeaning to have to court this Sicilian who had been a fisherman in Greece and a farmer in Italy, and had risen to power because of his luck in breeding racehorses. "If I learn anything, you will know of it. But," he could not resist the temptation to add with ill-concealed malice, "those who stand revealed may be more than you bargained for. Roman nobility has enjoyed its intrigues for as long as there have been buildings on the Palatine Hill."

"It does no one credit to be part of illicit dealings." He no longer wanted to deal with Justus, and would have ordered him to leave. On the chance that Justus might know something else of worth, Tigellinus decided to ask a few more questions. "Your wife is a Clemens, is she not?"

"Atta Olivia, yes. It is sad to see so great a house fallen on such difficult times. Maximus Tarquinus Clemens, my honored father-in-law, has allowed me to give him certain . . . assistances on behalf of his family." Justus could never speak of that without gloating.

Tigellinus nodded. So the speculation about the nature of Justus' marriage was not inaccurate. The girl had been sold for the sake of restoring the family fortunes. As he looked through the steam at Justus, Tigellinus thought that there were few men he would like less to be indebted to. "I am certain he is grateful," he said, knowing that Justus was the sort who would use his power over his wife's family mercilessly.

There was one other barb that Justus wanted to plant before he left the wretchedly hot room for the frigidarium, where he could relax in the cool water and ogle the young women who waited in the tepidarium for men to spend a few hours alone with them. "There is something worrying me, Commander," he said slowly.

"What?" The question was short.

"That foreigner, the one who brought Petronius' will to Rome. I fear that he may be more dangerous than has been realized." He forced himself to speak thoughtfully as he relished the revenge he would have on Olivia. "He is quite rich, and lives very much apart from Roman society."

"Not quite apart. Petronius liked him well enough, and the Emperor himself has shown Franciscus favor." Tigellinus had no intention of embroiling himself in Justus' private feuds. "He owns no gladiators, only bestiarii and charioteers, which is hardly the way of a politically ambitious man. His stables house less than four hundred horses, so you can't say that he takes that enterprise too seriously. In his will, Petronius said that Sanct' Germain was amusing himself in Rome, liking our society for its venality, and that it was his interest in music that made him a worthwhile companion, nothing more." That ought to be sufficient, Tigellinus thought, wondering what it was that the foreigner had done to earn Justus' enmity.

"A very useful deception," Justus said, feeling annoyed by Tigellinus' indifference. "Petronius himself had such a pose, and you know what it masked." Too late, Justus remembered that it was Tigellinus who had manufactured the evidence that had condemned Titus Petronius Niger.

"Yes," Tigellinus said, sounding very bored, "I know precisely what it masked."

Justus was determined to salvage his argument. "Perhaps that was not as it appeared, but I tell you, the man Franciscus is more sinister than you think. He goes everywhere, has access to the highest ranks in the empire, and is welcomed by almost everyone." For an instant the memory of his wife in Sanct' Germain's arms, languid with desire, rose in his mind. "He is insufferably arrogant! He mocks us all! When you finally recognize the danger he represents, it will be too late. I warn you."

"It would do no harm to keep watch on his movements," Tigellinus said reflectively. "His villa is beyond the Praetorian camp, as I recall. It should not be too difficult to have the Watch at the Viminalis and Collina Gates keep note of his coming and going."

"And why there only? Why not the Capena and Salutaris as well?" Inadvertently he struck the water with his clenched hand. The sound was pleasant, and reduced the force of Justus' demands to childish petulance.

"There are seventeen gates of various sizes in the walls, Senator, and that does not include the bridges. The Watch can be better employed in guarding the city than they can be in searching for one foreigner. Those who keep guard at the Gates he is likely to use will know him in any case." He sank farther back into the water so that just his head and neck were above the surface. "I cannot help but think that you are too zealous, Senator. If there were few foreigners in Rome, or if Franciscus had demonstrated his intent to harm the citizens or the state, it might be different. But Rome is a city of foreigners now, and we have learned to tolerate them. It is true that this one has known unlucky men, but which of us has not?"

Justus ground his teeth with vexation. "I had thought to make an unsuspected danger known to you, but I see I need not have bothered." He got to his feet, the water falling from him. It was good to be out of the bath, and away from this Praetorian commander, who was little more than a peasant. He stepped out of the pool and glared at the two procurators. Judging by the watch they kept over their commander, Justus scoffed, one would think that *he* was suspect. He kept his contempt to himself, saying, "I hope that your health improves, Ofonius," before he sought the frigidarium.

When he was certain that Justus was gone, Tigellinus motioned to the nearer of the two procurators. "Antoninus," he said, "what do you know of Cornelius Justus Silius?"

The procurator thought before he answered. "He's got a reputation for craftiness. He has never been accused of a crime, he has not been part of any conspiracy. His cousin was the lover of—"

Tigellinus sighed impatiently. "Yes, Valeria Messalina, Claudius' wife. That's ancient history. Is there anything recent?"

Antoninus pursed his lips. "His wife is reputed to sleep with gladiators. Silius does not seem to mind. He was one of the men Claudius most disliked and he went into unofficial exile for a time. That might have been because of his cousin."

"And it might have been a whim of Claudius'." Tigellinus sighed. He had learned long ago to pay attention to his hunches, and he had one now about Cornelius Justus Silius, but no matter where he looked he could find nothing to support his misgivings. Musing aloud, he said, "Those who have been out of favor rarely forget it. That may account for his officious interests."

The procurator said nothing.

"This other man, the foreigner. What do you know about him?" Tigellinus turned slowly in the shallow pool, searching for a more comfortable position.

"He raises horses and mules. The horses are bred for the arena, most of the time, though apparently he has some larger animals for battle and long marches. The army buys most of the mules, and there have been no complaints. His villa is an odd design with two atria instead of one. The larger is at one end of a long colonnaded portico, and is more on the Greek style, with a garden and a dining chamber that opens onto it. The other is smaller, and only Sanct' Germain himself and his body slave, who is an Egyptian, are allowed to enter it." Antoninus hesitated. "We might be able to bribe one of the slaves. It is said that one of his bestiarii goes to his bed."

"A man?" Tigellinus had not heard that the foreigner was so inclined, not even from his spies who had been in Petronius' household and had had ample opportunity to observe such things.

"That Armenian woman with the specially trained team. You've seen her." Antoninus smiled a moment, then once again was serious. "She has been at his disposal since he bought her. We might be able to approach her. Enough money to buy her freedom would be more inviting than her master's cock, I should think."

Tigellinus nodded deliberately. "It must be done carefully. We don't want the man alerted, or it could become unpleasant for us. Choose one of the spies who is not associated with the Guard in any way, an Armenian, if possible. Pay her in halves, or there may be nothing to show for it." Although he had no sense of danger from the odd black-clad foreigner, Tigellinus had learned to be cautious.

"Is the need urgent?" Antoninus asked. It was his job to see that the commander's orders were carried out in the proper sequence. If this were high priority, it would be difficult.

"No, I don't think so. Let's call it being careful. Have his comings and goings through the gates watched and make note if any of the very suspect men seek his company. He's sufficiently conspicuous that there should be no trouble observing him. His clothes are foreign, his manner is quite compelling, and he's fairly tall. Not the sort of man you can lose in a crowd. Be a little circumspect, and if the opportunity presents itself, suborn the woman." He thought of the documents waiting for him on his desk that Antoninus had brought him earlier that day. They needed his attention, and he would not trust Nymphidius Sabinus to handle the matters. It was time to leave the pool of hot water. As he got laboriously to his feet, he reflected that the shallow caldarium was rapidly becoming his only pleasure. He looked through the steam to the other caldaria and wondered if it was true for any of the other men there. As he drew a drying sheet around his shoulders, he considered his other pleasure—the exercise of power. He straightened himself and spoke briskly. "Bring my chariot, Antoninus. I will be ready to leave shortly."

Antoninus nodded, gave a quick salute and went quickly out of the large, steamy room.

Tigellinus addressed the remaining Praetorian procurator. "I want Antoninus watched. Find someone who will give him a slave, and make sure the slave stays close to him."

"But Antoninus—" his fellow protested, making no attempt to conceal his shock.

"Antoninus has been sending messages to Gaius Julius Vindex in Lugdunum. One was intercepted a few days ago. If I revealed its contents to the Emperor or the Senate, Antoninus would have his last kiss from the plumbatae. He is playing a very dangerous game." He was almost dry now and he reached for his rust-red Praetorian tunica, which he wore in preference to a toga.

"It's a mistake," the procurator blurted out.

"Lucius Antoninus Sulper is committing treason, Fulvius, and there is a price he must pay for it. He and his companions will forfeit their lives for this foolishness." Tigellinus closed his hand over his beautiful gold-plated lorica. "I want to catch them all, stamp out the plot entirely, eradicate the villainy so that no portion of it will survive to flower again." He stood while Fulvius helped him buckle on his lorica. "The caracalla," he said, holding out his hand for the red soldier's cape. Finally he sat down on one of the benches along the wall to pull on his caligulae. He took up his scabbard and began to buckle it on as he walked. Even the Praetorians were allowed to carry nothing more formidable than a short sword inside the walls of Rome, and although Tigellinus knew that the edict was wise, he missed the long blade of Damascus steel that hung in his quarters at the Praetorian camp.

In the tepidarium, six young men were being instructed in wrestling by a freedman of very mixed parentage. Tigellinus might have stopped to watch if he had had more time and fewer urgent matters pressing him. He passed through the tepidarium and out into the street. By the time he stepped into his chariot, he had consigned his talk with Justus to insignificance as he wondered what to do about the procurator who held the reins for him.

Text of a letter from Maximus Tarquinus Clemens to his oldest son, Pontius Virginius Clemens, lost in transit when the ship carrying mail to Narbo went down in a squall off Sardinia.

To my beloved son and the hope of my family, Pontius Virginius, greetings:

I am loath to write to you, my son, for there is nothing I can say to you that will be welcome to you, I fear. Yet I have obligations to you and to our house and it is my hope that the Lares need not suffer any more disgrace from me and mine.

I have heard through various of our family that you have been active in the cause of Gaius Julius Vindex. While he is a fine military leader, what you propose is not a matter that honorable men should undertake, particularly when the position of this family is so precarious.

Your objections to the Emperor are not unjust, but I must remind you that he does rule us, and that to rise against him is a grave and terrible crime. We are no longer powerful. I have put us into the debt of Cornelius Justus Silius, which though necessary, was and is most unpleasant, but you propose to add dishonor to our name which is already tarnished. I have heard the arguments your group has used, and if they come to light, the entire family will be disgraced. Silius has intimated that should your part in this conspiracy be known, all of us would be exiled. I have done enough damage to this family without this addition from you. Let me beseech you to draw back from your involvement. If you cannot honor my request as a son would honor a father, then consider the plight of your brothers, your mother, even your sisters, who might also pay for your behavior. Silius has said he does not know if he could give Olivia his protection if we were exiled. Consider what Olivia has done for us already, and do not impose this additional burden on her.

Should you persist on this dangerous enterprise, I would have no choice but to disown you, which I do not wish to do. You are my favorite child, although I should not admit it. I love you with all the fervor that parent has ever loved child. It would pain me mortally to deprive myself of you forever, but I must protect your brothers, your sisters and your mother. Do not force so terrible an act upon me, Virginius.

On the nineteenth day of May in the 818th Year of the City, this from my own hand.

Maximus Tarquinus Clemens

11

HIS MOVEMENT through the shadowed night was fluid, was powerful, was beautiful. His grace was not the grace of a dancer, whose splendid ease is born of meticulous, disciplined years, but rather it was his natural condition, an aspect of self as much as his musical voice and arresting eyes.

He had entered Rome at dusk through the Rudusculana Gate on the south side of the city. This was one visit he did not want the officious Praetorians to know of, and he had realized that his movements were noted only through the Viminalis and Collina Gates at the northeast end of the city walls. As an added precaution, he had worn a long red cloak and wide-brimmed hat which were the mark of Greek mercenaries. He had answered the officer of the Watch in heavily accented Latin, and swore long and comprehensively by Ares when he was required to surrender his sword.

The first touch of summer was on the air, and the night was warm. Streets were filled with people though the sun had been down for more than an hour. Near the Circus Maximus, the wine shops and whores were doing a brisk business, and away on the Oppius Hill, the Golden House glittered with lights.

Sanct' Germain had discarded the red cloak and hat near the entrance to a shop that sold meat-filled breads, knowing that it would not be remarkable there, where many soldiers ate. He had made his way up the Aventine Hill behind the Temple of Juno toward the luxurious houses near the crest. Now his dark Persian clothes blended with the night, his soft tread unheard over the omnipresent roar of the city.

At the house of Cornelius Justus Silius, he had climbed into the stableyard by way of a tree that overgrew the high walls. He had hesitated on the high branch, crouching low as he listened to the conversation of the slaves who cleaned out the stables. Their language was an odd mixture of Latin, Cimric and the dialect of Roman Africa. From the sound of them, they had been drinking, and in confirmation, two of the voices burst out in a loud, tuneless rendition of the bawdiest, bloodiest of the gladiators' songs.

With this cacophony to cover any sound he might make, Sanct' Germain dropped from the branch and slipped across the stableyard unseen and unheard. He went swiftly, darkness moving against darkness, until he had worked his way around the house to the new wing where Olivia's room was.

As he stopped beside a gnarled apple tree, a soft, agonized wail sliced the night. Sanct' Germain felt the sound go through him like steel. It was Olivia's voice. There followed sounds of a scuffle and another cry, and then Justus' voice, strangely breathless.

"Lie still for him! There!"

Sanct' Germain had already begun to move toward the window when he saw the slave who had guided him to Olivia's room waiting near the garden entrance to her wing. Cautiously he sank back into the shadows. He wanted a moment, only a moment, and then he would be across the narrow garden and in her window.

Peculiar, panting laughter came from the room, a quick, scrabbling sound, and then Justus' hoarse order, "Away! Let me!"

Sanct' Germain's hands had tightened into fists and it was an effort not to rush into the house, regardless of the slave who waited at the door. Only his concern for Olivia, and knowing that a reckless attempt on her behalf would be more dangerous to her than none at all, kept him from this action.

Some little time later the door opened and a ruggedly built Greek came out. He swaggered a little as he walked, and in response to the waiting slave's question, he said, "Oh, he won't be satisfied until he sees her split in two by an ass' cock." His laughter was low and contemptuous. With the other slave, he strolled away toward the low building near the stables.

The sounds from Olivia's room continued awhile, and Sanct' Germain moved to the window. The stonework was regular and left enough projections that Sanct' Germain knew he could climb it. He set his fingers on the stones and began to move up the side of the building toward the tall windows of Olivia's room.

Justus had left her as soon as he was finished, and now Olivia lay alone on her disordered bed. The lamps were still burning, and it made her shame worse. It was bad enough that she be treated this way, but with so much light . . . She shook her head miserably. Justus had been pleased with his

Boetian bodyguard, and her body ached from his assault. She wanted to cross her arms to cover her breasts, but there were too many scrapes and bruises for her to stand to touch them.

A noise at the window brought her upright in her bed. What would Justus require of her now? She bit her fingers to keep from screaming, refusing to give him that satisfaction.

It was not the door that opened. For an instant it seemed that the night was invading her room, and then Sanct' Germain stepped off the sill and came silently across the room toward her.

Olivia stretched out her arms toward him, feeling suddenly giddy. Then she wondered. He was so silent that she feared he was a dream conjured by her mind to soothe her.

Sanct' Germain saw her hesitate even as he noticed the marks of cruelty on her flesh. He stopped. "Olivia?" he said so softly that the murmur of the wind seemed louder.

"Sanct' Germain?" Her voice was only a little louder. "It *is* you?"

He took her outstretched hands. "Of course. I had your note this morning, and you said you had to see me. For you to attempt something so dangerous as that note, I knew your need was urgent. Was it this?" His eyes went to the bruises on her arms and breasts.

Fatalistically she shook her head. "No. Not really. It's nothing new." Her fingers tightened. "I am frightened, Sanct' Germain, and there is no one—"

"Not your family?" he asked quickly, thinking that they would be surer protection than himself.

"No." She swallowed against the despair she felt rising within her. She had no one else to turn to, no one else she felt she could trust, yet there was no reason for Sanct' Germain to help her. She was just a woman whom he had pleasured.

He wanted to ask her why she could not go to her family, but instead, as he sat beside her, said, "Surely you haven't done anything to merit their anger. What is so dreadful that you can't speak of it to your father?"

It was a sensible question, she knew, but her face turned scarlet and she tried to pull her hands away from him. "It isn't anything they could help with."

"Could, Olivia? Or would." He bent to kiss both her hands. "Why do they tolerate what Justus does to you? Have you told them?"

"I can't," she said in a suffocated tone.

"Do you want me to speak to them? Is that why you asked me to come to you?" Sanct' Germain met her eyes fully, and felt that strange pull she exercised on him.

"No. I don't know why I asked you. I can't do anything about it. You can't, either. But I felt so terrible." She was determined not to weep. Her father had taught her the Stoic philosophy, and her mother had told her to accept her station with dignity. To shed tears before this stranger, again, was too daunting.

"Worse than this?" he demanded, his eyes lighting with fury.

"Not . . . like this. He's selling my slaves. When we married, I came to him with five slaves, and now they're all being sold, and he's replacing them with his own creatures." Her voice caught, but she went on resolutely. "He told my father that I would be allowed to keep my slaves. He would have sold them last year if he hadn't given his word to my father. Now, it isn't important." At last her indignation was sparked. "They aren't his! They're mine! The law says that a husband has no right to any portion of his wife's property, even if he's bankrupt. That's his precious Divus Claudius' law! But he's selling my slaves!" Suddenly she realized she was shouting, and she stopped, frightened. "Is there . . . ?" she whispered uneasily.

He made a quick gesture, listening. They waited in silence but no one came. Sanct' Germain moved closer to her. "Where does he watch?" he asked softly.

She nodded toward the hidden door, then glanced back at him, her fright reborn. "You don't think he's there now, do you?"

He knew it was possible, so he avoided her question. "Get up and cross the room. Open the door as if you're expecting him. If you can, smile." Sanct' Germain slid away from her into the shadow of the bed hanging as Olivia got up.

Walking across the room, which seemed now to be huge, she tried to convince herself that this was a foolish precaution, but her inward quaking could not be touched by this stern good sense. She had experienced too much of Justus' caprice to feel protected from him in any way. At last she got to the door and pressed the release. It swung open and she held her breath, fixing a grimace on her mouth.

The little room was empty. She stepped into it and tried

the latch on the door to the connecting passage that led to Justus' rooms, but it was locked. With a deep sigh she closed the door once again. Until that moment she had not known how much she dreaded facing her husband a second time that night. She turned toward Sanct' Germain. "Nothing," she said quietly.

He had stepped out of his concealment behind the hangings. "How long have you lived this way, Olivia?" A frown clouded his face. Judging by the new wing on the house and the elaborate preparations for observing Olivia, Justus had intended this for some time.

"At first it didn't happen very often," she said unhappily. "He would tell me to ask this man or that to sleep with me. They weren't men I would have wanted to ask." She stopped and looked at Sanct' Germain, about to apologize, but saw his knowing expression and went on. "I thought it would stop, or I would get used to it, but . . . Justus never comes to my bed unless someone else does first. He says that it is necessary for him. I'm afraid to try to show him . . . otherwise." Again she faltered. The sympathy in Sanct' Germain's face was almost forbidding. "He wants to see the act done without affection or tenderness or any pleasure but his. Tonight was the first time he helped. He held me for his bodyguard." Her face had paled.

"Then we must be more careful next time," Sanct' Germain said as he reached to pinch out the lamps. "I cannot erase what has been done to you, but if you will let me, Olivia, I will do all I know to give you those things you want: affection and tenderness and pleasure." He opened his arms to her.

Three steps brought her to his side, and she leaned gratefully against him. He was more than a head taller than she, his body was stockily trim and strong, and as his arms circled her waist, she felt him bend to her, moving to be closer to her.

Sanct' Germain held her so, unmoving, for some little time. The shape and pressure of Olivia's body filled his mind. From the gentle motion of her breathing to the upward stretch of her arms, he felt how real she was. There her hip nudged him, slightly below his own, and there the curve of her arm rested inside his arm. It was a kind of privacy that he wanted and had not dared to seek.

Finally he kissed her. Her body trembled as her lips parted

and she clung to him with an unexpected ferocity. He lifted his head and looked down into her face. "I want you, Olivia," he said in a low, deliberate voice. "You know how I want you."

Her answer was a tightening of her arms. There were no words for her to tell him, but they were not necessary. She loosened her hold as he lifted her into his arms and carried her easily the few steps back to her bed. He kicked the rumpled blankets aside and lowered her to the unblemished sheet, bending over her as he did, his mouth close enough to hers to brush kisses there. It was joyous to give her will, which had sustained her through all the torment Justus had forced upon her, over to an even stronger will that was set on seeing her fulfilled. Her eyes closed as he sank down beside her.

In the past when Sanct' Germain had experienced such merging of desire, it had been cloaked in the compelling bonds of religion. This had all that convergence of purpose, but now it was done for its own sake. Everywhere he touched Olivia, he could feel the passion of her in his hands. Her demand increased with his, and she strained to draw him nearer. Sanct' Germain moved eagerly over her body, riding the inexorable tide of her longing. He received her with elation, sharing her release. His arms sheltered her as she pressed against him in sweet delirium.

Only much later did his doubts return. He lay looking up at the bed hangings and painted ceiling in the gloom. Olivia slept with her arm across his chest, her head in the curve of his neck. Was Aumtehoutep right, after all? Had he been right all along? Sanct' Germain tightened his hold on Olivia as his senses flooded with the whole force of his loneliness, so long denied. What was it about this woman that called him so? Why did she and her uncertain smile penetrate his long-established defenses so effortlessly? If her life had been otherwise, had she married an honorable man, she would have found this affair repugnant. She turned in her sleep and he moved to accommodate her, rolling toward his side and lifting his arm so that she could nestle in the curve of his body. The sound of her breathing was precious to him, and the way fawn-brown hair lay in disorder against her neck.

She curled nearer, smiling, and with a little yawn came awake. "Oh. Good." Her head nuzzled his shoulder. It was wonderful, she thought dreamily, to wake in Sanct' Germain's embrace.

"Sleep, Olivia," he murmured, lightly kissing the curve of her ear. "Sleep."

It was tempting to obey him, but she heard the rueful tone in the soft words and she looked at him. "Is anything wrong?"

"No, nothing's wrong." His hands stroked her, soothing and relaxing. "Hush."

She was quiet some little time, then said, "I know that you're concerned. If it's about what you do to me, I don't mind, truly." She put one hand to his hair, letting the loose short curls slide around her fingers.

"It's not that, not entirely." He stared up at the ceiling, thoughts, memories, shifting, and finally he spoke. "Most people, when I have come to them, have regarded me with awe and fear. Both emotions have their uses. A few others accept my ways because there are advantages in compliance." His face twisted briefly with distaste. Tishtry was good to him, and his admiration for her was genuine, but her matter-of-fact tolerance of his favor was not binding, and she had never denied that, given her choice, she would prefer more ordinary pleasures. "I have been willing to make do with adoration or terror or concession. Now, I don't know. I don't know." He closed his eyes, but that didn't help. Too many images crowded in on him, too many losses, too much isolation. Making a strange sound that was compounded of grief and hope, he pulled Olivia closer to him, holding her tightly as his turbulent feelings roiled within him.

Olivia put her arms around him almost absentmindedly. This outburst of emotion perplexed her. She had been so caught up in the prison of her own torment that she had little comprehension of the distress in others. Now, in the dark with Sanct' Germain enfolding her in his desperate embrace, she felt the somnambulistic nightmare that had become her life loosen its hold on her, so that she would be able, in time, to break free of it; in Sanct' Germain's anguish, she found salvation from her own.

There was a kind of peace, a tentative calm that descended on Sanct' Germain as he clung to Olivia. He had not been able to speak those words before, to admit how keenly he felt his separation from humankind. He took her face between his hands. "For whatever forlorn reason you've accepted me, I am grateful. I give you my word that I will not desert you, that I will not repudiate this union."

"And is this all our union?" Olivia asked wistfully. She had not wanted her ravishers to touch her, but Sanct' Germain she welcomed with her whole being.

Sanct' Germain shrugged slightly, a sad, rueful smile on his lips. "Yes. Among my kind, nothing else is possible."

"But it must be possible," she objected reasonably. "How else do you continue?"

This was a question Sanct' Germain anticipated with dread. "We continue . . . through contamination. Those whom we take to ourselves, if they come knowingly, eventually become like us. If you were to taste my blood, the change would be certain, but if you give yourself to me, that, in time, will accomplish the same thing." He explained this flatly, meeting her eyes with difficulty.

"And I? Will I be like you?"

"Eventually. If we continue to love each other." It was a hard task to say these words while Olivia studied him, uncertainty in her eyes. "Perhaps I should have warned you. You may still send me away and suffer no hurt from me. As I have said, it takes time to change."

Send him away? The thought itself was painful and she reached for him convulsively. "No."

Misunderstanding her, he said, "If we lie together five or six more times, it is likely to happen. More than that and it is assured. Listen to me, Olivia—I will be your ally, if you like, and ask nothing more of you. But I will not abandon you to your husband. With the blood there is a bond, and I may not, I *cannot* refuse it." He had seen more beautiful women, he thought as he spoke to her. He had slept beside them or visited them as a dream, and had left them, sated but hungry. With Olivia, he could feast on the light in her eyes. This was not the strength of the bond holding him to her, it was not even his need. Olivia herself, her unique self, was the tie, and would have been, he thought, if he had never touched her.

"Don't leave me," she said softly.

"I have said that I won't."

"And lie with me. Love me." She was caught in his arms, engulfed by the force of his passion. As his beautiful small hands warmed and opened her, she had the fleeting thought that if this rapture was what it was to be like him, she would delight in the change he spoke of, seek it eagerly. Then the thought was gone and all that remained in the universe was his searching nearness, and the soul-shaking spasms and elation.

Neither of them wanted to part, though the quickening of the breeze indicated that dawn was near. "A little while more," Olivia murmured to Sanct' Germain's shoulder.

"A little while more,"—he paused to kiss the place below her ear where her jaw and neck made a sweet indentation—"and your slaves will be up, and I might be discovered."

She knew this was so, and reluctantly released him. "Go quickly, or I'll call you back."

Those words alone were enough to stop him. "Do not be too long, Olivia. Send for me as soon as possible." He had one foot up on the sill of her tall windows.

"Soon. Yes." Her bed already felt empty and cold, and the gathering of the sheet around her did not make her warmer.

"Each day at sunset," he said in a different tone, remembering that they would need to be very cautious in future, "a fruit seller will pass your house. If you have need of me, ask for berries from Dacia, and say on what day you will want them. On that night, I will be here. I will not fail you if you call me, Olivia." He saw her start to extend her arms to him, and he knew he must leave. With a quick, affectionate gesture he turned away and dropped silently into the garden below.

He had traversed the garden and was almost to the tree over the stableyard when he heard a voice behind him.

"A moment!" The accent was that of Roman Africa, and when Sanct' Germain turned, he saw a huge man of swarthy complexion and rough, scarred features. "What's this? What's this?" the Tingitanian demanded as he hefted a large club.

Sanct' Germain made no answer. He silently cursed himself for the folly of being seen, but there was no time to be cautious or they would be discovered, which would put Olivia, and himself, in great danger.

The club moved in a quick whooshing arc as the stablehand swung it at Sanct' Germain's head. "Sending Persians to spy on Senators now, are they?" the Tingitanian demanded.

By the time the club passed the spot where it would have struck Sanct' Germain, he had turned and taken the Tingitanian's shoulder, letting his opponent's weight be pulled by the motion of the club. Another two steps and he was behind the stablehand.

Surprise turned to fury as the Tingitanian fell heavily to

the ground. He took up the club, scrambling quickly to his feet to avoid the second kick the foreigner had aimed at his ribs. "Treacherous Persian!" he shouted, thrusting the club at Sanct' Germain.

He had to be quick. That shout would be certain to rouse the slaves in the stables. Sanct' Germain sprang forward, pushing the club aside and leaping upward at the same time to drive his feet into the Tingitanian's wide, flat stomach. The stablehand collapsed, folding in the middle like a faulty hinge. As he lunged forward, Sanct' Germain reached for his chin and snapped his head back with practiced, deadly efficiency. The Tingitanian slumped to the ground and did not move again.

By the time two of the stable slaves had run from their quarters in answer to the shout they had heard about Persians, Sanct' Germain was two houses away, going down the hill toward the Circus Maximus, where half a dozen of his bestiarii would appear that day.

As he walked through the gate leading under the stands, he heard the cough of a leopard nearby, and farther away, the sleepy, halfhearted protests of the gladiators' whore.

Text of a letter from the Emperor Nero to the foreigner Ragoczy Sanct' Germain Franciscus.

> To the distinguished stranger from Dacia, who is not a Daci, Ragoczy Sanct' Germain Franciscus, my imperial greetings:
>
> Doubtless you have heard that the Emperor of Armenia is to honor me and all Rome with an official visit, and you must be aware of the importance of this visit, which will seal the peace between Rome and Armenia forever.
>
> You have, among your slaves, an Armenian woman,

called Tishtry, I believe, who is a bestiarii with two teams of trained horses. This Tishtry has appeared in many of the Games and has won singular recognition for her skills and her beauty. It would be a great compliment if this woman would prepare new feats to honor Tiridates on his visit, for she is not only a woman of great skill, but as an Armenian, any honor given to her must be a compliment to King Tiridates as well. I am gratified to know that you will do everything in your power to aid in my plans to receive Tiridates with all the splendor that Rome can offer a visiting monarch.

There are a few other matters I wish to mention about this visit: I plan to have a great venation, and I am told that your supply of animals is quite remarkable. You have half a dozen pards in your stock at present, and, I am reliably informed, may get more. I will want all you have and double that amount. Those magnificent cats will certainly impress the Armenian and Persian guests. Some of those African big-horned deer would be good to have. Also a few of those Asiatic goats, the large ones with the heavy coats. Wild boars are always good in venations, for they are strong, bad-tempered and unpredictable. If you should happen to know of some easily available, they would be most effective for the hunt. I would be particularly pleased if you happen to find any ounces. Pards are well enough, but the ounce is so fine a cat, and so rarely seen, that I would be eternally grateful to you for procuring me half a dozen of them for the venation. That big black-and-white bear you imported from the East would also be more than welcome.

If it seems to you that I impose upon you, it is more a token of my respect for your expertise and abilities. I would not make such demands of most of my Romans, for I know that they would not be capable of accomplishing them. You are another matter. You have demonstrated again and again your capacity for doing what would appear impossible.

The time is short, and it is necessary that you go to work at once to get these creatures. I have delayed coming to you because I believed the promises of my Romans, who have yet to procure me more than fifteen hippopotami and one white rhinoceros and a few dozen lions who have yet to be trained to eat men. I look forward to hearing of your progress on my behalf.

From my own hand on the sixth day of June in the 818th Year of the City,

Nero Caesar

12

WHEN THE SLAVE had withdrawn, Justus turned to his visitor. "Well, Drusillus, I am sorry that your sister is not here to receive you. Olivia has gone for the day to the Springs of Faelius to bathe and be treated by the water. Is there anything I may do for you in her place? Is there a message I can deliver?"

Drusillus, who at age eighteen was still awed by the presence of his brother-in-law, shifted from one foot to the other. It was not appropriate for a newly commissioned tribune of the Ninth Legion to feel embarrassed, but it was not so long ago that his family had been so impoverished that Drusillus had seriously considered enlisting as a common soldier. Now, with the help of his sister's husband, he had the rank he longed for, and the opportunity for advancement that would otherwise have been lost to him. "May I talk to you?"

The atrium of Justus' house was in the old fashion—a large square room with a hole in the ceiling to let in light. The newer houses were more Greek in their design, the atrium resembling a Greek peristyle, almost an interior garden. Justus indicated one of the rooms off the atrium. "If you would like to talk, perhaps we should sit down." He clapped twice, and three slaves rushed forward. "I will want wine and cakes in my study."

As he followed his host into the room, Drusillus could not help but compare these rich surroundings to the shabbiness of his family's house. They were roughly the same age, but where the murals had cracked and faded in the Clemens house, here they were fresh, the doors were of neatly carved rosewood with golden handles, and Justus' study was lined with open-fronted chests filled with expensive volumes and neat stacks of *Acta Diurna* that were sold daily throughout

Rome. The shutters were thrown back from the window, revealing part of the garden and the new wing that Justus had added six years before. The air was thickly warm, close as a blanket.

"Why not take that chair?" Justus suggested, indicating one of the two diamond-seated chairs near the window.

Drusillus sat down carefully, his new scale lorica jingling and clattering. "I'll try to be brief," he promised.

May Prometheus' eagle consume his liver! Justus thought, and smiled ingenuously at Drusillus. "Is it about that Persian spy that killed my stable slave?" he suggested. "I have talked to Tigellinus, but he, predictably, has done nothing. Yet the slaves swear they heard the Tingitanian cry out 'Treacherous Persian!' and then a fight. I want that spy caught. I want to see his head lopped off." He crossed his thick arms over his chest and stared at the very young man who was his brother-in-law.

"It's not about that," Drusillus said unhappily. "The Watch and the Praetorians . . ." His smile was as self-effacing as he could make it. "There are other matters I must discuss with you."

"Very well," Justus said, letting a little of his impatience show, "discuss them. I'm curious to hear what you have to say to me."

Now that he actually faced Justus, Drusillus found that all the well-reasoned arguments he had rehearsed had fled. He stared at his sandaled feet. "You know my brother, Virginius?"

"The one in Gallia, isn't he? I have met him once or twice. Why?" Justus felt his inner sense come alive. There were rumors of conspiracies again, and some of them came from Gallia.

"He's there, yes. At Narbo. There are certain matters that have come up . . ." He faltered, wonderng for the first time if Justus would give away the plans his brother had asked him to reveal in confidence. "The matter is private. . . ."

"By which you mean secret?" Justus said, inwardly delighted. Here was another chance to unmask traitors and gain the favor of the Emperor. He nodded sagely and leaned forward. "A question concerning Lucius Domitius Ahenobarbus?" That had been Nero's name at birth, before Nero was adopted by his stepfather, the Emperor Claudius. "It is only a few short weeks since Vinician conspirators were arrested.

Surely there is not another one being hatched, and summer hardly begun?" He studied Drusillus, his ferret's eyes bright.

"You know that Julius Vindex is gathering support for another revolt?" Drusillus asked, strangely breathless. "The men around Piso and Annius Vinicianus were careless. They let themselves be discovered and betrayed. They were too close to Rome and the power here. But Vindex is in Gallia, and he has the might of his legions to fight for him. My brother has already committed himself to this cause, and has urged me to join with him." The words tumbled out of him, and he looked eagerly at Justus.

Justus pretended to give the matter some thought. "This follows closely on the Vinician effort, perhaps too closely. It would be a simple thing to surprise Nero"—he carefully avoided calling the Emperor by his rank—"if he had not had so many other attempts made already. He is a young man, with foolish delights and demanding appetites. We could indulge him, win his confidence, if he had not become so suspicious." He looked past Drusillus' shoulder toward one of his open chests. "So far, the daily journals have not got wind of this, except to say that Vindex is active in Gallia. If he dreams of the purple, he has chosen a difficult task."

Drusillus was encouraged. "You say that Nero is young, and that he is wayward. I am younger than he, much younger, and yet I have not indulged myself and given youth as my excuse." He was keenly aware that any such opportunities had been denied him by the poverty of his family. "Nero spends his nights in debauch, and builds a palace that may consume the entire city before he's through, and sings Greek tragedies. He's even having the king of Armenia on a state visit to make peace instead of letting Corbulo take the Cat's Paw Legion and . . . and make Armenia a mouse." His color heightened with his indignation.

"Nero," Justus said with a cultured sneer, "is not fond of war. Peace, he says, is the greater ideal. That's more Greek nonsense, for though Seneca was a Stoic, he taught Nero true Roman virtues."

"Which he has discarded for effeminate Greek philosophies." Impetuously Drusillus got to his feet, his fists clenched. "It's bad enough that we must honor these foreigners, when it's Romans who conquered them. Vindex may not be born to the manner, but he is more of an Emperor in Gallia right now than Nero is in Rome, for all his splendor!" His voice had risen to a childish treble and he stared around the study in confusion. "How can you abide to live in his shadow, Silius?"

Justus smiled easily. "We can't all abandon Rome to Nero and his favorites. The entire city would be Greek, if we did. Who would have thought to see so many of them in such high places? You would hardly think that Greece has been conquered at all." It was so absurdly simple to make this armored child betray himself, Justus thought. "There are those of us who know that Rome must endure, no matter what our rulers may do in their folly."

"Folly?" Drusillus said hotly. "Madness, rather."

"Perhaps," Justus said silkily. "That is not for any of us to judge. No . . ."—he raised his hand—"say nothing more of madness. You never knew Gaius Caligula. There was madness, my boy. Nero is nothing to him. I am amazed that we have any equestrian ranks left, after the way he butchered them." He studied Drusillus carefully. "What do you want from me, Drusillus? Money? Assurances? Aid? Protection? What?"

Drusillus was anxious for this invitation, and he sat on the chair again, leaning forward with his elbows on his knees. "We want you with us. We want you in our numbers, those of us who wish to put Vindex in power and bring down this . . . this painted actor who calls himself Caesar. What do you say?"

"I am a cautious man, Drusillus. I have survived when others were less fortunate because of that caution. Yet there is a great deal in what you say. Your complaints about Nero are most persuasive and I have a sympathy with your cause. Let me agree to this: I will lend you support when Vindex marches to Rome. Until then, it would be too grave a risk to support you, for it would not only endanger me, but all of your family: your father, your brothers, your sister and your mother. If your plan were to be found out, there is nothing I could do to save any of them." He did an admirable job of convincing the lad that it was his concern for others that kept him from joining with Drusillus and Virginius in their foolish plot to unseat the Emperor. "You cannot know what your trust means to me, Drusillus, but there is much more at stake here than just my honor. How could I endanger so many to feel myself a true Roman again?" He spread his big, thick hands wide.

"Yes," Drusillus nodded, deeply moved that Justus would

be so concerned for his family. "The head of the house who honors his obligations has Roman virtues, too." He wished there was something more he could say to his impressive brother-in-law. His awe of Justus until then had been accompanied by a feeling of doubt, but now that doubt was banished. He realized how much Justus took his familial responsibilities to heart.

By the Balls of Mars, the boy was gullible, Justus said to himself, almost smiling with satisfaction. With an effort he kept his features severe and sighed heavily. "If there were a way for me to satisfy my honor without hazarding those who depend on me, I would be with you in a moment. . . . Well, I don't know what to do." He smacked his palms together and twisted the hands, one against the other.

Drusillus hurriedly filled the conversational gap. "I will be most happy to apprise you of all our plans and progress as we go. In a few months, our hopes should be realized. Before then, I will bring you happy news, and you will be able to speak for us with a clear conscience." He got to his feet, very pleased with the way things had gone.

There was almost no sport to this deception, Justus lamented inwardly. Drusillus was so blind, so willing. "As you gather your allies," he said hesitantly, as though it was all he dared to do, "will you tell me who they are? When the time is a little more . . . auspicious, perhaps I can do something with them on Vindex's behalf."

Pride at his success with his imposing brother-in-law was growing in Drusillus with every breath he took. "Oh, certainly," he said importantly with a wave of the hand that showed the matter was trivial.

"I'd like to know that soon, so that we might arrange things here more to the advantage of Vindex." This request, if made of a more experienced man, would be dangerous, but when dealing with Drusillus, no concern at all.

Drusillus realized he should have thought of that himself and knew a moment's chagrin. "Naturally. I'll see that you have the names today. I'll send my body slave."

"Do you think that's wise?" Justus asked, smothering a spurt of annoyance at Drusillus. If all the men Vindex depended upon were as inept as this one, his rebellion was doomed before it began.

"Oh, yes. Cyncadis is completely devoted to me." The Greek-Syrian slave had been given to Drusillus when he was ten years old and since then they had lived as closely together as twins. Drusillus never considered the inequality of their positions as important, and would have been genuinely disbelieving if anyone had told him that Cyncadis hated him.

"I think, perhaps," Justus said thoughtfully, "that I will send one of your sister's slaves to fetch the list. I have bought her a new household of her own, you know." He made this treacherous act sound like the most gallant generosity. "One of her creatures, coming to you, will not be suspect. Sisters and brothers are always sending messages between one another. Aren't they?"

Drusillus found the idea very clever. "Yes. And no one will think anything about it. It's good of you to take so many precautions, Justus. Not that anyone will notice." He straightened his lorica, and the scales tapped and rang.

"Let us hope not," Justus said heavily, knowing how many spies Ofonius Tigellinus had in the city. He knew that much of the army was watched, and the families of discontented nobles were checked often. Justus was reasonably sure that someone had made note of Drusillus' visit today, and might also learn that Olivia's slave had visited her brother, and the whole thing would appear innocent. "It is better to be too careful than not careful enough."

"Yes." He nodded earnestly. "I must leave you. I will look for my sister's slave . . . when?"

"The hour before sundown, if that's satisfactory. Most of your men will be going to supper then, and this should not inconvenience you." He rose at last and put his big hand on Drusillus' shoulder. "This is quite an enterprise to be entrusted to one so young."

"Younger men than I have toppled nations," Drusillus responded, his cheeks flushing again. "To be an officer at my age is not unusual."

"That's true," Justus agreed, recalling how much of the senior military staff Gaius Caligula had had killed for their involvements in the plots that had tortured his imagination. "Advancement has been fairly swift of late."

"That's changing." Drusillus sulked. "Nero refuses to fight any wars, and there are soldiers enough in Judea. There may be another uprising among the Jews, but it would not be enough for all the officers."

"Are you eager for such a battle?" It was an unnecessary question, but he was glad of the reaction it got.

"I have proved my mettle," Drusillus insisted because he knew he had not.

"Certainly," Justus said soothingly, with a moment of sympathy for the soldiers who served under such an inexperienced leader. He consoled himself with the thought that Drusillus would not survive his plot against the Emperor long enough to lead his men in battle. "However, conspiracies are not like war. The secret path to power is difficult to tread. Those older and more accomplished than you or I have lost everything to that path. Think of Piso and Vinicianus. Both were sponsored by some of the most powerful men in the empire, men close to the Emperor and enjoying his highest esteem, and where are they now?—Seneca, who was guilty, is dead, and so is that fop Petronius, who was not." He sighed again and favored Drusillus with his gravest expression. "I depend upon you, Drusillus, but I must warn you that it is harder to come through this pass to victory than it is to conquer Persia with half a legion." He sank back into his chair as if fatigued.

"I will not fail you," Drusillus promised with youthful intensity. He turned on his heel and left the study, crossed the atrium with long strides and was let out of the house by the large Boetian who guarded the door at this hour.

Justus stayed in his chair, one finger pressed into the curve of his lower lip. How best to do this? he asked himself. It was tempting to wait to see what Drusillus might bring him, but it might also seem that he was actually supporting Vindex. Better to dispatch a note at once to Tigellinus, with a promise of more to come. That would alert the Praetorian spies, but it was a chance he was willing to take. As he glanced around the room and it occurred to him that no one had brought the wine and cakes he had requested, he grew irritated. He rose, clapping sharply.

"Master?" The slave was bent humbly, her blonde hair in thick braids.

"I ordered cakes and wine. They are not here." His voice was flat, emotionless, and everyone in the house lived in fear of it.

"They were sent for. I saw Nyso go for them upon your order." Her voice was hushed.

"Then where is he?" was the honeyed question.

"He has not returned. Perhaps he could not get the wine

from the steward. You yourself ordered that only the steward could dispense wine."

The audacity of the slave was reprimanded quickly by a blow to the head. Justus stood over the woman as she fell, so that when she began to crawl away from him, he kicked her, catching her just below the ribs with such force that she made hardly a sound as she collapsed to the mosaic floor.

Three other slaves had hurried to the atrium in answer to the imperious sound of Justus' hands. They faltered as they saw the blonde woman lying unconscious at her master's feet, blood at the corner of her mouth.

"Where are the cakes and wine I requested?" Justus demanded of the three. "Where is Nyso?"

"In . . . in the kitchen. . . ." the nearest responded unwisely. "Shall I get him for you, master?"

"No, no, little man." Justus was starting to enjoy himself. "I won't have any of you scum warning him. Take that"—he nudged the prone woman with his foot—"and drag it out of here. Drag it, I say. Don't carry her. Leave her in the stableyard until she wakens." He waited while two of the men took the blonde woman by the heels and set about pulling her from the atrium. The slaves made no complaint, only exchanged quick, cold glances as they tugged at the woman's thin ankles.

Justus paced as he waited for Nyso to return, his eyes going occasionally to the third slave, who stood away from him, clearly hoping to escape. "Fetch me my rods," Justus said to him at last. "I want the triple rod, with the long braided thongs."

The slave ducked his head, obviously very frightened. He moved slowly, for he had personal experience of that rod.

"Hurry, or you will share with Nyso in punishment." The sight of the slave scuttling away toward his private suite of rooms gave Justus a great deal of pleasure. He locked his hands behind his back, rocked onto his toes and gave a brief, tuneless whistle.

When the slave returned, he had the specified rod, which he held as if it were poisonous. "I must warn you," he said with the implacable calm that comes beyond desperation, "what you do is against the law. If you beat Nyso, he will bring suit against you. If you beat me, I will bring suit against you. We have not been rebellious, we have obeyed your orders. We have not stolen from you, made attempts on the well-being of any member of your household, profited by your misfortune, or corrupted anyone living within these walls." He folded his arms and waited for the blows that would have to kill him.

Justus had stared in disbelief as the slave recited the law in that cold voice. Rage welled up in him, and he wanted nothing more than to lay the slave's back open to the ribs and hang him like meat while he bled to death. With formidable effort he kept his temper, as he realized the other slaves must also have learned something of the law. "You want to be rid of me as a master?" Justus mocked when he could trust himself to speak.

"Yes," was the answer. There was no flicker of fear in the word, no quaver.

"Very well. Since you wish it. I have no desire to keep those slaves who cannot and will not do as they are required. You will have a new master? So be it." He turned abruptly and strode back into his study, reaching for a sheet of parchment and the container of ink as he sat down. His slaves wanted a new master, did they? He began to write quickly, smiling as he wrote. Nyso and . . . what was the other's name? Fidelis. Yes, Fidelis, they would have their wish. It was a pity he was not empowered to send slaves to the galleys, but there were other tasks almost as unpleasant. Titus Flavius Vespasianus required thousands of slaves to maintain the quarries in Syria and Egypt. Two more slaves, both fairly young and strong, would be welcome to him. Justus finished the deed and signed it with a flourish, then scrawled a short letter to accompany the slaves. At last he rose, and without turning, addressed Fidelis.

"I have granted your request. A new master you shall have. In five days, when the next transport of soldiers leaves for Egypt, you will leave with them. I am sending you to Ostia tomorrow, under guard."

The slave was silent as new apprehension turned to fear.

"And while you labor with the stones and ropes in the full glare of the sun, think of this place, and remember it was your wish to leave." He faced Fidelis, and was gratified by the expression in the slave's eyes. "Go now."

Fidelis stumbled from the room, his feet leaden.

Justus watched him leave, then resumed his seat, to write to Ofonius Tigellinus of the morning's development. He was almost finished with the letter when Sibinus slipped through the door and waited, expectant, in the shadows. "Well?" Justus did not look around at this slave.

"I have found a gladiator for your wife," he said, an unpleasant laugh rising through the words.

"A gladiator?" Justus asked, disappointed. There had been so many gladiators, but Sibinus had never found one that was as brutal with his wife as he was in the arena.

"I think this one is somewhat different. I think he will surprise you." Sibinus moved a little nearer his master. "You have heard about him, haven't you, the one who is endowed most . . . lavishly. They say his spike hangs halfway to his knees."

"And does it?" Justus wanted to know. He was familiar with such boasts.

"I didn't bother to assess that," Sibinus answered, his rat's face brightening. "I did determine that it is as long as his foot. He is quite robust, and it is not like some with great length who never stiffen sufficiently."

"You begin to interest me," Justus admitted.

"I have asked three gladiators' whores about him, and most of them would not discuss him at all, beyond saying that he is capable and willing. I learned more in the lupanar. The whores there don't like him at all. Pulcheria says that she will never have to do with him again, because when he was through with her, she could not take another man for three days, and he did not pay enough to compensate her for the business she lost." Sibinus had waited to be certain that Justus would want to see this gladiator. "He will come tonight, if I send him word. He's never had a patrician lady before, he said. I doubt he'll disappoint you," Sibinus said more earnestly.

"He had better not," was Justus' answer. "What is the name of this paragon?"

"Something unpronounceable. He's from somewhere beyond Dacia. He'll answer to Maius."

"In other words, a barbarian," Justus said with a condemning shrug. "There's nothing to them. A few pants and the whole thing is over."

"That's not what the whores say," Sibinus reminded him cautiously. "He's a big man, master, quite tall, and broad as a wagon in the chest. The rumor is that he was the torturer for one of the local rulers; he developed a taste for it, and the ruler had to get rid of him. You've seen him in the arena, remember? The one you said fought for the joy of it?"

In an instant Justus recalled the man—he was large, with thick, heavily muscled arms, who had disdained to use his sword on a fallen opponent, but had crushed the life from him slowly, with his foot. Justus began to smile. "You may be right about this gladiator. Very well. Tonight, then. I will deal with Olivia when she returns from the springs." He looked over the letter before him, then folded and sealed it. "Sibinus," he said.

"Yes, master?" The little slave had been edging toward the door.

"On your way to arrange things with this gladiator, I want you to go to the Praetorian camp." It was a long way to the camp, and in a different direction from the Great School, where the working gladiators were barracked during the Games, but if Justus was aware of this, he gave no indication of it. "This letter is most private. It is for the eyes of the Commander Ofonius Tigellinus and none other, not even Sabinus. I want you to hand it to him yourself. Tell him that it concerns a private matter. If you fail me in this, I will have you turned over to the Emperor to work on the Golden House." He held out the letter and waited while Sibinus, with a sour expression, took it. "I have told Tigellinus that the seal is intact. If it is not, he will make short work of you."

Sibinus slipped the letter inside his tunic, under the belt. "No one will know I carry it, master. You may rely on me." He lowered his head and left the room. It was a short time later that he left the house on his inconvenient errand.

In his study, Justus sat back to read. He had chosen a book of tales of the Greek gods, and as he read, he imagined the gladiator as Hercules, and Olivia as Iole, and the time passed quickly.

A letter from C. Ofonius Tigellinus, with Nymphidius Sabinus, co-commander of the Praetorian Guard, to the Roman garrisons at Athens.

Greetings to the soldiers and citizens of Rome who are stationed in Athens, from Ofonius Tigellinus and the Praetorian Guard:

The Emperor Nero has decided to honor Greece with a visit at a time when he may compete in the great Olympian Games, as a show of his affection and respect for that great and antique nation. It will be your rare privilege to guard your Emperor while he is in attendance there, and to see that all things progress without undue complications.

It is rare that the Emperor of all Rome should be moved to give such a great tribute to a client nation, but Nero has been known for his remarkable statesmanship, as is demonstrated with his great reception of the king of Armenia and the peace terms recently concluded with Parthia. This latest gesture of imperial magnanimity clearly indicates his commitment to stability and prosperity throughout the empire.

In such a climate of international trust and goodwill, your work should be most pleasant. You need only escort Nero to the Games, be with him while he is there, and then return to your various posts when he has departed. Though the legions are known to love war, this is a time when peace will give you more opportunity for advancement than the bloodiest conflict, for Nero has expressed his desire to acknowledge all meritorious service done for him while in Greece. You may be assured that your accomplishments on his behalf will shine as brightly at the Olympic Games as they would shine in the glow of victory.

You may have qualms about this Emperor, who puts more worth on culture than on military strength, and I can assure you that there are sensible men in Rome who share your concerns and who are close to Nero, advising him on these and other delicate matters. Your opinions will be heard if you wish to address me or any of my associates. Truly Nero is a man of many accomplishments and is sincerely dedicated to the good of the empire, but it is true his experience is limited and there are those with more understanding of the nature of battle and the conflict of nations, who are eager to protect and expand the limits of our empire.

Let none of you doubt that these Games serve the cause of Rome. I have heard soldiers here muttering against what they consider to be a senseless indulgence and display, but we must admit that Nero has proven more shrewd than expected in the past. Those misguided men who sought to overthrow him quickly discovered they had underestimated his understanding and the devotion of the men near to him. While I, with you, could wish for a more militant posture from Nero in certain matters, I will not condemn his efforts and his gestures of rare diplomatic grace toward our client nations.

This is sent so that you will have time to prepare for the arrival of Nero and those of his court who will accompany him. It is August now, and his departure is planned for early September. You have time to make ready to do honor to your Emperor. Use the time well and you will find ample rewards for your efforts.

By my own hand on this, the nineteenth day of August, in the 818th Year of the City.

C. Ofonius Tigellinus,
with Nymphidius Sabinus, co-commander
The Praetorian Guard

13

TISHTRY PULLED in her chariot beside the long-legged blue roan her master rode. There was dust everywhere in the orchards; and the practice track that wound through them, around the lake and behind the vineyards was clouded from the passage of chariots during the morning.

"How are they?" Sanct' Germain inquired, though his practiced eye told him that the bay mare on the right was flagging. "I think you've got the yoke too tight."

"Yes." Tishtry sighed. "I have been working them for over a week now, and they still aren't ready. Canvo there"—she nodded toward the horse on the right, the only one not yoked with the other three—"he holds his own on the inner turns, of course, but I can't get him to get speed enough when he's on the outside. It's habit. In the Circus Maximus, he always turns on the inside, so he's used to holding the pivot. I wish there were a way to explain it to him."

As if in disapproval of this, Canvo tugged at his rein and sidled away from the other three yoked horses. Tishtry reached for the reins tied around her waist and pulled him back. "You see how it is?" she said to Sanct' Germain. "He's been like that for more than a month, ever since I took that toss in Nero's Circus in May. I think he was confused, an empty arena without a spina to guide him down the center."

"Would you rather not participate there again? I can refuse you to anyone who requests." He leaned forward in the padded, stirrupless Roman saddle. "Is all well with you, Tishtry?"

"Well?" she repeated, her strong, angular, sun-bronzed face revealing little. "I suppose so. My horses are learning, I am getting money of my own, I have learned a great deal." As she spoke she steadied her horses.

"Is that all?" He had felt himself withdraw from her before now, but had not been certain she was aware of how much he had changed. Looking down at her with the hot, diamond-bright sun hiding nothing, he realized he had not understood how sensitive she had become to him.

"It's enough." She could feel his concern, as intense as the heat. "I have liked sharing my master's bed, but you want more now. Wrongly or not, I don't have what you need. This"—she touched the reins that were tied around her waist—"is my life. The other, well, it is pleasant enough, but not what you've demanded of me. I can't do it, my master. When you took me to your bed the first time and were willing to be honest with me, I told you my feelings. They haven't changed. If you want to send me away from you, it's your right." She shaded her eyes with one hand in the hope that she could read his expression, but the sun was behind him and her eyes were dazzled.

"I've always appreciated your frankness," he said, feeling a sensation that bothered him. He was pleased not to have to make a choice between Tishtry and Olivia, since such choices were foreign to him. Yet he was sorry that in the four years he had shared the night with Tishtry, none of those delightful, sensual contests had moved her sufficiently to feel a bond with him. He wondered now how she would feel when she woke from death into his life, and he worried for her.

"Will you send me away?" There was a little apprehension

in her question. She liked Rome, reveled in her fame and was well-treated by her master.

"No. Should you wish another master, you must tell me." He straightened in the saddle. "If I send for you tonight, will you come?" He had not seen Olivia for many days, and then they had had only a few moments to talk. Though his hunger for her was growing strong, he could not risk entering her house again so soon, while her husband still feared Persian spies.

"You are my master," she said with a slight hitch to her shoulders.

"Would it displease you?"

She looked away from him, toward the orchard and the hill beyond. "You've never displeased me, my master, not as you mean. I think sometimes that I disappoint you, but you've never said so. If I do disappoint you, it is not what I want to do. We're so different, you and I, that I think we often misunderstand each other." To change the subject, she looked at Sanct' Germain's feet. "You wear Scythian charioteer's boots all the time, even when you ride. I wear proper sandals. You see."

Sanct' Germain knew that their differences were otherwise. "Footgear isn't the problem," he said sardonically. "I accept your terms, Tishtry. I won't impose too much on you. I thank you for being willing to share my bed, and for your honesty."

"And if I weren't willing?" she asked, watching him, thinking how like a shadow he was, standing between her and the sun. "You could order me."

"Yes, I could order you," he said wearily. "It's a master's right. I wish you would believe that I would never order you." He thought briefly, painfully, on those years he had been a slave, and though they were long ago, he recalled them clearly.

"You haven't yet," she allowed. "My master, my horses are restless, and we have a long way to go to complete the course."

Sanct' Germain pulled his blue roan back to give her chariot room to pass; then as the dust rose around her, he turned his horse and made his way down the slope toward his villa.

It had changed since he built it. Where there had been one large U-shaped stable, there were now three, and a heavily fenced animal compound beyond. The barracks and cottages for his slaves extended along the edge of his vineyards to the eastern limit of his land. The villa itself, with its double atrium, was completely finished, and the extensive garden between the atria was full of flourishing rare plants and large roof-high cages containing many strange, gorgeously plumed birds. Three intricate fountains cascaded in this garden, cooling the air and adding a delicate music to the hot afternoon. Two artificial streams flowed from those fountains through the stableyard, passed the slaves' barracks and cottages and into a small, artificial lake in the animals' compound where, at the moment, a pair of tigers was lolling to be rid of the heat.

Drawing up at his colonnaded portico, Sanct' Germain slid out of his saddle and called for a slave to lead his horse around to the stables. "I will come later to feed him," he added as the boy took the reins from his hand. "Be sure to put the saddle on its rack immediately. It could be ruined otherwise." Padded saddles were still something of a novelty in Rome, and many of the older stablehands treated them with contempt. To avoid that, Sanct' Germain had two Parthian slaves to care for his tack, but he had learned to be sure that orders were given for proper care.

The slave nodded, bowed slightly, and led the horse away.

Sanct' Germain went swiftly through the garden and entered the larger wing of the house through one of a series of huge windows that opened onto his main dining room. There were nine couches there, the proper number, and the little tables before them were lacquered with fantastic designs. A long table on a dais at the end of the room was reserved for women, since at formal dinners women did not recline. Sanct' Germain's eyes flicked over the room, looking for signs of poor preparation, but he could find none. His guests would be pleased, which was what he wanted.

As he left the dining room, Aumtehoutep approached him. "I've been looking for you, my master."

"And you have found me. What is it?" He crossed the mosaic-inlaid atrium to his main reception chamber, Aumtehoutep falling into step beside him.

"There were two Praetorians here today, conducting what they called a routine inspection." The Egyptian's expressionless face was unreadable to anyone but Sanct' Germain.

"Why does that worry you?" he asked as he opened the gold-fitted doors of palest northern pine.

The reception room was the most splendid apartment in the larger wing of Villa Ragoczy. Its style was distinctly not Roman. Tall narrow windows let in light, so that the very air seemed to glisten. There were no murals on the high walls; they were painted a fine, pale blue, and the false columns that rose to the ceiling at regular intervals were silver. Instead of mosaics, there was a carpet on the floor, of colors to match the walls. This extravagance was unusual enough, and had taken Persian weavers a year to make, but more outstanding were the rosewood chairs with pale blue silk cushions, which had come the entire length of the Silk Road, from that fabulous land that was so rich the very skins of its people were golden.

"It worries me," Aumtehoutep said carefully, "because it means someone wants you watched."

"Why do you say that?" He looked around the room carefully. "Do we have any white flowers? Have them arranged in the three silver-and-lapis bowls, and bring in the rosewood tables for them."

"Of course," Aumtehoutep said, and scribbled a note on his tablet with his stylus. "I think there are some white blooms, still. I'll put one of the household slaves to work on it shortly. You said that you wanted your black cotton Egyptian robe tonight, the long kalasiris and the black shenti . . ."

"Yes. The silver girdle, I think, and my ruby-and-silver collar. No headdress, no earrings."

"Bracelets?" Aumtehoutep asked hopefully.

"Oh, I think not. I'll seem foreign enough without that. And," he added with a slight smile, "since I'm on my own ground, as it were, I think I will go barefoot." He tugged at his short-sleeved black tunica. "It will be good to wear something a little lighter than this." At last he relented. "Very well, Aumtehoutep. About the Praetorians."

"They were polite, but I would not like to have denied them too much. They wanted to see the private wing, of course, but I told them I had no authority to admit anyone there. They accepted that, and by Thoth's Feather, it is so. All the barracks and stables and compounds were inspected." He closed his fingers tightly around his stylus. "If you owned gladiators, it would have been bad for you today, I think."

"Yes," Sanct' Germain agreed. "That's one of the reasons I

don't own any. Did the charioteers and bestiarii disappoint them?"

"One of them, indeed. With all the plots that have been afoot, and the conspiracies, it would be easier for them if they could find proof of a foreign plan to overthrow the whole empire. That would be more easily dealt with than a plot against Caesar." His brown, impassive eyes rested on Sanct' Germain's face. "There are those in Rome who wish you ill, my master. They will not rest until they have made you guilty and condemned."

Sanct' Germain shrugged. "It's not the first time, Aumtehoutep. Is it?" He clenched his hands together. "You're right. I should make a few provisions against that day. Babylon taught me that, if nothing else." He turned quickly on his booted heel. "Come to my library. We'll take care of this now."

Aumtehoutep moved after him, holding his tablet ready and his stylus poised. If anyone else in Sanct' Germain's household had seen the tablet, except for Sanct' Germain himself, he would have been bewildered by what was written there, for Aumtehoutep wrote in the language of his youth, the elegant modified hieroglyphic script of Egypt's Eighteenth Dynasty.

"Have the oysters arrived?" Sanct' Germain asked as they went through the garden.

"A barrel of them. They are in the cold room, packed in ice and wood shavings." He knitted his brows. "The plovers' eggs haven't been sent yet."

"Send one of the slaves to Scimindar in the Old Market. He'll have them. What about wine?"

"The best from your own estates in Gallia. The red is twenty years old. I had the master cook test one of them. He said it's excellent."

"Good. Serve it unwatered. Are the musicians ready, and the cupbearers?"

Beside them, a peacock in full display made a raucous sound as it minced toward a Chinese pheasant.

"They'll be ready in two hours. Are you still planning to give the cupbearers to the men they serve as gifts?" Aumtehoutep nodded to the tall lean African who guarded the garden entrance to the north wing of Villa Ragoczy.

"Certainly. They expect that kind of gesture of me." He turned to close the door. The room they had entered was good-sized, of simple design and pleasing proportions. It would have been impossible to assign a style to it, for it was unique to its owner. The high walls were paneled in cedar that had been rubbed with wax until it glowed. The few articles of furniture were of the same wood, of simple and elegant lines. On the far wall there was a tall chest, and Sanct' Germain went to it, opening it and drawing out two thin parchment sheets and a small jar of ink.

"What are you doing, my master?" Aumtehoutep asked, as Sanct' Germain drew up a chair to his writing table.

"I'm taking precautions, as it seems I must." He had taken a fine brush and was writing quickly in a small, neat hand. "You will find my slave deeds in my Assyrian chest in the library, should you need to present them. There are copies in Rome, but they may not be secure if I have too-powerful enemies." He was silent as he wrote, filling all of one of the parchment sheets and half of the second. Finally he looked up. "There. I hope that this is enough."

"Enough?" Aumtehoutep did his best to keep the fear from his flat voice.

Sanct' Germain looked down at the parchment. "This provides that should I be exiled, executed, imprisoned, arrested on capital charges, or disappear for more than sixty days without word to anyone, then every slave I own will be freed, without condition, and granted a plot of land on one of my estates. That won't help the household slaves much, or the bestiarii, but they will have something of value beyond their freedom. At least they need not starve." He rose and placed a small amethyst carving on the parchment. "I will have two or three of my guests witness this tonight, and that should be sufficient. Corbulo will do it, I know. If two others sign as well, it will be enough for any court."

"Will it come to that?" Aumtehoutep asked, studying Sanct' Germain's quiet face.

"I hope not. But it could." He turned away from the writing table. "You, Kosrozd and Tishtry are provided for elsewhere, but this covers you as well, in case the state moves against me and my grants are invalidated. They are blood of my blood now. And you . . . how many years have you been with me, old friend?" He did not expect an answer, and got none. "In time, it will be so with Olivia." For a moment his eyes were troubled. "She's in great danger, more than she knows. If her husband ever learned of her affection for me, he would use her much more brutally than he does now." Without being aware of it, he had lapsed into his native tongue. "He's looking for an excuse now."

"She isn't safe to know," Aumtehoutep said carefully.

Sanct' Germain raised his brows. "Yet it was you who told me that I was becoming too remote, too untouchable. You see, I have taken your advice. Now you warn me of the very thing you urged. How can I deal with all your strictures?" He was teasing, an ironic note in his voice.

Aumtehoutep responded seriously. "I don't question your need for her. You are changed since you've known her, and it is good to have it so. She has awakened something in you—I have no words for it, my master. You are like one recovering from a long illness, who rediscovers the world, and life. Yet this caring has become a grave risk for you, for her, perhaps for all of us."

"Yes," Sanct' Germain said, cutting him short. "Though it may be that the risk is necessary. What good is this awakening, as you call it, if it demands nothing of me in return?" He himself had no answer for the question he posed. He had thought of it several times as he walked alone in the night, unrested and filled with desire. At such times he had refused to read, or study, for he wanted nothing to interfere with his reflections. Aumtehoutep was correct in saying that he was changed, and the change was increasing, like ripples in a pond. Olivia drew him with the force of a tide. Twice since their last night together he had ventured into Rome to Cornelius Justus Silius' house on the Aventine Hill, but had not been able to gain entrance. He had seen Olivia a few times, but at a distance, and when he had tried to approach her, a tiny gesture on her part had kept him away.

"My master?" said Aumtehoutep.

Sanct' Germain forced his mind away from Olivia. "Yes, you're right." He started toward the door, saying, "We're having ducks cooked in honey, aren't we? Is the cook planning to serve those before or after the dates and chopped mushrooms?"

Text of a letter from Cornelius Justus Silius to Servius Sulpicius Galba in Toletum, delivered eventually in Tarraco.

To the revered and distinguished S. Sulpicius Galba, greetings:

In this unfortunate empire, filled with suspicions and hatred, there are few who command the respect that is given you, and fewer still who begrudge it to you. I say this, who have seen my wife's family suffer the full weight and fury of the law for their folly in allying themselves with hopeless causes and inadequate leaders. Certainly you have heard that Maximus Tarquinus Clemens has been convicted of conspiracy to overthrow the Emperor. His sons, Pontius Viriginius, Fortunatus Drusillus, Cassius Saultus and Martinus Licius, are all condemned with him, and my attempts to assist them have been to no avail. They have claimed that only two were involved in any plotting and that the others are blameless, and one must admire their heroism, if not their sense. They insist that their cause was betrayed, and it is with grief that I hear them speak so. Who would have thought that so valiant men would rely on that ancient excuse for their lamentable failures?

Word has reached me that your legions want to hail you as Emperor and displace Nero. With the Emperor prepared at last to embark to Greece, some say that this would be a fine opportunity to march on Rome, providing Nero does not delay again. Surely a man as wise as you, one who has grown nobly old in the service of Rome, must realize that such an act would be disastrous to his hopes, for Rome is readied for just such an attempt. Think on your many years of service to the empire, and bide your time. Should Nero prove intolerable, then the Senate must listen to wisdom, and where better to seek it than from one with your experience. Do not let the zeal of your men lead you into unwise decisions. There is time yet to hope for reform, and more than that, many still have hopes for Nero, who, for all his extravagance, has been an Emperor of peace with an astute grasp on many of our needs. Those needs may well be the key to his rule.

Be patient, and watch to see the changes in the Emperor, so that you may not be led into unwise alliances or precipitate endeavors. Reflect that greater houses than yours have fallen on fewer suspicions than are now directed toward you. The ruin of my wife's family has taught me a great deal. Profit by my experience.

Should your plans change, I hope you will let me know of them so that proper steps may be taken. I am ever eager to advance the cause of the Roman Empire, as are you.

From my own hand, on the twenty-fourth day of October in the 818th Year of the City,

Cornelius Justus Silius

14

FROM HIS vantage point near the Gates of Life, Sanct' Germain watched the Circus Maximus fill with more than seventy-five thousand Romans. As much of the populace of the city as might cram themselves into the public stands had turned out for Nero's last Games before he left for Greece.

The great tarred ships' beams were in place so that the arena could be flooded for an aquatic entertainment. Slaves were already stationed at the sluices, ready to let in the torrent that would flood the floor of the amphitheater to a depth almost twice the height of a man.

"They didn't used to do this," remarked the old, freed gladiator who stood beside Sanct' Germain. "The spina was lower, too, and the metae were standing on it, to keep chariots from running onto it when they turned too tightly. Now they have to have the metae on the ground and the spina is almost as tall as they are. They've raised the stands, of course. Well, they had to after that leopard climbed into that old Senator's box and mauled him and his slave." He rubbed at his neck. "Hot day."

"Yes," Sanct' Germain said.

"That bestiaria of yours going to be here today? I saw her last time she was in the arena. It's a pity she doesn't know how to fight. A woman like that, with a sword and those horses . . ." He ducked his head in respect. "Fine woman, your Armenian."

"Thank you," Sanct' Germain responded. "I will tell her you said so."

The old gladiator snorted. "Why, she wouldn't know Tsoudes from a savage. It's good of you to offer."

A shout went up from the various managers of the Games, and the slaves waiting at the sluices bent to turn the stiff brass handles. There was a throaty rumble under the susurrus of the crowd as the water began to rush into the arena.

"Where's the court?" Tsoudes muttered. "You can't tell me a showman like Nero'd let the Games begin without him." The old gladiator folded his thick arms across his massive scarred chest. "Sometimes I think the only thing they care about now is the spectacle. Not so long ago, it took skill to fight in the arena. We had pride, all the fighters, because we were the best-trained warriors in the empire, and that includes the legions. Now"—he tossed his head scornfully—"it's blood they're after and blood they get. Last month, those Greek hoplites were in the arena. I tell you, they are soldiers, those men. It was a joy to watch them. But the crowd hated them. There wasn't enough blood on the sands for them. The hoplites fight too efficiently and too well."

"Did you fight when the spina was lower?" Sanct' Germain asked, eager to turn the conversation.

"By Mithras' Bull!" A low, rumbling laugh shook him. "That was done before my grandfather was made a slave; Divus Julius or Divus Augustus did it."

"Nero has talked about adding more stands. There were two people killed in the rush to get seats this morning, and so long as part of the stands are being rebuilt, they might as well be made higher." Sanct' Germain looked up into the packed stands and toward the multicolored awning of finespun wool.

Tsoudes followed his glance. "I was here the day that

Caligula had the awning removed and the exits blocked. He wanted to punish the people for laughing at one of his displays. It was very effective, really. The sun and the heat were terrible. A handful of them died of the sun."

Through the thick tar-coated logs came the scent of roses. The water filling the arena had been perfumed. Sanct' Germain recalled Petronius and his aversion to roses, and was saddened.

"Yes," Tsoudes went on, delighted to have so distinguished an audience for his ramblings, "it was dangerous being a gladiator for old Gaius Caligula. Never knew where you stood with him. I remember watching him in the parades, very tall and gangly, forever looking about. And Claudius . . . well, I never liked Claudius. There were unpleasant rumors about him, and there was something in his eye. See this scar?" He pointed to a jagged white line that ran from his collarbone to the top of his hip. "That happened under Claudius' podium. I killed my opponent, straight and fair, but it wasn't enough for Claudius. He ordered one of the others to kill me. Screamed at him, telling someone I had not fought with to kill me. If it hadn't been for the crowd, I'd have gone out through the Gates of Death that day."

Sanct' Germain, who had seen Claudius once, in Britannia, held his peace, though he agreed with Tsoudes.

"Two of the fighters I trained will appear today," Tsoudes went on. "I had less than a year with each of them. They're nowhere near ready for a combat, but that's the way of things now." He hooked his thumbs into the wide leather belt pulled tight across his hips. "There isn't the pride there used to be. No one cares for skill and training. It used to be there was honor in the arena, but now, it's disgusting the way—"

His words were lost in the sudden blare of trumpets and the drone of the hydraulic organ on the spina. From the awning lines high above the crowd, beautiful young boys with gilt wings tied to their shoulders were lowered to hang like cherubs over the heads of the people. They had been given roses and gold to toss to the crowd, and various gifts from the Emperor, among them deeds for land, large estates, a brace of wild boars, fine jewels, a fully manned bireme, a charioteer, half a dozen ostriches, bolts of silken cloth, an invitation to dine with the Emperor on his pleasure barge, a man-eating tiger, an Egyptian mummy, and other equally whimsical expressions of the Emperor's favor, all of which would be signed over to the new owners at the end of the Games.

Just as the crowd had grasped at the last of this largess, the boys were once again drawn up to the awning and the trumpets pealed out their fanfare announcing the arrival of the Emperor. There were rustlings and murmurs as the people looked toward the podium. It, and many of the nobility's boxes, stood empty. The noise of the crowd grew louder and the trumpets were almost overwhelmed by the din.

Then, at the far end of the Circus Maximus, three huge doors that rose above the logs at waterline lifted, and six fine barges, each drawn by fifty beautiful youths trained to swim in precise coordination together, surged onto the perfumed water.

In the foremost of these barges was Nero himself, resplendent in silver-and-blue cloth, with a fanciful wreath of seashells in his dark blond hair. Around him were part of his court, and most of the nobility followed on the other barges. The last barge was ornamented with flowers and gauze to resemble a seashell borne on the waves, and in it rode the Vestal Virgins, stiff with disapproval.

This amazing procession circled the spina twice as the crowd voiced its approval. At last the barges drew up before the various boxes of their passengers, and from the marble stands, gold-painted steps were lowered by slaves dressed as fauns, and the nobles climbed out of the barges into their boxes to the wild acclaim of the people crowded together in the stands.

As Nero took his seat in the imperial box, the fanfare came to a glorious climax and the nearly hysterical Aves began. Nero stood with arms raised, his usually discontented expression changed to one of genuine delight. Then he gave a sign and turned to take his seat.

The youths, still swimming with fine precision, were tugging their barges toward the far side of the arena where two doors waited, open.

A cry went up from more than seventy-five thousand voices, and the swimmers broke their rhythm, wondering what had occasioned the sound that rang around them, as vast as the sound of ocean waves. The leader trod water long enough to shout a few terse orders, and once again the barges moved forward through the water.

But now there were other shapes in the water with them,

long, dark lizardlike shapes that moved with deadly swiftness toward the barges. These were the great crocodiles from the Nile, some of them three and four times as long as the height of a tall man. Every motion of the reptiles was filled with purpose as they sped forward.

The swimmers knew now that something was terribly wrong, and they faltered in their smooth strokes, looking around, looking above for archers, or for more boats that might be filled with armed men. Finally one of the swimmers looked down into the water, and shrieked out his terror.

The confusion among the swimmers was brief. The first of the crocodiles struck, jaws gaping, and closed on the lead swimmer, dragging him underwater before he could scream.

In the stands, the expectant silence that had fallen a few moments before now erupted in excited yells. From the highest tiers to the finest senatorial boxes, the spectators leaned forward with avidity as the water began to churn with thrashing bodies and hungry crocodiles. One of the swimmers was caught between two of the huge beasts: one crocodile seized the swimmer's shoulder, the other took both legs in his hideous jaws, and then each crocodile turned over in opposite directions, twisting the young man apart with appalling ease.

Sanct' Germain turned away from his stand by the Gates of Life, sickened.

"Ah, you foreigners," Tsoudes said with a sympathetic wag of his head. "You're not like Romans. The sight of blood strengthens a man." He peered toward the arena again, where only two swimmers were in sight, and one of them was fighting hopelessly with the crocodile who had his arm in his teeth. "I don't like this sort of thing myself," he added inconsistently. "There's no point to it."

"What is next, after this?" Sanct' Germain asked, looking toward the cages that were being drawn up near them.

"A venation for the crocodiles from rafts, naturally, and then a series of combats between blinded soldiers. That always pleases the crowd." He nodded as if remembering an engagement. "I should look their gear over. Sometimes, to be amusing, they're given defective weapons." Tsoudes got down from his position with uncharacteristic haste. "I believe your Armenian races after that. She's doing that alone, isn't she?"

"Yes. The Emperor has requested a repetition of the performance she gave for the visit of the king of Armenia." He was concerned, for Tishtry had one new horse in her team, and she was not convinced that he was ready to work in the arena, with all the noise and the huge press of bodies in the stands.

"A great honor for her," Tsoudes said, and lumbered away.

There was a last great scream from the stands, and then Sanct' Germain watched as new rafts maneuvered out of the narrow gates, floating over the water, smelling now of blood and ordure instead of roses. On the rafts rode tall Nubian slaves, each with two long, deep-pointed spears held at the ready.

Another flurry of activity near him caught Sanct' Germain's attention, and he gratefully left the watch station by the Gates of Life.

He had just stepped into the twilight world of caverns and passages under the stands when a voice behind him stopped him.

"Franciscus!" Necredes spat out the name like a curse.

Sanct' Germain stopped, but did not turn. "What do you want, Necredes?"

"I want to warn you, foreigner, that I haven't forgotten the shame you brought upon me. The time will come when you'll wish you had never made me your enemy." The Master of the Bestiarii strode up to Sanct' Germain. "I saw you watching the crocodiles. You don't like them, do you?"

"I don't like slaughter, Necredes. I don't like waste of life." His face was set as he forced himself to respond coldly to the man who confronted him.

Necredes glared into Sanct' Germain's dark eyes. "One day I will have my vengeance, Franciscus. I'm willing to wait for it."

"I trust you won't mind being disappointed?" Sanct' Germain asked quietly. "I have to see to my slave who performs today."

"Yes!" Necredes declared. "The disobedient woman, who is the favorite of Nero now. Make your conquest of him complete, and send her to his bed. They say he's come to like barbarians." With a smug glow in his eyes, he waited for Sanct' Germain to challenge him.

"I don't fight with slaves and freedmen," Sanct' Germain said. "You are not worth my notice or my contempt. If you take any action against me or my slaves, now or in the future, I will see you in the arena, the way those swimmers were." He shouldered past Necredes and started down the nearest passageway.

"If I don't see you there first!" Necredes shouted after him.

By the time he found Tishtry, Sanct' Germain had decided to say nothing to her about his encounter with Necredes. He had told her before to avoid the Master of the Bestiarii, and now, with this difficult performance facing her, he had no wish to add to her worries.

"I still don't know about Shinzu," she said as she patted her new horse in the hitch. "I wish Immit hadn't gone lame. Well, I'll do all my somersaults on the straight parts and keep to the standing bits on the turns. He can hold through that, I'm certain." She was gaudily decked out, with many copper bracelets on her arms and her most startlingly woven Armenian fringed tunic belted twice around her.

"Don't take any chances, Tishtry. And don't try that handstand if you have any question whatever about the new horse." He put his hand on her shoulder. "I'll take responsibility for that. I'll tell the Emperor that you are acting under my orders, and I'll have a good reason for it." His degree of concern for her surprised him—it went beyond their shared satisfaction to an abiding affection. He knew that his growing ardor for Olivia had brought an unexpected fondness for Tishtry in its wake, and this disturbed him.

"I don't want to disappoint the Emperor," she said rather sharply. "He wants to see everything I performed for Tiridates, and I will do all of it." She flicked the short switch that was attached by a thong to her wrist. "I've gone over all the equipment twice, so I know that won't fail."

"Are the leathers new?" Sanct' Germain asked as he glanced quickly at the wide girths and collars that attached to the abbreviated racing yoke.

"Fairly. I've been aging these a few months so they won't chafe." She put her hand on her lightweight racing chariot. "I'm going to need another chariot in a while. This one is getting old."

"How long have you had it?" Sanct' Germain felt his concern flicker again as he looked at the wood-and-wicker vehicle.

"Not quite two years. Long enough." She grinned up at him. "May I have scrollwork on the next one?"

Sanct' Germain laughed. "If it doesn't alter the balance or

weight, of course. Tell me what you want and I'll put the chariotmakers to work on it tomorrow."

"Oh, good." Her eyes danced. "And paintings on the sides? I'd like pictures of horses racing through the clouds."

"Whatever you want," he promised her as he ran one finger along her jaw. "Do well, Tishtry. Keep safe."

It was her turn to laugh. "You're kind to me, my master." She gave him a roguish look, then climbed into the chariot and secured the reins around her waist. "I've got to take the team out and warm them up." So that it would not sound as if she were dismissing him, she added, "I like that new tunica. It isn't Persian, is it?"

"I had it from a merchant from Hind. It has the virtue of being cool."

"If you want to be cool, why do you always wear black?" She expected no answer to this inquiry and got none. A flick of the wrist and her horses moved off smartly and Tishtry turned her whole attention to them.

When he had seen her enter the practice track beside the Circus Maximus, Sanct' Germain sought the stairs that led to the stands and the marble-seated boxes of the nobility. He passed a squad of black dwarfs armed with throwing knives and spears, and beyond them, in narrow, foul-smelling cells, Jewish prisoners waited to be sent into the arena with wild beasts. One of the tunnels that ran under the arena to the spina opened onto the main passage a little farther on, and there a few custodial slaves gathered, two of them dressed in tunicae of cloth-of-gold with gilded laurel leaves in their hair. These, later in the day, would present various gifts and tributes to the victors in the Games, but now were attempting to get something to eat before they began the long, hot watch on the spina. Fifty paces farther on, a bestiarius struggled to bridle his unruly mount—a white rhinoceros.

At last Sanct' Germain came to the stairs that led upward, and squinting upward into the subdued light, he entered the world of the spectators. The sound was constant, like swarms of bees but much louder, and occasionally punctuated with cries and oaths. In the marble boxes of the patricians, slaves were serving fruits and cooked meats to the high-ranking Romans while hawkers of various foodstuffs made their way through the stands above, calling their goods and prices. On the sands, in the full glare of sunlight, Gallic cavalry was slaughtering a small, determined squad of Daci bowmen.

Sanct' Germain had rented a marble box of his own, and Aumtehoutep waited there for him, a somber figure in a white shenti and linen headdress. Sanct' Germain raised his hand as he approached, and saw Aumtehoutep nod his acknowledgment when a very beautiful young slave with a collar of jewel-studded gold and dressed in a Greek chiton of sheerest Coan linen approached him.

"Nero Caesar would be happy to have a word with you," the slave said, making what was clearly a command seem like a polite request.

"Now?" Sanct' Germain asked, apprehension pricking along his spine.

"Certainly. He has sent me to escort you." The beautiful young man beamed at him.

"Then, by all means, lead the way." Almost everyone in the Circus Maximus knew where the imperial box was, but plainly, Nero wanted to be sure that Sanct' Germain came quickly. "Will you send one of your companions to tell my slave why I am called away?" This was not an unreasonable request, coming, as it did, at midday, when many had a light meal. Sanct' Germain was willing to have Nero's slave assume that such was the case with him.

"It will be done as soon as you greet the Emperor. I will go myself." With the same engaging smile, the young slave stepped into the mural-lined corridor that ran behind all the patrician boxes.

They walked briskly past slaves with food and wine who eyed the fare set out for their masters. Some of the nobility loitered here as well, searching with famished, jaded glances for that special beauty or ugliness that promised novelty. Finally they entered a heavily guarded corridor that ended in five steep steps. The slave stood aside and inclined his head to Sanct' Germain.

Nero was licking the last of a fruit sauce from his fingers as Sanct' Germain entered the imperial box. His pale, intelligent eyes were cold with fright in that instant before he recognized the newcomer; then he smiled and waved Sanct' Germain to the chair on his right. "Ragoczy Sanct' Germain Franciscus," he said with delight, as if his arrival were wholly unexpected. "The man with the very impressive name. Sacred freedom, isn't it?" He smiled at Sanct' Germain and made an expansive gesture to the others in the imperial box.

"Actually, the meaning is closer to 'one with the god's

liberation,' " Sanct' Germain answered smoothly as he looked at the others.

"Let me see," Nero said. "You know Justus Silius, I believe, and Adamenedes, who is to be one of the judges of the Olympic Games. My wife you've met. Aeneas Savinian is a poet, newly come from Treviri. His companion is Placidus Reggianus. You know Sabinus of the Praetorians, and Viridius Fondi, his tribune. We're all waiting to see your wonderful Armenian charioteer demonstrate her skill. Tiridates was quite thrilled with her performance."

Sanct' Germain nodded to each as they were introduced, taking care to conceal his disturbance. Why did Nero want him here? What did he want of Tishtry, or himself? In the past, Nero had forced his guests to make him lavish gifts during the Games in tribute to the Emperor's genius. Sanct' Germain was certain he could not sign Tishtry away, so he waited while a place was made for him under the wide green awning.

"Did you see the Games last month?" Nero asked, interrupting himself to indicate the food that was spread on low tables. "Have what you want. The goose is particularly good, and so are the larks' tongues."

"Thank you, but among my kind, dining in public is considered very rude conduct." He was glad to be seated out of the sun, for even with his earth-lined boots, sitting in direct sunlight, which the imperial box was, would be severely uncomfortable in very little time.

Nero's crowing laughter was dutifully echoed by the others in the box. "How quaint foreigners are," he said as he wiped his kohl-lined eyes with the hem of his robe, leaving a black smudge on his cheek.

"About the Games," Sanct' Germain prompted him as he took his couch and propped himself on his elbow.

"Ah, yes, there was the most exquisite joke. Everyone enjoyed it." He chuckled at the thought. "There was a criminal sentenced to the arena, for fraud. He had debased coins, being a goldsmith. Well, it was found out, and he was condemned. The poor fool was ready to die of fright. They put him out on the sands alone, and the slaves dragged out one of those huge cages they use for tigers, all very solid and closed, and then they hurried off with just the catch line running to the side so that the cage door could be opened." Nero reached for a large goblet of silver inlaid with pearls and drank from it greedily. "The goldsmith was certain he was going to be torn apart, and he very nearly fainted. Finally, the editor of the Games gave the signal and the catch line was pulled. Everyone leaned forward for the terrible minute, because they, too, thought a tiger would leap out and rend the criminal in pieces. But after a moment, a chicken came from the cage. The criminal collapsed, and the entire crowd laughed, and the editor reminded the criminal and the crowd that one fraud deserved another."

The guffaws that greeted this were more than polite, and Sanct' Germain joined them. "Very clever," he said.

"Appropriate," Nero concurred. "But that's not why you're here. I want to honor your slave, and it would be most fitting to honor you at the same time."

"Honor me?" Sanct' Germain asked, wishing he knew what Nero had planned. "I have done nothing deserving of honor."

"That is for me to determine," Nero said, and waited while his company nodded.

Justus cleared his throat, and without once looking at Sanct' Germain, addressed Nero. "It is not wise to invest too much attention in foreigners while deserving Romans go without imperial favor," he said with a portentous frown. "Since there are those who disapprove of your plan to go to Greece shortly, they will feel even more abused that you should take time to distinguish Franciscus."

For once Sanct' Germain found himself in agreement with Justus. "That's true. And it is not my intent to take credit from Romans, who have been willing to have me as a guest for so long."

Nero waved both these objections away. "Nonsense. You're being too self-effacing. You've supplied me with animals for these Games and those of Tiridates' visit. You've shown me how to play on the tall Egyptian harp. You've sent your slaves into the arena at my request. Show me a Roman who has done so much." This was obviously a challenge, but no one chose to respond to it.

"This is home for a Roman, and as such, it is a place where he can feel, and rightly, that he has certain rank and privileges not granted to those of us who are guests." As he spoke, Sanct' Germain was still troubled.

"All sons," Nero said, turning suddenly petulant, "should be a credit to their houses. They should be eager to bring praises to it and to show civic virtue." He stared moodily into his cup. "My mother was a terrible woman, a terrible woman, but she was right about one thing—those who wear the purple are surrounded by traitors and liars, and Caesar is a fool to trust any of them."

A tension thrummed through the imperial box, and though no one spoke, the guests stiffened and looked away.

It was Sanct' Germain who broke the silence. "Am I suspect, Caesar?"

"You?" Nero shook his head. "No, not you." He held his cup out for more wine, and while the slave filled it, he said, "No, what I want from you, Sanct' Germain, is your advice about a new project I have in mind. These others, well, it was friends who killed Divus Julius. I must remember that."

On the spina, trumpets brayed and the victorious gladiator was cheered by the crowd while he lifted bloody arms in response to the ovation.

"Your slave is next," Nero reminded Sanct' Germain unnecessarily.

"She is ready, I'm sure," Sanct' Germain answered.

"Sanct' Germain," Nero said abruptly with a slight wistful smile, "do you think she would be willing to teach me to do that? I'd love to be able to stand on my hands, balanced on the backs of two racing horses."

"It's very dangerous," Sanct' Germain responded quickly, knowing that Nero's enthusiasm for racing had led him to rash acts before. He was anxious to avoid any difficulties with the capricious Emperor. "Tishtry herself said that it took her most of her youth to learn how. Her family has done such feats for three generations, and the training begins as soon as the children can walk." He tried to sound calm as he added, "Such stunts aren't part of a leader's skill, Caesar. Great leaders should know how to drive chariots in war, not use them for tricks to amuse a mob."

"You're right, of course," Nero said when he had considered the matter. "But what a splendid trick it is." He looked at the other men in the imperial box. "What of the rest of you? Would you like to see me do that, and fail? It would be easier for you, wouldn't it, if I'd kill myself driving a chariot. Then you could take command of the government without your plots and intrigues. And in no time, you'd be at each other's throats, each one wishing Nero were still with you, so you could be agreed in hatred, if nothing else." He met the eyes of each of his guests in turn, then looked into the bright arena.

The Gates of Life were flung open and Tishtry galloped her team onto the sands and down the length of the spina. Cheers met her and became louder than thunder.

In his imperial box, Nero leaned far forward and watched the Armenian slave with yearning eyes.

Text of an official dispatch from Greece to the Senate and people of Rome.

> To the august Senators and knights, and the people of Rome, from the Greek garrison of Athens, hail!
>
> By order of the Emperor, Nero Caesar, the treacherous general Cnaeus Domitius Corbulo has taken his life upon his arrival in Greece for the Olympic Games. The general, once the hero of wars on the eastern borders of the empire, redeemed his honor by his prompt obedience to the Emperor's orders, and died a good death upon his own sword.
>
> His last word was *Axios,* which in the Olympic Games is the shout that greets the victor, signifying approval of a victory justly won. In this Corbulo expressed his recognition of the Emperor's right to his life. Those malcontented and misinformed Romans who say otherwise harm the memory of this valiant and sadly deceived warrior who did so much for the empire.
>
> May this commend the Greek garrison to you and to all Romans.
>
> Titianus Sassius Bursa
> Centurion, Athens garrison
> on the fourteenth day of May in the
> 819th Year of the City

15

AS OLIVIA STEPPED from the enclosed two-wheeled chariot, no slaves rushed to meet her. The house seemed old and neglected, with dry leaves drifting at the door and rickety shutters over the windows. Yet this was the house she had been born in, an old and honorable building on the Palatine Hill, built in the days of the Republic by her three-times-great granduncle, and had been one of the grandest houses in Rome when Augustus Caesar ruled. Now the gentle spring sunlight was cruel to the building, for it showed the neglect and poverty that ate at the house like a disease.

Olivia hesitated on the threshold, distressed by what she saw. This was the first time since the death of her father and the condemnation of her brothers that Justus had allowed her to visit her mother. A bell chain hung beside the door, and Olivia pulled it to summon the doorkeeper, thinking that when she was a child, there had been no need for such a bell because a footman slave had waited at the door at all times. She heard the unmelodious clang echo in the house. She turned to the slave that drove her chariot. "You're blocking the street, Joab. Take the chariot around to the stables and I'll come there when my mother and I are through with our talk."

Joab twitched the reins to obey, but was not pleased with the order. But Olivia was right. The street, as was typical of most Roman streets, was narrow and there were those with carts and sedan chairs who could not pass him.

Once Joab was gone, Olivia pulled the bell chain again, suddenly very concerned. She was almost prepared to try the door herself when she heard a step, and then the scrape as the bolt was pulled back.

"Oh! It's Olivia!" said the ancient porter as he held the door wide, indicating out of habit that she should cross the threshold on her right foot.

"Yes, Eteocles, it's Olivia." She had smiled quickly to conceal the shock she felt at seeing the Greek slave in a badly frayed tunic and patched sandals.

Eteocles gave an understanding sigh. "Yes," he said, "it's

sad to have this come out so. Only those of us who belong to your mother were spared. All the rest, they were condemned along with your father and brothers. All of them. All." He closed the door as he coughed.

Though Olivia had heard of the breaking up of the household, she had not known how sweeping it would be. "Just my mother's slaves were spared?" she said, thinking that there could not be more than a dozen people living in the house now.

"The law is specific, mistress. It is required that nothing be left of the sedition, and so—"

"But slaves can't be held responsible." Olivia's voice had risen. "That law hasn't been enforced so strictly since the Republic. Now all they do is sell the slaves, not condemn them." She looked down the corridor toward the library, where her father had often gone to study. The floor had not been swept recently and one oil lamp burned where four had shone before. Olivia felt her throat tighten. "Who was so barbaric as to condemn slaves for the master's folly? The Emperor is more reasonable than that." It was true most of the time, she knew. She also knew that Nero was often frightened, with good reason, and that at such times he was dangerous and impulsive.

"I don't know that, mistress. I only know that it happened, and that there was no one who would help us."

Olivia felt chagrin at that. She wanted to explain that Justus had ordered her to avoid her family when they were condemned, and still disapproved of her affection. She was aware that Eteocles probably felt she was much to blame for the severity of the judgment that had fallen on her house. Olivia herself felt that, and knew that under other circumstances she might have done a great deal for her father and brothers. She could find nothing to say.

"No one blames you, mistress," Eteocles said gently as he led the way toward her mother's room.

Much of the furniture was gone, seized at imperial order and sold at auction. The tables her great-grandfather had sent from Egypt were missing; and the fine chairs, all matching, made of pine brought from forests far to the north, no longer stood in the reception room. One of the old chests remained, but the larger and newer one where her father had kept the scrolls of household accounts had been taken.

"This is . . ." She could find no word sufficiently bad. "When did this happen, Eteocles?"

"The month after your father was imprisoned. They took little at first, but as time went on, more and more things were confiscated, and your mother had no one to help. Her brother was afraid to speak to her, her sister is still in Gallia with her husband, your sisters have been forbidden to write, and your husband never answered the messages she sent to him." There was rancor in his voice now, and though it stung, Olivia welcomed it.

"My husband never told me about messages. If he had, I would have seen that something was done. He told me that all my family had been ordered not to send or receive messages." Her hands tightened. It was like Justus to tell her such a lie.

Eteocles held a door open for her, and waited while Olivia passed into her mother's private apartments.

Here there was not so much missing, but the same oppressive air of want filled the room. At the window, Decima Romola Nolus, Domita Clemens, stood arranging a few flowers in a vase in an attempt to brighten the room. Her hair, which she had liked to wear in careful, ordered curls, was done now in a single knot at the back of her neck, and instead of being a rich, honey-brown color, it was blighted with gray. She was dressed in an old wool stola to keep off the chill, for the room was no longer heated. One last rose was put into place, and then she turned to her daughter. "Olivia," she said, and almost choked on the word. Blindly she moved into Olivia's opened arms.

Both women were embarrassed to weep and neither could restrain their tears. They clung together, not daring to meet each other's eyes, until they both regained control of their emotions.

Romola was the first to succeed. She dashed her hand over her face and stood back, straightening her clothes and trying to appear unconcerned. "It is good to see you again," she said with difficulty. "I apologize for the house. They left us very little, and I haven't enough wood for heating, so the floors are cold and there are drafts everywhere." She went to one of the three chairs in the room. "The furniture here is mine, and so I have it still, but the rest, it's been taken, even to the kitchen supplies. I have Gedrica to cook for me still, but she is very old, and I don't like to ask much of her, so I hope you won't be offended if I don't offer you anything more than bread and fruit juice." Her hands folded tightly together. "They took the wine, or I would give you that."

Olivia stifled the indignant outburst that welled within her. It was useless to speak out now. The time for that had been and gone. "I'll see that you have wine again, Mother. Justus will have to do that much for me, if nothing else."

"*No!*" Romola cried, thrusting out her hands as if to ward off a blow. "I want nothing more from that man. I have had all that I can bear from him, and more."

"What do you mean?" Olivia demanded, fearing that her suspicions might be proven true.

"I'm sorry," Romola said in a strained voice. "I have no proof, of course, and the man is your husband." She made a jerky motion toward one of the other two chairs. "There. Be seated. I'll have Eteocles bring our refreshments."

"But I didn't come for refreshments," Olivia protested. "I came because I've wanted to see you. Justus is angry that I'm here, but I'd rather endure his anger than stay away from you any longer." Her voice almost broke, but she was silent a moment. "Mother, I wanted to be with you. I pleaded with Justus to let me come sooner. He forbade it. If he hadn't sold my slaves and replaced them with his own, I would have come in spite of him, but none of his slaves will disobey him for me." She sighed.

"He's sold your slaves?" Romola said as if she had not heard the rest. "By what right? Why did you let him?"

"Let him?" Olivia repeated shakily. "There was no question asked of me. There was no permission given. He said he would do it and that if I objected, he would foreclose on all the loans and other considerations he'd given father just before we were married. Sometimes he threatened to have the whole family banished for debt." She put her hand to her mouth. "I didn't know what to do. He never let me talk to Father alone, he . . . forced me to agree with him on . . . Well, that doesn't matter. He said if I refused, it would mean disgrace and ruin for the rest of the family."

Romola nodded, saying bitterly, "I understand. I feared it was like that. Your father never thought that Justus would actually prosecute him, since the family is so old and noble."

"The junior branch, however," Olivia said, as she had heard her cousins say it all through her youth.

"The junior branch. I've never doubted that if he were

given a chance, your husband would harm us." She said this defiantly, lifting her head and staring at Olivia. Her deep, new wrinkles were revealed uncompromisingly; what had remained of her youthful beauty had gone, but in its place there was a majesty she had not possessed before, a look of strength that had come only on the far side of suffering.

"Yes," Olivia said quietly. "He likes to harm people."

There was a discreet knock at the door and Romola called, "Enter."

Eteocles brought in a tray with refreshments piled on it. There were sweet cakes dripping with date syrup, flaky little pastries with spiced meats in them, plump buns that had been cut open and heaped with savory pork, thin batter breads folded around ground nuts and then cooked in hot oil. Because the room was cold, a glass jug of well-spiced apple juice steamed in the center of the tray, crowned with a cloud of whipped egg whites.

"But this is a feast!" Olivia protested as the old slave set the tray down on the antique scarred table by the door.

"Gedrica wouldn't hear of you coming home to nothing but little wheaten cakes, like a freedman. She said that this was to be a proper celebration." Eteocles folded his arms in determination. "She says that there's plenty of extra in the kitchen for us, and so that's not to come back with nothing eaten."

Olivia flushed with confusion and gave a quick, inquiring glance to her mother. "Tell Gedrica that I've missed her cooking, and that nothing could have pleased me more than to have her willing to make such a delicious meal for us."

Apparently this was the response that Eteocles expected. He unfolded his arms and relaxed his stance. "I'll do that, mistress, and it will please her that you said so." With that he left the room, closing the door behind him.

"Do you really think that there is enough for them in the kitchen?" Olivia asked softly as she looked at the food.

"Probably not." Romola sighed. "We haven't very much, and little money to buy it with. I've thought of selling one of the slaves, but most of them are fairly old and wouldn't fetch much at market, in any case. It would be cruel to send them to a new master now, when they've been with me so long."

Olivia reached out impulsively to take her mother's hand. "I'll see that you have money. I know I can get some."

"I want nothing from your husband," Romola said harshly.

"I am touched that you would do this for me, but I won't accept anything from him. There has been too much evil from him already."

"If not from Justus, would you take it from someone else?" She told herself that she was being rash to assume that Sanct' Germain would aid her. She had so little contact with him, and most of their meetings had been furtive, hardly more than a few words and rushed kisses. Yet she knew he was rich, and had offered her help before.

"Who else?" Romola demanded.

"A friend." Olivia looked away.

"A lover?" her mother asked critically. "Before you have an heir?"

Olivia's sudden laughter sounded hideous in her own ears, and she saw the alarm in Romola's face. She stopped almost as abruptly as she had begun. "I've had countless lovers, Mother." She shook her head. "No, that's not true. I suppose I could count them if I could bring myself to think about them."

Romola was shocked. "Does Justus know? Is that why he's been so determined to hurt us?" She felt a terrible, hot anger inside her.

"Oh, yes, Justus knows. He brings them to me." Olivia's voice had risen and this time it was hard to control it. "He makes me ask them—terrible men, Mother. Some of them are banned from the lupanar because the whores are afraid of them. Then, when they come, he has a place where he watches. Lately that's changed. Now he wants to help them with me." Her face was hot and she could barely whisper out the last few words.

"I see." Romola sat still, the icy majesty stamped on her face like a mask in a Greek play. "How long has he done this?"

"From the first." She was shamed to admit this, and dared not meet Romola's eyes. "I tried to tell you once."

"Mother Isis shrivel him!" Romola cursed as her hands tightened in her lap once again. "He has destroyed our house!"

Olivia nodded miserably. "I hoped to reason with him, Mother, but he would not heed me. He said I had been bought and paid for like a slave, and he expected the same obedience from me." She pulled at the corner of her stola, winding it about her fingers. "I wanted to tell you before, but he's made threats and I was frightened. He meant what he said."

"But you tell me now," Romola said in a flat voice. "Why now, after all that's happened?"

"Because it has happened. It doesn't matter that he threatens to destroy my father and my brothers, because it has been done. They are gone, and all the household. He showed me the tally. Three hundred forty-eight slaves were sent to the arena because they belonged to my father. They weren't tried or given any of the rights that Divus Julius assigned them. They were sent to die." She had not felt so helpless as she did at this moment, talking to her mother in this empty house.

"When they beheaded your father, Justus was there. He watched the whole thing." She looked at the table. "The meal is growing cold."

"I don't think I can eat it," Olivia said as she stared at the big tray.

"You must. Otherwise poor, lonely Gedrica would be desolate. Have some of the juice while it's still hot, and as we go along, we will eat the rest. You have time, don't you? You needn't go at once."

"No, not at once." She accepted the warm apple juice that her mother offered her in a plain glass cup.

"The silver and gold goblets were sold," Romola explained with little emotion. "We have the glass, and the slaves have earthenware plates and cups, those that are left."

"How much money do you need?" Olivia asked bluntly after she had tasted the hot juice.

"I don't know, Olivia. Eteocles might be able to tell you, if he has the figures. The household has never been so small, and our position so precarious."

"Find out and send me word. I'll see that you have it." She was not certain how she would be able to get money from Sanct' Germain, but she believed in her heart that he would not deny her what she asked.

"Your lover has no interest in me," Romola said as she watched her daughter's face.

"But he has an interest in me, and he is rich." She was surprised at how coldly she said it. To speak of Sanct' Germain thus, as if he were a tolerated favorite instead of a man whose nearness brought her to life, whose touch could transform her.

"I don't want to know who he is. It's wiser not to know such things. If he is willing, I fear I would have to accept what you give me. I don't have anything else." For a little time she trembled and could say nothing more. "That Decima Romola Nolus, Domita Clemens, should come to this! I might as well join the women who collect the grain dole each morning. They say almost a third of the population gets free grain now. Why shouldn't I join them?"

Olivia had no answer for her. She drank the rest of the hot juice and then nibbled at one of the little cakes. Though the food was tasteless to her, it was welcome because it saved her from having to speak with her mother. As she ate, she promised herself that she would see that Romola was better provided for, and living decently again. Justus could not forbid that now.

"Your husband," Romola said in a somewhat distant tone, "was the one who betrayed your family. I thought you knew that, but perhaps you don't. Virginius found out, and before he was condemned, he sent me word."

"Justus?" Olivia asked stupidly. She had thought that he had refused to help her father and brothers for fear of being condemned along with them. "Who told him?"

"He heard it from Tigellinus himself, when Drusillus was being beaten. Tigellinus declared that he had learned of their treachery from their own brother-in-law, and that if he was so shamed by their actions to inform against them, then it showed that they were acting not out of honor but from greed and spite." Romola rose and walked to the window, where she touched the flowers in the vase.

Olivia sat very still, afraid that if she moved the earth would open or the building would collapse around her. She had thought she knew the worst of Justus when he had delighted in her suffering at the hands of the brutal men he sent to her. She had taught herself to accept that to ensure the protection of her family. Now that sacrifice seemed empty and of no worth at all. Fear and rage warred within her. She wanted now to take a long dagger and push it into his chest while he writhed. She wanted to watch Justus' blood, steaming and spurting, drain from him while she laughed.

Her mother recalled her from this imagining, saying, "Let me give you the rest of the juice, and then we can eat the buns while we talk."

Text of an official proclamation from Nero to the Senate and people of Rome.

To the Senate and the People who are the soul of all Rome, your Emperor sends you greetings from Greece:

At Corinth, on the twenty-eighth day of November in the 819th Year of the City, I proclaimed the liberation of Greece. It is inappropriate that Rome, who has been given so much from Greece, should put the foot of oppression upon the neck of this splendid nation. The freedom of this country is a tribute to Rome, for it was a shame upon us all that we maintained the trappings of conquest here where we instead should have come as devoted suitors and admired the glory of this place.

The Olympic Games have now concluded and I am determined to return to Rome, and to that end, notify you that I will set out within a month of signing this decree. The Games were a great triumph for Rome, as we have demonstrated our skills and talents beyond question. I myself competed in many events, and for that, have been awarded 1,808 prizes in all the Games in which I participated, being the Olympic, the Pythian, the Isthmian and the Nemean. Such great honor is not just for myself, but for the might of Rome.

My agent Helius has begged me to return quickly, and I am taking his advice to heart. Before February is ended, I will return. I am axious to see my city once again, to note the progress on my Golden House, and to touch the sacred soil of Rome with renewed devotion.

Be prepared to make me welcome, who is bringing you so much glory. Tell all the people that my love for them is increased and that I am as anxious to see them as a lover is to hold his beloved to his breast. The winter storms alone have stopped my return until now, and soon, even they will not have sufficient force to keep me from the place I love best.

With assurances to you all and anticipation of my welcome, I look forward to our reunion with joy.

Nero Caesar
Emperor
on the third day of February in the 820th Year of the City

16

KOSROZD PAUSED at the door to the private wing of Villa Ragoczy. He had been in the restricted rooms half a dozen times since his master had taken him there from the arena, to tend his wounds and restore him to life. He raised his hand and knocked twice. The slave who guarded the door watched him carefully.

A few moments later, Aumtehoutep opened the door carefully. "Yes?"

"It's Kosrozd. I must see my master." He moved restlessly, black eyes flicking from the face to the door to the slave beside it and back again. "It's important, Aumtehoutep. I wouldn't come here for something trivial. Let me in."

The Egyptian studied the beautiful young Persian. The ravages of his accident more than two years before were gone except for the deep, angry scars on his shoulder. "Follow me, Kosrozd," he said with little inflection.

"Thank you," was the grateful response as Kosrozd stepped inside the door. "Where is my master?"

"In the clock room. I don't believe you've been there. It's on the far side of his bath. Would you like me to take you there?" Aumtehoutep held wax tablets in his hands and had obviously been interrupted at his work.

"The far side of the bath. I'll find it." He started down the long corridor, the tap of the Scythian boots he now wore instead of sandals clicking sharply on the mosaic and marble.

Sanct' Germain sat in his clock room, frowning over a fan-folded manuscript. He was dressed in his familiar Persian clothes—a black sleeved tunic over black trousers. The only jewelry he wore was a silver ring engraved with his signet, the eclipse. He was very much preoccupied, and did not look around until Kosrozd called his name. "You."

Kosrozd looked uneasily at all the clocks in the room. There were Roman clocks, carefully designed to run by weights, dividing the day and the night into an equal number of hours, and geared to adjust to the changing lengths of day and night. There were clocks that ran by water and ratchets and sand. Most were silent in their operation, or nearly so, but a few squeaked and hissed as they marked their particular divisions of night and day.

"Kosrozd?" Sanct' Germain asked gently.

He gave his attention to his master. "I'm concerned. I came to tell you."

"What concerns you?" He folded the scroll along its ancient creases. "I should have a library slave do this, I suppose, but I'm always afraid that the scrolls will be broken, they're so old and fragile."

Now that he was in Sanct' Germain's company, it was hard for Kosrozd to speak. "I've heard things. I thought you should know about them."

"If you mean about Nero's return, I've probably heard every rumor twice, and met a few coming back from other sources." He put the long folded papyrus on his desk and got to his feet. "There's rebellion in the air."

"More than one," Kosrozd warned.

"Of course. Nero was gone too long. If he'd stayed away a few months, there wouldn't have been time to organize an opposition, but it's more than a year now." He looked at the various clocks that stood on tables and shelves, each inexorably recording the passage of time. "He's given his enemies a chance to form an effective resistance to him. It was foolish to order Corbulo's death—the legions would follow him, but now, there's no one to swing them to the Emperor, and they will give their support to the first man strong enough to take Corbulo's place."

"It's worse than that," Kosrozd said emphatically. "There have always been rumors. Since I started racing, I have heard rumors of rebellions and uprisings. The legions were never behind the rebellions, but that's what is said now." His black eyes glittered. "This does not sound the same as the other rumors. This time the whole idea has substance. There is no useless bragging now, and none of the vainglory I've always heard before. There are real men speaking about real leaders, not a few discontented soldiers and gladiators trading dreams. There have been many men coming from the legions in Gallia and Lusitania. They stay here a little while, speak in whispers and meet in shadows, then return to their garrisons, and no one is quite sure why." He held his hands open, wishing that Sanct' Germain's expression of polite interest would change.

"And you are suspicious, as you ought to be." Reaching out, he put one hand on Kosrozd's shoulder, covering the scars there with his small fingers. "It's not time to worry yet. Oh, I agree. There's much more than simple discontent in the air. We're likely to get a few attempts on Nero's life before long, and then we'll have another spate of executions. It's a common enough pattern. But there will be no real trouble until the Senate turns against him. When that happens, it will be chaotic in Rome."

"You speak as if you expected it!" Kosrozd shook himself free of Sanct' Germain's hand. "Don't you know what could happen to you if there is rebellion?"

"I have some idea," he said dryly. "And I do expect something of the sort to be attempted." He moved away from Kosrozd. "When you are . . . older, as our kind is older, you'll know why I feel as I do." He opened one of the chests, revealing several cubicles with fan-folded scrolls and an assortment of very old Egyptian timepieces which no longer ran. "These scrolls," Sanct' Germain said remotely, "talk about a similar occurrence. It took place more than a thousand years ago. There are countless others. Your family was part of one. Mine fell to one, with the assistance of a neighboring king." He stared rather blankly at the timepieces. "It's an effort to remember. I've often thought that something that important would be fresh in my mind forever."

"But Rome," Kosrozd protested. "Rome is rich, and rules half the world."

"Not quite half." Sanct' Germain smiled. "Wealth, plenty and power breed their own particular kind of dissatisfaction, and when it erupts, it becomes rebellion, so that the leaders are cast down. If that fails to cure the ills—and it usually does fail to, because the leaders are often very much alike—then the people turn to religion, the more extreme the better. A hundred years from now, unless Rome is tested by another power as mighty as she, religion will become an obsession with her people. Conquest brings its own invisible chains to the victor." He went to the window and threw open the shutters so that light streamed in, golden with spring. The courtyard revealed was half-atrium, half-peristyle, filled with tubs of flowering plants around a central fountain.

"Don't you want to do something?" Kosrozd demanded, moving closer to Sanct' Germain.

"There's nothing I can do. I'm not Roman. I have no real power beyond my wealth. My foreignness is some protection, and it should extend to all of mine. Even if I had political power, I don't know how I would use it." He stopped a moment. "Not long ago, I wouldn't have cared what became of Rome, so long as I could avoid the worst of it." His brow twitched into a frown. "That's no longer the case."

"My master?" Kosrozd still felt Sanct' Germain to be alien to him when such moods were on him.

"Forgive me. I'm not quite myself." He turned away from the window. "You're right to tell me what you hear. I need to know if I'm to guard you and the others. I don't make light of what you've said, but by now, rebellion seems so familiar to me that I feel odd at my fear. Oh, yes," he said, seeing the alarm in Kosrozd's black eyes. "I feel fear. Even we are vulnerable. The sword that beheaded Maximus Tarquinus Clemens would be as deadly to us as it was to him. Sever our spine and we die. Fire will kill us. We can be broken and crushed as easily as anyone. We have weaknesses. Take off those boots and walk in the sunshine, and you will learn quickly. You will be scalded as if you embraced hot metal. The night, the earth, are our friends, but they can't save us from the true death. For that we need our wits and luck, as does every man."

"But what about all those compliments that Nero gave you before he left? People haven't forgotten that, my master. You could be drawn into the fight whether or not you wish it. I've heard some say that you should be condemned along with the Emperor." Kosrozd moved anxiously nearer the door. "The danger is real. You have enemies."

Sanct' Germain folded his hands and stared down at them. "One of them is Necredes, the Master of the Bestiarii." He had no doubt that this was so. "He would like to see me cut in pieces for that day when I stopped him whipping Tishtry. He hasn't excused that humiliation, and he probably never will. So. And, as you say, Nero has shown me public favor. Quite a precarious honor, it seems. There are those other than Necredes who will assume that I am one of his supporters because he has singled me out and because I am foreign." He looked toward Kosrozd, studying the young charioteer, looking for signs of the change in him. There was a slight difference, he told himself. Under the straight black brows, Kosrozd's black eyes were more arresting than they had been three years ago. His movement was lithe and forceful as his new strength emerged, and though his face was unaltered from the time he had become one of Sanct' Germain's blood, and would remain unaltered until he died the true death, there was a subtle difference in his expression, a quality that would one day be mastery. "I've thought about leaving, I admit," he went on. "I have other homes, in other places. But that would mean added risk to those who stayed behind." His thoughts turned to Olivia as he spoke. "I can't do that. I can't let . . . them suffer for me. If you wish, Kosrozd, I will free you, and send you to an estate I own in Parthia. You may live there as long as you like, provided you are careful in your conduct. Or you might return from there to Persia, if you think it worthwhile."

"Leave?" Kosrozd asked incredulously, glaring at Sanct' Germain. "I am not a coward."

"I didn't say you were," he answered, not knowing how to tell this very young man what the centuries had taught him. For all the ties that blood gave them, he could not bridge the gulf of years. "Listen to me, my friend. You are valiant and full of courage, which is admirable, but not if it makes you rash. You might think it would be good to throw our luck in with one of the rebels. And, naturally, you assume that we would choose the man who will succeed. It's not so easy." He put his hands on his hips, sighing. "Learn, if you can, to avoid such choices."

"You say that, but you won't leave." It was very nearly a challenge, and Kosrozd shifted his stance as if anticipating a blow, though he had never received one from Sanct' Germain.

"I can't. And if I could, I'm not certain I would. Rome has a lot to hold me." He said the last reflectively, looking toward the window and the flowering garden.

"There are others." Kosrozd shrugged.

"You've learned that already?" Sanct' Germain asked, feeling saddened. He had believed that once, himself.

"Some are more desirable," Kosrozd admitted after a pause. "One nearly fainted from fear, and another would have opened her body from breast to thigh if only I would continue to give her pleasure." There was a certain embarrassed boastfulness to his words and he could not quite meet Sanct' Germain's piercing eyes. "Why is it different for you?"

Sanct' Germain shook his head, a little motion, almost imperceptible. "I don't know. I don't know."

Kosrozd paced the room, a feeling akin to anger spurring him. "Then are you simply going to wait? It might be too difficult to leave later."

"So it might," Sanct' Germain agreed quietly. "I don't insist that you stay. You have my permission to go when you want. I doubt very much that there will be real trouble until summer, and there will have to be a great many more rumors before the real danger appears. If Nero acts quickly, the opposition may not succeed. If he doesn't act quickly, the Senate may delay past the time of change. There are many things that could happen."

One of the clocks clicked loudly and a small gong sounded.

Whatever tension that had flared between Kosrozd and Sanct' Germain was broken by that tinny clang.

"You race again soon?" Sanct' Germain asked in another voice, as if Kosrozd had just come in.

"Ten days. I'll be racing for the Blues this time, instead of the Reds. That faction would like to buy me so that I would drive for them all the time." He slapped at the dust on his tunica, and rubbed at his bare arms. "I've been out on the practice roads."

"You'll have to tell the Blues that I'm afraid I am not prepared to sell you." As he took his seat again, he added, "May all the forgotten gods protect Rome if the racing factions ever become too political. Then there would be real trouble. You'd have people betting on chariots for political favor, and the races would not be tests of skill, but manipulations for power. It has happened before, on a small scale. It could happen again."

Suddenly Kosrozd grinned, and it had all the force and charm of his youth. "Mithras bleed you, my master. Very well, I will go bathe. But believe me, I came to you honestly."

"I know that," Sanct' Germain said ruefully. "I value your concern, truly. By all means, bathe, and later, if you like, we'll talk again. But not about Nero and Rome."

Kosrozd chuckled and went out of the room, starting to whistle as his boots clicked down the hall.

Sanct' Germain did not move from his chair. When he was sure that Kosrozd had left the private wing, he called out, "Aumtehoutep!" and a little later, when the Egyptian stepped into the clock room, he said, "The rumors are increasing, according to Kosrozd. I think we may have been lax in our observations." His face was set in hard lines, and there was a bite to his words that had not been there when he talked with Kosrozd.

"The rumors have not seemed serious," Aumtehoutep said with a degree of puzzlement. "With Nero's return, you expected more of them."

"I think this may be more than rumors now. There's gossip of the legions being involved, and that is not usual." He rose suddenly. "I want to know what is being said. I want to know what the Praetorians are saying among themselves. If there's to be real trouble, we'll need time to prepare for it." He had picked up a staff with a small winged bull carved into one end of it, and this he tapped on his open palm. "Kosrozd has heard of messengers from Gallia and Lusitania, and the legions there are very strong. If they are determined to rise against the Emperor, or establish one of their own, there could be battles in the streets before the year is over. I want you to choose a few of the slaves—and be very careful in your choice. Give them to a few key men, and learn as much from them as we can. Those two library slaves, the ones you recommended I buy last winter, they might be willing to help us. There's that groom from the north, and he would be observant. Certainly a young tribune would find him useful. If he should want to talk to Tishtry upon occasion, there would probably be no objection."

"How soon must the slaves be chosen?" Aumtehoutep asked calmly.

"As soon as possible. I'd like a few of them established by the time Nero passes through that new gate they're cutting in the walls for him." He slammed the rod down on one of the tables and the clocks there jumped. "What fools they are! All of them!"

Aumtehoutep's face revealed nothing. "Unlike you, my master."

Sanct' Germain raised his brows sardonically. "Oh, I am a fool as well. I have no illusions on that point." Slowly he took hold of the rod again. "At least I know it."

"As you say, my master." The Egyptian was silent while Sanct' Germain crossed the room to the window once again.

"How many times have I promised myself to learn from my past errors? Yet Rome is near the brink of civil war, and I cannot leave. So much for my hard-won wisdom."

"There are all sorts of wisdom, my master," Aumtehoutep said quietly.

"So I tell myself, old friend. And sometimes, when I'm not quite honest, I believe it." He shook off this ironic frame of mind. "About the slaves: I'll want a list of the ones you think most capable of doing what is required, in two days. We'll make a decision then."

Aumtehoutep heard the familiar note of self-mockery in Sanct' Germain's voice, but forbore to mention it. "What of Kosrozd? Do you plan to use him in this?"

"By the eternal Styx, no." He gave a rueful, dismayed laugh. "He's obvious enough as it is. If I told him how much I want information, he would rush out and demand it of every slave in the arena. The ones with real information would flee from him and the others would provide him with every fantastic rumor about, and if the time came that the rebellion occurred, we would be in even greater danger, because everyone would remember that it was Kosrozd who asked so many questions. Also, if he's to get any valid news, he must come upon it by accident. Real conspirators don't brag about their plans; they keep them to themselves. Let Kosrozd think I'm being blind, and let him tell me what he hears by chance. We'll learn more that way."

"Very well. In two days I'll provide you with the names of your slaves." He gestured his agreement and set about the task his master had set for him.

Text of a letter to Cornelius Justus Silius from the co-commander of the Praetorian Guard, Nymphidius Sabinus.

To the distinguished and noble Senator, Cornelius Justus Silius, greetings:

I have been asked by my co-commander, C. Ofonius Tigellinus, to inform you of his retirement from office. His health has forced him to leave Rome and live quietly on his estates in the north, where, it is hoped, the care of his physician and the more restful setting will soon restore him to his former vigor. Certainly you must feel as I do that the Praetorian Guard has lost a respected and able leader at a time of great need. Had it not been for his deteriorating condition, you may be sure that Tigellinus would be here with me now, helping to reorganize our men into a more effective unit.

Since the Emperor has been gone so long, his return has thrown us into something of a quandary. We have new troops who have yet to serve the Emperor in person, and for that reason there are many new demands of the Guard while we prepare to assume the full weight of our responsibilities once again. There is a very high standard of conduct demanded of the Praetorians, and it will be a little time, I am sad to say, before we are once again at the level of that standard. The constructive advice of men such as you will get our fullest attention at this time.

Tigellinus informed me that you have been of service to him in the past, and so I ask that you will be kind enough to have the same regard for me now that the whole burden of command has fallen to my shoulders. How greatly I have come to value those noble and honorable Romans who have taken the interests of the empire to their hearts and have sworn to protect all that we have gained, here and abroad, and are not seduced by the new waves of treason that are lapping at the very gates of Rome. Those subtle enemies who work from within are more dangerous than those who besiege us from without, for they gnaw at the very heart of the empire.

Perhaps you are aware that some of the legions far from Rome, in their discontent, have spoken of rebellion and the raising to power of their various governors and commanders. We have had information here within the last two days, from truly reliable sources, that the legions in Tarraconensis and Baetica, and possibly those in Lusitania as well, are about to hail their governor, Servius Sulpicius Galba, as Emperor of the Roman Empire. It seems incredible that a man of Galba's years—he is close on seventy, as you may know—should embark on so dishonorable and rebellious a venture at this time. It is true that many of the legions do not love Nero, and that the recent prolonged stay in Greece has in part contributed to the unrest abroad, and has helped bring this uncharacteristic action about.

You have long observed the ways of Rome, and Tigellinus has assured me of your deep loyalty. For that reason I would like to request that should you at any time hear from those legions, or others, who have plans to unseat the rightful Caesar and set another in his place, that you will be at pains to inform me of what you have learned so that the Praetorians may fulfill their sworn oath and protect the Emperor.

This on the tenth day of April in the 820th Year of the City, by my own hand and under seal.

Nymphidius Sabinus
Commander, the Praetorian Guard

17

OUT ON THE lake of the Golden House there were boats filled with musicians and singers, and they played Greek songs to the guests on the banks. The evening was warm and soft, scented with herbs and flowers. It was a bright evening, with stars pricking through the last touch of daylight. A small herd of tame deer wandered among the guests, who offered them fruits that slaves had given them for that purpose. Nero himself walked along the banks of the lake, strumming his lyre and singing bits of new songs he had learned while he had been competing in the Olympic and other Games.

"Yes, the Greeks are far ahead of us in matters of art," Nero interrupted a bit of *Ariadne on Naxos* to remark to the men beside him. "Their halls are alive with song, their statues make ours look stiff and paltry, their conversation is elegant and philosophical. Until you've spent time among them, you can have no idea how profound their culture is."

"You may bring it to us, Caesar," Cornelius Justus Silius said with a nod to the other three men accompanying the Emperor. "You've had an opportunity that is given to few."

"But the burdens of my rank," Nero sighed and plucked at the big lyre. "There are times I envy the meanest shepherd in Greece, who has time to watch the wind and explore the full extent of his thoughts."

"You express your genius in other ways," Nymphidius Sabinus assured him. "This great Golden House with grounds that would make me think I was deep in the country if I had not seen for myself that we are in the heart of the mightiest city of the world."

The third man, Constantinus Modestinus Datus, was newly arrived from Gallia Belgica, and was still somewhat stunned to find himself in such exalted company. "Indeed, Caesar, I had heard of the Golden House, but nothing, nothing had prepared me for its . . . grandeur."

Nero smiled broadly. "It is my tribute to the empire," he said, and struck a deep chord on his lyre.

Modestinus nodded rather grimly. "It requires a wealthy empire to create such a lavish palace."

"What of my statue?" Nero asked eagerly. "Have you seen it yet? Doesn't it impress you? A few critics have compared it with statues of Apollo." He chuckled to show that he did not agree with this extravagant praise. "It flatters me particularly because Apollo is the god of music, which has always been my first love."

"And no one can question the depth of your devotion," Justus said quickly. "You have made yourself the first acolyte at the altar of art."

Nero regarded the fourth man in the group, who walked a little apart from them. "And you, Sanct' Germain. Would you agree with the Senator?"

"Your dedication is rare for an Emperor," Sanct' Germain said evenly. "It does you a great deal of credit. But if you were a singer and not the Emperor, you would have to be twenty times more devoted to your art to excel to the fullest." It was a calculated risk to speak so to Nero, but Sanct' Germain thought it might be worthwhile.

"There, good companions, is an honest man," Nero cried in delight. "My prizes say that you are too severe, but I believe you are not dissembling."

"Prizes," Justus said at his most ponderous, "are not given for art alone, but for skill in presentation and in the quality of majesty of the singers. You have such an impact on those who see you, Caesar, that no one could deny the merit of your prizes."

Sanct' Germain refused to be drawn into such an argument. He lifted his shoulders negligently. "I did not hear Caesar in competition, and therefore have no judgment to offer on his prizes."

Justus gave him an angry look, then turned his attention to Nero once more. "The statue is a wonder, and everyone who sees it is struck with its beauty and richness. There is gold enough there to supply three or four kings with an ample treasury."

Or, Sanct' Germain thought to himself, several thousand slaves and freedmen with food for five years. He directed his next comment to Modestinus. "In Gallia, what have you got for entertainment? I have heard you have several excellent arenae, and a few theatres, but I'm not sure where these are."

"It's not on the scale, of course," Modestinus said, glad for the deft change of subject. "There are a few arenae, nothing so large as you have in Rome, and not so many. We have a theatre a day's ride from the garrison, and there are times I've gone there, but the actors are not usually the best, and many of the plays are not very well-performed. We did have some jugglers and acrobats come through a few years ago, and they were marvelous. It doesn't sound like much to someone living in Rome, but in Gallia Belgica, it means a great deal to us, I can assure you."

"I think," Nero said, overriding the conversation once again, "that at the end of next year, I will visit Gallia and see how the garrisons live there. I may even perform for them. I remember how well the legions there like the song I wrote for them."

"They still sing it, Caesar," Modestinus said with real sincerity.

Nero was pleased. "Do they? How kind of them. It was a pleasure to write a song for soldiers."

"Sometimes the troops sing it while they march," Modestinus assured the Emperor, but did not mention that the soldiers had added many verses of their own, far less patriotic in tone than those Nero had written.

"Do they? Sing my song?" He flicked his fingers over the strings and began the first verse. "As far as any eagle flies, the might of Rome will go. / From out of steaming Africa to Hyperboric snow / Oh, hear the awesome marching beat / The steady tread of legions' feet / Advancing while the foes retreat; / Advancing on the foe!"

Modestinus had joined in the song, which pleased Nero so much that he offered to sing all fifteen verses. "I'm afraid my memory isn't as good as yours, Caesar," Modestinus said quickly with a little self-deprecating bow. "I've never been good at remembering the words to songs. It says a great deal that I can remember so much of this one."

Nero was too satisfied to be offended by this. "Well, it does me good to know that my efforts on behalf of the legions are appreciated." He turned to Sanct' Germain. "I have wanted to speak to you since my return."

Sanct' Germain's response was prompt. "Tishtry's not for sale."

"Excellent!" Nero laughed, his head thrown back, his dark blond hair in disarray around a silver wreath. "No, no, it is not about that fabulous charioteer of yours, though if she were for sale, I would be the first to make an offer for her."

"In which case, should I ever decide to part with her, I will give her to you, since no one would bid against you for her."

If Nero heard how sardonic the remark was, he gave no indication of it. "She would be a rare present, indeed. I will remember that, Sanct' Germain, and remind you of it." He smiled at the other two men. "She is an amazing woman, this Armenian charioteer of his. Even in Greece, I saw nothing to equal her." Then he turned back to Sanct' Germain. "I've had a project in mind for some months now, and it occurs to me that you are the very man to help me bring it to a full realization."

Sanct' Germain felt a certain dread at that announcement, but kept his tone carefully even. "A great honor, Caesar. Though I admit I wonder why you should ask me, and not another Roman."

"Because of your skill with musical instruments and metal," Nero said, as if it were obvious. "I've noticed that the hydraulic organ in the Circus Maximus is in need of repair, and so long as the work is to be done anyway, the instrument might as well be replaced with a better one. You're gifted in such matters, and I would like you to help me with the design. I have already worked out what will be required, but I'm unsure of the actual limits of the metal in the instrument. I rely on you to help me there. I've studied the plans of the organ as it exists now, and I am certain that the sound can be improved. It's loud enough now, but it would be more appropriate for the pipes to ring like bells rather than bray like asses." This was a carefully turned phrase, and Nero waited for admiration.

Justus did not disappoint him. "You have much felicity in your speech, great Caesar. There are orators older than I who, in all their years, have not learned to speak as well as you do."

Nero made an expansive gesture. "It is a point of honor with me to use the language as elegantly as I can." Suddenly he flung out his arm and pointed to where slaves were carrying a tall crucifix to which a man was tied. "Ah! The Jews!"

"Jews?" Modestinus wondered aloud.

"Oh, I'm sure you've heard of them. They're the ones that are always starting a war with the garrison in Jerusalem. Stiff-necked and fractious as any in the empire. This group petitioned the Master of the Games to be spared the humility of dying with heretics—other Jews with a different point of view, is what they meant. They are condemned to be executed, and so, since the leader of this particular sect was crucified, I decided to let them emulate him." He watched excitedly as the slaves placed the unusually tall upright beam in a waiting, reinforced hole.

"But what is he wearing?" Modestinus asked, plainly becoming distressed.

"A tunica soaked in pitch," Nero explained delightedly. "There are several dozen of them about the gardens. The tunicae will be set on fire and then we, too, can see the light they claim to have seen. I have ordered them gagged so that their screams will not disturb us."

The furtive pleasure in Justus' eyes was worse than the greedy anticipation in Nero's. "Great Caesar, your genius extends everywhere, even to your wit."

"Yes," Nero responded automatically. "I considered letting them run free in the garden, but there was no saying whether or not one of them might seize a Roman and carry both down in flames. This is more appropriate, somehow." Nero gave an exasperated sigh. "If they would stop attacking the garrison, none of this would happen. I've told their representatives time after time that they can worship their gods in any way they like, in their country and in Rome, and they respond by saying that there is only one god"—Nero almost laughed—"and that all others must be destroyed. They see the presence of our garrison as a religious matter. What can anyone do with such a people? I wish to be a just and merciful man, yet they make it impossible to pardon them. I have tried to be reasonable, but they won't accept my offers, and they continue to rebel."

Over the centuries Sanct' Germain had seen such barbarity, and acts much more atrocious, but they always gave him the same cold horror ever since he had found himself alone on a battlefield with a sea of corpses around him. "Don't you think that this will only spur them to further rebellion?" he suggested gently.

"I hope it will spur them to sense and moderation," Nero snapped.

"They will think you monstrous for such an act." There was no threat, only certainty in Sanct' Germain's voice.

"Monstrous?" Nero repeated, testing the word. "But how else will they know how powerful I am?"

"There are those who respect the limitation of power," Sanct' Germain said carefully, knowing that he was treading on dangerous ground. "The Jews could be like that."

Nero looked askance. "But how can I limit myself when I have yet to discover the extent of my power? Perhaps it would be possible for me to destroy all of Jerusalem with one order, and if that is the case, then this is moderate. Isn't it?" The question was almost innocent in tone.

"With the might of Rome at your command," Justus said quickly, "you are most restrained with that difficult nation. It is a worthwhile plan to make an example of a few of the people, and then once again offer your terms to their leaders."

Modestinus regarded Justus with disgust. "If this is the good counsel that Caesar receives, it is a wonder that there is a rebel left alive."

"Don't provoke him, you hothead," Sanct' Germain murmured to Modestinus, and said aloud, "History is full of tales of great feats of conquest, but the more honored are those who sued for peace and goodwill. Greece gave homage to the warlike and brave Spartans, but it is the Athenians who are revered, they who ruled by statesmanship and moderation." It was not entirely true, he recalled, but it was what Nero believed and might respect.

The Emperor's face took on a mulish cast. "If it weren't for the Spartans at Thermopylae, Darius would have slept in Athens."

Sanct' Germain had difficulty picturing the forces of Rome as the beleaguered Spartans, and the handful of rebellious Jews as the entire military might of Persia, but he did not point this out. "Unlike the Greeks, then, you still have time to settle the matter with the Jews. You need not be drawn into a war with them."

"But they're the ones who are rebelling, and if they are allowed to go unpunished, then others will do it as well. Judging from the report on the legions who want Galba to be Caesar, I have been too lenient already. And the Jews are near our weakest border. If we are lax there, then the Parthians will be upon us in force and we'll have a much worse war going on, and the Jews will think that dealing with the Roman garrison was a feast by comparison." He was genuinely irritated. "You don't understand this, Sanct' Germain. You haven't been in Rome very long, and you don't know our traditions and how much we have done to secure the empire."

"Perhaps you are right," Sanct' Germain allowed, doubting it. "But I will sue for peace whenever possible." Then he gave a dismissing shrug. "What I tell you isn't important, after all. I am a foreigner, as you say, and your problems are not mine."

"It is a credit to you that you ask," Nero said, willing to be generous now that Sanct' Germain had turned away from the matter.

Modestinus scowled first at Sanct' Germain and then at Nero. "If these men are the enemies of the state, then they deserve to die, but you do not leave them much dignity, Caesar."

"Dignity?" Justus said. "What dignity do they deserve? They have continued to fight against us, and in so doing, have relinquished any claim they might have had to dignity."

One of Nero's slaves approached him, waiting silently to get the Emperor's attention.

"Yes?" Nero demanded. "What is it?"

"You are required, great Caesar. We cannot begin . . . the . . . torches . . . without your order."

Nero clicked his tongue impatiently. "I'm afraid I must see to this," he said to the three men with him. "Perhaps we can continue the discussion after the meal."

"You have planned a meal, too?" Modestinus asked.

"Yes, of course. There are tables set about the gardens, and there are gongs to summon slaves when you want to eat." Nero chuckled. "I've moved out of doors for many reasons, but the most demanding one is to demonstrate that all is well with me. The last banquet I gave indoors, there was a storm and lightning struck my dining table. If any of the gods are minded to do it again, this provides them a splendid opportunity, though, of course, the night is clear." He nodded to the men, then turned to go with the slave.

"I had not realized that Nero was . . . the kind of man he is." Modestinus turned to look across the lake. "These gardens are truly beautiful, and the Golden House is remarkable." There was a doubtful tone to this and he looked to Sanct' Germain for help. "I have nothing against the punishment of prisoners and the just condemnation of rebels, but . . ."

"You've been away too long," Justus told him. "That's the trouble. You live in Gallia or Syria or Egypt and you forget what Rome demands of its citizens. The Emperor has more responsibility than you or I can imagine, and it is to Nero's credit that he works so devotedly for our good."

"Your brothers-in-law didn't think so," Modestinus said. "I had occasion to speak with Virginius before he was condemned, and he did not share your opinion." He looked up at the figure tied to the crucifix. "Rebel or not, he doesn't deserve this."

"Would you rather see him torn to pieces by wild beasts in the arena?" Sanct' Germain asked, and did not wait for an answer. They had come to a fork in the path, and with a parting nod to the two Romans, he turned down the narrower one toward an artificial spring. The last he heard of the conversation was Justus telling Modestinus that foreigners were not to be trusted in situations such as these, for they were not truly interested in the protection of Rome. Sanct' Germain smiled ruefully, knowing that by the end of the evening his character would be painted as black as his clothing through Justus' skillful insinuations. He wondered if Modestinus would believe the Senator.

The pleasant murmur of water over rock grew louder as the path neared the little stream that led from the ingeniously constructed spring in a pleasant grotto. The builders of the garden had tapped into the Virgo Aqueduct for the water here, running their pipes six handbreadths underground for several hundred paces. The rocks of the grotto were mostly quartz and they still glowed in the waning light. Sanct' Germain stepped off the trail into the shelter of a small grove of laurel trees.

A sudden flare of light from a distant point of the huge gardens told him that the first of the human torches had been set alight. He closed his eyes, hating the brightness. As he opened them, another torch began to burn.

The sound of footsteps on the path drove him deeper into the shadow of the laurels, where he crouched down, watching.

Attracted by the gently falling water, a doe stepped into the clearing and looked about, delicate head poised on her graceful neck, ears pricked forward in curiosity. She turned to the spring with dainty, fussy steps and lowered her head to drink. Then a vagrant breeze brought the stench of burning pitch and flesh to the doe and her head came up in alarm. A moment later she had crashed away through the low shrubs.

The approaching footsteps had stopped, and when they resumed, their progress was more uncertain. Sanct' Germain kept to his place, his dark eyes intent on the clearing.

When Olivia finally neared the spring, she sighed heavily. Her face was pale except for the livid bruise on her jaw. She had grown thinner of late and her hair had lost much of its shine. Choosing a low-lying boulder, she sank down upon it and buried her head in her hands.

Sanct' Germain moved swiftly, coming up beside her as silent as a shadow.

At the last instant she turned, eyes frightened, shrinking back from his light touch. One outward-turned palm protected her face, and her body quivered with sudden tension.

"Olivia?" Sanct' Germain hesitated, distressed by what he saw.

Relief swept through her, and she opened her arms. "You. You did come."

He lifted her as he caught her in his arms, holding her close, happy as she returned his embrace. "I've missed you, Olivia," he said softly as he bent to kiss her. Their lips met briefly, but with overwhelming intensity, then Sanct' Germain drew her toward the laurel grove, and the darkness.

"I was afraid you wouldn't come. I saw you talking to Justus and I thought he might have found out. . . ." She spoke in fast, whispered spurts of words.

"He would learn nothing from me," Sanct' Germain told her, and led her to the spot where the trees grew most thickly. "This will do for now. We're not likely to be disturbed for a little while. Everyone is watching the torches."

"They're not torches, they're men!" she said, trying to keep her voice low. "It sickens me."

"But you go to the Games," he said without criticism. "Why is this any different?"

"I can't tell you why, but it is." She leaned her head against his shoulder, feeling that splendid peace he gave her.

"Yes, it is different." He kissed her brow. "What has he done to you now, Olivia? Why the bruises?" It was an effort to keep the fury he felt out of his voice.

"Justus, of course. I fought the Cappadocian soldier he hired, and it angered him. Particularly when the Cappadocian refused to assault me at my husband's order." She bit her lower lip. "It was a victory of sorts. Justus took no pleasure with me that night."

"He beat you." How he would have liked to number Justus among the tortured figures on the crucifixes!

"He's done that before." She was so tired. It would be easy, she thought, to stay here with Sanct' Germain, ignoring the danger of their meeting. "I want to divorce him. I have grounds. If my mother and my sisters weren't alive, I would." She twisted a stray lock of hair around her finger. "He still has them to threaten me with. He lost my father and brothers when he betrayed them, but he still has them."

Sanct' Germain was very still. "He betrayed your father and brothers? You're certain?"

"My mother believes it, and I don't think she's a foolish woman." She put her hands on his shoulders. "Let's not talk about it. I have that with me always, but you, I have you in precious little moments." She pulled his head down and kissed him, letting him feel her need in her eager mouth.

"I want you with me, Olivia. I want you away from Justus and safe with me." He could feel her desire rising, and his hands moved gently over her body. He looked quickly into the grotto, and saw that it was still empty. It would be foolish to stay with her longer, knowing they might be discovered. There was no room to lie down; the trees rose up around them and hemmed them in. "Lean back on the trunk," he said softly, and as she did, he loosened the clasp of the fibula that held her palla, spreading the soft garment behind her. Her only other garment was a flowing dalmatica of thin cotton caught at the waist with a narrow jeweled girdle. This he untied, then slid the dalmatica off her shoulders.

She made one soft moan, half of anticipation, half of protest, then leaned back to receive his love, pulling him to her tightly when she felt she could endure no more of the rapture he gave her.

As he pressed against her, he felt the tremors of her fulfillment shake her. He was held by the depth of her passion much more than by her arms. He forgot the danger around them, the risk of discovery, as his lips brushed her face, her breast, her neck. Then the urgency of his need joined with hers as the laurel shook above them.

By the artificial lake, the last terrible torch flared alight.

A letter to the Office of Food Distribution in Rome, from Statilius Draco, captain of a supply ship operating between Ostia and Alexandria.

To the officer in charge of wheat for the Food Distribution Ministry, greetings:

I have taken it upon myself to address you in a matter that has caused me a great deal of concern, in the hope that you will be able to remedy the situation promptly.

My ship, the *Reliable,* should be known to your office, for it has been used to bring Egyptian grain to Rome many times in the past. It is a small, worthy ship, with a single bank of oars and a large cargo hold. Although it is not a very speedy craft, it has earned its name many times over.

When last I loaded in Alexandria, where it has been the custom to take on grain, there was no wheat for us, but only a large load of white sand for the Circus Maximus. We have carried sand before, but never a cargo of it exclusively. We were told that this was ordered by the governor-prefect himself, T. Flavius Vespasianus, and with this official sanction, we thought nothing more of the consignment, but loaded as we were instructed and brought the sand to Ostia.

Soon after we landed, I came to Rome to see the cargo properly delivered. I was amazed to discover, upon my arrival in the city, that there was a serious grain shortage and that the dole had been short for more than three weeks. Had I known that in Alexandria, I would have pursued the matter more completely and attempted then to find out why we were not given grain to carry, as well as sand.

I have considered the matter and decided that the only course I could follow was to inform you of what transpired in Egypt. It would seem that there is some lack of understanding between your office and the prefecture of Egypt. Surely no official would deny the citizens of Rome the grain they have been guaranteed for so many years. If Vespasianus was aware of how desperate matters are in Rome, he would undoubtedly take swift steps to remedy the situation.

Two days ago I witnessed a riot on the part of those waiting for their dole, and I am told that this is not the first. Certainly this is a dangerous state of affairs. Because of this emergency, since it is no less than that, I am offering my ship and crew to you at once. We will return to Egypt without waiting for a new cargo and load up with wheat if you will only give us the authorization to present to the officials there. It is a national disgrace to see starving faces on the citizens of the most powerful city on earth.

We are at your disposal and eagerly await your mandate.

Statilius Draco
Captain and owner
The *Reliable,* docked at Ostia
on the second day of May in the
820th Year of the City

18

DARK CLOUDS had been building up in the west and the first low mutters of thunder, like the sound of a distant army marching, echoed along the sky. The day was hot and oppressive, with very little breeze from the storm that was hovering near the ocean. The air over Rome seemed filled with a nameless menace, as if rent by an unheard scream.

There were no Games at the Circus Maximus that day, "For which," said the manager of the vast amphitheatre, "I am heartily grateful. In weather like this, the way things are, we'd have fighting in the stands before the day was half over." He was standing on the spina, looking out across the sands to the tiers of seats and benches. Below him, a bestiarius was working with his performing bears while slaves spread the new sand.

Sanct' Germain, who had been inspecting the hydraulic organ, agreed. "There is something worse than lightning in the air." He was dressed in the Egyptian manner, in a short military kalasiris of pleated black linen, with red Scythian boots that reached almost to his knees.

"The grain dole has been cut again and the distribution of oil was stopped day before yesterday." The manager said this calmly, though he was aware what such shortages would mean.

"What has the Emperor done?" In spite of himself, he was concerned now. If Nero did not respond to the people, they would turn against him, forgetting their enthusiastic affection for him.

"He says he's trying to get grain for them, but that Vespasianus has refused to send any grain." The manager leaned over the low rail of the spina to call to the bestiarius, "Get them to run, fool! If you can't do any better than this, I'll turn the tigers loose on you!"

The bestiarius responded with a loud, savage cry that set his animals lumbering down the sands.

"What do you think, then?" the manager asked of Sanct' Germain, turning to him once again. "I know the Emperor wants the organ improved, but I can't see how it's to be accomplished."

"I think there are some things that can be done with it," he responded thoughtfully. "The pipes are old and their shape isn't true. A more perfect casting is possible, I think, and that should improve the sound. Also, the pitches are not carefully made, and that I know I can improve. It will take time, of course, but I have specialized equipment that might do what's needed. There are always problems casting brass pipes of that length; however, I'm reasonably certain that I can get what's required."

The manager, a Greek freedman, clasped his hands over his ample belly and sighed. "I'll confess that any change will be welcome. The organ has been in need of repair for some time, but there has never been anyone willing to undertake it."

"That's no longer a problem, is it?" Sanct' Germain asked sweetly, then gestured toward the stairs that led to the passages beneath the floor of the arena. "I've seen enough. I'll do my calculations, and then return to get specific measurements for my work. I'll give you ample notice before I come to do the work."

"Yes, yes," said the manager, leading the way down the steep flight. "I'll need to keep the time free and make plans so that no one else is on the spina. You'll be able to work in privacy that way. We have our annual cleaning of the dolphins and eggs coming up shortly, but there shouldn't be any conflict then."

Sanct' Germain acknowledged this with a wave of the hand. "I doubt we'd be in each other's way, but it will be as you wish. My body slave will bring you my message. He's with me today. You met him earlier."

The manager's expression was slightly more grim. "Oh, yes. The Egyptian."

"He's seeing to the chariot we brought for the next races. It's a new design, something borrowed from the Scythians, with deep grooves in the floor of the vehicle. You need to wear heeled boots like these"—he gestured toward his feet—"to use the grooves as braces, but one of my charioteers has been practicing with it. He claims that he can hold the team steadier this way."

They were in the underground passage now, and the air was fairly cool, filled with the odors of animals and old blood. "That's the Persian, isn't it?"

"Yes," Sanct' Germain said, adding, "since that accident he had three years ago, he's been anxious to have a more stable chariot without losing any of the maneuverability he requires. I'll admit the project intrigued me."

"He's fortunate in his master," the manager said, an odd irritation in his tone. "Most owners of charioteers don't care anything about the chariots except that they be fast. If the drivers get maimed or killed, they blame their skill and not the vehicle."

This unexpected vehemence surprised Sanct' Germain. He had not thought that the manager would be so sympathetic to the dangers of racing. "This design, if it proves successful, would be available to anyone who wanted to use it."

They were nearing the end of the tunnel now, and the air was very close, almost cloying. Nearby a leopard coughed and padded in a holding cage, and there was another strange sound which Sanct' Germain realized was the distressed whimper of wild dogs.

"I'll let it be known, but I don't expect much. They're all used to the old designs." He stepped into the corridor that led to the stableyard. "I'm afraid I have to leave you here. There are other duties I must attend to. But I'm glad that someone is finally going to do something about that instrument. It's getting so the trumpets can't keep with its sequence." He bobbed his head once or twice, for all the world like a gigantic bird, then hurried away into the gloom under the stands.

Sanct' Germain made his way along the corridor to the stableyard. His mind was preoccupied with the design problems for improving the hydraulic organ, and it was not until he was almost across the wide expanse that he became aware of a sound stronger and more near at hand than the thunder. He stopped, listening. He knew what he heard then, for he had experienced it before while watching the Games; it was the eerie drone of thousands of voices. This time it was not the buzz and rush of anticipation of the Games, but a different sound, one more chaotic, echoing off the tall walls of the insulae near the Circus Maximus where much of the population lived.

Aumtehoutep stood beside the new chariot with a stable slave, instructing him in the method of harnessing the team with the new yoke that Sanct' Germain had developed, which lessened the drag of the collar strap on the horse's neck. Occasionally he would give an uneasy glance to the gates as the noise outside grew louder.

The stable slave was visibly frightened, and paying little attention to what he was being told. He was young, hardly more than a boy, and his slave's collar identifying him as the Emperor's property was fairly new.

"This," Aumtehoutep said, fingering the strap in question on the nearest of the four horses, "is a new feature as well. It runs from the collar strap to the girth, and prevents the collar riding up as well as helping to hold the girth in place. You may see how this works with the new, smaller yoke, binding less on the shoulders and making it possible for the horse to breathe more freely as it runs."

It was likely that the stable slave did not see any such thing. The noise from outside was growing louder as the mob neared the Circus Maximus, starting to mill around the huge, narrow structure.

"I am giving you instructions," Aumtehoutep reminded the stable slave sharply.

The slave gave one frightened cry of agreement, then bolted from the stableyard seeking a haven in the gigantic stables.

"He wasn't listening to you." Sanct' Germain had to shout to be heard. "He's terrified."

Aumtehoutep looked severe. "The walls are stout and he was told to learn this new system of harnessing."

"Consider his position a moment," Sanct' Germain suggested. "Out there are he doesn't know how many people, and they are making more noise than hungry lions. He is familiar enough with lions to recognize them in human form. Let him go, Aumtehoutep."

The large wooden gate that blocked the far end of the stableyard began to sound as fists, rocks and other things were hurled against it.

"They may break in here." Aumtehoutep said it quite calmly, his manner unafraid.

"They're probably after the food stores that are kept for the animals. There's a lot of grain brought in especially for the horses." Sanct' Germain looked quickly around the suddenly empty stableyard. "I think that's their purpose, if they have one—to get the grain."

As if in acknowledgment of this assessment, the pounding on the gate grew louder, more intense, and the huge timbers began to groan under the assault. The sound of the mob had become a feral howl, like some monster out of legend hunting its victim.

There was a splintering crash and one of the thick hinges tore away from the wood. A ragged cheer rose beyond the gate and the efforts of the crowd were redoubled.

"Into the chariot," Sanct' Germain said to Aumtehoutep, his manner now brisk and not open to question. He stepped into the light racing vehicle himself as he spoke, making room beside him for his slave.

The horses were restless, tossing their heads and sidling as far as their harness would allow. As a second timber splintered, the big bay on the far left side of the team, the horse that would in a race be on the inside of the sharp turns in the Circus Maximus, neighed shrilly and leaped forward, pulling the other horses with him and almost overturning the chariot.

A grating, creaking, snapping moan came from the gate as the wood gave way at last. The mob pressed against the falling timbers, frenzied with success.

Sanct' Germain already had the reins in his hands as the first few figures rushed into the stableyard. With all his great strength, he dragged the horses around to face the rushing hordes of desperate Romans who poured through the broken gate like a floodtide. As the mob came on, he started the horses walking into that maddened mass of people, who were beginning to spread through the stableyards and into the passages under the stands.

The horses minced forward, their eyes showing whites, and foam flecking their mouths as their coats darkened with sweat. Sanct' Germain held them steadily even as the chariot rocked as people knocked against it or grabbed it to keep from falling.

A young man in a cheap torn tunica tried to climb onto the back of the bay, and the horse reared up, whinnying and pawing the air as the other three horses strained at their bits, ready to bolt.

Sanct' Germain reached for the light whip that was used to guide the outer two horses in the turns and with a quick, expert motion sent the lash across the forearms of the man clinging to the bay's yoke. The man shouted as he lost his grip, sliding off the horse and almost falling under the press of people before he disappeared in the mob.

For what seemed hours, Sanct' Germain held the horses on a firm path for the gate. Their progress was made in inches as the pressure of the mob increased around them. The horses answered the rein reluctantly, only out of habit, kept in check by Sanct' Germain's rigorous hands and the limits of their harness.

The crowd became denser as they neared the gate, and the chariot jostled and rocked. Hands, arms, clubs, refuse and other things appeared around them out of the vast swarm of bodies. The noise was as powerful as the physical presence of the mob.

Looking through the gate, Sanct' Germain could see that an equally large mass of people waited beyond the stableyard as those thousands who had already forced their way into it. The street would be more difficult, with the narrow spaces and the limiting walls of the insulae decreasing their movement more than the expanse of the stableyard.

Aumtehoutep gave a cry, and clapped one hand over his eye.

"Don't let go!" Sanct' Germain ordered, not daring to look around. "Are you hurt?"

"A stone struck me." Aumtehoutep reached back and fixed his grip on the top rail of the chariot's frame. His fingers were bright with blood.

There was a little break in the crowd, and Sanct' Germain gave the horses their head, taking care to keep enough tension in the reins so that they would not take their bits in their teeth and run into the crowd.

Now they were almost through the gate and the noise that had been a senseless roar became the repeated cry for "Bread! Bread! Bread! Bread! Bread!" until the word made no sense and the chant itself drove the people on.

Just as they got to the gate, they were very nearly overturned as several youths with cudgels rushed at the chariot, yelling incoherently, brandishing their weapons and ready to do as much harm as possible. Sanct' Germain braced himself, and as the first of these clubs swung toward him, he lifted one arm to meet it and turn it aside, knocking his assailant off his feet. It was a calculated risk, for he had to loosen his hold on the reins while he dealt with the cudgel, and for that moment the horses might have bolted.

Then they were through the gate and into the pandemonium of the streets. People milled before the gate, turning into whirlpools and eddies like the ocean, pounding at the narrow entrance to the stableyard. Women holding infants in their arms rushed with the crowd, their eyes crazed. Great numbers of young men pushed and shoved, each one eager to break into the rumored storehouses of grain and bread that were kept for the animals and slaves of the Circus Maximus. A few rushed at the chariot, but most of them were put off by the danger of the hooves and the intensity of the eyes of the foreigner who drove it.

"Master," Aumtehoutep shouted, though his voice was faint in the overwhelming sound. "There are more coming!"

Sanct' Germain nodded to indicate he had heard. He could see the crush of people grow denser as they fought their way to the huge amphitheatre. It was foolish to continue against the tide. There was another, dangerous way, and for an instant he debated taking it. Once he committed himself, there could be no turning back, no restraining the crowd if the horses bolted out of control. The crowd thickened around the chariot, and soon they would not be able to move.

"Hold tightly!" Sanct' Germain shouted to Aumtehoutep as he slowly, carefully turned the chariot broadside to the rush.

The horses trembled and the bay almost went down on his haunches, his ears laid back and teeth bared as the crowd pressed nearer. Sanct' Germain could feel the team tremble through the reins as he continued to turn them.

It seemed that they must be overset, that the constant battering of countless bodies would dash the fragile chariot to pieces. It had never been intended for this sort of use. It was a racing vehicle, as lightweight as possible, designed for nothing more than the seven frantic laps around the spina of the Circus Maximus. The force of the mob against it shook the frame and nearly dislodged one of the two large wheels. Sanct' Germain held the team steady and the chariot crept farther into the turn, moving into the current of the mob. A little more, and they would be pulled into the rush for the gate to the stableyard.

At the most hazardous instant, Sanct' Germain pulled the horses away from the gate to the narrow street that ran beside the high walls of the Circus. Here the crowd was thinner, but moving more quickly, the whole motion more frenetic. With a shift of balance, Sanct' Germain lowered his hands and let the horses run.

The streets of Rome were narrow, and here the paving stones were rutted and uneven. The chariot lurched like a drunkard over the pavement as the horses lengthened their stride.

Around them ran those parts of the mob that could not get into the stableyard, and with them came the denizens of the dark world under the stands. These were the gamblers, the prostitutes who served the gladiators and the patrons of the Games who found a dark satisfaction in lying with a woman or man or child while the bloody sports raged, the old and useless fighters with their wits gone, the abandoned children who begged, the debauched who reveled in the presence of the condemned and maimed, the traders in misery who corrupted servants and slaves in order to seduce and ruin their mistresses. This bizarre assortment of the exploited and depraved joined the madness with a rare enthusiasm, mocking and jeering as they ran.

Sanct' Germain's team plunged onward through the avalanche of people, swaying, curvetting, dragging the chariot after them. They were trained for speed, bred for it, and the nearness of the mob had driven them to a state of panic. There was foamy sweat on their flanks and their breath was taken in sobbing gulps, but they ran gratefully, and Sanct' Germain held them on the road.

A long peal of thunder cracked and rumbled across the sky and the horses nearly broke stride. Sanct' Germain yelled at them and reached for the light whip at his right elbow as he strained to keep the team moving. With a last wrenching effort he turned the chariot into a side street, away from the Circus Maximus, where few people ran and where the keeper of a wine shop, standing idle while less than a hundred paces away the poor of Rome rioted, cursed the racing vehicle for ruining his business, though the street was empty.

The next clap of thunder was louder still, a deep, awesome crescendo that drowned the shout of the mob. The dark clouds had moved and now commenced to blot out the sun as they roiled in from the west.

Carefully Sanct' Germain began to rein in his team. It was nerve-racking to careen through the close, squalid streets, fearing that at any moment something, someone would appear out of nowhere to block their path. The chariot would certainly run down any but the most durable obstruction. With the added boom of the thunder, the horses rushed onward in a new burst of speed, seeking to escape the terrifying noises that surrounded them.

At last, when they were several blocks away from the Circus Maximus, Sanct' Germain pulled the team to a dazed, tired walk. He took the reins into one hand and turned to Aumtehoutep just as the Egyptian reeled against him. For the first time he saw the deep gash in his slave's forehead and the blood that covered his face like an elaborate funerary mask. "Aumtehoutep!" He reached out his free hand to brace the other man.

The Egyptian tried to speak, but the words were slurred, and in a language that had never been spoken on the banks of the Tiber. Finally he dropped to his knees on the floor of the chariot. "Drive," he muttered.

Sanct' Germain looked at his quivering, steaming horses. They were breathing hard, but they were bred to run. If he required it of them, he knew they could gallop most of the way to Villa Ragoczy, though it would exhaust them. What worried him the most was their hooves, for the paving stones were notoriously hard on even the toughest hooves.

On the floor of the chariot, Aumtehoutep bit back a groan. It was enough. Sanct' Germain had seen his slave take an arrow in the arm and only wince. He reached for the whip in its brace and snaked it over the head of his team.

The bay faltered, stumbling as the tip of the lash flicked over his rump. Then he collected himself and set the pace for the other three horses, taking as fast a trot as the horses could maintain together without breaking into a gallop.

He was well along the Vicus Patricus between the Cespius and Viminalis hills when he heard another sound, the ordered tramping of feet coming from the north. Sanct' Germain pulled his team to the side of the road and waited anxiously.

Within a few minutes a century of the Praetorian Guard appeared, marching four abreast so that little could get past them. As they came to Sanct' Germain's chariot, the centurion bawled an order, and one side of the wide column dropped out of line with the rest so that the Guard could pass. The centurion paused beside the chariot. "You come from the Circus Maximus, foreigner?"

"Yes. We got away just as the mob broke in the gate to the stableyard." He spoke briskly, with a certain touch of haughtiness.

"We?" questioned the centurion.

"Yes. My body slave lies on the floor of this chariot with a gash on his face. Worse would have been done if we had not got away when we did." Sanct' Germain made no effort to hide his impatience.

Apparently the centurion chose not to notice. "That's a racing rig you've got there. Not the kind of vehicle I'd want to take on the streets, though it's small enough for the law to allow it."

"I hadn't planned to," Sanct' Germain said sardonically, wishing that the centurion would not detain him any longer.

"They say it's the biggest riot yet," the centurion went on. "We've had three estimates, twenty thousand, thirty thousand and seventy thousand. It's probably around thirty thousand." He made a face. "Well, who can blame them? They haven't had the grain dole for close to a month and there's been no oil distributed for ten days. They're hungry." He slapped the rail of the chariot and it sagged under the impact. "Well, if your slave is wounded, you probably want to get him to a physician, if he's worth anything to you. I won't keep you. But you know," he added as the thought occurred to him, "when Galba is Caesar, he'll get the dole going again soon enough." With a wave he fell in with his column as the last twelve soldiers marched by.

As he whipped his team up again, Sanct' Germain wondered if many others agreed with the centurion, and now supported Galba's claim to the purple. Then he turned his whole attention to his driving as he sped toward the Viminalis Gate and the road to Villa Ragoczy that lay beyond.

Text of a report to the Senate of Rome by the tribune Marcus Antoninus Deva.

To the august and revered Senators of Rome, hail!

It has been said of the Ahenobarbus family that their bronze beards are a fitting match for their iron faces and leaden hearts, though in the case of Lucius Domitius Ahenobarbus, who ruled as Nero Claudius Caesar Drusus Germanicus, the matter is open to question. His death, when he finally accomplished it, showed him to have a few virtues left, and indicated that he was not entirely given over to the effeminate conduct of the Greeks.

When news of the battle of Vesontio was brought to him a few days ago, on the seventh, and though he rejoiced to hear of the death of Vindex, he realized that the situation was much more serious than he had previously believed. Until then he had planned to go to Gallia and into the west, perhaps as far as Lusitania, for the purposes of appealing to his troops and singing new songs for them that would win them to him again, as he had done years before. He had not taken into account the action of the legions at Carthago Nova who had already hailed Galba their Emperor, and who, in spite of Nero's attempts to seize his lands and property, and even take on the role of counsel for himself, had found many among you Senators to side with him in open defiance of Nero.

With Tigellinus gone, Nymphidius Sabinus could make no decision, and so the Praetorian Guard was left to flounder, with those who opposed Nero having the stronger voice.

On the night of the eighth, the troops guarding Nero

left their posts, his personal guard taking his box of poisons with them. According to his slaves and others at the Golden House, his freedman Phaon suggested that they leave the palace and go to his house outside of the city. Phaon had heard some of the troops talking earlier that night about a plan to kill Nero as he slept, and so thought to remove him from danger this way.

One of the Praetorians claims that he paid Phaon to reveal Nero's hiding place in the storage shed behind Phaon's house, but that may be an idle boast. Phaon himself did not go with the Emperor, but sent him two messages, one assuring Nero that all would be well, and one informing him of the sentence handed down by your rule: that he was to be stripped and beaten to death with heavy staves. According to Epaphroditus, his minister who had accompanied him to Phaon's house with Sporus, it was then that Nero decided to take his own life, and had a grave dug to his measure. He lacked the courage to throw himself in the river, though Sporus said that he made a joke about cold water having always been his favorite drink. He sang a few choruses in Greek, chiding himself for indecision and cowardice, and lamented how ugly his life had become. Epaphroditus tells us that Nero was particularly upset that he would no longer enjoy the arts. He was confident that if he could restore the dole and remove Vespasianus from office in Egypt, the people would love him as they always had.

It was when he heard the sound of approaching horses that he made up his mind to use his knives, or so Sporus says.

I had ridden there with four other Praetorians on your orders, anxious to arrest Nero and deliver him up for the death you had decreed for him. It had taken almost an hour to get the information we needed to find him, and then we rode fast, for we feared he would escape.

When I found him, he was already dying from a cut in his throat, and as I raised his head, he gave me a look of greatest derision and with an obscene gesture said, "You are too late, my loyal Praetorian." My three companions entered soon after, and Nero's attendant ministers were taken into custody, and you have their statements as well as my own as to what transpired.

I recommend that the petition of Nero's old mistress Acte be granted and that she be given charge of the body so that the former Emperor may have a proper funeral. For all his faults, he was much loved by the people and they will want to do him honor. It is not suitable that he be cast into the river like a beggar or burned with refuse in the fields. Nero has already lain two days without cremation or burial, and it is imperative that proper disposal be made as soon as possible.

It is the opinion of Sporus that Phaon was tricked into betraying Nero's hiding place, but if that is so, I very much doubt that he was unaware of what he did. There is a rumor that Phaon was trying to find a captain to carry Nero away from Rome until he could rebuild his support and return to Rome in victory. It may be that, driven by desperation, Phaon did such a foolish thing. Any captain in Rome approached by Nero's freedman on the morning of the ninth would have known what was being planned, and would have come to the Praetorians or to the Senate with the report, for feeling was running high in the city. I only know that Nymphidius Sabinus gave us our orders at midmorning, and that Nero was hiding where we were told he would be.

By my own hand, under seal, on the eleventh day of June in the 820th Year of the City.

Hail Galba!

Marcus Antoninus Deva
Tribune, the Praetorian Guard

19

IN THE PRIVACY of Justus' study, the man in the outrageous wig paused by the window. He was in his middle thirties, with rather deep eyes, a long nose and a dissatisfied mouth. "I admit that your caution is understandable, Justus. The rumors from Germania are distressing, and it is perfectly true that Aulus Vitellius is an ambitious man. I admit that Galba is old. But then, I am not. And Caesar has assured me that I will be designated his heir."

"But it hasn't happened yet," Justus pointed out. He had

been talking with Marcus Salvius Otho for the better part of an hour, and he had yet to be convinced to give public support to the new Emperor, Servius Sulpicius Galba.

"You have my word on it," Salvius said grimly.

Justus could not resist provoking his guest. "And if he does not? What if Galba names another heir?"

This time Salvius glared at Justus. "If Galba appoints another heir, he will regret it."

"Why should he?" Justus asked, for the first time beginning to be interested.

"Because if he does not live up to our agreement, I will rebel against him. More than one Caesar has fallen for forgotten promises. Most of the troops are with me, and they will fight if it comes to that." He began to pace the room.

"Do you know that? Have you asked?" Justus found Salvius' all-consuming vanity difficult to deal with; the wig, the spectacles he refused to wear in public although without them he could not see more than a dozen paces, his elaborate armor and jewelry, his silk clothing, mitigated against him in Justus' mind, though he respected Salvius' ambition.

"Yes," Salvius admitted after a moment. "There seemed a time when Nero had declared Galba an enemy and was seizing his property and lands, that Galba might not carry his claim. I made sure then that if support failed for him, it would come to me. I know that it is true now. I have guarantees of that." He tapped his lorica that was decorated with a representation of Mars ravishing Rhea Silvia while his woodpecker and vulture hovered above.

"And are you willing to gamble on it? Galba is well thought of in Rome."

"Galba is *old!*" Salvius shouted. "He's seventy! I'm thirty-six. I have experience. I'm willing to wait my turn. But I've got to be certain that there is support for me so that we can keep the state moving without interruption." He looked at one of the low chairs with two soft pillows lying in it. With a sigh he sat down. "Justus, listen to me. There are real advantages to be gained now. Galba will honor those who give their support to me, since I will be his heir, and that will mean that you will have my goodwill as well as Galba's."

"Provided you are the heir, and that this business in Germania doesn't become worse and that you can solve the problem with Vespasianus about Egyptian grain. Water theft is so common that a third of the Claudian Aqueduct is siphoned.

There's also the matter of the pay owed the legions." Justus ticked these problems off on his fingers. "The situation here in Rome is far from stable."

"But that will change soon," Salvius insisted.

"I have only your word for that," Justus reminded him gently, deciding that it would not be wise to antagonize his visitor any further. "You weren't in Rome during the last of Nero's reign. Oh, I understand your position quite well, and I don't envy you. Your . . . association with Poppaea, and after you gave her up so that Nero could marry her, you couldn't very well remain here. I know that. But I think perhaps you don't know what those last few years were like. We've all learned to be very cautious. My own father-in-law, you know, was executed and his sons condemned to die in the arena because they were foolish in their choice of allies." He gave a fatalistic gesture. "It's made me very circumspect, Salvius. You can't imagine how shocked I was when I learned about my wife's family. The Clemens house is one of the oldest and most respected, and then this happened. . . ."

Salvius hesitated. "I had forgotten about that. Yes, I do see why you want to be careful." He held out a rolled scroll to Justus. "You might take time to look this over. It's the reforms that Galba is planning. If you have anything you think should be added or deleted, make a note of it and we'll discuss it again in a few days, if I may call on you then?"

"Of course, of course. I'm flattered that you'd think of me in such circumstances. I want you to believe that I don't oppose you or Galba, but there have been so many rapid changes that I haven't quite had time to deal with it all." He rose, adjusting his toga and bowing. "It was good of you to come. I'm sorry I can't give you a prompt decision, but I want to be sure of how we all stand." He gave his best self-deprecating smile as he stood over Salvius.

Salvius got to his feet slowly. "I appreciate your position, Justus. May I tell the Emperor that you do not oppose him, in any case?"

"Of course you may do that," Justus said heartily and clapped one large hand to Salvius' back. "I can see you're doing the honorable thing, watching after the Emperor's interests so very carefully."

"I'm not entirely disinterested in the matter myself." Salvius made an attempt at humor. "You could say that your cooperation is less a present issue than a future present."

Dutifully Justus chuckled, taking smug satisfaction in knowing that he had won over Marcus Salvius Otho. He walked beside him to the door. "My doorman will show you out, Salvius. I'm very much looking forward to reading this." He held up the scroll with a grave, friendly look. "It bodes well that this Emperor, unlike the last, considers the wishes of the Senate as well as his own whims."

Salvius wore a self-satisfied expression. "You may be sure that the next Emperor will do so, as well." He turned away then and strode across the atrium toward the door.

He would have been less confident of Justus if he had been able to see his face then. His eyes narrowed with cunning and all the pleasure had gone out of his smile. He tapped the scroll against his leg, then went back into his library, calling to his new secretary. "Monostades, I will see the centurion from Germania now."

Monostades inclined his head as he paused in the doorway. "Do you want to see him in your study, or elsewhere?"

"Here will be fine. Make sure that we are left alone." He gestured his dismissal and sat back. So Marcus Salvius Otho wanted to wear the purple, did he? And was counting on the death of the aged Galba to give it to him. That path was an uncertain one. But if Salvius was aware of that, he might still have the advantage. Justus considered the matter dispassionately. Whatever the immediate advantages might be to siding with Salvius, there was the whole question of Galba's strength and public support. After the lavish young, flamboyant Nero, the old, stern Galba would be a disappointment to a populace grown used to spectacle and excitement. Salvius was another matter, having much of Nero's vanity and his luxurious tastes, but out of touch with Rome. Perhaps in time this would change. But Justus was not sure that time was available.

His thoughts were interrupted by the arrival of Monostades with his other guest. "Master, this is Caius Tuller, centurion under Aulus Caecina Alienus in Germania."

Tuller walked heavily into the room. He had the look of a career soldier. He was of a powerful build, and though he wore the toga virilis, he was obviously more used to lorica, caracalla and weapons. As was the fashion among the troops in the north, he had a short beard and his hair was somewhat longer than the prevailing mode in Rome.

"Tell me," Justus said as he rose to greet his visitor,

smiling as if they were old companions having a reunion, "does your general still take his wife with him on campaigns and does she still wear that long purple cloak?"

The centurion's face relaxed. "Yes. And Caecina hasn't given up his taste in bright colors, either."

Justus gave an indulgent chuckle. "I haven't seen Caecina in years, but I can recall hearing him speak. He's a fine orator, your general."

"That he is," Tuller agreed. He was uncomfortable in these fine and unfamiliar surroundings. He looked to his host for help and Justus indicated the chair that Salvius had left but a few minutes before.

"I understand you have a message for me from Caecina. I'd like very much to hear it." Justus settled himself comfortably once more.

"Caecina is concerned about the new Emperor. He likes Galba well enough, but doubts that he is truly capable of assuming the duties of Emperor." Tuller ran a square, scarred hand over his beard. "I can't say that I blame him."

"Ah," Justus said smoothly, "but I understand that he intends to appoint Marcus Salvius Otho his heir, and he might be capable of handling those duties." He watched to see what effect this might have on the centurion.

"Otho . . ." He stared at Justus. "Otho will be Galba's heir? There's been no announcement."

"It is my understanding that he will be proclaimed heir quite shortly. Does that complicate your mission?" With one hand he touched the rolled parchment that lay on his desk.

"It might." The centurion nodded slowly. "But I said I would speak to you, and I will." He drew a deep breath and began what was obviously a carefully rehearsed speech. "You're aware how great abuses have been made with imperial power in the last few years. It is apparent that this cannot be allowed to continue if the Roman Empire is to remain the strongest power in the world. We need to find a leader who combines the appeal that Nero had for the common citizens and freedmen as well as someone who is respected by the Senate and the patricians. Caecina feels that, in spite of the many honors that have been given Galba, and with merit, he is not a man for the people and for that reason will not be a good ruler. He believes that Aulus Vitellius, who is now serving as governor-prefect of Germania, is the better choice and that it would be for the benefit of Rome to declare him Emperor."

"And that way, Caecina can keep a hand in government without any imperial risks, is that it?" Justus knew from the alarm he read in the centurion's eyes that his guess was very close. "I see. I begin to understand. How many Senators are you supposed to see before you return to Germania?"

Tuller looked terribly unhappy as he answered. "There are fifteen on my list. I've seen six."

"Good. Good. Let me know what success you have with them." He rose, concluding the brief interview.

"Don't you want to discuss this with me?" Tuller asked in a deeply offended voice.

"No, not yet. Because if you've seen so many of the Senators already, you may be certain that one of the Praetorian spies is watching you now, and will certainly make a report of everywhere you go. If you don't tell me anything more, then there will be little I can say to them when they come here asking for information."

"Praetorian spies," Tuller repeated heavily. "I had not thought that they would watch a fellow soldier."

"Praetorians aren't your fellow soldiers, Caius Tuller. They are a very special force, and no one knows that more than they do. Be careful of them. They've made Emperors more often than the legions have ever dreamt of doing." Justus stood by his study door, one hand on the latch. "I will send for you in a few days, and we will meet safely then."

The centurion had no choice but to leave. He accepted the dismissal with understanding. "Thanks for the warning. I'll have to be more careful, I see. I wish one of the others had told me about the spies."

"We don't like to mention such things in Rome," Justus said smoothly. "Where will a message find you?"

Tuller answered, "I am at the Inn of the Dancing Bear, near the old forum. I can read, so you may leave a sealed message for me there."

"Excellent. Expect to hear from me in three days." He stood aside to let the centurion out. When he had heard the soldier walk away through the atrium, Justus once again sat at his desk, and pulled a sheet of parchment from the chest beside him. He prepared his pen, then began a letter to Titus Flavius Vespasianus, governor-prefect of Egypt.

He was almost finished with the letter when the door behind him opened. "I am not to be disturbed, Monostades," he said without turning.

"I am not Monostades," Olivia said in a small, tight voice.

"Olivia," Justus exclaimed, his eyes still on the parchment as he wrote. "You have not been to my study in months. What will you ask me to do for you this time, I wonder?" The mockery was plain and his light brown eyes brightened with pleasure.

"You may tell me what's become of my mother." It was not easy to keep from screaming at him, but that she knew was what he wanted her to do. Sanct' Germain had taught her that, and now she refused to give Justus any of the satisfaction he wanted from her.

"Your mother?" He stopped to sign his name, then rolled the parchment into a scroll and reached for his signet.

"Surely you remember her," Olivia said sarcastically. "The wife of the man you betrayed? The mother of the sons you saw condemned? Her name is Romola. That may remind you." She stayed by the door. Being in her husband's presence was disgusting to her, and she was in his company as little as possible now. "What have you done to her? Where is she?"

Justus' expression as he turned to face his wife was one of the most ingenuous innocence. "She had so long expressed a wish to live away from Rome that I took her at her word. She has been moved to my estate near Brixillum on the Padus. You might not recall the property at first. I confess it is not my best holding."

"It is very likely your worst. You see, I do remember it. You once offered to sell it for two teams of racehorses." Her anger was hot within her, and she nurtured it, for it fought down her revulsion and gave her strength.

"How fortunate that I did not." His hot gaze rested on her. "Why do you want your mother, Olivia?"

"Why? She's all I have left in this world. I want to visit her, I want to be with her . . ." Here her voice cracked and she hesitated while she mastered herself. "I don't care if you sent her to the wildest outpost in the empire. I want to join her."

"It is unfortunate that she did not want to remain in Rome," Justus went on as if he had not heard what Olivia had said. "I offered to repair her house—in fact, I sent builders to do the work, and she refused to admit them or take anything from me." He toyed with the pen in his hand.

"I won't stop asking, Justus. I want to join her. I want to leave Rome. I want to leave you." It was a temptation, to be in the same room with him. She wanted so much to throw herself upon him with every weapon she had ever heard of in her hands so that she could return some little portion of the pain he had given her.

"But if you go to that estate, you won't be here to meet the new soldier I've found for you. He's reputed to be quite remarkable. Think of what you would miss, Olivia, if you left here." He put the pen aside. "You're planning to set your will against mine. Let me warn you now that just because your mother is out of Rome, it doesn't mean that she is out of my reach. It might take a few days longer, but my orders still protect her and your sister and her family." Slowly he stood up and advanced on Olivia.

In spite of all her good resolutions, she cowered as he came near her, one hand raised to fend him off. "Send me to her," she said.

Justus laid his hands on Olivia's shoulders and was delighted to feel a shaking that she could not control. "I've told you that you may not. And though it is true that you can petition the Senate for a divorce or separate maintenance, that would mean your mother would starve, and you with her. Your sister in Gallia might be posted to Armenia. It would also mean that you would have to endure having your reputation dragged through the courts, and that would make it impossible for you to marry again. Do you think that any man of honor would want to possess a woman who preferred to sleep with the lowest class of gladiators, men who were so brutal that the whores of the lupanar would not have them? Do you? And that is what would happen, little wife, I promise you. There are plenty to testify, including some of those very men." He relished the hatred in her eyes. "Do as you think best, Olivia. If you prefer dishonoring yourself and your family and a pauper's death to our marriage, you have only to tell me."

"One day, Justus, I will. When you cannot threaten me with my mother. On that day, I will denounce you, and all that you've done to me, and it won't matter what you say of me, because then at least I will be free of you, without any necessity to see you again." Her voice was steady and calm as she fixed him with a strange stare. In her mind, she thought of Sanct' Germain, and the last time they had met. It had been shortly after Nero's death a few months ago, and they had taken advantage of the confusion to spend a few short hours in each other's arms. She could remember even now the tenderness of his touch and the gentle power of his lips.

"I prefer you this way, Olivia," Justus told her with a snide laugh. "I don't enjoy it when you cringe or become passive. You must tell me again sometime what it is you're going to do to me. I'll be interested to hear it." His hands tightened and he saw her go white around the mouth. "You'd like it better if I beat you now? Of course not. But you provoke me with this defiance. I am amused by it now, but at another time I might not be."

Through the hurt, Olivia watched her husband. "You're loathsome," she whispered, and the words were more terrible for the quiet, "you aren't worth my hatred. Contempt is all you deserve." With a single fast movement she broke out of his grip, ignoring the hurt that came as she did. She unlatched the door and stepped out of the study, saying as she did, "You are a sickness, my husband." Then she slammed the door, and apparently oblivious of the stares of the slaves around her, walked toward her wing of the house.

When Justus called Monostades to him a little later to hand him the scroll and give him instructions for its delivery, he was brusque with his secretary. "Go. Do as I've told you. I don't want anyone to disturb me again today," he snapped as Monostades hurried toward the door. "Not anyone, is that clear? Not anyone!"

Text of a proclamation of the Emperor Galba.

To all loyal citizens of Rome, the empire, and to the nobility and freedmen, my greetings:

It nears the time of the festival of the Saturnalia, a time of gifts and the pleasures of rejoicing. I will rejoice with you as well, for my heir will be with me, sharing with me responsibility and power so that he will not come to the purple unprepared and unknown to you.

Lucius Calpurnius Piso Licianus has officially been made my heir, and I know that you all will be proud that so noble a young man has consented to be part of my administration and to follow after me.

It is always a difficult decision to make, this selection of an heir. There are those who believe that they deserve such recognition more than others, and a few are misled into thinking that they have earned the honor through service. But though such actions are laudable, they are not sufficient. Piso Licianus will bring to the empire his faultless lineage and a character of the most dedicated and honorable.

As we approach the new year, let me remind all of you that there are a great many tasks before all of us, and that we must renew our dedication to the empire so that the great rifts of the past year may be mended. To that end, I caution you all against the various rumors that always make themselves heard in Rome. It is true that there are those who have been disappointed by recent events, but such matters are soon resolved among honorable men. The rumors that have come from Germania are not sufficiently important to be given attention. As an old soldier, I know how such rumors are subject to exaggeration. Do not be deceived by those who tell you that there will be a revolt in this province or that one. Our upheavals and battles are over. The great injustices that you all endured under Nero will be corrected, and we will return once again to those stern virtues that have made the empire as mighty as it is.

I hope you will share my satisfaction in my choice of heir and will join with me in lifting us from the mire of self-indulgence and vanity that almost engulfed us.

The next year will be the 821st Year of the City. Let us strive to make it the finest Rome has ever known.

Servius Sulpicius Galba Caesar
on the nineteenth day of November
in the 820th Year of the City

PART II

Ragoczy Sanct' Germain Franciscus

Text of a letter from the centurion Caius Tuller to his commander, Aulus Caecina Alienus, in Germania.

To the general A. Caecina Alienus, greetings:

Less than a month has passed since Galba and his heir Piso met their deaths here in Rome. That happened on the fifteenth of January, and already the purple is awarded to Marcus Salvius Otho. The people like Otho better than they did Galba: the old general was too stern for them, too full of the talk of virtue and not much given to pleasure. Piso Licianus, poor fool, has had the worst of this affair. Galba attempted to resign in his favor, in order to prevent the rebellion that overtook him. For five days Piso reigned as Caesar, hardly long enough to review the coinage. They died together on that cold, bright morning while the wind rode down the Tiber.

Otho has already had word of the movements in Germania, and is planning to take his legions north to meet any advancement toward Rome before the city is reached. He is quite flamboyant, this Marcus Salvius Otho, and the people are pleased with him. The taxes he has tried to impose do not meet with the same enthusiasm. So far the Senate has not responded to his demands, and therefore Otho will take into battle troops who have not recently been paid, which may affect their loyalty. Otho has declared that the whole question will be resolved by May, and that the shipments of grain will be at their usual level. He has arranged for loaves to be distributed to those on the dole, and for a portion of pork to be given twice a week. The Senate has said that this is a dangerous precedent, and it may be that, but Otho knows that he must earn the respect of the people if he is to fulfill his promise to them, and this is the quickest way to do it.

The Great Games have been suspended for a time, but Otho has promised a full five days of Games, with grants and awards distributed on each day. He has already promised that some of the imperial gifts will be of certain items owned by Nero himself.

Work on the Golden House has stopped completely. Galba hated the place, Piso said he wanted to pull it down, and Otho has not been Caesar long enough to know what to do with it. Many of the people of Rome have come to dislike the building, but they are still sentimental about Nero and would oppose taking the palace down because Nero loved it so much.

There has been talk in the Senate about water theft again. Twelve illegal taps have been found on the Claudian Aqueduct alone, and the inspection of the others hasn't begun. The price of aqueduct water has soared this last year, and some of the builders of insulae for the poor have threatened to leave out the plumbing entirely unless some adjustment is made. If Vitellius would address himself to this issue, he would find a great deal of support and little opposition, for to oppose such reform is very nearly an admission of water theft.

I have attempted to contact all the Senators you listed, but it has been difficult. There are three Praetorians who watch me constantly and report all my activities. More than one patrician has told me that the Praetorians are a government unto themselves and none dare oppose them. All have warned me that if Vitellius is victorious, he will have to accept the demands of the Praetorian Guard if he intends to rule for more than a month. Many of the high-ranking officers are openly courted by men of rank, as if they were minor rulers. They're a very haughty unit, without regard for the legions and any soldier who is not of equestrian rank, at the very least. They're dangerous, those Praetorians, and much more powerful than I'd ever realized. Let Vitellius be warned.

There has been an increase in spying, which is to be expected. Very few citizens will speak their minds, but the walls of every street in Rome reflect their discontent. Everywhere there are threats and slogans scrawled, and those who read them laugh and nod.

The conflict with Otho must be settled quickly, as

Rome is growing tired of rebellion and confusion. By no means should the current Caesar be allowed to fight from the city, so do not follow the plan you made to drive him back to Rome and kill him here. It would go badly for you that way. Otho must die away from the city, where there will be no chance for the Romans to take up sides. See that the Emperor falls on the battlefield in the north, so that there can be no disputing it within the city walls.

I await the good day when you enter the ancient gates bringing a new and finer Emperor with you. I will work toward that day with all my capabilities. I have even hired sign writers to go about the streets and paint Vitellius' praises on the walls during the night.

Caius Tuller
Centurion, XI Legion
on the fifth day of February
in the 821st Year of the City

P.S. There was a banquet two nights ago, with lavish entertainment, as in the days of Nero. Dancing girls from Egypt and musicians from somewhere in Africa to entertain. Greek wines served unwatered, fifteen dishes for each course. Very grand. Otho was as liberal a guest as he was a host, and after his fourth cup of wine, he threw his wig into the air and rubbed oil on his pate to make it shine. Everyone is still laughing about it. Except Otho, of course.

1

THERE WAS a dark place on the paving where the water ran down from the garden of the villa of Constantinus Modestinus Datus on the hill above. In the fading dusk, as the shadows grew denser the wetness seemed to resemble a lean, elongated, cloaked figure, all the more sinister for lying toward the sun instead of away from it. One or two late travelers who hurried toward the gates of Rome hesitated as they neared this ominous mark, then, discovering it was only water, were filled with relief as they crossed the spreading trickle. From the villa came the perfume of the garden's flowers, which the rising wind carried away.

Shortly after the Roman gates had been closed for the night and the Watch posted, Sanct' Germain approached the villa, dismounting some distance from it. He had expected this summons for more than a year. The last letter from Sennistis had warned him that he had received a visit from a man claiming to be an Armenian scholar, but who spoke with a marked Persian accent. The high priest of Imhotep said that the scholar had demanded information about both Sanct' Germain and Kosrozd. Then there had been no more letters from Egypt. When the polite invitation had been delivered to Sanct' Germain the day before, he had welcomed it. At last he would have an opportunity to investigate further. In the note the Armenian scholar had said that he had heard of Sanct' Germain in Egypt. He would have to learn from whom, and how much.

As he walked down the Vicus Tusculis, Sanct' Germain studied the villa on the brow of the hill. He sensed he was being watched, but there was no movement in the garden to give his observer away. When he came to the rivulet that ran from the wall of the garden, an unpleasant smile touched his lips. "Running water," he said softly. Did anyone truly believe it would stop him? His heeled Scythian boots raised two little splashes as he strode through the wet toward the villa of Constantinus Modestinus Datus.

The slave who opened the door to his knock was not quick enough to disguise his fear of the visitor, and he stammered a welcome, adding that "The foreign scholar and his escort are in the garden, at the end of the corridor. Shall I show you . . . ?"

"Thank you, I know the way." Sanct' Germain inclined his head slightly and stepped into the house. He had departed from his usual custom of dressing in Persian and Egyptian garments. Tonight he wore a toga draped a little shorter than was most fashionable. It was of black linen, and the border, instead of being Roman eagles or Greek keys, was of his signet, the eclipse with raised wings, and was embroidered in silver thread.

There were three men in the garden. Two were dressed in the uniforms of the palace guard of Tiridates, king of Armenia, but the swords they carried were of Parthian design, as were their sandals. Both men were massively tall, and fixed their eyes on some invisible point near the horizon. Sanct' Germain glanced once at them and raised his fine brows in inquiry.

The third man rose from a bench by the fountain. He, too, was wearing Armenian clothing, but not the military gear of his bodyguard. His was the long tunic and fringed cape of a favored and courtly scholar. His young face was craggy and intelligent, and though he smiled readily enough, his dark eyes were wary. "Ragoczy Sanct' Germain Franciscus?" he asked unnecessarily.

"I understood from your invitation that you would be expecting me." He looked about. "Modestinus is not here?" He was grateful that this interview would take place in private, though it was remarkable for a guest to entertain without his host in a private villa. "A pity." This formality was not lost on the Armenian.

"The unpleasant difficulty in the north has called him away. Word has come that there is to be a battle between Otho and the generals of Vitellius. Modestinus has chosen to befriend Otho and protect his interests in Gallia. Do you think this entirely wise?" He gave a short, cynical laugh.

"My opinion can have no bearing on Modestinus' actions." He decided to let the scholar have the direction of the conversation for the moment, in the hope that he would reveal more than he had intended. As he moved to the bench across the fountain from the scholar, he asked, "Are you interested in Roman politics? It seems a perilous study just at present."

"Hardly perilous," the Armenian disclaimed. "I'm a foreigner."

"All the more hazard, I should have thought. Is what you learn worth the risk?" He saw the other man's eyes narrow once quickly. "War is not a scholarly matter," he said at his blandest.

"Politics do intrigue me, and Roman politics are fascinating just now. Three Caesars since January. Remarkable." He resumed his seat on the opposite side of the fountain, watching Sanct' Germain through the falling water.

"Particularly to Parthia and Persia?" Sanct' Germain suggested with gentle irony.

The scholar's hard bright eyes narrowed, but he said with great aplomb, "Parthia and Persia are as important to Armenia as Rome is. You will agree that the current . . . I hesitate to call it a civil war, but you must have noticed that it appears to be like one . . . civil war, then, is apt to have a lasting effect on Armenia."

"And on Persia and Parthia. They have been at war with Rome since the days of the Republic." Sanct' Germain had spoken in Armenian, and noted with satisfaction that the scholar was startled by this. "It would be to Persian advantage to keep the war going."

"I know nothing of Persia," the scholar said, too quickly, in Armenian, his eyes flicking away from Sanct' Germain's ironic gaze.

"Surely, one of Tiridates' court must be aware . . ." he said and let his voice trail off.

"No more than any other. I am a scholar, not a diplomat. It isn't fitting that I spend my time on politics. There are great schools in Parthia and Persia that interest me, of course," he went on hurriedly. "I have spent a little time studying in those countries. But as to this conflict with Rome . . ."

Sanct' Germain nodded sagely. "As you say, it's hardly a matter for scholars. And yet"—he gazed dreamily beyond the garden—"I cannot help but find it strange that you speak Armenian with a Persian accent. No doubt it's the current fashion at court." He knew beyond doubt that this was not the case. At other times he might have found the game amusing, and would have taken time to lead the scholar into more and deeper lies, but not now.

The scholar's glance was quick and poisonous, but he managed to give a smooth answer. "My first tutor was Persian, and I learned the accent from him. I am the son of my father's second marriage," he improvised unnecessarily, "and had no brothers or sisters near me in age."

Though Sanct' Germain gave the scholar mental credit for facile wit, he also recognized in him the common failing of liars, that he made things too complicated, and explained too much. "No doubt that isolation drew you toward learning," he said gravely, then went on deferentially, "You must forgive me, but I thought I knew all the scholars traveling from Armenia. Modestinus has been host to many of them, and they have often mentioned their colleagues. Your invitation this afternoon did not say much more than your name, which I confess I don't recognize. No doubt it slipped my mind. Led Arashnur . . ." He contemplated the name. "No, I'm afraid I can't place you."

"I'm . . . I had not planned to come to Rome so soon. But then an opportunity presented itself, and I took it." Arashnur was decidedly nervous now, and the Persian accent was much more pronounced. "Such things happen."

"Certainly," Sanct' Germain said with a self-deprecating smile. "But what do you study, that brought you here so quickly?"

Led Arashnur licked his lips. "I'm a student of practical mathematics. I study the designs of bridges and buildings . . ."

And military fortifications, Sanct' Germain was certain. "And with such turmoil in the city, you came here to study?"

The self-proclaimed Armenian scowled, and his striking young face became menacing. "I must take advantage of opportunities as they arise. If there is turmoil in the city, it's unfortunate but I must not let it deter me."

"Indeed," Sanct' Germain said softly. "Precisely how great a fool do you think me, Led Arashnur?"

"Franciscus?" the scholar demanded as his eyes flew to his silent bodyguards.

"Call them at your peril, Arashnur," Sanct' Germain murmured as he fixed an apparently friendly expression on his features. He made a point of reclining on the bench, supporting himself on his elbow as he watched the tension settle in the scholar's face.

"There are two of them, and they're armed," Arashnur said at last.

"Do you really think that would make a difference?" Sanct' Germain's amusement lit his dark eyes. "Well, you're welcome to try."

Arashnur hesitated before he answered. "No," he said slowly. "I don't think they could best you."

"Very wise." Sanct' Germain busied himself with the drape of his toga. "Now, what does a Persian spy from Armenia want with me?"

"I am not a spy!" the scholar protested with an abrupt, angry shout. "I am a scholar."

"I asked you not to treat me like a fool," Sanct' Germain reminded him silkily. "You want something of me; what is it?"

Arashnur was clearly taken aback. He had not dealt before with someone who thought so little of the threat he represented. "There's nothing . . ." he began, then saw the sardonic light in his visitor's eyes. "You have a slave."

"I have three hundred slaves," Sanct' Germain corrected him. He hoped that the spy would not lie again, for he knew that they had begun very dangerous talk.

"Only one interests me and . . . my associates," Arashnur said curtly.

"Your masters, rather," Sanct' Germain amended. "Which of my three-hundred-and-some-odd slaves deserves this attention?" He knew who it must be, but suggested, "It can't be my Armenian bestiaria, can it? Tishtry is not for sale, not to you or anyone, at any price. If your masters want to curry favor with Tiridates, they'll have to think of another present."

Arashnur looked disgusted. "We're not interested in an arena performer. Not *that* performer."

It was Kosrozd, then, as Sanct' Germain had feared from the first. "I have over sixty bestiarii and thirteen charioteers. Who among them has caught your fancy?"

"You're flippant," Arashnur snapped.

"Am I." His voice grew hard. "Led Arashnur, I fear you will have to disappoint your masters. None of my slaves is for sale."

"One of your slaves is a Persian prince!" Arashnur burst out, and the bodyguards turned toward him, one of them reaching for his sword. Arashnur gave him a stern look and a sharp gesture. The bodyguards returned to their positions, silent as ever, but they no longer stared abstractedly at the horizon. Now their attention was on the two men by the fountain.

"No, Led Arashnur," Sanct' Germain said quietly, "one of my slaves *was* a Persian prince. Now he wears a collar and races a four-horse quadriga in the Circus Maximus."

Torches had been lit in the garden by the household slaves, and now the flames, licked by the wind, flickered over the marble of the fountain and touched the falling water with tints of gold, amber and red.

"Kosrozd Kaivan is the oldest son of—"

"Prince Sraosha, third heir to the throne of Persia until his death for treason." He saw the cunning in Arashnur's eyes. "No, spy, my slave did not confide in me. I knew who he was when I bought him. Let me guess," Sanct' Germain went on with a sardonic laugh. "There is yet another conspiracy brewing, and you intend to benefit no matter who wins. If the conspirators succeed, you will be the one to give them their rightful prince, and if they do not, you will be able to bargain for favor by turning Kosrozd over to the king. That is your intention, is it not?"

Led Arashnur was silent, his eyes like shards of flint. "Yes," he said at last.

"And you are in Rome, not to study practical mathematics, but to learn how much damage this civil war has done to Rome, so that Persia and Parthia can decide whether or not they want to break their current truce with Rome."

"Yes," growled Arashnur.

Sanct' Germain was not surprised to learn this. He had been expecting something of the sort since Galba and Piso died in January. "I wonder," he said reflectively, "why you're willing to admit this to me."

This time Arashnur's voice was decidedly unpleasant. "I learned a few things while in Egypt."

"About the wheat supply?" Sanct' Germain suggested with feigned innocence.

"Until the wheat dole is reinstated in Rome, there will be civil war," Arashnur said, scoffing. "There is no shortage of grain in Egypt, only a canny and ambitious governor-prefect named Vespasianus."

"On that, at least, we can agree." Sanct' Germain nodded. "What else did you learn in Egypt?" He kept his tone gently mocking, but his mind was wholly alert. Led Arashnur might prove to be more of a threat than he had seemed at first.

"There was an old man," Arashnur explained. "He sold herbs and spices and had the reputation for being skilled in medicine. There were those who called him a priest. His name was Sennistis."

"Was?" Sanct' Germain asked in spite of himself. He had an instant of vivid memory of the tall, dignified Sennistis in his white robes and pectoral.

Arashnur shrugged. "He was not very strong, and toward the end his mind wandered. He thought he was back in the temple of Imhotep. He spoke a great deal of his predecessor. It was a curious tale. Perhaps you'd like to hear it?"

How much had Sennistis revealed before he died? Sanct' Germain asked himself. The old priest had had full knowledge of him, but would have resisted telling what he knew. He could see the gloating curve of Led Arashnur's full mouth and wished that he had the opportunity to peel the flesh from bone and teeth. His anger was hazardous, and he kept it banked within himself. "I am often entertained by curious stories."

"This former high priest of Imhotep, according to old Sennistis, was a foreigner. That, in itself, was unusual, but apparently this man was more remarkable. He had many strange habits, including that he neither ate nor drank except in private, and then, he claimed, only of the Elixir of Life. He was attributed with miracles. It was said that his body slave had been brought to him a dead man, the victim of plague, a novice from the Temple of Thoth, and that after two days, life returned to him."

"Another drinker of the Elixir of Life, no doubt," Sanct' Germain said with feigned boredom. If Sennistis had been brought to speak of Aumtehoutep, he had revealed more than Sanct' Germain had thought.

"Not according to Sennistis. He said that the slave was not like his master, but what the difference was, he would not reveal." He gave Sanct' Germain a careful, expectant look. "You have a body slave who is an Egyptian, or so I have heard."

"Yes."

Arashnur waited, but Sanct' Germain said nothing further. "The old man died before he told us more," he admitted.

Sanct' Germain's dark eyes grew hard. "How did he die, that good old man?"

"Bravely, if that pleases you. Almost a year ago. I stumbled on him by accident, you know, after I learned something of the man who had bought Kosrozd. My task might have taken longer if the priest had not kept your portrait. The inscription with it tells an amazing tale. How old are you, Franciscus? If that's your name."

"Older than you think me," was his grave answer. "And Ragoczy Sanct' Germain Franciscus is as much my name as any that Sennistis knew." He rested his compelling eyes on Arashnur. "I am surprised, spy, that knowing what you do, you have attempted anything so rash as this interview."

Led Arashnur got hastily to his feet. "I know something of you, Franciscus, and it's written down. If you and I do not come to some understanding tonight, I will dispatch that record to Otho in the morning. It should reach him at mid-April. He'll ask the Senate to act on the information, civil war or no."

"And if I refuse?" Sanct' Germain forced himself to

maintain his relaxed, reclined posture on the bench. "In ten days, I can be gone from Rome."

"From the city, but not the empire, and Roman law is persistent," the spy said with satisfaction. "You're vulnerable, Franciscus, and unless you come to terms with me, you will regret it. For example, one of your captains, a Greek, often uses his ship for smuggling. He might be willing to testify that he did so on your instructions. He was the one who found the old priest for me; his uncle. Were you aware of that?"

"No," Sanct' Germain lied, not adding that he had suspected that Kyrillos might be bringing in illegal grain to Ostia in order to profit from the high price on the illegal market.

"It would take little to have his entire cargo impounded, and from there it could mean that your other ships would be seized. That would be a blow to your finances, and then you might have to take advantage of the offer I have to make."

Sanct' Germain recognized the boasting in Arashnur's voice, and decided to draw him out some more. "I can't see why any Roman would take the word of a Persian—your pardon, an Armenian—scholar about any ship, Roman, Greek, African or unknown."

"I would not give the warning myself. It would come from a faithful but unknown Roman." Suddenly his expression turned crafty. "Oh, no, Franciscus. None of that. I won't give myself away to you so easily." He came around the curve of the fountain and stood over Sanct' Germain, his face flushed in the torchlight. "I want Kosrozd. I will have him. You think that because of your age and your blood that you are clever and safe, but you're not. Try to keep the prince and I will ruin you."

"Will you," Sanct' Germain sat up slowly. "You will find that a difficult task, spy."

"Say the same thing when you see your household disbanded. Then the Senate will be delighted to let me purchase Kosrozd. The slaves of a condemned foreigner are not welcome in Rome. The Emperor might even require that your slaves be sold outside of Rome. Otho cannot afford much more unrest. In your case, it would go very hard. Otho has a great distrust of foreign magicians."

Sanct' Germain had seen the fear in Arashnur's eyes that lurked behind the bravado. "And you share his distrust, it seems."

"You . . ." He made a sign with his hand to ward off evil, breathing more quickly. "Unnatural creature!" he cried out rather wildly, moving back to the other side of the fountain.

There was an ironic gleam in Sanct' Germain's eyes again. "You do believe the myth about running water. I crossed some on the road as I came here." Had the thick soles and heels of his Scythian boots not been filled with his native earth, a sufficient amount of water, especially running water, would be very difficult and painful to cross, but he thought it best to keep that to himself. "Shall I stride through the fountain, spy?"

Arashnur was paler and he looked aghast at his black-togaed visitor. "You can't."

A narrow stream ran from the fountain into the garden, winding between trees and banks of flowers, shining like molten metal in the torchlight. Sanct' Germain rose from the bench and stepped across it, then followed it through the garden, making a show of crossing it at every bend. He walked back to Led Arashnur and looked down at him. "You've mistaken your opponent, spy."

With a quick motion Arashnur summoned one of the soldiers to his side, but before the formidable bodyguard could reach his master, Sanct' Germain had stepped up to him and had touched him on the arms, using a firm pressure of his small hands. The bodyguard faltered and his drawn sword clattered to the mosaic walkway. With a swift motion Sanct' Germain stepped to the side and with one seemingly gentle blow sent the soldier crashing to the ground. He had confronted the second bodyguard before he had his sword out of his scabbard, and grabbed the soldier's sword arm above the elbow.

Startled, the soldier tried to pull his sword into play, but gave an agonized shriek as the hands tightened. A moment later his arm dangled uselessly, and he had sunk to his knees, holding his broken arm to his chest.

Sanct' Germain turned back toward Led Arashnur and laughed. "Spy, I have fought ten times this number alone. And that is no boast."

White-faced, Led Arashnur stepped backward. "I . . . I . . ." He fumbled in his belt for the knife there.

"Since you were unwise enough to reveal your plans to me, Persian, I think it had better be you who leaves Rome. The Praetorians might get a message about a spy at the house of

Constantinus Modestinus Datus if you are not gone." Contemptuously he turned his back on Led Arashnur. "Three days should be ample time."

"You would not dare! I will tell Otho what you are!" His voice had risen and fright made him stink.

"Send your message, if you think it will help you. Otho has other things on his mind just now. I doubt he'll be worried by . . . unnatural creatures like me." He looked at the Persian again. "Don't make it necessary for me to kill you, spy. Be glad that you can escape me." He looked at the bodyguard who whimpered over his broken arm. "See that the bone is set, or he'll be useless to you. The other . . . well, it's a shame. He'll be dead by the end of the month, probably within fifteen days." He saw the horror in Led Arashnur's face. "Oh, there's nothing unnatural about it. Men as mortal as you are can learn the blows. His organs are bruised, and they will stop working. When that happens he will die." His face became sardonic. "Think of this when you are back in Persia, and if you decide to come to Rome again, or send others to bargain for Kosrozd, remember this soldier's death before you act."

Led Arashnur made a frantic attempt to recover his dignity. "You dare not risk open court!"

"And who is to accuse me? You?" Before the Persian could answer, Sanct' Germain had turned on his heel and moved off through the garden toward the wall. With practiced ease he vaulted the wall and was gone into the night, leaving the villa of Modestinus and its torchlit garden behind.

Text of a letter from Cornelius Justus Silius to Titus Flavius Vespasianus, in Egypt.

To T. Flavius Vespasianus, greetings:

It is many months since I have written to you, and

for that I must crave your indulgence. No doubt you have had news of all the troubles that have beset this city, shaking us like so many political earthquakes. Fantastic rumors are repeated everywhere and it is only with diligence and care that the truth can be learned, although that is strange enough. The latest revelation is little more than a continuation of what has gone before. I have recently had news that Otho died by his own hand only a few days ago. This is not yet generally known in Rome, though, doubtless, the word will be abroad by the time the sun sets tomorrow. The Senate is prepared to proclaim for Aulus Vitellius. What a year this has been: Galba, his heir Piso, and now Otho dead and spring is not over.

Vitellius is supported by his generals, of course, and Aulus Caecina Alienus is a very ambitious man. I don't know that much about Fabius Valens, though I am willing to wager a considerable part of my fortune that he's in Caecina's sphere. Caecina is really the one we must watch. He is clever, handsome and a persuasive orator. I think he sees Vitellius as a ladder to imperial power. It would not be the first time such things have been attempted.

Assuming that there are no more disruptions, Vitellius should arrive in Rome in June, though he may want to come slowly to allow matters to calm themselves before he enters the city.

The hippos you sent for the Great Games of last month were a great success. Where you get these gigantic animals, I do not know, but the crowd was delighted with them, and many have spoken well of you. We haven't used all the animals yet; there are more Games coming in May, and I have arranged with the Master of the Bestiarii, Necredes, that there will be a long aquatic venation. These new sorts of hunts are becoming very popular with the people, who greatly appreciate the variety of strange animals that take to the water. One of the bestiarii told us that tigers can swim, and we've decided that it would be very exciting to add a few of them to this splendid venation. So far, we have had no luck in getting porpoises to battle in the water, and they are most difficult to transport. There was an attempt to bring a few sharks into the arena, but it failed when the transport case broke and the huge fish escaped and killed eight slaves before it died. We have got eels and ocean-bats, but they are no longer the novelty they were, and do not do well in fresh water.

Permit me to say that your handling of the grain situation has been most astute. I realize the crisis is apt to continue a little while longer, and when it ends, you will be very high in the esteem of the people. There is some grain reaching the city, of course, being brought from farther east, and from Gallia. It would be impossible to make up for the loss of Egyptian grain, and the success of these small traders has been unpredictable, as grain is now worth stealing. I would imagine that by fall, any genuine relief would be hailed as the gift of the gods.

I had occasion to speak to your nephew Tullius, and he assures me that you have not abandoned the plans we discussed last year. I'm certain that your enterprise will be successful, and for that reason alone, I am happy for any opportunity I might have to contribute to its outcome.

There have been two minor fires in the poorer insulae. Those buildings, you know, are not well built. In the worst of these, half the building is underground, and so there is little circulation of air. There are always complaints about the dripping of water there, for the plumbing works badly, and now that so many are trying to prepare what little grain they are given at home, in makeshift ovens, there have been fires and will probably be more. Most of the very poor no longer take their grain to the public mills because they are apt not to get it back again. There will be a great deal of rebuilding to do in the next year, particularly of the insulae. It has been a rule that there be no more than seven apartments per building, but I think that could be increased to ten or eleven without significant danger. Housing is always an important matter in Rome, but just at present, it is even more so. You might want to give it some thought.

I look to a happy reunion before too many more months go by. You and I, Flavius, are not so young that we can postpone such occasions indefinitely. I will be fifty-two shortly. A sobering thought, isn't it? Yet I am hoping that the decline of my life will be less of a disappointment than the rise of it has been.

Until our next meeting, this by my own hand on the twenty-third day of April in the 821st Year of the City,

Cornelius Justus Silius
Senator

2

VITELLIUS BELCHED as he moved his hand over his massive belly. On the other couches his guests reclined, men and women alike, for the new Emperor disliked any formality that distracted from the food set before them. "Best thing I ever did," he said, wagging a finger at the disapproving patrician across the room from him. "If I hadn't disbanded the Praetorians, they would have had one of them into the palace and then one of their number would ascend to the purple." He motioned to one of the slaves to remove the whole pig that lay in the center of their couches. There were seven other U-shaped clusters of couches and diners around the enormous banquet room, each with a similar dish in the center.

The patrician Vitellius had addressed kept a noncommittal expression. "Your generals are wise men, Emperor. They are aware of . . . many things." He stopped as he licked honey from his fingers. "But the Praetorian Guard is part of Rome, and the people aren't used to any other. It won't make your establishment here any easier."

Now Vitellius was scowling. "Remigeus," he said to the patrician, "your sympathies are well-known in Rome. Nine members of your family have been part of the Praetorians. I will excuse your zeal on their behalf this time, but I refuse to continue to do it for your convenience." He motioned to the cupbearer nearest him. "Refill Remigeus' cup, Linus. Get his mind off this subject."

The Senator on the couch beside Remigeus took up the argument. "He's right, Emperor," he said with a knowing expression. "The people of Rome, they're used to certain things—"

This time Vitellius was not so indulgent. "Fabricus, I have done it. There is no more time for discussion." He beckoned to his two attendants who stood near his couch. "I've got to relieve myself so I'll have room for the next course.

Peacocks' tongues, calves' brains and fish roe. It's a dish of my own. If any of you have suggestions as to how I could make it better . . . I'm not pleased with it yet." He lumbered to his feet and went off between his two attendants to the vomitorium.

Remigeus looked over at Fabricus. "He'll regret his action with the Praetorians. They won't forgive him."

"That's certain," Fabricus agreed. "Has there been any news from Egypt?"

"Talk to Justus. He's the one who seems to know everything." Remigeus stared ahead rather blankly at the table from which the pig had just been removed. "How many more courses tonight?"

"Four," Fabricus answered. "And a supper after the entertainment."

Fabricus sighed. "It's like the old days. Except that Vitellius likes wine better than iced water." At this oblique reference to Nero, he looked about furtively. "I don't know what will happen to us all if we keep living like this."

Remigeus laughed uneasily. "We've ridden out three Caesars this year; four if you count Piso. If there's one thing we do well as Senators, it's keep power. Emperors may come and go, but the Senate remains."

Behind him, one of the slaves leaned a little nearer.

"Loose talk," Fabricus admonished him, and was pleased to see that there were slaves coming with the next course. "Delicious," he called out with enthusiastic sycophancy.

Vitellius had required two feathers down his throat before he felt himself ready to return to the banquet room. His slaves had given him a wet towel to wipe his face and hands, and he had had to adjust his toga, which was hanging untidily about him. As he stepped into the hall, he was startled to see one of his guests there.

"Sanct' Germain," he said to the foreigner. "How are you enjoying the meal?"

Sanct' Germain nodded casually to the Emperor. "I was certain that you were aware that one of my idiosyncrasies is that I never eat in public. Among my kind, taking nourishment is considered to be too . . . intimate to be shared with a room full of people." He was very grand tonight, and quite aloof. He wore a long pleated gown of black silk with a deep, open neck. Against his chest lay a wide pectoral of silver, jet and polished rubies in the form of his signet, the eclipse disk with raised wings. Tonight he wore thick-soled sandals on his small feet instead of his usual Scythian boots.

This understated magnificence was lost on Vitellius. He gave Sanct' Germain an annoyed smile. "Surely you can make an exception for the Emperor."

"Ah, but, Caesar, you are not my Emperor. I am not a citizen of Rome." He spoke with such deference that it was nearly impossible for Vitellius to take offense. "Your invitation, considering my status, was a great honor."

Vitellius was somewhat mollified. "It isn't the usual way, but with all the things you've been doing for me and . . ."—he paused awkwardly—"my predecessors, it seemed appropriate to have you here. And there is the matter of the fish roe," he added in a rush.

One of his slaves had gone to the banquet room and now returned with a cup of wine, which he handed to the Emperor.

"Good." Vitellius drank deeply, and his already high color flushed a little darker. "I don't know about this, Franciscus. I don't like this refusal to eat."

"My customs no doubt seem strange to you, but as a Roman, you should understand the honoring of tradition." Sanct' Germain decided that he did not like this tall, lame man in the disarrayed toga who stood before him. "You, yourself, evoked old tradition tonight at this feast, did you not?"

The announced purpose of the evening was a tribute to Romulus and Remus, the legendary founders of Rome. "Well," Vitellius said slowly to keep from slurring his words, "it has been a neglected tradition among us, and I thought it would be beneficial to revive it. It's a mark of Romans that we honor our heritage."

Sanct' Germain would have liked to challenge this unctuous declaration, and to tell Vitellius that it was the Emperor's main purpose to lend an air of permanency to his shaky rule, but he was experienced enough to hold back the question that rose to his lips, and contented himself with saying, "A fortuitous time to restore it. The people cheer you and the Senate calls you a statesman."

Visibly irritated, Vitellius drew himself up and fussed with his toga. At last he hit upon a way to give this polished foreigner back his own coin. "About that hydraulic organ you're working on. When do you think you'll be able to install it?"

With a bland smile Sanct' Germain answered, "I should imagine it would be a month or two before I've finished the work, and once the instrument is in place, I will need a few days to adjust it." If he minded being suddenly relegated to the role of hired artisan, he gave no sign of it. "Do you want to inspect it?"

"There will be Games in twenty days. Can you have it ready by then?" He fixed his small, bright eyes on Sanct' Germain and waited, feeling smug.

"It could be ready, of course," Sanct' Germain answered without the least show of discomfort. "And if that is your wish, I will do all that I can to have it installed for those Games. However, it would mean that the instrument will not be completely tested and its tone and pitch might not be all that you desire. These organs are very delicate—as delicate as a lyre. It is through neglect and lack of adjustment that the old one has come to make a sound like"—he recalled Nero's description and took delight in using it now—"braying asses. Surely the new instrument should be an improvement on the old." His slight smile was polite and his tone at its most deferential, but Vitellius was not satisfied. Under that elegant manner lurked mockery.

"Are you saying that you won't install the organ for me?" he demanded angrily, his voice becoming very loud.

"No, Caesar," Sanct' Germain responded with every show of respect. "I am only telling you that if you wish the instrument installed before it has been tested and adjusted, it might not be as successful as it would be with proper preparation. If you are willing to wait, the organ will be more pleasant to hear, and its sound will be truer. But I will carry out your orders, whatever they are."

Vitellius gnawed at his lower lip, measuring Sanct' Germain's arguments. "Very well," he said curtly. "Do as you think best. But do not take too long." He turned between his slaves and stamped back toward the banqueting room.

Sanct' Germain was about to follow the Emperor when an officer of the new Imperial Guard stepped up to him. Sanct' Germain realized that he had been watched, that the soldier had been waiting for such an opportunity. "Yes, Guardsman?" he said, letting his hauteur mask his sudden apprehension.

The officer, a newly appointed tribune whose battle-scarred features were at odds with his fine silver lorica with its chased fittings, cleared his throat. "I am sorry to detain you, Franciscus. There are some questions, however, that you must answer."

"Indeed?" Sanct' Germain felt all his senses sharpen. "Questions about what?" He did not give ground before the tribune; he stood very straight and directed his penetrating gaze at the soldier.

"I am acting on orders from my general. You must realize that with this new regime"—he put his hand to the hilt of his short sword, as if he expected to have to fight his way out of the hall—"there are certain matters that have come to our attention . . ."

"Certain matters?" Sanct' Germain repeated lazily while his mind raced. What had happened? Had there been trouble with his slaves through that spy, Led Arashnur? Had he found some way to take Kosrozd? Had the accusations he had sent to Otho been found, after all? Had his importing rights been revoked, as they had been for so many other foreigners? Had someone broken into the private wing of Villa Ragoczy and found too much there? He caught his breath. Had Justus forced the truth from Olivia? Had she told him at last of their long, desperate, joyous affair? Was she safe?

The tribune hated dealing with the foreigner in this way. It should, he told himself sourly, be unnecessary to detain the man during a state banquet, on something of which he probably had no knowledge whatever. It was demeaning to be forced to speak this way, while the sounds of revelry echoed eerily through the lavish marble halls of the Golden House. He looked involuntarily at the empty pedestal where a bust of Nero had stood only a year before. Since then the busts of Galba and Otho had been there, and now it was once again empty, awaiting the new likeness of Vitellius.

"Well, tribune?" Sanct' Germain prompted.

"The captain of one of your ships has been smuggling grain. He was apprehended at Ostia with a load of fifteen barrels that were not listed on the manifest and for which he had no authorization." The words came out in a rush, and ended abruptly. "If he had your permission to do this, you, as well as he, are in violation of Roman law."

Sanct' Germain favored the tribune with a half-smile that disguised his worry. "And does he say that he had my permission?"

"He hasn't been questioned yet. For the moment he's being held by the garrison." He cleared his throat and made a small fatalistic gesture. "The man is a Greek, and a freedman. Official orders will be needed before we can question him."

That fool Kyrillos! Sanct' Germain thought in sudden anger. To have taken the Persian's bribe! "How did you come to know of this? I have a number of ships, and it hasn't been usual for such a thorough inspection to be made. I would think you must have had some information that made the inspection very careful. The *Gull of Byzantium* has a cargo capacity of two hundred thirty barrels. To have found fifteen in so many . . ."

"There was a warning," the tribune admitted.

"Anonymous?" Sanct' Germain asked, knowing the answer.

"Yes," the tribune admitted miserably.

"I see. Well, tribune, all my captains are authorized to purchase cargoes and sell them at a profit, but I would have to be more of a fool than I am to encourage any of the captains in my employ to break the law, particularly that law." He nodded brusquely to the tribune. "Tell me to whom I should speak. I want this matter settled as soon as possible."

The tribune's attitude changed, and instead of addressing the foreigner in the formal tones he had used at first, he adopted a more understanding attitude. "Well, on the sea, what's to be done? Captains have exceeded their authority before now, and this may be more of the same."

"Have any of the captains of my other craft broken this law?" Sanct' Germain asked, fervently hoping that they had not. "I own thirty-eight ships of various sizes. If there is some conspiracy between the captains, tell me now so that I can see they are reprimanded."

"Thirty-eight ships?" the tribune echoed, surprised. "I did not know there were so many. Thirty-eight, you say?"

"Yes." He modified his approach a little. "What is your name, tribune? If there is to be an investigation, I would like to know with whom I'm dealing."

"I'm Caius Tuller. Until last month I was a centurion in the Eleventh Legion. When Vit . . . the Emperor founded his new guard, I was promoted."

"No doubt that was recognition long overdue," Sanct' Germain said, knowing how every soldier felt about promotion. "Well, take me to your superior so that this unfortunate matter may be cleared up." He started down the hall ahead of the tribune Tuller.

"It might not be necessary to speak to Fabius tonight,"

Tuller said, as much to himself as to Sanct' Germain. "We were not aware that you had so many ships and—"

"And you'd like to investigate before you talk to me, is that it?" Sanct' Germain said quickly. "It would be wise. I would appreciate hearing anything you learn." He had already decided that he would have to dispatch one of his slaves to Ostia that night to make sure that Kyrillos left with the tide. No doubt his villa would be watched. It would have to be one of the bestiarii, then, for they often went to the seaport to bring new shipments of beasts back to his compound at Villa Ragoczy.

"We will inform you," the tribune agreed. He was in an awkward position now, not knowing what to do with the foreigner. If only he had been aware of the other ships. The Emperor was already angry at the amount of illegal wheat that was making its way to Rome, and now when he seemed to have found a safe and acceptable target for imperial wrath, this complication occurred.

"Do you wish to detain me?" Sanct' Germain asked without hostility. Now that tribune Tuller was less certain of his success, it was an easy matter to be cooperative.

"No. No, not under the circumstances." He met Sanct' Germain's unnerving eyes. "After our investigation, perhaps, but not now."

"I am at your disposal, of course," Sanct' Germain assured the tribune. "You may tell your commander that for me. Or, if you like, I will tell him, since he is dining with the others."

This offer made Tuller grind his teeth. "No, that will not be necessary." He had never had a man volunteer to place himself under arrest before. "I'll speak with him tomorrow."

"Then may I return to the banquet room?" The silence hung between them for a moment, and Sanct' Germain broke it. "Tribune Tuller, I realize that you have more tasks than you know how to discharge. If it is of any help, I will be willing to make available all the official shipping records of my captains for your examinations. It might be easier for you to spot irregularities that way."

Caius Tuller was glad to have this face-saving offer made to him. "Yes, that would be most useful." He stood aside as a drunken Senator lurched down the hall toward the vomitorium. "Shall I send a messenger?"

"If you like," Sanct' Germain responded. "Or I will have one of my slaves bring the records to the Golden House." He quickly saw that he had misjudged the tribune. "You may want to inspect my office. You are welcome to do so." He made himself smile. "You'll be fortunate, tribune. Almost no one has been into the private wing of my villa."

A loud shout went up from the banquet room and both Sanct' Germain and Tuller turned. A loud babble of voices followed this.

"What now?" Sanct' Germain asked aloud, not aware of how much contempt was in his voice.

The tribune looked unhappy. "It's the Emperor. He and his generals are going out in disguise."

Sanct' Germain looked at Tuller. "Like Nero used to do?"

Tuller was embarrassed now. "Not just that. He goes to the lupanar, to sport with the whores, and he goes to the gladiators' taverns, to hear them talk of blood and fighting."

"With or without escort?"

His question was interrupted as Vitellius appeared in the hallway with the handsome Caecina beside him. Both men were quite drunk and the general had started to sing a bawdy song as he reeled along beside the Emperor.

"You!" Vitellius shouted as he saw Sanct' Germain. "Still here! Come with us!"

Sanct' Germain addressed the tribune who stood beside him, a miserable expression in his downcast eyes. "A fortunate night for you, Tuller, to be the companion of your Emperor."

"I think," Tuller said quietly, "that you were the one—"

"It would hardly be appropriate for the Emperor to be seen with a foreigner of my reputation," Sanct' Germain protested.

Vitellius had come up to Sanct' Germain and now he wagged a thick finger at him. "No, no. I'm going in disguise. You'll see. Caecina here, he's got it all worked out. Linen tunicae. Leather belts. No one will know us."

Sanct' Germain doubted that, for though Vitellius had been in Rome for less than two months, his regular excursions to the lupanar were already legendary. "Great Caesar," he said in a controlled tone, "you may be able to disguise yourself, but I, sadly, am well-known to the gladiators and bestiarii. I would be deeply shocked if any should come to recognize you through me."

This argument got through the wine fumes that clouded the Emperor's mind. He reached for his companion and clapped an arm around Caecina's shoulder. "Maybe we better not take him," he said dubiously.

"Maybe we better not," Caecina agreed, interrupting his song.

"Take the tribune," Vitellius said with the sagacity of drunkenness. "Tuller's a good fellow. Let him take his pick of the whores. He'll pound 'em. It'll be good sport."

From the expression in Caius Tuller's eyes, the last thing he wanted to do was share this intoxicated adventure with the Emperor and his favorite general, though such an evening might mean recognition and promotion. He studied his large square hands. "I am not worthy—"

"Nonsense!" Vitellius draped his other arm over Tuller's shoulder and pulled both Caecina and the tribune closer. "If we leave now," he said in what was supposed to be a conspiratorial whisper, "then by the time dinner's over, we'll be out of range of this pile. We can be pronging whores and listening to the gladiators boast."

Caecina struck up his song again, laughing as it grew more outrageous.

Sanct' Germain stepped back, away from the strange trio that moved off down the hall erratically. He watched until the three men had stumbled through the tall doors to the vestibule, then turned toward a side room that gave onto the extensive neglected gardens. He went quickly through the overgrown paths to the wall.

By the time the Emperor and his two companions had reached the lupanar, Sanct' Germain was outside the city walls, walking swiftly toward Villa Ragoczy.

Contents of a note scribbled on a handkerchief and dropped before Aumtehoutep for his master.

Sanct' Germain:

It hasn't been possible for me to avoid Justus' guards. I have longed to be with you, but I haven't dared to act.

Now I must see you. I must speak with you. I must be with you again.

In six days Justus will leave for the imperial villa near Antium. He has set his slaves to guard me and spy on me, but there must be a way. You have told me that you will not desert me. Come to me while he is gone.

There are times I fear I will become distracted, like his first wife. She is still alive, you know, and kept in seclusion. All the slaves say that she is mad. Poor Corinna, if Justus used her as he has me. At least he can no longer touch her where she has gone. She has escaped him.

Sanct' Germain, as you love me, help me.

Olivia

3

AUTUMN HAD turned warm, giving a last, lingering kiss to the seven hills before the chill winds would sweep in from the north. Harvest festivals had lasted longer than usual, to take advantage of the splendid weather. The Games had been extended by order of the Emperor, so that all Rome buzzed with enthusiasm. On this last day, the new hydraulic organ in the Circus Maximus was to be played for the first time. Vitellius had declared that at the end of the day all victors would be awarded their freedom, and for that reason, if no other, betting was carried on with even greater avidity than normal for such Games.

Kosrozd, his arm still stiff from a recent accident, turned to Sanct' Germain as he tugged at the special harness that Sanct' Germain had made for his racing chariot. "I'm not quite used to handling eight reins instead of four, but it makes a difference, having each side of the horse under control." Satisfied, he gave the left-hand stallion a reassuring pat. "It would be a real military advantage, to be able to handle all four horses individually. The mobility alone would be worth the time and trouble necessary to train the charioteers."

Amused by this martial enthusiasm, Sanct' Germain asked, "If you win today, will you offer yourself to the army, to train their charioteers with this new rig?"

"You mean you will free me if I win?" He was very serious, and his eyes searched his master's face.

"I don't imagine I'll have much choice. Vitellius has declared that all winners are to be free, and I don't think he's going to allow any exceptions. The crowd wouldn't let him." Then Sanct' Germain realized that Kosrozd was seriously upset. "There is no question of you leaving my service if you don't want to. You are of my blood now, Kosrozd. There is nothing that will change that, short of the true death."

"Then I have nothing to worry about," Kosrozd said with a sudden smile.

"That's not quite so," Sanct' Germain told him, growing somber.

"Isn't it?" Kosrozd looked about swiftly, making sure they were not being closely observed. "That fall I took in the summer, it would have been a near thing if I hadn't . . . changed. As it is, all that's left is a little stiffness."

"Kosrozd," Sanct' Germain said measuringly, "how many miraculous escapes do you think you can have before some people start asking questions? No, don't answer me yet. I want you to think it over awhile. You've been through a lot and you're learning more than I thought you would. I have no complaints with that. But there is more to this than you might think. You must learn to be circumspect. Otherwise there is real danger that you will not be able to deal well in the world."

"What do you mean?" Kosrozd stared at Sanct' Germain. "I haven't taken blood from anyone unwilling. I haven't bound myself to anyone. Where's the danger?"

"All around you, my friend," Sanct' Germain said quietly. "You are being watched. For that reason alone, you should be cautious, but it's doubly important now. Suppose you were captured, kidnapped, held prisoner. How could you explain your needs? Where would you find sustenance? What would you tell your captors when they tried to harm you and you felt no effect? How would you convince them that you must have your native earth in the soles of your boots or be unable to cross running water, or stay in the sunlight without terrible burns? Have you thought about that?" He waited patiently.

"That spy is gone." Kosrozd was truculent. He knew that Sanct' Germain was right, that he had been flamboyant and foolish, but he hated to admit it.

"You're not sure of that, and neither am I. We know that

someone speaking Armenian left Ostia with one tall bodyguard a few days after I spoke to Arashnur. However, someone informed on Kyrillos, and he is in prison now because of that. Arashnur may be afraid of me, but he will not give up so easily, I think. He wants you, and he'll do everything he can to have you. Never doubt that."

Kosrozd looked down at his feet. "Perhaps you're right, my master. But you forget what it is to change. It happened to you a long time ago, and for me, it's only a few short years." He tried to laugh. "What shall I do, then? Should I lose?"

Sanct' Germain could not quite smile but there was deep compassion in his eyes. "I leave that up to you. You shouldn't be ostentatious about it, whatever you decide to do. But if there is another accident in the arena, this time you cannot entirely escape from it. I will set you to training other charioteers and their teams, but there can be no more recoveries." He put one small hand on Kosrozd's shoulder. "If you win your freedom, so much the better. But it has been yours for the taking for three years. You had only to ask."

There was a warning shout behind them as the teams for a novelty race were led up toward the Gates of Life.

Kosrozd looked with contempt on the teams. The first was a tall chariot drawn by two ostriches. The charioteer held the reins tightly since the unpleasant tempers of these birds were well-known. A second chariot was behind it, held by six nervous bestiarii. This chariot was drawn by two dark brown Scythian bears that made low distressed sounds to each other and fretted at the restraints of yoke and harness.

"Ever since Nero had those chariot races with camels, these foolish novelty races have gained in popularity," Kosrozd said with a disgusted shake of his head. "It's a disgrace to the art. There's no skill in driving such a team, aside from luck and survival. The confusion of the animals is all the crowd wants to see. It's a waste of chariots and animals, and it cheapens real racing."

"You're a purist," Sanct' Germain said. "You don't have to bristle like that. I agree with you. What else goes into the arena against those?" He thought that ostriches and bears were quite enough, but there were never less than four chariots in a race. "The other teams are equally appropriate, I assume."

"There's a team of oryx and a team of leopards. Quite a challenge, in their own way. They'll be fortunate if any of them come out through the Gates of Life." Kosrozd put his hand on the flank of his team leader. "He's sweating." He motioned to one of the grooms. "Take my team into the holding stable. These beasts are upsetting them." As the groom obeyed, he looked back at Sanct' Germain. "I'll avoid collisions, if I can."

"All I ask of you is that you use good judgment," Sanct' Germain replied. "That, and remind you to be careful of strangers. I've learned to heed my feelings and I've felt the pricking of danger along my spine since that night in Modestinus' garden."

"That was months ago," Kosrozd said, dismissing the matter.

"If Arashnur was willing to take years to find you, and learn about me, a few months are not apt to discourage him." He folded his arms and the silver bracelets on his wrists glowed in the muted light. "Have a care, Kosrozd."

"I will. I will." He touched his amber slave collar. "But it would be a delight to lose this before all Rome."

"That can happen anytime you ask. The Reds will like it if you win, and you can have your moment of triumph. Remember, though, that the loss of that collar might lead to the loss of other things, including the liberty you desire." He glanced over his shoulder as the cry of a leopard sounded nearby. "I had better leave. This is getting too crowded." He waved to the bestiarii handling the chariots with the two big cats yoked to it.

Kosrozd frowned at the leopards. "I've seen them before. They're both killers. Necredes wants blood on the sand."

Sanct' Germain nodded. He had sensed the lust in the crowd, the eager anticipation of slaughter. Two years before, Nero would have forbidden a race like the one being readied now, but the Emperor had changed and tastes had changed with him. Vitellius enjoyed the sight of carnage, and the people of Rome were happy to follow his example. "He only supplies what's wanted."

"Sometimes I think that one day that's all it will be—blood and death and spectacle." He shook off his mood and gave Sanct' Germain a grin. "By then, I'll be out of it."

"You've only to ask. Don't forget your danger now, though." He stepped back.

"You'll watch from the imperial box?" Kosrozd called after him.

"Yes." He turned away, and in a few long strides entered the passageway under the stands. He moved quickly through the shadows, past trainers and animals, past cells into which the condemned were jammed, awaiting the last few minutes of sunlight and space they would know, past the professional fighters, each jealous and proud of his skill at killing. Sanct' Germain had been there too often to notice them. Now his dark eyes were distant and his thoughts turned to Olivia. He had managed to see her twice while Justus was away, and both times, though she had not complained, there had been too little time and too much risk. It was no longer enough to give her pleasure and fulfillment; nothing he could do could erase the brutal use her husband forced on her. She told him little, and that reluctance to speak was more eloquent of her suffering than any words would be.

An imperial slave greeted Sanct' Germain as he stepped into the mural-lined hall that led to the imperial box. "Vitellius Caesar awaits you."

"I'm honored." The exchange was automatic, almost senseless. Sanct' Germain fell into step behind the slave as they made their way between officers of the new Imperial Guard. The sound of the crowd echoed through the narrow hallway like the rush of the sea.

Then the slave stood aside, and Sanct' Germain stepped into the imperial box and inclined his head to Aulus Vitellius.

"Greetings, Ragoczy Sanct' Germain Franciscus," Vitellius bellowed, holding up a thick-fingered hand. He was slumped amid pillows on the marble throne, his imperial toga sloppily draped and the wreath on his brow at a rakish angle. Beside him, two slaves tended a little table on which wine and cold meats were laid. "Have some wine, if you like." He broke off his hospitality as he flung himself forward, pointing delightedly toward the spina.

The oryx-drawn chariot had been brought down by the leopards, one of which had already climbed on the nearer antelope's back and was getting down to the serious business of killing the animal. Both charioteers were tugging uselessly on the reins, panic visible in their features. The second oryx made a futile attempt to pull the chariot free of the leopards, and in the next moment the two vehicles were tangled together and blood gouted onto the sand.

Succumbing to fear, the charioteer of the oryx scrambled out of the wreckage and started running toward the far end of the arena and the Gates of Life. He had not gone far when the ostrich chariot came around the end of the spina, and he ran toward the huge birds, shouting to the driver and waving his arms to slow them. He had almost reached the chariot when one of the birds kicked out in that vicious, forward thrust of a clawed foot and disemboweled the terrified charioteer. As he fell forward and the ostriches moved over him, the crowd hooted with laughter.

"A great show! I hope the bears last long enough to fight the leopards," Vitellius said, wiping his streaming eyes with the hem of his toga.

To the Emperor's right, his favorite general sprawled between four Imperial Guards. Today Aulus Caecina Alienus was very grand in golden lorica and silk caracalla, with rings clustered on his fingers like warts. If anything, he was more drunken than Vitellius. He gave Sanct' Germain a broad wink. "Good sport today," he declared, emphatically slurring the words.

"So it would seem," Sanct' Germain responded dryly. He went to the chair indicated, and seated himself.

"Now that's what irks me," Vitellius said as he gulped down another cup of wine. "That's what I don't like."

The ostriches had rounded the spina and were heading toward the far end of the Circus Maximus. The crowd broke into greedy shouts as the huge birds came up against the chariot drawn by bears.

"What?" Sanct' Germain asked, ignoring the sounds around him.

"That foreign clothing. Black, too. Hardly fitting for a true Roman." He held out his cup to the waiting slaves.

"But I am foreign," Sanct' Germain reminded the Emperor gently. "I wear this because it is similar to what I wore years ago in my own land."

"Dacia," Vitellius said sagely and turned to Caecina for confirmation.

"Yes, but I'm not a Daci," Sanct' Germain reminded him.

"From Dacia," Caecina agreed. "We talked about that, Vitellius. I said I didn't like it."

The bears had risen to their feet in order to deal with the ostriches, and had tossed their charioteer from the flimsy vehicle. Amusement erupted all over the Circus Maximus as the two bears tussled with each other, one trying to reach the battered charioteer, the other determined to seize the huge birds.

"The organ will be played while they pour fresh sand," the Emperor informed Sanct' Germain grandly. "A special moment today, the first call of that instrument. It had better be all you've promised."

"It is," Sanct' Germain said confidently. He had spent three nights working on the great brass pipes, adjusting each one with meticulous care so that they had the same clarion tongues as the military trumpets that called the legions to battle.

"We're all looking forward to it," Caecina told him with sudden intensity.

"I'm flattered," Sanct' Germain responded, making no attempt to hide his uninterest.

The bears had broken their yokes, and one of them was running free in pursuit of the ostriches while the other, trailing the remains of the chariot, mauled the unlucky slave who had been their driver. A hush fell over the Circus Maximus as the first bear rounded the end of the spina and saw the leopards.

"Hush!" Vitellius ordered, leaning forward again. "Look at that!"

The bear had started toward the leopards as they pulled apart the oryx. One of the leopards raised his head and growled a warning. The bear paused, then rose on his hind legs and advanced, huge curved claws swiping the air as he neared the big cats.

"Get him! Get him!" Vitellius shouted, though whether he addressed the bear or the leopard, not even he knew.

Forgotten by bear and cat alike, the ostriches sped on around the spina as the bear began its rush for the leopards.

Screams, hoarse shouts, clashed together as the battle between bear and leopards was joined. The sound was like a crashing ocean storm, battering at the walls of the Circus Maximus and the nearly eighty-thousand people who crowded together in the stands.

"We're going to have to add more seats," Caecina shouted to Vitellius as the cacophony grew.

"What?" The Emperor was less than an arm's length from his general, but could hardly hear him.

One of the leopards had sunk his fangs into the bear's shoulder as the bear raked the spotted fur with its claws. The animals went down, rolling on the blood-streaked sand, each tearing at the other while the people howled their pleasure.

When it ended there was one ostrich still alive, and Vitellius ordered it presented with a laurel wreath, since the huge, bad-tempered bird was clearly the victor.

Vitellius was decidedly unsteady on his feet when he rose to announce the first demonstration of the new hydraulic organ, which was to be played by a musician brought to Rome for the occasion.

As the stirring strains of *The Song of Jupiter Triumphant* rolled through the Circus, Vitellius turned a satisfied face to Sanct' Germain. "Very good. That's very good."

"It is what was required of me," Sanct' Germain said cautiously.

"A feat worthy of a Roman," the Emperor suggested slyly.

"It is kind of you to say so." Sanct' Germain glanced uneasily at the nine armored guards in the imperial box, and at the drunken Caecina, who gave him a fatuous smile.

"I have been thinking about that," Vitellius confided as he pushed his wreath farther back on his head. "You've done a great deal for Rome. Not just the hydraulic organ. No." He snapped his fingers for more wine. "There's the mules you raise and sell the army. That's patriotic of you."

"It's profitable business," Sanct' Germain corrected him.

"Same thing, same thing." He took a deep draft of wine. "It's a fine vintage. Not like the Greeks with their resins and honey. This is tipple for a man. Look at it. Red as blood, sweet as puncturing a virgin, strong as . . ."—he searched for a word—"strong as . . . good steel, by the she-wolf's tits!"

Sanct' Germain closed his eyes a moment before saying, "You do this foreigner great honor and I am grateful." He was also apprehensive, wondering what he could do or say that would allow him to leave the imperial box quickly.

"The foreigner part, that's what I wanted to see you about." The Emperor set down his wine cup. "You shouldn't have to be a foreigner. Be a Roman. I'll make you a citizen. Just like that. The Senate will approve. For once," he added darkly.

"But I can't do that," Sanct' Germain said as gently as he could. "It is a great compliment, and I am sincerely grateful to you for offering me Roman citizenship. But I must refuse."

"Refuse?" Vitellius' heavy face was starting to change color, from ruddy to plum.

"I must," Sanct' Germain insisted as kindly as he could. "I

have an obligation to those of my blood, and to my native soil. My first loyalty must remain there."

Vitellius drew back. "Loyalty to Dacia, and you not a Daci?"

He wished the offer had never been made, and certainly not here, with Caecina to watch. Sanct' Germain sighed, and hoped that the Emperor would interpret it as disappointment. "The Daci are not the only people who have lived there. Those of my blood are far older, and as I was their prince once, I cannot desert them." He looked squarely at Vitellius. "You have loyal troops, Caesar. Would you, for a treasured honor, turn away from them?"

"Troops? Do you head an army?" The Emperor folded his arms and smeared a pepper sauce on the front of his imperial toga.

"Not for many, many years. I have my followers, though, and they are as much a part of me as your Guard is of you."

Vitellius snorted, but it was easy to see that he was mollified by this comparison. "You're a fool, Franciscus. Become a Roman and the world is open to you."

"It would dishonor my house." This was usually a clinching argument with a Roman. He had used it once, a century before, to Divus Julius. That first canny, acute Emperor had turned tired, knowing eyes on him and said wryly, "And are the rest of . . . your blood . . . as clever? I could wish them for allies." This Emperor peered at him through red, bleary eyes and said, "Can't do that. Without honor to the house, the whole of Rome falls."

"So you see my predicament. What would you do, in my place?" Sanct' Germain asked, taking advantage of the Emperor's assertion.

Vitellius gave a ponderous wag of his head. "Yes. Yes. I understand now. Does you credit, your conviction, but it's a shame. When I think of the access you've got. Snow leopards, tigers, apes, all of them, and what it would mean to Rome . . ."

Sanct' Germain could not quite conceal his smile. "You're welcome to command me at any time, Caesar. If that is what you want of me."

"Good of you," Vitellius said, unaware of the ironic edge in Sanct' Germain's voice. "If you change your mind about being a citizen, let me know. Make you a Roman overnight. You'd like it. You could own dozens of gladiators."

At the end of the spina the hydraulic orgân fell silent and the crowd cheered anew. The musician rose and took off the rag that bound his ears and prevented him from being deafened by the blare of the instrument he played.

"If you wish to do something for me," Sanct' Germain said with a nod toward the hydraulic organ, "you might give that player his freedom. He has done well and deserves recognition. Very few musicians can perform so skillfully."

The blurry lines of the Emperor's face were not promising. "I'll consider it," Vitellius said indistinctly and loftily as he motioned for the next event to begin.

Report to the Emperor in the investigation of the smuggling activities of Kyrillos, captain of the merchant vessel *Gull of Byzantium.*

> To the Procurator Senior:
>
> Following the instructions of your office and the Senate, and upon behalf of the Emperor, we have detained the captain, Kyrillos, who was identified in our first report as being the master of the vessel the *Gull of Byzantium,* which is owned by the distinguished foreigner, Ragoczy Sanct' Germain Franciscus, who resides near Rome.
>
> Acting on the recommendation of an unknown citizen, officers of the port inspected this vessel and found that it was carrying wheat, and that such did not appear on the manifest.
>
> We have questioned the captain repeatedly, with only moderate application of torture, and he remains adamant on three points that were disputed at the time of his arrest.
>
> I) that the purchase of wheat was a fortunate accident

and not part of a continuing plan to smuggle forbidden goods into Roman ports,

II) that the opportunity to purchase the wheat came from men who approached him, identified themselves as Armenian and told him that the grain was available. Since Kyrillos was aware of the situation in Rome, he says that he decided to take a chance and sell the grain covertly after he arrived in Ostia. He claims now that the whole venture was a plot against him from mariners jealous of his success in trade.

III) that at no time was his patron, said Ragoczy Sanct' Germain Franciscus, part of his plan to carry illegal grain, that Franciscus had no knowledge of the transaction and that he was acting on his own and without instructions from the owner of his ship. Further, he declares that Ragoczy Sanct' Germain Franciscus has often admonished him to obey the laws of Rome to the letter and at no time to seek to circumvent those laws. Interviews with captains of other vessels owned by this man confirm what Kyrillos has said.

Therefore, we seek to know how to dispose of this case. The captain, Kyrillos, has been denied the right to sail from Ostia or any Roman port, and until he appears in court there is no way to determine how he should be treated. Because this is a first offense and because his record is good, we would recommend a light sentence. With his background, he could be bonded and his bond remanded to the state until the full amount of his contraband be returned. It seems a waste to send him to the galleys, where he would die within a year from the severity of the labor. Condemnation to the arena is not commensurate with the nature of his crime.

We await your opinion and will be diligent in carrying out your orders. Included with this letter is a full and accurate transcription of the statement given by Kyrillos. For the eyes of the procurator and Emperor only, and for their action.

Hail Vitellius,
Cyprius Laeteur
Customs Magistrate, Port of Ostia
on the twenty-third day of
September in the 821st
Year of the City

4

THREE DAYS BEFORE, the moon had been full, and now it floated through the sky, leaving a thin wake of clouds. The season was turning, bringing cold nights and the promise of rain.

Sanct' Germain stood in the window of his bedroom, looking out at the tarnished silver of the night. His loose robe dangled half-open, caught at the waist with a carelessly tied sash. To his particular eyes, the night was filled with splendor that the brightness of the day hid. Now, in the time when owls hunted and cats slunk and scampered in the hills, the world seemed to be more truly his. Sanct' Germain loved the night, was part of it.

"My master?" From the bed Tishtry's voice followed him and cut into his contemplation.

"Yes?" He did not turn, but he spoke affectionately to her. "Come to the window, Tishtry."

Obediently she rose from the bed and padded across the mosaic floor. "What is it?"

"Look at the night." His dark eyes saw far into the moon-shadowed dimness. He spoke distantly even as he put his arm around her shoulder. "There. By the orchard. There's a bat flitting like a bit of soot. Look at the trees—they're like storm clouds anchored to the soil. They're like us in that." He bent and kissed her shiny dark hair, but still looked out the window. "Oh, Tishtry, I haven't wanted to be cruel."

"Well, you haven't been," she said heartily. "You've been more kind to me than many." She was naked and the night was chilly, but her good nature kept her at his side, shivering faintly.

"Does it matter that I'm sending you away?" The darkness was familiar, but tonight it only served to reinforce his loneliness.

"From your bed?" She turned her head to rest it on his shoulder. "You know how I feel about this. It is my decision, not yours. You're the master and you're good to me. Your ways aren't my ways, but it's your right." She put her strong arm around his waist. "You've given me pleasure and you've been more than fair with me."

"Do you regret this?" His small hand touched the curve of her breast, her hip, with familiar affection.

"No. You don't just use me, the way some have. I won't say I wouldn't like it better if you functioned as other men— I would. You've known that all along. But it isn't that important, really." She was getting colder and there was gooseflesh all over her.

"Isn't it?" For the first time he looked at her.

"No, not really. Think how long this lasts, even your way. An hour, perhaps two, and all the rest are left open. I am in your bed twice in a month, certainly not more than a dozen hours. The rest of the time I'm with my horses, or in the arena or cleaning tack or one of all the other things I do in my life. Why should I trade all that for a dozen hours, no matter how pleasant?" She leaned forward and kissed him heartily. "I'll miss you, because you care so much for my pleasure."

The sad, ironic smile he gave her was lost in the darkness. He hugged her, then said, "You're freezing, Tishtry."

"It's getting cold," she admitted. "I'm fine."

Sanct' Germain untied the sash he wore and drew her close to him inside his voluminous robe. "Better?"

"Of course," she said with an indulgent giggle.

He gazed out into the night one last time. "It's beautiful," he said dreamily.

"You always like the night better than day," she reminded him as she laid one hand on his chest.

"Night and I, we're part of each other." It had been that way for as long as his memories reached back. In legends, his kind were inexorably linked with the dark. At night, he had no need of his earth-lined boots, except to cross running water. At no other time did he feel the same relaxed surge of power, or the same elusive peace. "You will share the night, eventually."

Tishtry pressed her powerful, taut body close to his. "There are a few hours yet until dawn. Since this is the last time, shall we lie together again?"

He had always liked her forthrightness, however bluntly she spoke. Even when she had asked that there be an end between them, he felt neither regret nor rancor. It was impossible to feel those things with Tishtry. "Would you like that?"

With one hand he smoothed back her hair as he bent to kiss her.

She shrugged and nodded at once. "I enjoy what you do. Since this is the last time, it would please me." She stopped and stared into his enigmatic eyes. "Why were you willing to let me go? Why did you accept? You are my master, and could have commanded that I stay with you."

"And have you unwilling?" The question did not surprise him, but he sighed anyway. "You have given me a great deal, Tishtry, and I know that though my ways are not your ways, or not yet your ways, you have learned to take pleasure in what we do. It was enough for me, and I like you. But I suppose now I've come to want . . . to need, something more. Not long ago it was enough to bring one to the height of fulfillment or terror. It satisfied me. I was, if not content, resigned. Now . . ." The word ended and he was silent.

"It's because of that patrician lady, isn't it?" There was no blame in the question, not yet. She waited while he sought for an answer to give her, that he could accept himself.

"If I hadn't been changing, Olivia might not have attracted me. I have lived long enough to accept change." Even as he said it, he knew it was not entirely true. He had never learned to regard loss as inevitable. There had been times when he had closed himself off from humanity, taking the aloof stance he had learned when he was a boy and a prince. Something always broke through, and there was the full weight and pain of grief to endure again. Olivia had surprised him, touched him before he was aware how deeply she moved him. The memory of their last meeting, more than two months before, filled his mind, an overwhelming presence. Every motion, every glance, every nuance of speech was vivid in his mind.

"Will you give me to Kosrozd?" Tishtry asked, wondering if he heard her.

"To Kosrozd? Why? Do you want him? Since he changed, he is as I am." He had thought she understood that.

"I know that. It seemed likely." She hesitated.

"What is it? Is there someone you'd prefer?" He lifted her chin up and smiled down at her. "As your master, the least I can do is see that you're properly provided for. Roman law requires that of me."

Now that she was in a position to ask a favor of him, she

became shy. "I don't want you to think that I prefer a slave to you."

"But you do, don't you?" He held her a little more tightly. "Who is it, then? If it's in my power, I'll give him to you, and free both of you, if that's your wish."

"Free?" She made a sound not unlike a snort. "When my days in the arena are through, then I'll want my freedom, but until then, I'd rather have a master who is generous and kind than be cast out into the world with my skills and my teams and turn bondservant in order to support myself."

"All right then," Sanct' Germain promised her. "When you are ready to leave the arena, tell me and I will free you and whatever man you wish, and see that you have a house and stables of your own." He hugged her impulsively. "Tishtry, you have been a joy to bed. I'm grateful to you, and I want you to know it."

"You don't have to tell me." She grinned because he had.

He pulled the robe tightly around them both, trying to hold off the melancholy that had got hold of him. "What do you want of me, this last time?"

"I don't know," she said rather slowly. "It would be nice to have something extraordinary, but I don't know what it would be." Her arms, strong from her life as a charioteer, held him increasingly forcefully. "I want . . . I want . . ." she murmured, her lips brushing his chest as she thought. At last she had it. "I want to lie atop you and have you move under me, so that nothing, not even your touch, can hinder my pleasure." She laughed at her own audacity, knowing that he might refuse her. She knew always, if he did not, that she was the slave and he the master, and that, given a free choice, she would have preferred a lover who used her as a man uses a woman, and who would give her children.

Sanct' Germain's brows rose with amusement. "Very well, if that's what you wish." With his arm and his robe around her, he walked through the dark bedchamber. As they reached the bed, he stopped. "Tell me where you would like me to lie, and I will do it."

"Really?" No man had made such an offer to her, and the satisfaction of the moment was delicious to her. "I want you to lie back. You may have a pillow, if you wish," she added magnanimously. "Lie across the bed, so that your feet touch the floor."

He turned, dropping the robe at his feet, and sank back. "Like this, Tishtry?"

"A little higher, my master. That's better." She stood, studying him in the gloom as he lay back. "You must caress and kiss me until I tell you to stop." Fleetingly she realized this would be the only time in her life when she could order a lover so completely to her own satisfaction, and that certainly held her a moment, almost reluctant to continue for fear there would be too much pleasure and it would shake her resolve to leave him. Sanct' Germain had been a considerate partner, willing to indulge her, anxious to gratify her as well as himself. She doubted very much that she would ever find a lover more expert in all things sensual but one. Expertise was not everything, and she had begun to feel the first touch of age within her, which, at twenty-eight, did not surprise her. It was time for her to establish herself with children, and she would never, could never get them with her master. Giving a tiny, fatalistic sigh, she decided to make the most of his offer for this last evening. Following the dictates of her senses, she said, "First I will lie so that our lips may meet and you will kiss me in many ways. I will tell you when to stop."

"Very well," he said gravely, though there was amusement in his dark eyes.

"And then I will tell you how we're to proceed." She announced this as if expecting a last-minute contradiction.

"As you like." His voice in the cool darkness warmed her with desire.

"If you think of anything more that I might like, you are to ask me if I want to do it. Let me decide everything." She knew she was postponing their lovemaking, fearing that the reality would be less than her imagination promised her. "I'm ready now."

His arms opened. "Then come to me, Tishtry."

Slowly, luxuriously, she stretched out atop him; her well-muscled, compact body was trained to respond to balance and movement so this new experience awakened her senses much the way that racing did when she stood on the backs of her horses as they galloped around the spina while the crowd roared above them. Sanct' Germain was of trim, stocky build and his strength was, as she knew, enormous. She did not worry about crushing him or inadvertently hurting him as she lay on him. Her mouth touched his, lips parting.

She moved over him leisurely, lingering when his lips discovered another of those mysterious sites that produced a new spurt of delight or deeper satisfaction. She pushed herself up on her arms, arching her body away from him as her thighs responded to his gentle coaxing, spreading to admit his questing hands and kisses.

There was a sound in the garden, and for a moment both were tensely still, alert and listening.

"What was it?" Tishtry whispered.

"I don't know. Don't be concerned." He reached around her and drew her tight against him once more.

"I . . ." she began, feeling the exultation slipping away from her.

"Shush." His hands were amorous and sure, knowing precisely where to touch her to restore and inflame her desires. His mouth sought out the center of her passion, drawing new pleasure from her as water is drawn from a well.

For Tishtry it was difficult to speak, to breathe. She feared for that instant when the spasm finally released her—joyously feared that she would burst apart. Her eyes were half-closed and there was a sound in her throat between laughter and moaning. Her body became a vortex of fulfillment, and she was caught in the rapturous whirlpool that coiled and spun from that one pulsing point of almost unendurable pleasure.

When at last Tishtry fell beside Sanct' Germain, her breath had nearly returned to normal. She lay beside him, silent, eyes on the pale, moon-clear night beyond the window. There were things in her mind that she wanted to say to her master, but she found words for none of them.

Sanct' Germain understood something of this, and accepted her quiet. He relaxed, listening to the rhythm of the night that he knew so well. When he spoke to her, he said, "I will miss you, Tishtry."

She turned a startled face toward him. "I will miss you as well, my master."

"But you will not change your mind?" He did not expect that of her, but it was easy to ask.

"No," she said slowly when she had given the question her consideration. "That was . . . more than I've ever had. But I don't think I could stand to have it too often. You were something like those fig pastries the Egyptians make—the first and second bites are delicious as the food of the gods, but after that, there is too much sweetness, with the honey and the almonds and the cinnamon, and the dates are cloying instead of rich. If I did this too often, I would become like those Persian soldiers who eat the poppy dust. Soon there would be nothing in the world but the hunger, the craving, and all the pleasure would be gone, not only from this, but from everything."

Her insight surprised him. "It can happen that way," he admitted, remembering too many times when it had. There had been a time when that was no consideration with him, but that was before King Shalmaneser raised the walls of Nimrud, when he felt more rage than loneliness.

Tishtry reached blindly for his hand. "It will be strange, not to be the master's woman. . . ."

"You are always of my blood," he said somberly.

"That is not the same. I don't know if I'll like the next one. There must be a next one, I suppose. For many reasons." She was suddenly, irrationally angry. "Why didn't you have more of us? Then I wouldn't have to get used to seeing another woman with you when there had not been one before. You've never met the patrician woman here."

"You've never objected to Kosrozd," he pointed out.

"Kosrozd is different. Once he changed, he did not lie with you. You told me that such things do not happen. When you change, you lie with those unchanged, not one another." There was an accusation in these words and she waited for him to try to mollify her.

He looked away from her, saying in a remote way, "I have never experienced it for myself but it was said when I was young, that if there is true acceptance and deep love, such things can happen. Those of my blood can lie together. I have never known of it. After all this time, I doubt it is possible, that kind of intimacy, but the wish for it still remains." It was an effort to turn his mind from such unfruitful speculations.

She had known him long enough to feel his pain, and she was aware that she had overstepped that unspoken limit behind which he hid his anguish. "My master," she said, contrite. "I did not mean . . ."

"I know." He turned toward her again. "Well, we must deal with this problem. What would you like me to do? Do you want to leave Rome?" he asked her gently. "You might prefer to be sent away. I have other estates, and you may live at any one you like with whomever you like, until you want to retire and be freed."

"If you wish to send me away," she said after a pause, her voice so small it was hardly audible, "that is your right. You may do with me as you will. And I would not blame you, truly I would not. But I would be very sad." She had no intention of weeping for this strange man. Romans despised tears, she knew, and though Sanct' Germain was not a Roman, she had never seen his eyes moist.

"Of course I don't want to send you away," he assured her, feeling a touch of annoyance. Tishtry in general was a sensible woman. It had been her wish that they part. She had asked him to let her choose one of the charioteers or bestiarii who liked her and would give her children. Now this. He propped himself on his elbow and studied her. "Tishtry, tell me what is disturbing you." He said it casually, as if they were talking about the merits of his new harness design, but it was an order and he expected to be obeyed.

"Nothing," she said curtly.

Patiently he thought of her life, and from what he knew of her he formed his next questions. "Would you like to return home to Armenia? Do you still miss your family? Tell me." He touched her cheek where there was a trail of wetness.

Her answer was not direct. She had no intention of telling him that she had come to prefer Rome to the rugged hills of her own land. "The last time I raced, there was a scholar from Armenia who talked to me afterward. He was very pleased with my team and my skill. He asked a great many questions about my racing and training. He said that it had been a great mistake to have such a treasure sold to Rome." She was staring at the ceiling where the murals were almost invisible in the dark, picturing in her mind the bright glare of the Circus Maximus.

Sanct' Germain felt himself grow cold. "An Armenian scholar?" he inquired casually.

"Very distinguished. He spoke with Necredes in Greek. You must not think that he was bent and gray, however—he was fairly young with a strong face." She wondered why it was so important that Sanct' Germain know how much she was admired. It was more than the petty satisfaction she felt in making him jealous. "He was respectful and attentive."

"I'm not surprised," Sanct' Germain said dryly. "Tell me, did this Armenian scholar have an accent?"

Tishtry laughed. "*All* courtiers have accents," she said. "The whole court speaks strangely."

That was true enough, Sanct' Germain told himself. And it would be unusual for Tishtry to recognize whether the scholar spoke in the courtly manner, or whether there was a touch of the Persian in his words. He tried to convince himself that this was needless worry—that Led Arashnur had left Rome months ago. "Tell me more about this Armenian scholar: what kinds of questions did he ask you?"

"Oh," she said blithly, beginning to enjoy herself, "he wanted to know everything. He said he was going to make a report to the king, and I told him I had already appeared before Tiridates when he came to Rome to see Nero. That impressed this scholar, and he inquired about when I had come here, and how long I had been performing in the arena. I told him quite a lot about that. Even about that time Necredes wanted me to take my team through lions and you protected me when I refused. That impressed him a great deal, my master."

"Did it?" Sanct' Germain asked ironically.

"Yes," she insisted. "I told him all about you. He didn't believe much of it."

"All?" he repeated.

She stifled a chuckle. "Well, not quite all. But it was enough for him to know that you don't abuse your slaves and that though you're not a noble or a citizen of Rome, you're still no one to meddle with."

Sanct' Germain reached for a pillow and dragged it under him. "I'm grateful for that. I wonder why this Armenian scholar took so much time on such matters. Surely he can't be planning to include that in his report to the king."

"There aren't a lot of Armenians in Rome," she pointed out, her momentary pique entirely forgotten. She was pleased that the scholar had been so attentive, and wanted Sanct' Germain to understand that this was no idle compliment she had been given. There were many men who admired her, and some who regarded her with avid, lustful eyes. The scholar had been different. He had cared about how she lived. "Try to understand, my master, that I was something new to him. My father and brothers often performed at the king's command, but that was years ago, before my brothers were sent to the army to train the charioteers for battle. Since then, not many of the court of Tiridates have seen the kind of demonstration I do. He was curious about it. He wanted to know how I came by my skill, who had bought me and why, and how I was treated. He wanted to know if there were others who had my abilities, and I said that so far none had been seen in Rome. No one has ever cared about that before."

"Ah." Sanct' Germain kissed her forehead lightly.

"Should I not have spoken?" she asked, suddenly anxious.

"It may not have been entirely wise," he said after a moment. "Never mind, Tishtry. It's good to know that someone appreciates your skill. Be glad that he was good enough to tell you. In future, however," he added in a more astringent tone, "do not be too open with such strangers, even if they are from Armenia."

Tishtry turned to huddle close to his side. "I only wanted to praise you, my master."

He put his arm over her shoulder. "I'm flattered," he said with weary sincerity. "Yet be circumspect. With the Emperor in so much trouble, and the people of Rome ready to pull down the city walls if it will bring them grain, there are many who want to turn this to their own advantage. Strangers, even those who give you genuine compliments, may have hidden reasons to do so. Being strangers ourselves, we must be particularly careful, since if there is to be trouble, it will be our own first." He did not want his last night with Tishtry to end so badly. With an affectionate squeeze he took her in his arms. "I am being very cautious because I have learned that it is necessary. Don't be distraught." He kissed her again, more determinedly.

"Are you angry?" she asked, still very concerned.

"No. Why should I be? If anyone deserves anger, it's myself. Don't put too much stock in my worry." His hands followed the line of her breasts, her hips.

"Are we in danger?" She said it quickly, as if the question were all one word.

"Those like me are always in danger. In time we get used to it. When you have changed, you will learn."

Their next kiss was interrupted by a sound from the animal pens, some distance from Villa Ragoczy. Sanct' Germain looked up sharply.

"What is that?" Tishtry asked as the distressed yapping came again.

"Something's bothering the wolves," he answered, frowning. The wolves had come from Carnuntum two months ago, and though nervous at first, had quickly learned to be calm.

The sounds increased, and over the sounds of the wolves there was added the coughing cry of leopards.

Sanct' Germain rose and pulled his robe about him. "I'd better find out what it is."

"The keepers can do that," Tishtry said softly.

"If your horses were neighing, would you say the same thing?" He asked it gently, and did not expect an answer as he bent to pull on his soft high-heeled boots.

She had no argument to make, and in fact was growing alarmed over the noise from the compound. She drew herself into a ball in the middle of the bed as Sanct' Germain rose. A moment later he strode from the room, calling for Aumtehoutep as he went.

Saddened, Tishtry pulled the largest pillow toward her and wrapped her arm around it, trying to recall the splendor of their last night together.

Text of a letter from Caecilia Meda Clemens, Domita Janusian, to her sister, Atta Olivia Clemens, Domita Silius.

> To Olivia, Domita Silius, familial greetings:
>
> I confess I was amazed to have your letter of October 2, which did not arrive for almost two months, due to severe weather and difficult road conditions. The military dispatches traveled swiftly enough, you may be certain, but a letter such as yours, though you are the wife of a powerful Senator, must wait while the twelfth report of the least experienced tribune is hurried south. Also, there have been certain difficulties on the borders, but that is a state of life here in Lugdunensis. Lutetia is a fairly tolerable city, but there is little to be done to make it really acceptable. The winter begins early here in the north and since we were posted here after our father's

and brothers' misfortunes, I've come to long for that splendid sun that shines on Rome with such profligate glory. Until you have lived in places like this, you can have no idea how truly delightful a place Rome is. To call it the very center of the world is not sufficient.

Which, my dear sister, is why I am puzzled by your request to visit us. How could you bear to leave Rome, even for so short a period as six months, and if you must come, why in the dead of winter, when there is little to do and nothing but hours of boredom?

I told my husband something about you, though I admit it has been very nearly fourteen years since I've seen you. I'm certain you're no longer that awkward child with the berry stains all over her best palla. Strange that I should remember that about you more than any other thing. Do you remember that holiday near Neapolis, visiting our mother's uncle? He had quite a grand estate (or so it seems in retrospect, though after Lutetia, a pigsty in Ostia or an apartment in the worst, most rat-infested insula behind the Forum of Augustus would be preferable to the grandest palace here) and it was near enough to the sea that we could go there for a swim. How long ago that seems. You could not have been more than eight or nine. It is a pity that we didn't spend more time together as children, I suppose, but it might have been awkward. I am fully twelve years older than you are, and it is not remarkable that our education took different turns. I remember what a shock it was to learn that our father had lost so much money and land. How fortunate that Silius was willing to offer for you then.

In your letter you tell me that your husband is unkind, though he's protected our mother and housed her in spite of the disgrace our father and brothers have brought upon us. It may not be a great pleasure to be wed to an old man, but in one of the letters he sent to my husband, he said he has never objected to your lovers. It's foolish to abuse so good a man, Olivia. You must learn to control your desires and work with your husband in partnership. He was unfortunate in his first two wives, and now you treat him shabbily. That is not the way you were raised. I know that, for we had the same nurse and tutors; Isidoros and Bion taught us our obligations along with Greek, you know. Though I haven't used the language in years, the principles they gave us have served me well here.

You cannot imagine how inconvenient everything is. Our villa is never warm enough for four months out of the year. We have a holocaust, of course, but it isn't adequate to the task of heating the rooms. And I will not have the ceilings lowered or open fireplaces put in rooms the way the natives do. The thought of a room with a great open hearth belching out smoke and flames into the room—Romans must draw the line somewhere! I've taken to ordering my clothes made of heavier fabrics, and the people here do make a fairly good woolen cloth. It dyes unevenly, however, and for that reason when we have a rare guest, I insist that we dress properly, no matter what the season. I will not receive a visitor in coarse wool—linen or cotton must be worn. Occasionally Drusus loses patience with me for this, and I must remind him that we are Roman patricians with a certain obligation to our position.

Though we have few messages here, there is a persistent rumor that Vitellius will be brought down. Is not Rome satisfied with this latest Emperor? How dangerous for you, to be close to it all. If that is what is really distressing you, I can certainly understand why you might want to be out of Rome for a few months until all is once again quiet. The last year or so, it seems we've barely had time to change the plaques at the garrison, and we must do it again for the new Emperor.

How different things were when we were in Antioch. There we had a chance for advancement, and there was talk of a great promotion for my husband. Nero had said that after a few more years in Syria and Greece, he would be ready to become a Senator. Now, there is not the least chance in the world of that happening. If we are fortunate we will be shuffled from Gallia to Britannia to Mauretania, and never be one step closer to Rome. Drusus could retire, of course, and he has estates near Syracuse, but everyone would know that he had capitulated, and I won't hear of it.

You have never seen my children, certainly, but I think I have reason to be proud of them. Hilarius is now twelve, and very precocious. One of Drusus' uncles will adopt him and see to his advancement. Fontanus is almost ten, and his tutors say that he has an excellent mind, far superior to the other childrens'. They want to send him to Greece, naturally, to study there, but I think his time could be better spent in Rome. My husband and I have yet to decide the matter. Perhaps Drusus should write to your husband and ask his advice in the matter. Maius is only six, and it is difficult to tell yet how he will turn out. So far he has shown a great liking for soldiers, but there is little else here to attract his attention. Flora is nine and with some effort on my part, she may become a beauty, but it will be work because she has no idea how to dress, and refuses to listen to me when I seek to guide her. If you're willing to have her with you in a few years' time, you may find she alleviates your loneliness as well as doing some good for the family. Salvina is seven, quite robust, which is not a thing I'd encourage in a girl. My baby is Cornelia, who is little more than two. A very well-mannered baby, though, in spite of her foot. The physician here is trying to treat it, for with a limp she may never hope to make a mark for herself in the world. It would be a pity if we had to marry her badly because of that little defect.

I was sorry to hear of our sister's death. Arianus wrote last year to tell us, and I was quite upset. Viridis and I were very close, you know, being only two years apart in age. Imagine being overturned in a chariot on the road to Patavium, getting little more than a broken bone, easily set, and then to have the arm go black, and be killed by fever. I was shocked. What was Arianus thinking of, to let her be treated by local physicians? They're all nothing more than incompetent butchers. Now only you and I are left, my dear Olivia. Four brothers and a sister have left this world too early.

Let me hear from you again soon. It has been years since your last letter, but I thought it was because of our disgrace. How ironic to think that if things had gone as our father wished, I would be in Rome now, part of a powerful family, enjoying the honors my husband had worked so hard to obtain. Yet I don't complain, as that would be a dishonor to our father and our Lares. Certainly, I wish it had been otherwise, but there is little to be done now unless you know of someone willing to help us. I won't ask you to talk to your husband for us, since you seem to be having a little trouble there just now, but when things are easier between you, a word or two would be appreciated. That is, assuming he continues to have influence when matters of the purple are at last decided and someone is Caesar for more than a year continuously.

How much I have written to you! It shows you how I long for your company. Let me counsel you, little sister—strive to be more tolerant of Justus. Men are vain, it's sadly true, but if we are indulgent and don't regard them too critically, they do reward us in the end, and we can then exercise our accumulated power without hindrance. Give that your consideration. These difficulties pass, believe me. By the time my letter reaches you, you'll be wondering why you wrote to me in such dejection. Husbands may be a burden at times, but at least you have Rome to amuse you, and for that, I admit I envy you.

Until I see you again, in Rome, the greetings of my family and myself.

Caecilia Meda Clemens, Domita Janusian
the twenty-first day of November
in the 821st Year of the City,
in Lutetia, Lugdunensis

5

A JANUARY STORM blustered over the hills of Rome. Rain fell in what seemed like handfuls, drenching everything, making the world appear entirely one color, a uniform sandy gray. The stone-flagged streets were awash in the low places between the hills, and in those narrow alleys where there was no paving, carts and men alike sank deep in mud. Over the rattle of the rain there could be heard the occasional shouts and oaths of those who had been trapped by the mud or cut off by water standing too deep in the road. Few people ventured abroad, though the city still reeled under the latest change of government, and a few were grateful to the weather for the relief it brought, and the excuse to stay indoors.

In the house of Cornelius Justus Silius there was water on the floor of the atrium and several household slaves worked to mop it up as it fell. In a few places little wraiths of steam rose, formed by the hot air that circulated just below the marble flooring, heating the house from the great furnace that warmed the small baths as well as serving the ducts that gave access to the spaces between marble floor and brick foundation. Though the rooms were tolerably warm, they were drafty, and the shutters rattled on the windows. For that reason, if no other, Justus was supervising the hanging of heavy Eastern-style draperies in the smaller of the two dining rooms on the east side of the house. This little chamber was in the lee of the wind as well as being painted with particularly attractive murals, and furnished in magnificent style. It was an impressive room, which is precisely what Justus needed this rainy afternoon.

"There, you incompetent idiot!" Justus shouted as he indicated for the third time where the Asian slave should hammer the bracket.

"But, master, there isn't enough—" the slave started to object reasonably.

"I will accept no arguments from you," Justus informed him quietly. "The bracket must go there, or the hangings won't cover both windows and there'll be cold drafts down both our backs."

"Master, forgive me, but we must move the bracket either more to the left or the right or there won't be enough wood under the plaster to hold it. That's what I was trying to explain. . . ." He held out his hand to demonstrate.

"Arguments with me are settled with rod-stripes," Justus warned the Asian slave. "I bought you because I was told you were a carpenter. Now it turns out you don't know how to drive a nail. The last slave who defied me lived long enough to regret it, but no longer."

The Asian turned pale. "I will drive the nail as you wish," he muttered. "But it will not hold."

"Hope for your own sake that it does," Justus said firmly. "This room must be perfect. I will not hesitate to mete out punishment to those responsible, should anything go wrong."

With a drooping of his head, the Asian carpenter turned once again to the impossible site on the wall. Very carefully he moved the nail up a handbreadth and set to work putting in the bracket.

Justus watched from below, holding the leather-braided rod behind his back and flicking it occasionally.

Monostades came into the dining room and stood at a respectful distance behind his master. "The dinner . . ." he said quietly, to attract Justus' attention.

"The dinner?" Justus turned around and stared at the slave. "Is there some difficulty?" he demanded, almost as if he wanted an affirmative answer.

"No," Monostades promised him. "No difficulty at all. There was only the question of the wine, and you told me I should come to you for instructions. . . ." Three years with this master had taught Monostades a great deal, and he had assumed a manner that was at once subservient and arrogant.

"Of course," Justus said, and moved across the room toward his Greek slave. "We will want to warm it, I think, on a day like this. There's no reason to serve cold wine to so distinguished a visitor."

Monostades achieved a sour smile. "The cook has made a few recommendations you may want to consider."

Ordinarily Justus might have let this pass, but not now. He wanted the entire guiding of the meal, since it would mean so much to him in future. "The cook oversteps himself," he snapped as he strode from the room, glancing once at the water on the floor of the atrium.

"Your wife is in her chambers," Monostades said, anticipating Justus' inquiry. "Sibinus is keeping watch on her."

"Good," Justus said tersely as he entered the corridor that led to the kitchen. "I don't want any untoward interruptions tonight."

"She has much to do. You need not be concerned." He shivered and thought it was because the hall was chilly.

"You've arranged for the staffing of her father's house as I ordered it?" Plainly he would accept no answer but his desired affirmative.

"As you've instructed," Monostades agreed. "She may be sent there in a few more days, and Sibinus has already prepared the various guardian stations. There is no chance that anyone will visit her at any time without your permission and full knowledge. Three of the slaves will be set to watch her day and night, and one of them will always be no more than a room away. One will sleep during the day so that he can keep watch at night, and that way it will do no good for her to hope for a visitor to come late in the night so that you will know nothing about it." He was rather breathless as he followed his master into the cavernous kitchen.

Triges, the cook, raised his eyes from the slowly turning spit. "My master," he said, not diverting his attention from the young wild boar that was being basted with oil and honey.

"I understand you wish to advise me on the matter of wines," Justus said, drawing himself up.

The cook had heard that tone before—every one of his household slaves had. "I ventured a suggestion," he said cautiously. "I thought you might not want to be concerned with such a minor matter—"

"Wine," Justus interrupted him sweetly, "is not a minor matter, particularly when my guest is the son of the new Emperor."

The cook's shrug suggested that there had been four emperors in the past year, and one more could have little effect on them. He knew his master's temper, however, and so tried to mitigate his offense. "It is important to serve the best food—it is as important to my reputation as to yours, master, and I would not allow a wine that would disgrace you or the meal to be served. Two of the sauces I have prepared for the first time have a special savor and would be at their best with certain wines. I did not mean to overstep my authority."

Ordinarily this would have brought grudging approval from Justus, but he had gambled too much on this day to be forgiving. "You will learn, slave, that there is no will here but mine, and that all you do is for my use. The new sauces are a good idea, though Domitianus is not noted for his love of food. The wine must be the best, and I will select it."

Triges sighed. "Very well, master, but may I suggest that when the thrushes stuffed with pomegranates are served that there be a sweetish, light wine served with them? I have used mace and cinnamon and pepper cooked in garlic oil to baste them, and the sauce will be less flavorful if you do not serve a sweet, straw-colored wine. The spices were brought all the way from Hind and cost more than the rest of the food combined. It would be a shame to overwhelm them with too robust a wine." When all else failed, Triges had learned to appeal to his master's greed and love of luxury.

"From Hind? When did you buy them?" Justus was at once fascinated and affronted that such a purchase had been made without his approval.

"Six days ago," Triges lied with a quelling glance at his underlings, "there came a merchant from a ship anchored at Ostia. He had rare spices from Hind and the lands of the Silk Road. They were more valuable than jewels, he said, and gave me a sniff of the best. Knowing that you would have a distinguished guest, I decided that this would be the best time to buy new spices so you might serve a meal that would be remarkable in every way. It is impossible that the Emperor's son should have such a dinner from any other host." He waited, half-expecting the leather-braided rod that Justus carried to be slammed down on his shoulders.

"How much did it cost?" Justus asked, intrigued in spite of himself. The cook was right—it would be a triumph to serve Domitianus a dish he had never had.

"A great deal, master," Triges admitted. The amount had been more than Justus had paid to buy his cook six years before. "Sixteen gold denarii."

"Sixteen gold denarii?" Justus repeated. "The spices are worth more than a racehorse?"

Triges thought of a number of retorts, but kept them unsaid. "They are rarer than racehorses, certainly," he ventured.

"All right, slave," Justus said grandly. "If this meal is all that you have promised, then I will give you your freedom and sixteen gold denarii. If it is not, you will get one kiss of the flagellum for each of those gold denarii. If that does not spoil your uses, I will have you on the auction block afterward, or you will be set to hard labor on one of my estates." From his satisfied smile, it was plain that Justus had no intention of freeing his cook.

"As you wish," Triges muttered. He knew as well as every other slave in the kitchen that he had been given his death warrant, whether it came quickly from the lash, or slowly from torturous labor. It was so tempting to poison the meal. He wished now that he had taken the little packet the foreigner had offered him—who had not come ten days ago and was not off a ship at Ostia, but was the slave of one of his master's distant relatives. Triges thought he had been a fool to refuse the offer.

"Are you satisfied, slave?" Justus asked.

"I am satisfied to obey your will, master." Perhaps, he thought, he could open his veins when the last of the meal had been served. There were knives enough and it could be very quick.

Monostades made a deferential sound in his throat. "It is very nearly the hour when the Emperor's son is to arrive. You have yet to be shaved and perfumed, master."

This reminder got Justus' attention. "Yes. It grows late. While I am being shaved, I will order the wines, and you will send one of the household slaves to the kitchen with my instructions. And you"—he leveled a finger at Triges—"will do as I tell you and serve my choices . . . unwatered."

"As you command me, master," Triges answered, his face and voice both hard.

"See that you remember that," Justus said as he turned on his heel and walked away from the kitchen, oblivious of the panic he left behind him.

His body slave had wiped away the last of the lemon-scented water from Justus' face and was applying a perfume of rose, sandalwood and hyacinth when word was brought that the Emperor's son had arrived.

Justus turned in his chair. "Very good. I will be with him in a moment. See that his train is made comfortable in the slaves' wing and offer him a dry cloak. Make it the golden silk one, so that I may present it to him as a gift."

The slave Ixion had been given the task of serving young Titus Flavius Domitianus, and he accepted this order eagerly, hoping that among the other things that Justus was sure to give his guest, he would be included. The giving of slaves was not uncommon and Ixion wanted to be out of the Silius household more than he wanted his freedom.

Justus entered the atrium a short while later. He was resplendent in a toga virilis of rose linen with a border of gold eagles. He wore a profusion of rings and one wide bracelet, though at the last minute he had decided against painting his face. It had been the fashion for Nero and Otho, but there was no way of knowing what the styles of the new court would be. He made a rather grand gesture of welcome. "Domitianus! My house is much honored, and in this time of victory and grief, it is particularly gratifying that you are willing to visit me. And in such weather."

Titus Flavius Domitianus resembled his father, having the same wide brow and set mouth, though his lips had a dissatisfied turn to them and his large eyes were fretful, and there was already the start of a permanent crease above them. Unlike his older brother, Domitianus was not a handsome man, and at eighteen lacked any definite stamp of character on his face. He had contented himself with a pale green toga with a discreet border of dark red, and a single gold ring. "It was gracious of you to invite me, but it's my understanding that you have always been in the forefront of those sharing interests with my family."

Justus clapped him on the shoulder. "As well I should be, lad, for the good of Rome. I can tell you that I was much shocked at the death of your uncle. Sabinus was a good man, and one to be valued. I ordered an offering be made at the Temple of Jupiter the Biggest and Best on his behalf." It had been a very public gesture, one that he was certain would be reported to the new Emperor and place him in even higher esteem.

"I heard something of that," Domitianus said. He looked toward the opening in the atrium ceiling where the rain clouds were visible, and the water that streamed from them in bright, pale waves, like the bending of wheat in a high wind. "The storm has caused a great many problems."

"Yes, I'm certain it must have," Justus agreed promptly as he waved his hand toward the smaller dining room. "Come in, be comfortable. I'd love to hear what your plans are, but you will probably prefer to have a little spiced wine, served hot, and an opportunity to take your mind off your work." He preceded his guest to the door of the smaller dining room and flung it open.

The effect was all he could have wished. The Asian slave had worked hard, and now the room was one of Eastern splendor. There were worked hangings on three walls, and braziers as well as hanging lamps gave the chamber a rich light. Lamp oil and brazier charcoal had been scented, so that the room was redolent of cloves and lilac. The two couches had been moved close together, and each had large, down-filled pillows piled up artlessly, promising warmth and relaxation. There was only one table between the couches, a wide one of fancy inlaid woods. Golden and silver goblets stood on the table, and two small dishes filled with warmed rosewater.

Domitianus was still easily impressed, and this was the grandest reception he had yet been given in Rome, and it seemed all the more so for its intimacy. The other dinners he had attended, he had been overwhelmed by the number of important guests, all of whom crowded around him seeking his good opinion, and through him the approval of his father, who was still in Egypt.

As the young man reclined, Justus clapped his hands, and Ixion appeared. He had been dressed in a Doric chiton of fine wool, and he waited, rather shyly, three paces back from the table between the couches. The sound of Justus' hands brought him forward to kneel to Domitianus.

"Pour the spiced wine," Justus ordered, then turned to the other slave in the room, a frightened young man from the north, in whose yellow hair silver grape leaves were twined in a wreath. "We will have the pickled fish now," he ordered, having learned that Domitianus had a weakness for pickled fish.

When Ixion had poured the wine, he stepped back as he had been told to do. He felt very awkward now, wishing that he had had more time to learn what was expected of him. The Emperor's son, he told himself, would be willing to overlook his inexperience.

"Tell me, Domitianus," Justus began as he sank onto the couch opposite his guest, "are you looking forward to wearing the toga picta?" This garment was reserved for victors and Emperors: Justus would have been willing to give away half his wealth to have the right to wear it.

"It's only cloth," Domitianus said as he dipped his fingers in the rosewater and wiped them on a square of linen set out for that purpose. "My father will have to show more durability than his predecessors if mine is going to be anything more than a shroud."

Justus forced himself to laugh heartily at this. "At the worst, you could go back to Egypt and join your father."

"Nothing!" Domitianus said with vehemence surprising in someone who had appeared so self-effacing. "Nothing in the world would get me back to Egypt. All of that part of the empire is worse than an open grave. The people are contemptible, their manners are appalling, their conduct bestial, their leaders are criminals and degenerates, and their religions are farcical!" He waved his wine cup rather wildly in the air and a few drops fell on his toga. When he slammed down his other hand for emphasis, the little bowls of rosewater were overturned. Domitianus looked down, chagrined. He had been warned by his father's general, Licinius Mucianus, that he would have to behave in a circumspect manner, at least at first.

"Don't be bothered," Justus said indulgently. "A little matter, my lad, easily remedied," he assured the Emperor's son, and clapped for the blond slave. "Ferrado, see to this. At once."

The handsome blond youth obeyed immediately, almost clumsily, clearing away the bowls and finger cloths.

"After each course, bring us fresh rosewater," Justus reiterated for Domitianus' benefit. "The finger cloths are an idea I've picked up from the Parthians. They're worthy enemies, in their way, and have a few things to teach us. If we can continue the peace for a while, it might be profitable." He had his freedmen investigating the possibility of buying Parthian jewels, and as long as the two huge countries maintained their uneasy truce, there could be trade between them. It would take nothing more than two or three years for Justus to make enormous profits as well as establish some trade agreements which would guarantee that he continue to get jewels, whether Rome and Parthia were at peace or not.

"They're sending spies here all the time," Domitianus said petulantly. "Parthia and Persia both. Sometimes they do it through Armenia, and sometimes through Jerusalem."

"Now that the government will be stable again, that will stop," Justus said with a show of complacence. "I have great faith in your father, in your whole family. I was very pleased when Mucianus presented you to the Praetorian Guard as Caesar. It will do a great deal for Rome to have the Praetorians again. Vitellius' private Guard was not popular."

Ixion stepped forward carrying a platter of pickled fish. He put this down before Domitianus as a temple priest might offer sacrifice to his god.

"This is good, very good," Domitianus said when he had eaten two of the little fish.

"I have them sent from Britannia. Nothing south of there is as tasty, I've found." He picked up one of the fish by the tail and dropped it into his mouth. Actually, he disliked the salty northern fish, but that would not win the approval of the Emperor's son.

"They're very good," Domitianus said mechanically as he reached for more. "Is your wife away?" he asked between bites.

"My wife?" Justus said with distaste. "No, I fear that she is reluctant to join us tonight. Since that sad day when her father and brothers were condemned for political intrigue—that was during Nero's time, you wouldn't remember—she has been uninterested in political things, and I have ceased trying to persuade her. She is an odd woman, though I shouldn't say it. You may have heard something about her tastes in men. There has been some gossip. I know that having an old man for a husband can be difficult for a young woman, and so I cannot bring myself to criticize her for what she may do. Not that I favor adultery, but a man must make allowances." He let himself sigh heavily, and then showed a tolerant smile. "Women. What creatures they are."

Domitianus had another fish in his mouth and could not answer at once. When he did, he said, "It sounds to me as if you might consider divorce."

"What? You forget that I've been divorced once already, and it would not look well for me to do so a second time." He reached for the wine jug and refilled his guest's cup.

"Why not? There are plenty of others who've had any number of spouses in their lives. A wife like that," he went on, assuming the manner of a sage, "she's no credit to a man like you, Justus. I can understand why you wish to be loyal. No one would like others to think that he had put a wife away because of folly in her family, but you must consider your position and your future. There are women who would be a greater credit to you and who would not have the cloud of suspicion hanging over them."

This was precisely what Justus wanted to hear, and from someone as powerful and naive as Titus Flavius Domitianus. "I had hoped that in time she might come to regard the matter differently. She is generally not unreasonable."

The platter of pickled fish was empty except for a thin film of brine. Justus motioned for this to be taken away.

The next dish was stewed sows' udders stuffed with honeyed dormice. Dishes of tart and sweet sauces were set on the table along with little buns. A second jug of wine had been broached.

Justus was deep in conversation with Domitianus when he noticed that Ixion was hovering near their table. He stopped his conversation and looked up. "Why are you standing there?"

Ixion pointed to himself, turning scarlet. "You said I was to—"

"I said you were to serve us, not breathe on us!" He was feeling the effects of the wine as well as pleasure at the way the evening was going. "You're listening to us."

"I'm not!" Ixion protested, moving back and almost tripping over the end of Domitianus' couch.

A measuring, crafty look came into Justus' face. "You're still new in my house," he said as he glared at Ixion. "I got you last autumn. You came cheap."

"My master was bankrupt," Ixion said, feeling very frightened. There was something in his master's eyes that filled him with horror. "You said it was fortunate that he was bankrupt. You bought fifteen of his slaves."

"Sixtus Murens was a supporter of Otho," Justus said suddenly.

Ixion nodded, hoping to escape the wrath he could see gathering in Justus' face. "Because of Otho, master, he lost all his fortune, in defending that false Emperor. Vitellius would not honor the various pledges that Otho had given my master. There was nothing else he could do but sell off his slaves and land. It was all that he had." His voice had risen.

"Or perhaps he wants to buy favor. Perhaps someone has made him an offer, and in exchange for a few services will restore his fortune." Justus knew it was what he would do in the same circumstances, and he found it difficult to believe that anyone else would not behave as he would.

"No!" Ixion protested.

"No? How do you know that, slave?" Justus was on his feet now, coming toward Ixion with an expression of dreadful anticipation in his eyes.

Belatedly Domitianus looked up from his plate. "Have your houseman take him away, Justus. You can examine him at leisure."

Justus refused to be robbed of his pleasure when it was so close. "Pardon me, young Caesar. If there were any other guest but you in my house, I would, of course, do that. But you are too precious, and too high above me for me to expose you to any more threats. Gaius Sixtus Murens was a traitor, yet he lives. It would be like him to plant one of his creatures here where he might spy upon you, and gather information that would be used by your enemies."

"No," Ixion whispered as he took another step backward. "No. I never would . . ."

Now Domitianus was interested. It was little more than a month ago that he had been in danger of his life and his uncle had been killed. He paled as he regarded the slave. "Tell me, you, is there any truth in what your master says?"

Ixion dropped to his knees and crawled toward the young man on the couch. "No truth, Caesar. None. I have never been a spy. There is no reason I should be one. My master is . . . wrong. I would not—"

"Make a liar of me, would you?" Justus thundered. "Monostades!" he yelled as he reached down and dragged Ixion to his feet by the hair. "Monostades, bring the rods, quickly!"

"Master," Ixion protested, almost inaudibly. "Master, no. I swear to you that I never did anything contrary to your orders and interests. . . ."

Monostades opened the door, three long leather-and-wire-wrapped rods in his hand. "What do you wish, master?"

"This one!" With a shove, Justus sent Ixion sprawling. "He has been spying on the young Caesar, who has honored me as my guest, and he will not admit it. See that he does." He stood straddling the slave. "Ixion. An appropriate name. He suffered, and you will, too."

While Justus and Titus Flavius Domitianus dined on the special pomegranate-stuffed thrushes dipped in the secret sauce that Triges had made, Ixion was dragged to the stableyard and tied between two tall posts. As the rain fell and darkness came on, Monostades beat him until the required confession was obtained. Satisfied, he tossed the bloody rods away and went back into the house to report, leaving Ixion hanging in the rain while his life ran out of him.

Text of a letter written in code by Led Arashnur to an unnamed person, delivered sealed into the hands of a traveler from Seleucia in Mesopotamia shortly before he boarded a ship bound for Antioch.

To my superiors:

I regret that I can report no progress in the matter of the Prince Kosrozd Kaivan. Not only was I unsuccessful in purchasing him from his owner, the Ragoczy Sanct' Germain Franciscus we learned of in Egypt, but Kaivan himself is reluctant to return to Persia again. Two of the charioteers have told me that Kaivan has expressed himself on the question of his heritage with a degree of scorn, which is most unfortunate. We may have to resort to less subtle measures. I realize that it is essential that he not live out the year, but I will have to find a way to kill him here in Rome.

It may be possible to discredit this Franciscus, who is not Roman. He is said to be from Dacia and yet not a Daci. Although at first I doubted much of what that old priest said before he died, it seems there is something to it, and if only we can find proof, then the Senate will deal with him. I have been attempting to get that proof, but so far with little success. He is very careful and has many friends in high places. I have heard that one of the old Senators, a man of very ancient house and fortune, has expressed himself as being against Franciscus, though I have yet to learn why. This Senator, a Cornelius Justus Silius, has a great deal of political power, and if I can find a way to persuade him to exercise it upon our behalf, then the road to Kaivan is clear and he will be delivered into our hands.

Your message of three months ago has just reached me, and I was pleased to learn that two more of the heirs to the throne have gone their way into the black Mansion of Death. It would be a great mistake to have them left alive. There is too much to be lost if we allow them to live.

It would not be appropriate to send more soldiers, even Armenian ones, because I am currently living in a very poor district of Rome, not far from the Temple of Minerva. The building is old, no one dares to light the holocaust for fear the entire building will burn down. There are rats on the ground floor, but they rarely come higher because there are no cooking facilities in the apartments, and most of us buy our food from the little shops on the street below. The cheapest food is a thick wheat bun filled with cooked pork in a heavy pepper sauce. These are very popular. Everyone eats them. In such a setting, any soldiers would be noticed, and at the moment, I wish to be invisible. Should it seem desirable to find another place to live, or to establish myself in a grander setting, I will inform you, and would then welcome the soldiers you offer.

The Emperor is yet to arrive in Rome, though spring is well-advanced. He is still represented by his younger son, who has shown himself to be very popular with the reestablished Praetorian Guard. Though very young, Titus Flavius Domitianus demonstrates a good grasp of politics and his intellect is acute. His severity may lessen with age. If you can find a clever Greek who might be willing to do the work of a library slave or secretary, he could be very useful near Domitianus. Of the older son, who has the same name as his father, but who is called Titus to avoid confusion, I know no more now than I did two years ago. There is a degree of gossip about him, but I put little stock in any of it. Perhaps you might find someone close to him with an unguarded tongue.

If our plan is to succeed, then we must be very cautious. Kosrozd Kaivan is one of the more important of the princes, but only one. Should any of them be alive when our brotherhood makes its move to power, then we will have done it all for nothing.

Ours is a holy cause, and our course is clear. I will not fail in my task, I vow it with my blood and my life. It would be better that he die on Persian soil, but Rome will do. See that your dedication is as firm as mine, for though you are my military and religious superiors, you have chosen me to accomplish these important missions. When many of you would have faltered in Egypt, I carried on. I found the priest and had the truth out of him before his death. I will accept any reprimand you give me if it is warranted, but otherwise I must be allowed to act in the manner I think best.

You will have word from me again before the summer solstice. For the honor of the gods and the righteousness of our goals!

Led Arashnur
the fourth day of April in the
822nd Year of the City,
as it is styled in Rome

6

AUMTEHOUTEP'S EXPRESSION was impassive as he entered the private wing of Villa Ragoczy. "My master?"

Sanct' Germain looked up from the scroll he had been reading. In the slanted golden afternoon light it was just barely possible to read the spidery, faded scrawl in what appeared to be Greek. He handled the scroll with extreme care, as age had made it brittle and already bits of the papyrus had broken off the sides of the ancient document. "What is it?" He could read the distress in his old slave's eyes. "What's wrong?"

"There are three officers of the Praetorian Guard and a member of the Senate here, my master. They insist—'insist' is their word—that you see them at once." He looked toward the far wall rather blankly. "I have told them that you're occupied, but they won't accept that."

"Won't they?" Sanct' Germain set the scroll aside, placing a little statue of a dancing dwarf on the scroll to hold it. "Then, of course, I must obey. Tell them that I will be with them very shortly, and apologize for the delay. Show them into the main reception room and see that they have wine. Give them the good white wine, since it's so warm today and they undoubtedly have become thirsty on their journey out here." As he rose he put one small hand on Aumtehoutep's arm. "Don't worry, old friend. After more than a year of continuous upheaval in Rome, it's surprising that they're just getting around to me. This is not the first time such things have happened, as you recall."

The Egyptian nodded once. "I doubt that the matter is simple. I hope that it's nothing more than the usual distrust of foreigners. We've had our share of it. But three Praetorians and a Senator?"

"You forget, I'm very wealthy. Rome would not like to lose my taxes and the cheap mules I sell the legions." There was more resignation than cynicism in his voice. "Go, Aumtehoutep. Give them my message and see to the wine."

"As you wish," was the old slave's answer, though his eyes were unhappy.

As soon as the door was closed, Sanct' Germain moved quickly, slipping three small boxes into various parts of his desk so that they came to have the look of decorations instead of concealed drawers. It would not do, he thought, for the Praetorian Guard or the Senate to learn what was hidden in those boxes. He straightened up and smoothed the short dalmatica of black cotton he wore over his usual tight Persian trousers. Reaching for the pectoral he had removed while he worked, he wished, as he so often had for almost two thousand years, that he could see himself in mirrors. When he had adjusted the heavy silver collar of the pectoral, he left his library and went through the garden toward the public wing of Villa Ragoczy.

Two of the Praetorian officers rose from the couches as Sanct' Germain entered his blue-and-silver reception room. The third officer was busy refilling his wine cup and the Senator gave the foreigner a haughty stare, as if to inform him that a Roman noble was exempt from being courteous.

"I'm sorry to have kept you waiting," Sanct' Germain said with a pleasant, insincere smile. "My slave, I see, has extended you some of my poor hospitality. I hope you will do me the honor of taking your evening meal at my table."

"We won't be staying that long," one of the standing Praetorians said with a nervous glance at his fellows.

"From the grim sound of your words, officer, I assume that you have a specific request to make of me?" Sanct' Germain directed the full compelling force of his dark eyes toward the officer. "I regret, good Praetorian, that I don't know your name."

"Marcellus Octavius Publian, tribune," he said stiffly. "The others are Crispus Terentius Galen, tribune, Phillipus Dudo, procurator junior. The Senator," Marcellus Octavius Publian said with a badly concealed sneer, "is Regius Eugenius Este Bonaro. From a very distinguished house."

The Senator, who was no more than twenty-five and wearing a toga praetexta to which he had a dubious claim, gave the older soldier a quick frown, but did not pursue the matter. Instead, he turned his attention to Sanct' Germain. "You. Foreigner."

Sanct' Germain could sense the embarrassment felt by the soldiers, and decided to take advantage of it. "What will you give me the pleasure of doing for you?"

Phillipus Dudo, the procurator junior, cleared his throat in an apparent effort to direct attention away from the young, arrogant patrician. "We have received a report, Franciscus, that makes some alarming . . . allegations about you. . . ."

Once again the Senator spoke. "It is said that you are here to spy upon Rome, that you are in the pay of various princes in countries with which the state is at war. In proof of this, it is said that you have in your household a Persian prince who is working with you to bring about—"

All four men stared at Sanct' Germain, who had started to laugh. "Forgive me," he said when he had mastered himself. "I don't mean to insult you, but the credulity that can be given to such ridiculous rumors . . ." He had to stop again because his laughter almost overcame him. "If that is what has brought you to Villa Ragoczy, I don't know whether to be complimented or baffled."

His visitors waited uneasily, and Phillipus found nerve enough to ask, "Does this mean that there is no truth to the accusation?"

"You mean that one of my slaves was once a Persian prince? Of course it's true. I've never made a secret of it." He had never exploited the information, either, but it would not do to say so now.

"Then you *admit*—" the outraged young Senator began.

"I tell you that I have a slave who was once a Persian prince," Sanct' Germain repeated, more seriously. "My slave is a charioteer. You've probably seen him in races. Most of the time he races for the Reds' faction, but occasionally the Whites use him, as well. Both racing corporations have offered to buy him, but I have not wanted to sell him."

"Why is that?" demanded the procurator junior.

"Because he wins," Sanct' Germain said patiently. It was the obvious reason. "He has made me a great deal of money over the years and there is no good reason why I should give that to someone else. When he retires from racing, he will train more of my charioteers and I will continue to have winners." No Roman would find that at all suspicious.

"But a Persian prince?" the young Senator said with heavy sarcasm. "You keep him only for racing?"

"Considering that in the last two years he has earned me in the neighborhood of twenty million sesterces, I would be a greater fool than I am not to keep him." He gave a wry chuckle. "I don't imagine my motives are any different than yours would be in my place."

Crispus Terentius Galen, who had not spoken, found his voice at last. "It's convenient to have it so, and it's a simple matter for us to verify your claims."

"Do so," Sanct' Germain said promptly. "By all means. You may examine my records as well as those of the Circus Maximus and the Circus of Caligula and Nero."

Phillipus nodded. "I don't think you'd lie about that. Yet for a foreigner like yourself to have such a slave . . ."

"I don't come from Persia, good Praetorian, I come from Dacia. I have little interest in what happens between royal Persian cousins. If you mean to suggest that my slave is something more than a slave, then why haven't I freed him, or sent him to Persia to curry favor with the king?" He asked this quite reasonably, looking from one officer to the other, ignoring the petulant young Senator.

"Your explanation is not entirely sufficient," Senator Bonaro snapped, stung by Sanct' Germain's treatment. "You stand accused of conspiracy—"

"Accused?" Sanct' Germain's fine brows raised in polite disbelief. "Who accuses me?"

The Praetorians had the grace to be embarrassed. Publian stared up at the ceiling, saying, "The accusation against you is anonymous. That makes it very awkward, because you are a foreigner, and therefore not entitled to the same court proceedings as a citizen. We're willing to extend you every courtesy we can, of course, but since we can't examine the informant and have no real knowledge of his information or his motives, we must rely on you to show the charge to be false. We're not going to hold you for trial, not on such flimsy . . . material, but there are questions that must be answered."

"I see." Sanct' Germain looked away, eyes narrowing for an instant. "Very well, good Romans, I will tell you what I know of my Persian slave. He was bought by me at auction eight years ago. They said he had ability with horses and chariots, and I was seeking to expand my stables and teams. I bought him, rather cheaply because it was plain from his manner that he was defiant and unruly. This made me curious, because his manner was not that of one born to the collar. I own several ships, as I am sure you know, and I asked my captains to find out what they could of this charioteer. In time one of my captains found the answer. I learned from him that Kosrozd was the son of a man who had been executed for treason against the throne, and that his entire family had been sold into slavery. If I wanted to ingratiate myself with the courts of Persia, I would choose a different way than this. My slave, if he could return home, would be regarded as a fugitive and a traitor. His family is scattered, and none of them survive in positions of power. That is easily confirmed, good Senator," he said quickly, anticipating the young man's objections. "You may do it just as I did six years ago."

The Praetorians nodded at each other, clearly relieved, and Crispus Terentius Galen spoke for them. "It's only a formality, naturally, but because the situation is awkward, we'll have to do that. There will be no restrictions on you, however, so long as you make no attempt to leave the empire or send . . . things . . . abroad until this matter has been resolved. If you feel that this imposes on you too much . . ."

"I have no wish and no reason to leave Rome at this time," Sanct' Germain assured him quickly, thinking that he had been very cleverly maneuvered into a difficult position. Should he object now, there would be more stringent restraints put on him, he was certain. "I will be happy to put any of my accounts and records you may wish to see at your disposal, so that we may be finished with this regrettable misunderstanding as quickly as possible. You have only to tell my slave Aumtehoutep what you require and he will provide it."

Phillipus coughed diffidently. "We are going to have to make one more request of you. We've been instructed to place a guard here while we're completing our investigation. It's not what we would like to do," he added hurriedly after he licked his lips. "It is part of the instructions that have been given by the Emperor's son, and we are obliged to do as he orders."

This was definitely not usual procedure. "But why? Surely all this concern for one slave, though he was once a prince and belongs to a foreigner, is unmerited?" He wanted to challenge them, reminding them that this was against the letter of Roman law, but he held back. He would learn nothing more, once he opposed them; he needed information badly.

"Ordinarily," Marcellus Octavius Publian mumbled, "it would be, but there are special circumstances here." He was not happy saying so, and he looked to the others for support. It was very quiet in the blue-and-silver reception room.

The inward apprehension that had niggled in Sanct' Germain's mind became more intense, demanding. He had assumed from the first that this investigation was the work of the Persian spy Led Arashnur, but there might be more to it. He was aware that quite a few noble Romans coveted his wealth and his property. An investigation like this could provide them with the opportunity they desired. He allowed his geniality to be tinged with irritation. "I am willing to oblige you, of course, but it might be easier for all of us if you were a little more direct with me, good Praetorians. And you as well, Senator." He folded his arms and fixed a smile on his closed lips.

Phillipus stared at the wine cup in his hand as if he had just discovered it there. "As you know, one of your own captains was held on a matter of smuggling . . ." He looked at the Senator, who scowled but said nothing.

"Yes," Sanct' Germain prompted. "Kyrillos the Greek. He captained the *Gull of Byzantium,* a small merchant ship. I thought the matter was settled when I released Kyrillos from service, as I was asked to do." Perhaps, his racing thoughts suggested, someone had bribed Kyrillos—the captain doubtless felt little loyalty to an employer he had seen twice, and who had relieved him of command. It was even possible that Kyrillos had needed no bribe to act against his former employer, and had filed an accusation in revenge.

"Technically, it was," the procurator junior said, tugging at the strap that held his red caracalla. He wished now he had left the heavy cloak at the door, for now it seemed too warm and too tight at the neck.

"But that, it would appear, is not enough," Sanct' Germain said rather bitterly. "How am I to satisfy you, gentlemen? Tell me. I have a slave who was once a prince and you accuse me of trying to gain favor with him for some distant and unlikely day when he might return to his native land in victory. I dismiss a captain for smuggling, and now it seems that has made me more suspect than ever. What am I supposed to have done, that you deal with me this way?"

This time the uncomfortable silence was longer than before. Senator Regius Eugenius Este Bonaro occupied the time by filling his wine cup again. The sound of the liquid pouring was very loud.

"If you are not authorized to tell me," Sanct' Germain said quietly, "I will not press you for an explanation."

Phillipus muttered, "Under the circumstances . . ."

"*What* circumstances?" Sanct' Germain demanded, pausing for an answer that none of the four volunteered. "That is also a mystery, is it? Or is there some other reason you are not at liberty to discuss the matter with me?" He made no attempt to disguise his sarcasm now.

The young Senator, flushed with wine as much as choler, choked on an oath, then burst out, "You're defying us."

At that, Sanct' Germain managed to laugh. "If I were defying you, you would never have got through the door, Senator. I have borne with considerable patience this farrago of evasions and half-truths you've offered me. I'll do so until I find out what it is that you really want to know. But I will not tolerate being party to your deception. Let us be honest with each other this once: your true object in coming here has little to do with my Persian slave or my former captain. You have a different purpose that for some reason you are unwilling to reveal. For the moment I accept that, but I warn you right now, you, Senator, and you, good Praetorians, that I am not deceived." He gave them all an ironic little bow. "Is there anything else?"

Phillipus looked at the far wall. "Franciscus, it was not our decision to investigate you. We are obeying the orders of our superiors."

"And have no will or judgment of your own," Sanct' Germain said with his most friendly smile.

The Praetorians stiffened, and Marcellus Octavius Publian put one hand to the hilt of his sword. "You will not make things easier for yourself if you speak so, Franciscus."

"Nor will I make them easier for you," Sanct' Germain said quietly. "If you had told me at the first what it is you truly want, I would have done my utmost to cooperate with you, but as it stands . . ."—he lifted his hands helplessly—"you have chosen my course for me, gentlemen, and I must follow it as best I can. When you decide to be frank with me, we may talk again. Not until." Suddenly there was a subtle change in him, as if he had grown taller or his soft voice was louder. The four Romans moved back slightly, each in his own way, for it seemed that Sanct' Germain had become closer, more menacing, to each of them, though none could say how. "As long as you insist upon this deception, whatever it is, I will neither assist nor hinder you. If you want my aid and my interest, you must be prepared to be honest with me.

Believe that." He turned on his booted heel and strode quickly out the door, calling as he went, "Aumtehoutep! Get my shipping records for these men!" Without stopping to see that it was done, he went across the garden and into his private wing.

The reception room was silent for some little time; then Phillipus sighed. "I warned you that this was not the way to approach him. Our informant was mistaken about dealing with this Franciscus. He may," he added darkly, "have been mistaken about other things."

"Nonsense," snapped the young Senator. "There is no reason to think that the allegations are in error."

"There is also no reason to think that they are true," Crispus Terentius Galen observed dryly. "I'm afraid that I must agree with Octavius. I think we've blundered, and blundered badly. It was stupid of us to force the issue so soon."

The other two soldiers nodded glumly. The Senator poured himself more wine.

They had not spoken to each other again when Aumtehoutep arrived some little time later with a box under his arm. He paused to look at the men. "My master has asked that I bring these to you," he said in his most neutral voice which only his close associates would recognize as being his most condemning.

"Good." Phillipus sighed, and came across the room to take the box.

"The records go back ten years. If you need those before, you will have to send me word." He held out the box to the procurator junior. "We will need to have them back if we're to keep them accurate."

"Of course," Phillipus agreed. "I doubt we will need them for more than a month." He took the box with a strange sense of relief. He had not relished the thought of forcing Ragoczy Sanct' Germain Franciscus to do anything.

As soon as Aumtehoutep was gone from the room, the other three men crowded around Phillipus.

"Come," said Octavius. "Open it. Let's see what we've got." He almost knocked the box from Phillipus' hand in his eagerness to look inside.

There were eight neat stacks of fan-folded scrolls in the box, and each had a seal on it, showing the eclipse, a disk with wings spread above it with the Year of the City incised into each seal. The progression was neat and orderly.

"Here, let me have this one," Senator Bonaro said as he lifted one of the scrolls from the box.

Terentius took one of the fan-folded scrolls into his hands as well, then hesitated, looking at the other two Praetorians from under his lowered brows. "I don't know. We should have made him an ally."

Phillipus shrugged. "You know what Senator Silius told us when Domitianus asked his opinion on the man."

"I know. But all the same, what damage would have been done if he had been told that the unknown informant told us Franciscus is having illegal dealings with Egypt? I don't care if the Emperor is still in Egypt, there's no reason to think that Franciscus plots against him. What reason would he have? He said he would help us if we were candid with him." He worked to loosen the seal on the folded scroll.

"According to Senator Silius, all that is a ploy," Terentius repeated automatically.

"Why does he know any better than the rest of us, except that Domitianus dines with him?" Octavius remarked as he spread out the scroll before him. He stared at the page, and then started to laugh. "We'll have to confide in him, I think," he said when he could speak again, and held out his scroll for the others.

They took the proffered scroll, Senator Bonaro letting the one he held drop to the floor. As they passed the scroll from one to another, the reactions ranged from outrage to delight.

For the scroll was written in an ancient tongue that was old when Rome was founded.

Text of a letter to Atta Olivia Clemens, Domita Silius, from her mother, Decia Romola Nolus, Domita Clemens. Intercepted and destroyed by Cornelius Justus Silius.

To my unfortunate daughter Olivia, greetings:

I had hoped that there would be word from you this

month, but no letter has come, and I fear that you have not forgiven me. It would be easier for me now if I knew you do not hate me, though I realize that your hatred is completely justified. It was wrong of me, very wrong, to have agreed with your father in persuading you to marry Cornelius Justus Silius. It was not the same with your older sisters, for our fortunes were better when they married and it seemed that their husbands could only profit from alliance with us. When we lost so much, I was frightened. Surely you can understand that, my child. Senator Silius' offer was a gift of the gods, one which we would be fools to refuse, for it would establish us once again in the proper place of society. At one moment it seemed we would have to sell all the slaves and go live like peasants on our land in Dalmatia, and the next moment, there was the chance to save all, and present you with a splendid husband. Your reservations sounded so callow, so trivial, that I shut my ears and my heart to you, acts which I have come to regret most bitterly.

What you told me about Silius has disturbed me greatly. At first I did not want to believe that you were being treated so, and your father attributed your tales to disappointment. I admit that I thought you were exaggerating about the way he used you. Since I have lived on this barren patch of ground that Justus calls an estate, I have learned otherwise from the slaves that are sent here. To work here is a punishment, and for me it is a prison. One of the women arrived here two years ago and confirmed all that you had told me and much more. Olivia, if Mother Isis were to give me one gift now, it would be a way for me to undo the harm I have done you. But you must understand; it seemed so simple, so easy when Silius offered for you. I would never have insisted on the match if I had been aware of what he would do to you.

I have written to your sister, but she has not been able or willing to reply. Her husband, I am told, does not want her communicating with her family. It is easy to see why: he has a career to think of, and it has already been damaged by our folly and your husband's malice. Now I must turn to you, though I realize it is dangerous for you to act on my behalf, and there is no reason for you to do so. I have thrown away my right to your respect. Yet I hope that you have more kindness than I.

The weakness I wrote you of before has grown worse. My side aches much of the time, and it feels, on occasion, that there is a vast knot in my bowels. Nothing but syrup of poppies alleviates my suffering, and there is very little syrup of poppies to be had here. If you are willing to see that I am sent more, I would be grateful. The local physician is generally incompetent, but is willing to admit it in this case. He estimates that my death will come by winter. I think that it will be sooner. I hope it will be sooner.

At least you will be free when I am dead. I know now that Justus used your family as hostages, holding up their safety to keep you compliant. He saw to the death of your father and brothers, and left you with me. I will be glad, knowing that you may divorce Justus and reveal him in open court for what he is. Your sister will survive the scandal; do not be deterred by anxiety on her behalf.

Though you may not be able to forgive me, please accept from me this last and genuine token of my love for you: there is in our house in Rome a statue of Minerva, and within it is your father's record of what Justus had done to him. He wrote it the night he was condemned and hid it away so that the family might, at some later time, regain its honor and integrity. Go there. The statue of Minerva is in the niche opposite my room. It is yours, the only legacy I can leave you now.

If you despise me, do not scorn this record of your father's. It is the only document that will expose your husband. You told me the last time we spoke in Rome that you had one friend. Seek him out, if there is affection between you still. Then you need never again suffer at the hands of the man you married.

My daughter, my daughter, answer this letter, I beg of you. To die in pain without the comfort of your forgiveness is more anguish than I can bear. Let me know at least that you have found your father's papers and that you will use them in court against Justus. Without this assurance, I am in despair. Surely the Senate will act against Justus to condemn him when the full scope of his perfidy is known, and in that you will have some revenge. It may be little enough, but those with nothing must make banquets of such scraps, as I have learned.

It is a pity I did not learn to love you sooner.

Your mother,
Romola
on the twelfth day of June,
the 822nd Year of the City

7

In the peristyle of the Palace of Claudius, the roses were full-blown and starting to fade. The air was hot and still and not even the fountain that spurted perfumed water lessened the hammerlike force of the sun.

The two brothers lounged there, the older one nude, the younger in a short tunic of thin cotton. The family resemblance was strong, though Titus Flavius Vespasianus was handsome and his brother, Titus Flavius Domitianus, was not. As the older brother had the same name as his father, he was called Titus instead of Vespasianus, as his father was.

Titus scratched meditatively at the stubble on his chest, then squinted up at the sun. "I hope it's cooler tonight," he remarked.

"It won't be," Domitianus said, an unwelcome touch of jealousy giving him an odd satisfaction at his older brother's discomfort.

"At least it will be cooler when our father comes from Egypt. We have just under two months to prepare for that." Titus was tan, lean and athletic, just thirty-one.

"All will be ready," his younger brother said grimly. "You have my word on that."

Titus nodded. "You've been very good at that," he said in an offhanded way. "The Praetorians like you. It's a shame you aren't a little older. The people would like you better." He could not quite disguise the smug pleasure in his voice: he was a hero of the moment, and enjoying his fame. "To think that not so many days ago I was fighting Jews in Jerusalem. At least the revolt is over."

"Yet you have a fondness for Jews, don't you?" Domitianus said nastily. "What does Berenice think of this war of yours against her people?"

"We don't discuss it," Titus snapped, and lay back on the couch, letting the heat spread over him like hot oil.

"Too busy doing other things?" Domitianus suggested. Now that he had succeeded in irritating his brother, he was determined to make the most of it. "Romans won't like your affair with a foreign queen, you know. They'd be more tolerant of your boys and eunuchs than they'd be of her."

"Don't be an ass, Domi," Titus murmured. "No one will object to Berenice. A smart, lusty woman like her—she's just in the Roman style."

"Except that she's Jewish," Domitianus pointed out, pressing his advantage.

"You said you wanted to discuss the celebrations welcoming our father to the city. Why don't you get on with it?" He stretched languidly, wiping his forehead where damp curls clung. His searching fingers touched his receding hairline. How he hated the idea of going bald! In a few years, he thought unhappily, he would have to do as Otho had done, and have a wig made.

Domitianus glared at his brother. It infuriated him that Titus should be the favored one, the one to be the lover of the Jewish Queen Berenice, the handsome brother, the military hero, the one who had been raised at court, surrounded by favor and riches, while he, Domitianus, had to be satisfied with a few tutors in Egypt and Syria. Now he had word from his father that Titus would be replacing him as prefect of the Praetorian Guard, and that was worst of all, for it was in that capacity that Domitianus had known his first taste of success and power. He loathed the thought of giving that up to Titus, who had had so much already. "The city will have more than ten days of festival," he said as if reciting by rote. "There will be four days of Games, and a full Triumph with appropriate religious observances. There will be an imperial guard of honor at the temples of Jupiter the Biggest and Best and Mars the Victor. A special camp will be constructed for our father's legions on the south side of the city, and there will be displays of battle skills there on the days when there are no Games."

"A pity we can't change the law about the legions. It would be splendid to have them march into the city with our father at their head. Think of all the people cheering, and the great impression such a gesture would make." He grinned at Domitianus. "Tell me, Domi, do you think the Senate could be persuaded to make an exception to the law in this case?"

"I doubt it," Domitianus said. "It's a good law, and the day may come when you'll be grateful for it. If a general can't bring in legions inside the gates of the city, then there is likely to be easier going for the Emperor." He mopped at his brow with the hem of his tunic. What had possessed Titus to want to talk in the peristyle at this time of day? "There will be representatives from all our provinces and client nations here. We'll have to make some arrangements to house them properly, and that must be seen to quickly. There are Senators who would be willing to have a distinguished guest or two in their homes, so that they can use their influence. . . ."

"You're becoming a cynic," Titus said mildly.

"If you had been in Rome these last few months, instead of off looking for glory besieging Jerusalem," Domitianus shot back, "you might share my opinion. If you're going to have the kind of power our father seems determined to give you, then you'd better learn quickly whom you can trust and whom you can't. Most of the Senators are more interested in protecting their own fortunes than the fortunes of Rome. Face that now."

Titus stretched into a different position on the couch. "I have complete faith in you, little brother. If there is a Senator who is not worthy of our favor, no doubt you'll point him out to me, and save us all from embarrassment."

Never had Domitianus wanted so much to strangle his brother. The tranquil, unctuous assumption that he had no other purpose than to serve Titus rankled Domitianus increasingly. "I will give you my opinion if you ask for it. Otherwise, it is your place to find out these things. If our father restores the office of censor, it will probably fall to you, and you won't want to be coming to me every minute of the day."

"No," Titus agreed, "I won't. But you can give me that information later. For the time being, I should find out who is deserving of special attention at our father's entrance into Rome. I understand that you have a list of those who have helped us." There was an annoying sound to Domitianus' voice, Titus thought, a whine that bothered him.

"You know several of them yourself. There's Urbanus

Horatian, Nigrus Marco, Flaccus Aulus Semprius, Justus Silius, Italicus Livicus, Gaius Vitens . . ."

"Make a list of them." Titus sighed. "I'll look it over before I leave for Egypt. It's amazing, I spend a few days here, and then have to go back to Egypt so that I can return to Rome. It's good that our father is Emperor, of course, but these preparations are beginning to bore me."

"You haven't done enough of them to be bored." Domitianus sulked. "You've left most of it to me."

"Well, you've been here. Why shouldn't you help with it?" Titus asked reasonably. He cupped one large hand around his genitals. "All I'd need is sunburn."

"Saturn shrivel your precious balls!" Domitianus burst out, jumping to his feet. "I've been busy for months! Months! While you've been sitting outside Jerusalem whoring with your Jewish queen and your serving boys! I've talked to Senators until my throat felt like Cloaca Maxima, I've spent hours with the Praetorians, I've tried to keep Licinius Mucianus from seizing power for himself, and now you lie here and worry about toasting your famous golden prick!" He turned abruptly and walked the length of the peristyle garden. The sun was a bright glare in the sky, and Domitianus discovered he had a headache.

Startled, Titus rolled onto his side and levered himself up on his elbows. "Domi?" he said speculatively. "Domi, I didn't mean to offend you. I know how hard you've worked for us. You were here in the fighting, and you've done wonders with the Senate these last few months. I realize you've had a lot to deal with." He also knew that his younger brother was jealous of him, but thought he had better not mention it.

Domitianus stared down at the rosebush beside him. He wanted very much to believe his glorious older brother, but part of his mind rejected this sudden fellowship. "No one realizes how much I've done for our family. Not you, not our father, not anyone. I think you all assume that you can ask anything of me, and I'll do it for you without question." He did not know how petulant he sounded, though he wished for greater eloquence. "You have been in war, you say? Well, so have I. And I didn't have Berenice to comfort me, or all of the legions in the east to assist me and sing my praises."

"Oh, Domi." Titus sighed, exasperated. "You sound as if you were the only one who's had to sacrifice for our good. We've all given up things, worked hard, done without pleasures." He thought he had better not pursue that complaint, because he was aware that Domitianus had some basis for grievance there. "You've been valiant and effective. You deserve the respect that the Praetorians have given you. It's been difficult for all of us. You've had to bear the brunt of the work we've done in Rome, but all the family has had to struggle for this victory. You'll have your recognition in time, Domi."

"Will I?" he asked harshly. He did not turn to face his brother. "It's a simple thing to promise that, but it might not be possible to do as you intend. I'm tired of empty words." It was terrible to speak so, he told himself, but there was no way to stop the words now. "You're the heir. You're the one all this is for. It's a simple thing to make sacrifices when you know that it will all be to the good someday."

"Galba and Otho and Vitellius thought so, too," Titus reminded Domitianus. "Our father might outlive both of us, and then what would be the advantage?"

Domitianus pulled one of the roses off the bush and let the petals fall away between his fingers, his shrewd mind working quickly. "You don't believe that, Titus. If you thought that was so, you'd still be in Jerusalem with Berenice. This trip, ostensibly for our father, is really for you, isn't it?" The scent of the flower was left on his long fingers when the bloom had dropped to the ground.

"Nonsense," Titus said, without conviction. "There are many candidates for the purple, but how many of them ever wear it?" He got off the couch, slapping at a mosquito that had settled on the top of his hip. "Domi, don't fret. You'll have your credit and the respect you want."

"Another easy promise, Titus?" he asked, feeling very sad. "I should be thankful." At last he looked at his brother. "Rome will love you, unless it learns to know you."

"Rome loves you already," Titus said with false enthusiasm.

"No." Domitianus shook his head reluctantly. "No, Rome does not love me and will not love me ever. But Rome will accept me and that might be enough." He squinted upward; the sky was hot today, looking like hammered brass.

For one of the few times in his life, Titus found nothing to say. He put one hand on his brother's shoulder, only to have it shrugged off.

"You had better be careful with Licinius Mucianus. He's a

good general, the Romans know him, his soldiers have followed him faithfully, and he's energetic. Get him into a rivalry with one of the other generals, or there'll be another conspiracy before our father's boats arrive at Ostia. You should also spend a little time at the Senate and listen to the way talk is going. We've got to think about taxes soon, and about land grants for retiring legion soldiers. A few of the legions are behind on their pay. You'll have to change that. You said that our father wants to make a monument for himself in Rome. Let it be another circus, a very big one, because the Circus Maximus isn't big enough to hold all the people who want seats for the Games and wasn't designed for battle, anyway." He spoke flatly, his eyes on the far side of the peristyle.

"Domi?" Titus said, distressed by his brother's behavior.

Angrily Domitianus faced him. "This is what you want from me, isn't it? Then listen and act on what you learn."

Titus' face softened. "Domi, don't be angry. We didn't endure all that we have to end up angry with each other. Our father is Emperor now, and it is time we learned to enjoy our privileges as well as accept our responsibilities. Once we've got ourselves officially installed in whichever palace our father likes best, take a few months off. Find a few inventive companions and amuse yourself with them. You're feeling this way because you've had so little chance to take your full pleasure. You've been chiding me for Berenice. Isn't there some woman you'd like to bed? As the Emperor's son, you'll find many opportunities for that sport. Husbands and fathers will look the other way when you see a woman you like."

This wakened a lingering memory. "It's true, perhaps," Domitianus said to himself. "Justus offered his wife . . ."

"There." Titus smiled broadly. "You see? All you'll have to do is choose among the ones you want. No one would be stupid enough to deny you, especially the women. You'll have to reward them occasionally, but you're in a position to do that now." This time when he put his hand on Domitianus' shoulder, it stayed there. "I'll tell our father that you should be given public credit for all you've done. That will help. You'll see that it does. And in a year or so, you can establish a private villa of your own so that you may have privacy for your various recreations." He chuckled. "We've got to remember the question of public morals. Romans can be oddly priggish."

Domitianus heard only part of this. He was thinking of the subtle offer that Cornelius Justus Silius had made only ten days ago. He had said that his wife was passionate, and a woman of strange, submissive tastes. That covert offer had sounded echoes in his mind. Atta Olivia Clemens was not the sort of woman that attracted him, but if she had a desire that was the complement of his own . . . "What were you saying?" he asked Titus.

"Nothing," Titus answered blithely. "Come. It's hot. Let's go in. An hour or so in the frigidarium and we'll both feel better. Then we can get dressed and start evening visits to all these men that our father wants to know better." He sighed rather deeply. "After all this effort, there's more required still. We'll have to shoulder the weight awhile more, I fear."

"We can do it." Domitianus swallowed his resentment and let himself fall under the spell of his handsome, charming brother. He put an arm around his waist as he had when they were boys. "A bath would be welcome."

Titus cuffed his shoulder affectionately. "You're the most dependable of us all. Do you think the slaves will gossip if we go through the palace like this?"

"Slaves always gossip," Domitianus said philosophically, "and if there is nothing to gossip about, then they make it up." He began to walk toward the side of the house and the corridor that led to the baths in the palace. Once in the shade he looked back toward Titus, who still stood, beautifully nude, in the peristyle, posed like a piece of Greek sculpture. Domitianus sighed and resumed walking toward the palace baths.

Only when he was certain that Domitianus was no longer watching him did Titus abandon the pose he had worked so long to effect. He knew the posture had not been quite perfect. It would take a little more practice to achieve the resemblance to Apollo that he wanted. He rubbed his chest once more and thought it was time he was shaved again. Body stubble was nothing like Apollo, he thought wryly as he strode into the darkened corridor.

Portion of a report by the Praetorian Guard, submitted to the Senate and the new Emperor Titus Flavius Vespasianus.

In the matter of the merchant Titiano, we have found that the accusations against him are for the most part true. Dyes and textiles on which he has paid no tax have been found in his warehouse and there were spices seized at his warehouse near the Theatre of Marcellus. He has admitted that he lied in the testimony that we questioned him on before and he has refused to say more because of the others that are involved in his operations. It is our recommendation that the man be sentenced according to the law, and be given the chances to name his accomplices, in exchange for a lessening of the severity of his punishment. If he refuses, send him to the arena. We request authorization to subject him to the equuleus—stretching his limbs may stretch some truth out of him.

In the matter of the slave dealer Nurex, despite our exhaustive investigation, we can find no evidence that he was cheated by the Cappadocian who bought the three slaves from him. There was no way either Nurex or the Cappadocian could have known, from the beginning, of those slaves' particular talents. Nurex will have to bear his misfortune with fortitude.

In the matter of Ragoczy Sanct' Germain Franciscus, our investigation has not shown any indication that he has knowingly participated in smuggling operations, or other illegal activities. However, there has been no concrete proof to the contrary, either, and so far, our investigations have not turned up any further information either way. Were Franciscus a Roman, we would recommend that the matter be dropped, but as Franciscus is a foreigner and something of a mystery, we would prefer to continue our observations of him for another half-year at least. We have received two more anonymous letters about Franciscus, and still have not been able to discover who is the author of them and why he or she bears Franciscus a grudge, for such would seem to be the case. We would like not to make any final decisions regarding this man yet, but if more funds could be authorized, perhaps it would be possible to learn more about his associates in Egypt and other eastern countries. We would also like to discover who is writing those letters, and why.

In the matter of the murder of Janarius Oppoius Rufus, it has been found that two of his body slaves conspired in his death. Under the law, all his slaves must be condemned to death for their act, and in this case, we would recommend that the slaves be sent to the arena, where they would provide an excellent example of the work of Roman law. It would also discourage the gladiators and other combatants from rebelling, since this would demonstrate that justice is swift and sure.

In the matter of the shipbuilder Polyclitus . . . investigation has shown that he was not lax in his building, but that the wood supplied to him was not as specified, being too young and not treated as the shipbuilder so designated. The man responsible, Cradoc, is a freedman residing near Bononia. We would suggest that this Cradoc be fined and watched for a year, and that any further infractions of the law or the instructions of those who order wood from him be punishable by public flogging.

In the matter of Cerrinius Metellus Daecio, it has been found that he has indeed made use of his wife's monies and estates, and in violation of her marital rights as set down by Divus Julius and Divus Claudius. It is our recommendation that he be required to pay her full and complete restitution with an additional sum of damages not to exceed half of the actual sum to be restored. We further recommend that her request for a full divorce be granted immediately and that the claim of his family against her for slander be denied. Investigation has also shown that Daecio has many gambling debts that were pledged on the strength of his wife's fortune, and for that reason, we would stipulate that there may be no claim made upon her by his gaming creditors, who might otherwise approach her for settlement. If the Senate will authorize the sale of his property, both land and slaves, for the discharge of his debts and damages, the matter may quickly be settled and the conflict between husband and wife speedily resolved.

In the matter of the water theft from the Claudian Aqueduct . . .

8

HER FATHER'S HOUSE was cold. Olivia sat in a corner of what had been her mother's room, three stolae around her shoulders, a single oil lamp burning while she tried to read from the scroll she had brought from the library. Her attention wandered, but she was determined to postpone as long as possible the time she would rise and climb into the bed that waited against the far wall, for the blankets were thin, the mattress hard and the drafts through the room on this chilly night conspired to keep her awake. She hoped to make herself sufficiently exhausted to sleep, no matter how cold, how uncomfortable the room.

She sighed as she tried to make sense of the faded Greek letters on the scroll. Her knowledge of the language was adequate but not scholarly, and in the poor light she had a great deal of trouble deciphering the tale.

In the month she had lived in her father's empty house, she had felt hope ebb within her. At first she had been delighted at what seemed an escape from her husband's increasingly violent demands, but that had proved not to be the case, for when the need was on him, he would bring men to her here. He no longer bothered to hide while she was ravished, but stood nearby, watching critically.

A spot of moisture dropped onto the scroll and she wiped it away angrily. She would not weep! That had been her decision on the day that Vespasianus came to Rome, almost a month ago. All Rome spoke of new beginnings, and she had decided then that hers would be to abandon her futile sorrows. Her hands trembled on the scroll and she made a soft, strangled cry in her throat.

She looked up swiftly, hoping that those Justus had set to guard her had not heard the sound. They reported everything to him, and it had become increasingly important to her that he should not learn how much anguish he had caused her. She waited, hardly breathing, for the sliver of light from the hall that would show the servant she had come to think of as her jailer. There had been a sound beyond the door, she knew it, a slithery sound as if something had slipped along the floor. For one panic-filled moment she feared that Justus had decided to visit her again, bringing her some new horror.

The door opened at last, the slice of light amber in the gloom. Olivia shrank back into the shadows, trying to make herself as small as possible, or invisible.

A dark-cloaked figure stepped into the room, and a voice she thought never to hear again said, "Olivia."

She dropped the scroll as she got to her feet. "Sanct' Germain." Slowly she came across the room toward him, her voice husky with fear. "How did you get here. You must leave at once, before they find you. Oh, my love, I've missed you so much."

He held out his arms to her, and wrapped her within his cloak, close to him, his face against her hair as she, in sudden fierceness, clung to him. "Olivia. Olivia." With one hand he tilted her wet face up to him. "Olivia," he said again as he kissed her with a strange, quiet passion drawn from the depths of his soul.

When she could speak again, her words came in impulsive little starts, spoken hardly above a whisper, and all the while her hands plucked nervously at his tunica, as if wanting to reassure herself that he was not the product of her imagination. "How did you get here? How did you know where to look for me? You mustn't stay. How did you get in? They'll hurt you if they find you. They'll tell Justus. Sanct' Germain. Help me. Oh, my love, help me." Without warning she started to cry, great ragged sobs wrenching out of her.

His arms held her securely while the worst of her tears raged through her; then he lifted her easily and carried her across the room to the bed. As he walked, his heeled boots made a sharp report on the cold marble floor. When he had put her on the bed, he lay down beside her, his body close against her, his cloak spread over them both. He murmured quiet, endearing words to her while his small, beautiful hands smoothed the tears from her face.

"No," she said at last, trying feebly to break away from him. "No."

"No?" he asked, kissing her eyelids. "By all the forgotten gods, Olivia, you are precious to me."

She winced as if in pain. "Don't. Don't say that." Her voice had risen, and she quieted herself with an effort. There were those who were listening. He had to understand that. "Don't. If the guard finds us . . ."

"That's unlikely," he murmured as he loosened the stolae she had knotted around her shoulders in a futile attempt to keep warm. "Your guard, by some curious happenstance, drank drugged wine tonight, and will not awake until morning." He moved back far enough to get a clear look at her, and was secretly shocked by what he saw. Her face was thinner than ever, and there were new lines around her eyes and by her mouth that told more than words would of the suffering she had endured. There was a tightness in his chest when he spoke to her then, and though he tried to keep his words light, some of his anger and his concern colored them. "We have all night together, and there is nothing that the guards or Justus or the Emperor or Jupiter himself can do to stop us. I should have come earlier. I should have come when I found out where you were. I didn't want to take needless risks, but I see that I should have."

She put her hand to his lips. "No," she said, barely audibly. "Be quiet. There may be others still up."

"I'm not a fool," he reminded her gently. "No one else is awake. Only you and I." His mouth touched hers, the open lips parting hers with gentle persistence. He pressed closer to her, feeling the lines of her body through the garments that separated them. "Olivia." He had wanted her in all the days they had been apart, but now that he was beside her, his need was as sharp as steel within him.

"Sanct' Germain," she whispered, holding on to the last shreds of her resolution. "No, no, I can't. It's too hard, to love you, to have you with me, and then to have to subject myself to my husband. You know what he has done to me. I don't think I can stand this any longer, having your love when we can dare to be together, and then return to the demands that Justus makes of me. Don't ask it of me, my only, only love."

His lips grazed her neck. "I won't abandon you to your

husband. I've told you that before. I won't. You must not ask that of me, Olivia."

"Then what am I to do?" she asked, feeling the full weight of her misery once more. "I can't continue this way. Each day is worse than the last, and sometimes I'm afraid I'll go mad. I haven't heard from my mother in years. Here I am surrounded by nothing but spies, who find my state amusing. There are only a few scrolls left in the library, and I've read each of them at least twice. Justus has left me nothing. Even the statues that used to be in the niches are gone. He says that I have no need of them. Sanct' Germain, tell me. What am I to do?" This time she managed to hold her tears back.

"You must leave him. You must come to me. I've told you that for over a year." His hands worked to untie her clothes as he spoke to her in the dark.

"But the Praetorians . . ."

"If every officer of every legion and guard of Rome were in pursuit of me, it could not possibly make a difference between us. I don't say that idly, Olivia. I will have you with me, if I have to drag you through Rome by your hair." In token of this, he tugged at the pins that held her long hair in an untidy knot at her neck. Eagerly, slowly, he spread her hair over the rough pillow. "Listen to me, Olivia. You are part of me. Nothing in the world can change that, except the true death, and that has yet to touch me, though it's had almost two thousand years to do it." He was working lose the fibula that held her palla at the shoulder. "We've been together too often, too long for you to be free of me." His parted lips closed on hers again, less gently now as he felt his desire for her well within him. As their kiss lengthened and deepened, her breath quivered.

Then she pulled away, aching, her jaw tight. "I can't. My dearest Sanct' Germain, forgive me, but I can't." She tried to turn away from him, in the cradle of his arms. "Take what you need. I can do that, at least. It's what you must have." She closed her eyes so she would not have to see the compassion in his face. "Don't torture me with false hope. It's too hard, Sanct' Germain. I can't keep on this way with you. It's too painful when I have to return to . . . the other. I wish I were stronger . . ."

"You are strong," he said, moving to look more clearly into her face. "How many women do you know who could survive what you have? Justus' first wife is mad and his second dead. In spite of all that he does to you"—as he said it, rage pricked at him—"you have endured it. You haven't succumbed to his debauchery. You are sane. You are alive."

"No, Sanct' Germain. Please . . ." She shook her head.

He took her face in his hands. "Do you mean that? Do you want me to do nothing more than take what you think I require and leave you? Here? To this? Is that sufficient for you?"

Olivia could not meet his penetrating eyes. "No. It's not enough. But what else dare I have?" It was more difficult than she had imagined to deny him. There was no choice, she reminded herself, as she had so many times in the past month.

"Perhaps," he said in a low, caressing tone, "it could be enough for you. It would not be enough for me."

"It must be," she whispered as she reached to touch his good, loving face.

"But it can't be. I am not like other men. You know that. That was why you accepted me at first." With one finger he traced the line of her mouth. "I could never do to you what other men had done. Even if you desired it. Even if I desired it."

Hating herself for doing it, she braced her arm against his chest. "Sanct' Germain, what can we hope for?"

If he understood her, he chose to interpret her words in another light. "It's true that I can no longer serve you as another man would, but there are compensations. Would you like to spend all the night in loving? In seeking fulfillment and release in new ways, each unique, each wholly satisfying? There are myriad kisses to shower on you, touching that will bring sweet fire to the inmost part of you. Think of exploring the limits of your desires without fatigue and without disappointment." He moved the three stolae and the palla aside so that he could put his hand on the curve of her breast, an ardent, protective gesture that brought her out of the remote place of her mind where she had retreated from his concern and gentleness. "Whatever you desire, Olivia, for as long as you desire it, that I can do. My stamina is the same as your own. Have you forgotten that?" He bent to her lips again and this time she did not resist him, but lay passive beneath his demand. "Olivia," he said at last, more with sadness than reproach.

"I'm afraid," she said at last.

"Of me? After all this time?" He leaned above her, the muted glow of the oil lamp on the other side of the room touching the edge of his brow, the side of his nose, the curve of his mouth.

"I'm afraid of the things that I want." Longing for him grew within her with sudden intensity. She closed her fists in resistance to it.

"Why?" He had begun to pull her clothes away from her body. "Do you want to begin every hour of the night with a new expression of your love? It will be as you wish. I may never join my body with yours as others have, but my. . . soul . . . will share ecstasy with yours."

"And the blood?" Olivia asked, keeping the last little distance between them. "There is always blood."

"Yes." His dark eyes held hers with their intensity. "And there always will be. It is my life. What in you, what part of you is more truly yourself, if not your blood?" He held her closer, lying close above her, the arch of her hip pressing his. "My only gratification comes through your own. My pleasure is entirely drawn from yours. If you take no delight in what we do, then I cannot know any."

Olivia looked up at him, sensing, as she did occasionally, the isolation he had lived with so long, an isolation greater than her own. "Sanct' Germain . . ."

"I'd forgotten many things in my life, Olivia. Or I'd told myself that they were too ephemeral to matter, since I have lived so many years, and the rest of humanity lives so few. But that was foolishness and bitterness. An eternity of loneliness is more wretched than you can know." His arms tightened abruptly. "Let me love you, Olivia. There is so little else I can do. Let me help you put behind the bestiality of the men your husband has forced upon you, and his cruelty. If you cannot forget them, not even for the moment that we lie together, perhaps you can free yourself from the torment within you. We have been lovers for too long. I can't leave you. I can never leave you."

"What do you mean, Sanct' Germain?" she asked, startled out of the weariness that had clouded her mind. She had heard an unfamiliar note in his voice, an implacable promise.

"How many years have we been lovers? Five? And of those years, how often have we lain together in love, you and I? Thirty times? More? It requires six, possibly seven encounters with me and my kind before there is a change in you, a change that cannot be turned aside."

Her eyes had grown wide as he spoke. "What do you mean, a change in me?"

"I mean, Olivia, that when you die, as you surely will one day, you will walk again, as I do, to live as I do, in the taking of blood and the giving of love. I told you this long ago, when we first began—I thought you understood."

Vaguely she did recall some of the things he had told her when they had first become lovers, a warning of some sort that seemed insignificant then. All that had mattered then was his nearness, the release he gave her and the consolation his presence gave her. At the time, she had not cared what he said, or what he had promised, so long as there would be no more abuses by men who ravished and degraded her for her husband's amusement. "I don't think I did understand. Be like you? Entirely like you?" She felt bemused as she looked at him, opening her entire being to him now in a way she never had before.

"Entirely like me?" he repeated. "Very nearly." With one small hand he swept back her lackluster hair from her brow. His smile was rueful. "Unlike me, you will not lose your capacity to enjoy your flesh as women do."

She made a face. "I don't think I want a man inside me again, ever."

"Perhaps," he said rather sadly. "But ever is a very long time and you are apt to see quite a lot of it." He bent his head again, and this time his gentle, probing mouth touched her breast, passing over the nipples with a feather's touch, a light, elusive motion that drew all her desire after it.

"How will I feel when I change? What will I be like?" After the first moment of doubt and revulsion, she found that the prospect of being like her lover had little horror for her. She had known Sanct' Germain too long to find his nature disgusting.

"Much the way you are now, Olivia. You will be stronger, for all those of my blood are stronger, and you will sleep less, much less. The night will be another day to you. You will learn certain . . . precautions, and will never want to be far from your native earth, although you can carry that with you rather than remain atop it," he said with a wry half-smile.

"Are you really from Dacia, then?" she asked, realizing that it might be a convenient fiction he had invented.

"Oh, yes, that's quite true. I never lie about that. The Dacii came after my people by a considerable time, however. The names we give the land change often, but the earth is the same." It was, he realized, almost a thousand years since his people had lived in the part of the world that was now called Dacia. "Occasionally I return there for the pleasure of being on my home ground, but it is much changed since my youth and almost everything is unfamiliar to me but the earth itself." He looked away from her, saying almost dreamily, "The last time I was in my native mountains, they thought me a foreigner, just as you do. Those of my blood have become not memories, but legends. They've learned about the Greek lamia and confuse us with that." When his eyes met Olivia's once again, they were sad. "My cherished love, there are almost none of my blood left, and they are scattered over the face of the earth like grains broadcast in a field. We are few and vulnerable, for all our strength."

She nestled closer to him. "I think I'll enjoy being like you. I want to be like you." This was true. Until that evening, she might have resisted the idea of such a change, but not now, since Justus had sent her to her father's empty house, under guard, with the threat of worse if she opposed him. She remembered vividly his description, a few nights ago, of the brothel in Syria that specialized in Roman women. She had tried then to convince herself that life as a prostitute would not be as bad as what her husband had already done to her, and the pain of it was hard as the blow of a fist. There would be no escape from that brothel, and there was no escape now from Justus, though Sanct' Germain offered another way, one that pleased her. She lifted a hand to her eyes.

Sanct' Germain had watched the rapid, agonized changes in her expression. "What is it, Olivia? Have I upset you? Tell me."

"It's not you, Sanct' Germain. Never you. My husband . . ."—the words were spat out angrily—"my husband said a thing . . ." She stopped, misery closing off her voice. "I have earned the right to my own pleasure, haven't I?" She did not know how wistful she sounded in the cold, bleak room.

"Yes, if pleasure must be a right that is earned, you have done it." He kissed the line of her brow. He was alarmed by the tone of resignation that had come into her life. "Listen to me a moment, Olivia. You have never learned what it is to be moved as other women are. I do not want to give you up, not now. You are too much a part of me. There are things you must know, however, and a few things you and I must accept. In time, before you go to your tomb and walk again, you may want a man again. You deny that now," he said quickly, cutting off the objections that burst from her lips. "Not all men are like Justus. There will be those who will fire your blood and you will be drawn to them, when the bitterness and hatred have faded. You will be drawn to them, as you should be. Understand that, my love. You should desire others, and seek them. It is our life."

"But tonight, it is only between us?" Anxiety made her voice high and small. She had a dim comprehension of what he said, but she no longer wanted to listen. Now his nearness had become as inexorable a force to her as the moon to the tides. "The two of us, all night?"

"All night," he promised her, feeling her senses quicken under his hands. "We will do whatever you wish. Do you want me to caress you and embrace you until you have your release of your own accord? That is your right, and you may ask it of me. Do you want me to search for new expressions of love? You have only to tell me, and it will be as you wish. You've been ordered too long. Be abundantly selfish, Olivia, and you will be more generous to me than you know."

"But is this mine?" she mused aloud. "Or is this something else, foreign to me?" She had wondered this from the first time he had come to her, giving her pleasure when she had expected the worst brutality.

"Foreign." He laughed, though there was melancholy in his dark eyes. "Do you think that this is any more foreign than what you have been subjected to? Is what your husband forces on you more human because there is semen on the sheets at the end of it?" Centuries ago that question would have angered him, but he had answered it many times and the distaste it once engendered in him was gone. Now it was only a matter of reassuring Olivia so that she could set her anguish, her doubt and worry aside.

"I suppose it isn't important," she sighed. It was pleasant to lie back, Sanct' Germain's dark woolen cloak around them for warmth, the sure touch of his small hands, gently persuasive, waking her senses. She let her mind drift as he clothed her in kisses. Now her arms felt softer, less wooden, and she breathed faster. A delicious anticipatory shudder ran through her as her legs opened to his questioning hands. Nothing he did was urgent. His mouth, his hands, the pressure of his body, all were unhurried, as restful and as sensual as the lapping of the sea. Olivia reached for him, sinking her hands in the loose dark curls to pull his face to hers. "It will take time, Sanct' Germain. I'm . . ."

"I have time." He ran his hand lightly up her thigh, over the arch of her hip, along the line of her ribs, across her breast to her shoulder and down her arm. He saw some of her animation return to her face at last, and the tension and fear that held her locked in a shell of herself fell away from her as her garments had. "Ah, Olivia." Now his lips were more insistent, his mouth lingering over hers, summoning the need that was hidden in her, parting from her slowly before moving over the same path that his hand had taken.

The abysmal despair that had possessed her for so many days began to lift, like mist rising from the Tiber at the first morning light, turning from gray to silver to golden white before fading into the day. At last despondency loosened the dank hold it had on her mind. She gave a long, quiet sigh and her hands clenched and then opened as she gave herself over to the exaltation he found in her. *Let me love you. Let me love you.* She heard him say it in her mind as he had spoken the words so many times. Each time it had been a battle to accept him, to let herself know the depth of her pleasure, and each time the desire for him grew stronger. She felt her body was made of light, glowing, a fire, a star, a luminous mist at dawn, that would disappear for elation.

Deep within her she felt her senses contract so that the spasms that engulfed her were more frenzied than any she had ever felt. She cried out for the power and joy of it. In that cold little room she burned like the heart of molten gold.

It was some time before she released him, before the tremor of her passion left her breathing, before her bones felt solid within her. She lay back, her eyes half-closed. Then, with a start she realized that he had not satisfied his own need yet. She turned to him, questioning. "Sanct' Germain?"

He laughed softly, the sound low and musical, his eyes smoldering as he moved off her. The faintly mocking cast to his face was gone. "Now, Olivia," he said in a tone she had never heard him use, one that was unrestrainedly happy, "now we can begin to love each other."

There were tears in her eyes as she opened her arms to him, but not for hopelessness or despair. This time she wept with poignant longing as her desire soared to new life. As his lips brushed the curve of her neck she cradled his head in her hands, the immensity of their rapture filling them both.

Text of a proclamation of the Emperor Titus Flavius Vespasianus.

From the Emperor to the Senate and the People of Rome, greetings:

On the suggestion of my older son, who bears my name, I am pleased to announce to you all that it is my intention of celebrating my imperial reign by causing to be built a new amphitheatre for future Great Games. I have sought the advice of those knowledgeable in such matters, builders and arena workers alike, and their recommendations have been weighed and evaluated most conscientiously.

The location I have elected for the site of this amphitheatre is between the Esquiline and Palatine hills, where the lake in the gardens of Nero's Golden House currently lies. This lake will be drained, and in so doing will not only provide a superior location for the amphitheatre, but will help in the removal of that profligate Emperor's stamp on Rome.

This new amphitheatre will be large enough to accommodate those who wish to attend the Games without the serious overcrowding that has so often resulted in accidents and injuries in the Circus Maximus, the Hippodrome and the Circus of Caligula and Nero. So that it will be easier for all those who attend to see the full action of the Games, the circus will have no spina to block the view of many, and a special track will be constructed for the chariot races outside of the major arena, surrounding it. No more will chariots have to race where battles have just taken place. This will be beneficial to the charioteers, and will speed the flow of arena activities.

For those who worry about a conscription of slaves, I, as your Emperor, pledge to you that this will not happen. It is possible for us to use slaves already consigned to imperial use—the prisoners of the recently contained Jewish revolt. These prisoners will be given the task of building this fine circus. Before the end of summer, there will be ten thousand Jewish slaves in Rome to work on the amphitheatre.

Our plans are set, and we can tell that this will be a circus unlike others. This time it will not be necessary to cobble in improvements, for all the best architectural features have been planned, and the very latest in circus engineering has been studied for the construction of this amphitheatre.

The draining of the lake will begin in April, and as soon as the ground is sufficiently dry, formal building excavation will commence. When the circus is complete, it will be the glory of Rome.

Caesar Vespasianus
on the fourteenth day of March,
the 823rd Year of the City

9

KOSROZD SHADED his eyes so that he would not be dazzled by sunlight. He had just emerged from the dark stables of the Circus Maximus into the full noon glare. It was hot, and would be hotter tomorrow when he was scheduled to race.

"Persian!" called another charioteer, a flamboyant young man from Burdigala in Aquitania. "Come drink with us!" He waved his arm toward a group of other charioteers.

Kosrozd returned the wave. "Sorry! Maybe after we race."

"That's tomorrow," the Burdigalan objected. "A cup of wine won't fuddle you." He laughed his encouragement.

"After the race, perhaps," Kosrozd called again. "I'm not sixteen like you, but an old man of twenty-five." Among charioteers he was, in fact, at a fairly advanced age. His body, aside from the white seams of scars in his shoulder, had not changed since the night when he had tasted his master's blood and had become like him. He had not believed at first that his body would always be that of a nineteen-year-old, but it had been nearly six years since he made the change, and he had learned that it was true.

"Leave him alone, Havius," one of the others said. "The Persian doesn't drink." He added something under his breath that Kosrozd did not quite hear. The other charioteers chuckled and one of them gave Kosrozd an inquisitive stare.

Kosrozd knew that he had become an oddity among the charioteers, but his annoyance had worn off, just as Sanct' Germain had said it would. Two years before, he had got into a fistfight because he had refused to have a meal with Salamis, a famous charioteer who had won his freedom and a fortune in one afternoon. At the time, Kosrozd's honor was stung, and he had, he realized, acted very foolishly. "Have one for me," he called after Havius.

"Two!" came the prompt answer.

With a shrug Kosrozd turned away from them and found the Master of the Bestiarii facing him. "Good day, Necredes," he said with a minimum of cordiality.

"Kosrozd," Necredes answered with unsettling satisfaction. "I saw the woman here, as well." He folded his arms over his chest.

"It's her last appearance," Kosrozd remarked, feeling a touch of sadness. "She's going to be a trainer now. Our master has assigned four young charioteers to her already, and they're preparing to perform in the arena in two years or so." He was aware that Necredes knew this, but saying it gave him an excuse to study the Master of the Bestiarii closely. He was disquieted by what he saw. Necredes was smug.

"It certainly is her last appearance," Necredes agreed, "though she may be persuaded to one more presentation." He gave Kosrozd a curt nod and turned toward the corridor that ran under the stands. "We're getting new beasts today. Be careful of your horses. It wouldn't do to lose them."

"I appreciate your concern," Kosrozd said with heavy sarcasm. He shook his head and started across the stableyard to inspect his chariot and harness. The new rig that Sanct' Germain had developed was working well, but many of the slaves did not know how to handle and clean them properly.

"Persian!" Necredes shouted suddenly.

Kosrozd stopped. "What?"

"I have not forgotten!" Even at this distance, his rage was easy to see.

"Neither have I, Necredes," Kosrozd replied, and continued toward the quadrigium.

"Tell your master!" Necredes screamed, though Kosrozd gave no response. "Tell him!"

For an instant Kosrozd wanted to turn on Necredes, though Sanct' Germain had forbade such outbursts. He stifled his dislike and went on toward the long, low building where the chariots were stored.

Somewhat later, when the other charioteers had returned to the Circus Maximus bringing two skins of wine with them, and the new shipment of leopards had at last been unloaded into their holding cages, Kosrozd was sitting on the shady side of the stableyard watching three pairs of essedarii practice passes in their high-fronted chariots. His eyes narrowed critically as one of the pair completed a successful throw of the lasso on the target post.

Havius, his hand around the top of one of the wineskins, reeled toward the two-man chariots. "Catch me!" he cried out in challenge.

The other charioteers whooped their approval as the nearest of the essedarii shouted, "Right!" The driver pulled the two horses around and the roper began to spin his lasso. Havius let out a happy yell and sprinted across the stableyard. A second essedari chariot joined the chase.

A Greek charioteer shouted a wager on the impromptu contest and moments later there were bets being made on all sides.

"What's this?" Tishtry had come up beside Kosrozd. Her face was flushed and her rough tunica had a tear near the shoulder.

"Havius is playing tag with the essedarii," Kosrozd said rather obviously. "What happened?" He touched the flap of torn cloth, waiting for an explanation.

"It's Kalon. He mistimed a jump, and came close to getting his brains kicked out. He would have deserved it, too," she added with narrowed eyes. "He's learned to do one trick, and he thinks he knows everything it took me a lifetime to learn. If he keeps it up, he'll get killed." She sat down beside Kosrozd, her eyes bright with fresh indignation.

The third essedari chariot was after Havius now, who was

running in an irregular zigzag pattern to avoid the spinning ropes that snaked toward him. The charioteers on the sidelines shouted derision or encouragement, depending on their bets.

"Seen enough?" Kosrozd asked when Havius made his second escape. "Aumtehoutep is probably waiting for us. I'll call the others." He got to his feet.

Tishtry pulled at the hem of his tunica. "No, wait. I want to watch this. It shouldn't take much longer." There was the beginning of a smile in her eyes as the three chariots with their ropers pursued Havius. "They're doing better, the essedarii. They were getting in each other's way, but no more. Look."

Resigning himself to seeing the contest through to the last, Kosrozd leaned back against the stable wall, doing his best to duplicate his master's sardonic smile. "It won't be much longer."

Havius ran toward the target post, caught it with his outstretched arm and pulled himself around as one of the lassos dropped, narrowly missing him and snagging on the post. "Not good enough!" the charioteer mocked, and darted away again.

There were more spectators now. Other arena fighters as well as some of the denizens of that dark world under the stands, attracted by the shouting, had gathered to watch. They screamed their rowdy enthusiasm as Havius sprinted between two of the essedari chariots so that the high vehicles almost collided. Hoots of derision as well as cries of approval greeted this.

"He's doing fairly well," Tishtry said with a quick glance at Kosrozd.

He shrugged. "If the essedarii weren't playing, they'd have dragged him until the skin was off him on the first pass." Still, he thought, it was pleasant to watch the sport. He had lost his taste for betting, but the contest intrigued him.

The crowd was growing larger. A squad of gladiators had come from their practice area, and seeing the lassos, pushed their way through to the front of the crowd. No one refused these strong, ruthless fighters, whose only skill was killing.

In a moment of supreme defiance, Havius paused to drink from the wineskin he still carried, and very nearly was snagged by the roper in the nearest chariot. His bravado brought a wild reaction from the crowd around him, and he waved as he made a sudden leap away, and an essedari rumbled over the place he had been. An Egyptian bestiarius yelled something incomprehensible as the wheels of one of the chariots struck him a glancing blow.

Then Kosrozd noticed something beyond the crowd, and he pushed away from the wall, suddenly very tense. His knee-length black tunica brushed Tishtry's shoulder where she sat beside him, and she looked up. "What is it?"

Kosrozd shook his head and motioned her to silence, moving a few steps farther into the shadows. The essedarii raced past him, but he ignored them. He snapped his fingers. "Tishtry. Get up."

Puzzled, she turned toward him. "What is it?" The sharpness of his command startled her. "What—?"

"*Get up,*" he hissed, and held out an imperious hand.

Frowning, she got to her feet. "But what—?"

She was cut off by another shout as one of the ropers miscast his lasso and caught the driver of one of the other chariots. Before the essedarii could disengage from each other, one of the chariots was over on its side and Havius, winded, jumped to the fallen chariot and raised his arms in victory, letting wine spill on his upturned face.

With his eyes fixed on something beyond the gathered crowd, Kosrozd began to move toward the stable door. He had grabbed Tishtry's wrist, and pulled her after him.

"What is it?" she demanded just as Havius tumbled from his place on the overturned chariot.

"Soldiers," was the terse answer. "There's a century of them out there. Armed."

"They heard the shouts," Tishtry said impatiently, and tried to free herself from Kosrozd's grasp.

"I said armed," he told her. "They're bringing weapons inside the gates of Rome. It's no accident they're here."

"But what . . . ? Why . . . ?" She felt his urgency in his fingers. "Kosrozd, what's happening?"

"I don't want to stay to find out," he snapped as they stepped into the nearest stable door. Near them a horse whickered nervously, pawing at the sawdust-strewn earthen floor. "Where's your team?" he demanded. "Quickly!"

There was still no fear in Tishtry's eyes, but she was beginning to realize that Kosrozd was serious. "The next block of stalls."

"Good." Kosrozd nodded, releasing her wrist. "What about your chariot? Mine's in the quadrigium. I can't get to it."

"Why? What are we going to do?" Though the shouts from outside were undiminished, she had begun to whisper.

"We're going to get out of here, I hope. If those soldiers were sent here, for us . . ." He broke off, listening. There had been a crash and an answering roar from the crowd.

"That's crazy," she said, trying to reason with herself as much as with Kosrozd. "We're arena slaves. We're foreigners. Almost everyone out there is a foreigner. Why would anyone think there was any risk from us?" Her wide, high-cheeked face was earnest and she argued with intensity, punctuating each statement with a gesture.

"Spartacus made an army of arena slaves," Kosrozd reminded her.

"That was . . . years ago," she said, not very sure of how long ago that rebellion had been.

"About a hundred, I think," Kosrozd agreed. "They still remember, these Romans. They should remember." He looked down the row of stalls. Ordinarily there would be grooms to guard the horses, but as Kosrozd had hoped, they were out watching the contest in the stableyard. "No one around. Let's go. We'll get your horses. If there's time, we can try to go down to the south exercise ring. It's empty this time of day. We can go out through the side gate." He was planning aloud, thinking that his idea might work, if they had enough time.

"Do you think it will be unguarded?" she asked, trying to be practical. "It might be worse, if we try to leave."

The shouts outside turned to dismayed screams.

Kosrozd's expression changed. He grabbed Tishtry's arm and ran down the long corridor between the stalls. The noise from the stableyard grew louder, more intense.

"Hurry!" Kosrozd panted as they neared the stalls where her horses were housed.

As the sounds increased, the horses became restless, moving uneasily, whickering and snorting, one or two kicking nervously at the stall gates. Bred for speed in the arena, most of the Roman racehorses had skittish temperaments. Unpredictable at all times, when frightened they were apt to attack or bolt without warning. Kosrozd had driven enough of them to know that he would have to rely on Tishtry's team if he wanted to ride through the developing chaos on a horse that would not panic.

There were a few figures in the far door now, and the cries made strange, muffled echoes through the stable.

Seeing the figures silhouetted in the door, Tishtry brightened. "We could let the horses out." A dun stallion in a nearby stall was lunging repeatedly at the bars of his gate. "If ey were turned loose, they would—"

"Go after us first," Kosrozd said as he struggled with the latch on the first of her horses' stall gate. "If the horses get out, it will bring the soldiers even faster."

She sighed. "What do they want? Why are they here? You don't think that—"

A long, agony-filled scream sliced above the other garbled sounds. Kosrozd stopped his work a moment, feeling himself go cold.

"The essedarii caught Havius," Tishtry suggested, not believing it for a moment.

"You don't think at," Kosrozd said through clenched teech as he pulled on the latch and broke it open. "How is he in tight situations?" he asked, nodding toward the liver-chestnut waiting expectantly in the stall.

"Fine," she said, pride in her tone. "He's been doing tricks in the arena for five years, and I haven't had any trouble with him at all. I can wrap my legs around him and hang under his belly while he's at full gallop. He won't bolt." She reached out and stroked the dark, velvety nose.

"I hope not," Kosrozd said fervently. "What about the others?"

"The black, on the other side. He's very steady." Her face softened. The black was the first of the offspring of the stallion Sanct' Germain had given her six years before. He had the strength and steadiness of his sire, but a lighter, faster frame. "He will carry you as long as you need."

"Get mounted, then. Can I control the black by voice, or will I need reins?"

There were other figures running down the long central corridor of the stable, and more crowded the doorway. The clamor from outside had increased so that it was almost impossible to be heard when shouting. Kosrozd did not hear Tishtry's answer as he rushed to the stall she had indicated.

Tishtry pulled herself onto her horse's back, grabbing the mane in one hand and gripping with her legs. She shouted a terse command in her native language, and the horse sprang forward, out of the stall, loping toward the closed door at the far end away from the large mob that was forcing its way into the stables. She could hear wood splinter as horses fought their way out of their stalls, and their frenzied neighing added to the terrible sounds that flowed around her. She could feel her horse grow frightened and she spoke to him to calm him, not realizing that over the noise he could not possibly hear.

Kosrozd had just vaulted onto the black horse and was about to follow Tishtry when there was a groan of rending wood, and in a moment the door at the far end of the stables, the place he had thought offered safety, splintered inward, the huge braces bending as the soldiers forced their way in. As Kosrozd watched in horror, Tishtry rode into them, unable to pull up her fear-crazed horse. Long javelins struck out and the horse went down, hooves flying, as Tishtry fell under her wounded mount.

Unthinking, Kosrozd drove his heels into the black's flanks, determined to get to Tishtry before she could be hurt. The horse sidled under him, snorting in distress, his ears lying back. He moved forward in a mincing trot, perilously near bucking. Other horses were milling around in the wide corridor now, rearing and striking out with their hooves when the crowd from the stableyard got too near.

Tishtry's horse was still flailing his hooves weakly, but this was clearly a dying reaction. The horse was bleeding from many wounds, and somewhere under him, Tishtry was pinned. The soldiers were forcing themselves around the horse so that they could get into formation.

The black carried Kosrozd within range of the soldiers' javelins, then balked, whinnying loudly and tossing his head. "Go on," Kosrozd ordered as he once again slapped his heels into the horse's sides.

"You!" called out the nearest soldier. "Stop and dismount!"

"Get away from my companion!" Kosrozd shouted back.

An officer with a fan-crested centurion's helmet broke through to the front of the line and raised his baton to Kosrozd. "Get off that horse and give yourself up to my second in command." He nodded toward this individual. "And get out of the way."

Kosrozd scrambled off the black and moved quickly out of the way as the horse rose on his hind legs, wheeling away from the troops, back toward the confusion of horses and men at the other end of the stable. Ignoring the centurion's orders, he pushed between the soldiers to where Tishtry's horse lay still. He could see her head and shoulder protruding from under the horse's neck, immobile, eyes closed. He took the horse's head in his hands and pulled.

"Leave off," one of the soldiers said rather kindly. "We'll come back for her later. There's no rush for her."

Brusquely Kosrozd shook off the soldier's restraining hand and resumed his work, dragging at the inert body of the fallen horse with all his strength.

The soldier who had tried to restrain him stared as Kosrozd at last moved the horse's body just far enough to free Tishtry from his weight. "By both Twins!" he said, awed.

Hearing this, Kosrozd knew he had erred. Sanct' Germain had often warned him about showing too much of his strength, or any of those other characteristics that marked those of his blood. "He was not that hard to move," Kosrozd improvised. "Aside from the neck, he was badly balanced." He knew this was not true, but hoped that the soldier had not been paying enough attention to realize this. Then he dropped to his knee beside Tishtry, putting one hand to her forehead. "Tishtry?"

There was no response. She lay still, limp, and though one leg was still trapped under the body of her horse, he was certain it was broken.

"You've got to move," the centurion's second in command told Kosrozd, taking him firmly by the shoulder.

It took a considerable effort of will for Kosrozd not to turn on him with all the weight of his wrath, but he knew that would be greater folly than everything he had done until now. "This woman is alive," he said in a soft, angry voice. "She must be helped. My master would not want me to abandon another of his slaves." He folded his arms in the manner he had learned as a boy, when his uncles had taught him to be a leader of soldiers.

He had not lost his skill. The second in command glanced down at Tishtry, then looked at Kosrozd once again. "If you will stay here with one soldier to guard the both of you, then I will try to find the physician. If you attempt to escape, the soldier will kill her first, and then you." He turned on his heel and strode off into the sunlight.

In the stable, the troops advanced on the arena slaves and horses, pressing them back toward the far end of the corridor. The noise was continuous, demented, more horrible than the sound of blood-maddened leopards. Kosrozd turned his back on the battle and knelt beside Tishtry to guard her, thinking that his one hope was Aumtehoutep—if the Egyptian had seen the soldiers, he would carry the news to their master immediately.

Then he was aware that Tishtry's hand had closed on his, and he breathed his relief while he watched the first eager flies settle on her horse's drying blood.

Text of a letter from the slave Jaddeus to his brother Nahum.

> In the name of Jesus, who was the Christ, greetings, my brother:
>
> It may be some time before this reaches you, for it will be difficult to smuggle it out of our barracks at night, which is the only time it will be safe to make the attempt. Do not be distressed if there is a delay, as this is the way it must be, and we should not question the Great Will in this.
>
> The great lake is drained now, and the worst of the insects have disappeared since it became dry, though many of the slaves have fever and before the summer is gone, there will be need to replace those who have died. There are a great number of Jews here, of all persuasions and disciplines, though the number of Christians is rather few. That must be because so few of us joined the revolt in Jerusalem. Those of us who did, perhaps we deserve this condemnation for seeking worldly justice instead of heavenly salvation. This is a message I hope to preach to those who are prisoners with me. They have so little

hope and I have so much that it would be wrong of me to deny them the comforts of our faith and its promise.

The first of the foundation stones has been laid, and though there is very little of the structure yet above ground, yet already there are beggars and old whores and those who practice forbidden arts living in the crannies of this place. Most of them are proud to be living in what they already call the Flavian Circus, though it will be years before Games can be held here. I have wished I could go among these people and tell them how grave their errors are and tell them the joys that await them when they embrace the faith of Our Lord. Sadly, we slaves are not supposed to talk to these poor wretches, and for that reason, it will be dangerous to make the attempt. In a month or so, when the guards are less careful in their watching, I will make an attempt to reach a few of them. They may even be willing to aid in our correspondence. That is for the future, and as God wills it.

I have thought often of you and of our Brothers and Sisters in the name of the Risen Christ. When last I came to worship with all of you, there was such pleasure between us. You must tell Sister Philomena that her food would have satisfied Our Lord beyond any other on this earth, and the love that we gave each other afterward is still fresh in my mind. It is wrong, of course, to prefer one of our number to any other, for it is contrary to the teaching of Our Lord, but Sister Philomena delights me as none of the others do. Sister Jeremia chided me for it, and said that Our Lord would not approve of this in me. She was right. If we are to obtain His Grace, there must be no limitations in our love for each other, and all who desire it must have it freely. Think of the great love shared by Our Lord and His apostles, each of whom He embraced with the same holy passion that was known by the Greek philosophers long ago. Surely if ever I escape this pestilential hole, I will ask pardon of Sister Jeremia and lie by her side all one night. Brother Adrianus is here, but with another working crew and we do not often see each other or get to speak, but that may change with time.

I was appalled to meet one of those benighted followers of Paul and Timothy who call themselves Christians but who practice the most stringent and hateful austerity in complete contradiction of the rules of Our Lord. This man, Cephas, has told me that what we do is sinful, and despicable. He insists that the love Our Lord spoke of was the kind removed from the love of the body, which is not true. I tried to correct him in his error, and showed him how the words used by Our Lord to indicate love were those words that relate to the love in the body that exalts the soul, and that to deny this was to deny all the teachings of Our Lord and pervert their intent so that the very thing He most despised would be done in His Name. This poor Paulist sincerely believes that he must fast and deny the body and turn away from life so that all his mind is bent on the life that is to come. He calls women a snare. A snare! And insists that Jesus never embraced his apostles with love. He's most adamant in his error, and declares that only Paul has correctly interpreted the words of Our Lord. I hope that I may reason with him and persuade him that all he has come to believe is unfortunate error. Pray for me in this endeavor.

How I long to be with you once again and to join with you in the joys of worship. For now, this is not possible, but I must not despair, for that is the denial of the Holy Spirit, and it cannot enter where such inner darkness holds sway. In my prayers I remember you all, and give thanks that you are safe. Time will deliver me, either from the chains I wear or from the body. Be it soon or late, we will meet again. Say my name at your next Wedding Supper, and remember me to all those who have been my brides in the Name of Our Lord.

In the Name and the Sign,
Jaddeus
the second day of July in the
823rd Year of the City,
and the 71st Year of Our Lord

10

BEHIND HIS easygoing facade, the Emperor had an astute and crafty mind. His many years of uncertain fortune had given him a curious tolerance in some matters and complete inflexibility in others. Justus knew enough to be wary of this, and adapted his mood to that of his august host.

"The building on the new circus is going well?" he asked, solicitous of Vespasianus' pet project.

The Emperor stopped to pull a handful of grapes from those that trailed over the arbor. "Not as fast as I would like, but well. These Jews know how to build, I'll say that for them, but they don't like to have Roman collars." He sank onto a bench and began to eat the grapes.

Justus would have liked to emulate him, but knew that this would not serve his purpose with Vespasianus. He remained standing, hands clasped behind his back. "All Rome talks about the new circus. When do you think it will be ready?"

Vespasianus took a moment to swallow his grapes. "Five years is what the architects tell me, but I know something about that breed. Seven years at the least. Perhaps more." He gave a wry smile. "My son Titus is as fond of the project as I am, and if there are problems, he can finish it."

"Caesar!" Justus said, shocked. "You must not say that. It's because there has been so much imperial strife that you think that way. Consider Augustus' reign . . ."

"Augustus did not come to the purple so late in life. I am almost sixty-two. What I start, I intend that my sons and their sons shall finish. The Julian House did well enough, but I intend that the Flavian House will last longer." He said this flatly, with the calm of long ambition.

"Admirable," Justus responded promptly. "Rome needs a leader and a house that will endure, for only with that kind of continuity will the empire survive." He risked taking a more personable stance with Vespasianus. "When I had the pleasure to speak with your son Domitianus, we talked of this. You did well to have him put at the head of the Praetorian Guard."

"And as well to remove him and make Titus their prefect,"

said the Emperor as he reached for another bunch of grapes. The air was warm, almost sultry, and the soft drone of bees filled the arbor like a cat's purr.

"Didn't Domitianus object?" Justus wondered aloud. He had seen wounded pride in the young man then, and this would only make it worse, he was certain.

"Domi objects to everything," the Emperor responded, and paused to spit grape pips at the vines. "He complains that he lives in Titus' shadow, but he is a younger son. He's there to ensure the line, not to head it." From the tone of his voice, this was not a thing that Vespasianus cared to discuss.

At last Justus sat on the bench opposite the Emperor. "You have indicated that you are going to make some changes in the government. I thought that was what you wanted to discuss with me."

"Naturally. You have been most helpful to my . . . cause. I think it would be pleasant to have time alone with each Senator, but this is impossible, and I am more inclined to speak with those who supported me than with those who stood in opposition to my claim." His narrow, shrewd eyes flicked over Justus. "You aided me very nearly from the first. I've often wondered why."

Justus considered telling the truth, and decided on a modified form. "There's always been the question of wheat shipments, of course, and that put you in a powerful position. Yet, had there been a strong Emperor here, the wheat would have been shipped if it took soldiers to do it. So it was apparent that the men who wore the purple did not know how to manage their great office, while you, in Egypt, did. My first interest is for the benefit of Rome, which must mean a strong Caesar. Your actions showed that you are such a one, and despite your background, are of the mettle of the born patrician. Your father, I believe, was of equestrian rank and a tax collector, wasn't he?"

"He was," Vespasianus answered without embarrassment. "If it hadn't been for Claudius' freedman Narcissus, I wouldn't have been able to advance as I've done. There's no disgrace in admitting that." He finished the grapes and cast the stems aside. "I like your reasons for supporting me. It indicates you have sense, which is sadly lacking in Rome."

"I've thought so often," Justus agreed, nodding sagely. "I have had reason to think so, more than you know." He allowed himself to wear a distant, sad expression. "Never mind that. What is it you'd like to talk about."

"In a moment," Vespasianus said, intrigued by this turn in Justus, as he was meant to be. "What did you mean by that?"

"By what, Caesar?" he said with forced lightness.

"By that remark, that you have reason to think that there is little sense in Rome?" He wiped his fingers on the edge of the loose talaris he wore. This long-sleeved, ankle-length tunica was of thinnest Egyptian cotton and only the purple band, the augustus clavus, distinguished his rank. "Well?"

"It is merely a personal consideration, Caesar. It's not appropriate to talk about it here with you." He let his voice drop and he would not meet Vespasianus' bright eyes.

"Merely personal, you say? Personal fortunes can topple an empire, Justus. Tell me what troubles you." He made himself more comfortable on the marble bench, putting his feet up and crossing them at the ankles. "It's part of the Emperor's duty to be concerned for the lives of his people."

Again Justus hesitated, then said with a great show of reluctance, "You know I have a young wife?"

"Certainly. Her father and brothers were part of one of the conspiracies against Nero, weren't they? The sons went to the galleys or arena or some such, and the father was executed, I believe. The mother is living away from Rome, and there is one daughter other than your wife, somewhere in Gallia, if I remember correctly. I have not been idle since I came to Rome, Justus. I don't want any of those conspirators deciding that they would like to replace me." He looked at Justus. "What is it, man?"

"As I have said, she is young." He made a dismissing gesture. "It is nothing, Caesar. Let us talk about your plans, or the heat or the number of ships in the harbor at Ostia, but not, I must ask you, about my wife." He folded his arms and looked resigned, inwardly satisfied that now Vespasianus would begin an investigation and would learn precisely what Justus wanted him to learn. "I must admit," he said in another voice, "that I didn't understand why you had those arena slaves arrested last month. When I heard of it, I was quite shocked."

Vespasianus studied Justus for a bit before he spoke. "It seemed to be a wise thing to do," he said rather stiffly. "There are a great many skillful fighters who speak several languages in the arena. They have ways of passing messages.

I know that some of my own men received news through gladiators and charioteers. I also know that there are a few of the great patrician houses that are not pleased to have the son of a tax collector elevated above them. They cannot suborn the legions, since the legions must remain outside of Rome. I know that the Thunder-Clap Legion has been discontented for some time. Well, those opponents of mine can find a ready-made army in their arena slaves. Most of Rome knows them and worships them. I would not like to fight an army of those killers. Fifty gladiators and fifty charioteers to carry them, a few essedarii to pull a square to pieces and half a dozen retriari to net the stragglers, they'd be the most powerful, most destructive fighting force that Rome has ever faced. Add to it that most of them have foreign associations, and they would bring Rome to her knees in a matter of months." His face had grown hard and he leaned forward, hands closing to fists as he spoke. "You may think that this is a useless and unpopular precaution, but I assure you it is necessary. It's important that all the Roman nobles understand that I intend to remain on the throne, and that my son and his sons will follow after me. I won't allow anything to change that. They're anxious to put me to the test, I know, but this time I will move to thwart them before they can act against me. It's the only sensible thing I can do, short of open accusations against men of ancient and distinguished families. I don't intend to have another year of four Caesars."

"But surely some of those men object? Arena slaves are valuable and they're a major investment for some of the—"

"Would you sacrifice a dozen slaves in order to remove yourself from the ranks of suspected traitors?" He chuckled and it was not a pleasant sound. "Most of those distinguished Romans are rushing about to make sure their slaves are among those condemned, proving the masters are innocent of any wrongdoing. It's a master's right to punish a disloyal or rebellious slave." He waved at a bee that had come too close to his face.

"But what about the law forbidding slave abuse? Can't the condemned slaves sue their masters?" Justus was aware that the old law of Divus Julius would not be valid in these circumstances, but there might be those in the Senate who would want to test the interpretation.

"That," Vespasianus said with a smile of real satisfaction, "is possible, but what would be their defense? They can claim that the slaves were not rebelling, but how could it be proven? An arena fighter, Justus, is trained to kill. He is in the arena to defend his life in combat. That means that he's worth any four soldiers in any legion, most of the time. There are few men in the legions would be willing to go up against rebellious gladiators and charioteers. Opinion is with me, I think." He gave half a smile.

"I hope you're right," Justus said carefully. "If not, there will be a great outcry against you." He made his features sympathetic and gave the Emperor a searching look. "Have you had objections yet?"

"Certainly," Vespasianus admitted easily. "Most have not been from patricians, though. The freedman Chylos has objected most strenuously, and since he has a vested interest in his fighters, I have asked the Praetorians to take time to investigate his gladiators. He was one himself, once, and fought his way to freedom. I have decided to make him a citizen of Rome, and that will make the investigation go more easily, I imagine. Titus suggested it."

"Have you had others protest?" It would be helpful to know who was dissatisfied, for once in their confidence, Justus could turn the knowledge gained to good use.

"Foreigners, mainly, and there is some difficulty there. If the slaves are owned by foreigners, the law is less clear. I have asked the Senate to give the matter their consideration. There are more than fifteen slaves owned by the Greek Hector of Epirus. That Daci, Franciscus, owns four of the slaves who were arrested. Shabiran of Cyrene owns ten or so of the slaves. In those cases, we must do things carefully. It would be a bad thing to free the slaves, but under the law, there must be demonstration that the slaves were acting either on their masters' authority, in which case . . ."

"In which case," Justus said with an ingratiating nod, "the masters may also be condemned and the matter is easily solved. If the masters are not shown to be acting against Rome, then you must prove that the slaves were acting under the orders of others, and that might be difficult." He smiled sagely. "An awkward situation, Caesar, but I am certain that there is a way to deal with both the slaves and their masters. I can think of one way, but it would take time."

Vespasianus was immediately interested. He sat straighter and stared at Justus. "Go on."

"The masters you mention: none of them are part of a

royal court, though it is true that Hector and the man Franciscus claim to have noble relations. That means that you need not deal with Emperors or other such men. All three men have dealings abroad with merchants. It is certain that some of those merchants also deal with men who are openly opposed to Rome. That could prove that the masters had association with enemies of Rome, and for that can be tried and condemned, and their slaves may be sent to the arena. It would take time to gather such information, but it is certain to exist."

"It's very astute," Vespasianus said slowly. "I am no longer a persecutor of homeless foreigners, but the defender of Rome from insidious alien plots." His face became closed, crafty, as he thought over the suggestion. "If we could produce such associates, it still might not be possible to prove that the foreigners themselves had dealings with the opponents of Rome."

"If the merchants and agents in question who were the link between the foreigners and the enemies of Rome were dead, there would be no way to prove that the connections did *not* exist." This last was the gamble for Justus. If Vespasianus accepted this plan, he would have secured his position with the Emperor, for Vespasianus could never afford to turn away from him once he accepted this advice. Knowing that the Emperor had worked to condemn innocent men gave him a great deal of power. Justus sat back, hoping that none of his anxiety showed in his face.

"Dead," the Emperor said quietly, his eyes fixed on some spot far beyond the grape arbor. "It would be dangerous."

"Is the other way less dangerous, Caesar?" His fear that Vespasianus would reject the idea lent fear to his voice, and this the Emperor chose to interpret as concern for himself.

"You're probably right, Justus. How long do you think it would take to get the information?" His attention was sharply on Justus now. "It would have to be done carefully."

"In six to eight months you should learn enough to put your plan into effect." Justus was pleased at the deft way he made it sound as if the idea were Vespasianus' instead of his own. "If you ask your son, as prefect of the Praetorians, to take on a clandestine search, there would be few who knew of it, and once the proper documents had been filed, the men who had done the investigating might meet with unfortunate accidents. You would not be exposed by anyone then, Caesar."

"Except you?" Vespasianus suggested gently, one brow raising.

"Surely, Caesar . . ." Justus said, aghast, half-rising to his feet. "I see. You fear that I do this for my own benefit, and you wish to entrap me. Very well. I have given Rome most of my years. I do not refuse to give her my life." He stood now, quite straight.

Again Vespasianus made his unpleasant chuckle. "Sit down, Justus. For the sake of Apollo's arrows. Sit down." He waited until Justus had resumed his place on the bench, his back quite stiff, his face averted. "You need not make this display for me. I realize you have a desire for power. How could you be of the Silius House and not do so? There is nothing wrong in the desire for power, so long as it is not abused. Now, if you wished to wear the purple, there would be trouble between us, but I can see by all that you've done for me that this is not the case. If you will be content to be given distinction and to become part of my private council, then we may deal very well together. I would like to put your plan into effect, but I am sure you can see that if you don't accept my offer I must refuse what is really a most ingenious solution to this foreign-masters problem. You are a clever man, Justus, and you have survived in the Senate for many years. I need your advice and instruction and, it may surprise you to learn, I need your help." He had put his elbows on his knees and leaned forward. "Think about it, Justus. You can be very near me, second only to my sons. I need a man like you. You will have a great deal of power. If you wish to enrich yourself, I don't object so long as you are not too obviously greedy about it."

"Caesar . . ." Justus began, alarmed that Vespasianus had deduced so much of his intent. "You are correct in assuming I want power. I have seen the power of Rome frittered away and rent in pieces for too long. I am a rich man already, and I don't want to seize lands and goods for myself, but if I am to advise you, then I do want some compensation."

"What would that be?" Vespasianus asked, plainly skeptical of this avowal.

"Earlier you asked me about my wife," Justus said. "You know that she and I live apart. I have not sufficient proof yet, but I know that she has had many lovers and that her adulteries are common gossip among my slaves. When I have evidence enough to divorce her, would you consent to my marrying one of your nieces?"

"Need it be an heiress?" Vespasianus started to smile now. "If you are so eager to ally yourself with the Flavian House, would you be willing to accept a girl with little dowry?"

"I have said I am a rich man. The alliance is more important to me than money. If you care to investigate, you will find that I gave a settlement to my wife's family when we married. It turns out that I used my money unwisely," he added in what he hoped was a hollow tone. He cleared his throat. "You have said that you intend the Flavian House to wear the purple for many generations. If that is the case, I want the Silian House to share in that glory. I have no children alive, as you know, but if you have a niece who is marriageable, and if she is fertile, then I will have as much interest in the Flavian House as you have."

"You mean that your children would stand in line to the throne?" Vespasianus studied Justus' face and nodded once. "Very well. I will ask among my family. If there is a niece or cousin who will fit your requirements, I will inform you. I am willing to make her children provisional heirs after those of my sons, if that will please you?"

Justus was delighted, but he dared not show how well these concessions fitted with his plans. Vespasianus had two sons, and there were no legitimate heirs yet. If there were never to be, and if neither Titus nor Domitianus lived to reign, then it would be his children, the children of Cornelius Justus Silius, who would wear the purple. He kept his silence as if considering the matter carefully. "I want to accept. It would please me very much to accept. But before I can, there must be a way to deal with my wife. She may be more suited to the lupanar than to my house, but I have only her taunts and the whispers of my slaves to tell me that, and slaves can give no testimony. Let me search further to see if there is a way to settle the matter with Olivia, and then let me speak to you again."

Vespasianus rose. "Excellent. I see that we appreciate each other." He clapped a hand to Justus' shoulder. "I will await your word then, but I will make inquiries about a niece. That might spur you to deal more directly with your wife. If she demands a payment to leave you, why, take it, man, and be free of her."

Justus sighed heavily. "I have made that offer already, but she has refused. She says she will not give me the satisfaction of being rid of her."

The Emperor blotted a line of sweat from his forehead. "It might be worthwhile to approach her again, now that you know it would be profitable to be rid of her?" He let the suggestion hang between them on the grape-scented air.

"I'll make an attempt. It is a shame to disgrace her." He knew that he must not appear to be too anxious to rid himself of his wife, even one that was a harlot, for there were certain matters that a Roman husband should tolerate. If he showed himself too eager to be rid of Olivia, he sensed that Vespasianus would not be willing to make concessions to him once he found a suitable bride.

"It is her disgrace, Justus, not yours." He patted him once on the arm. "I'll expect you to come to the palace in three days and we can talk again." He turned away and headed off down the mosaic path toward the west wing of the Golden House.

Justus looked after him, for the first time letting himself smile.

A letter to the Emperor Titus Flavius Vespasianus from Hercules Ennius Peregrinian, tribune of the Mars' Favorites Legion, stationed at Amisus in Pontus.

To the Emperor Vespasianus and the Senate in Rome, hail:

A difficult situation has arisen here, and one that may seem comical to you, but must still be regarded as the serious threat it actually is. There is a man here claiming to be the Emperor Nero. He says that the announcement of his death was a lie, that he did not kill himself but escaped from Rome before the traitors at his court could assassinate him. He claims that he went to Greece, where he had won so much honor and was remembered with love, and there he remained until the rise of Vespasianus, when he knew he would have to get farther away from the large Roman garrisons. So now he is here, anxious to gather his faithful subjects around him and return to Rome and displace those who have assumed the purple illegally.

You know how much the people loved Nero, and their love for him has grown, not diminished in the five years since his death. Where he was a hero before, he is now almost a god. The people here follow him eagerly, Romans and Amisians alike. There are those of our legion, though it shames me to say it, who follow this impostor and praise him, call "Ave!" to him as they did to Nero. Many of them never saw the Emperor, and few of them had any close association with him, but, as you know, at one time I did. That, good Emperor and Senators, is why I am out here at the back of the world in Pontus instead of making useful friends in Rome. I trust you will remember this when this matter is concluded. I, as I have said, knew the Emperor slightly, and I tell you that this man who claims to be Nero has something of the look of him. His hair is light brown instead of the blond of Nero's, but that's a minor matter. He is not as tall and he is not as skillful with the lyre as Nero was, and does not know all the songs and epics that Nero used to sing. His accent in Greek, furthermore, is that of Moesia, and not the cultured Athenian that Nero spoke. Yet for those who never knew him, the match is close enough.

Be warned, Vespasianus, this man is a real danger. He is intelligent and cunning. He wants to ascend the throne. He already wears the augustus clavus on his garments as if it were his right, and none have denied him the privilege. Think of that, as you decide what to do. You may think that an impostor is no concern to you, but that would be a grave mistake. If the legions in the east were to support this man's claim, it could go badly with the Flavian House. I remind you that the legions raised Galba, Otho and Vitellius, and it was the legions in Egypt who won for Vespasianus; the legions and wheat. It may seem impossible that this man is a menace, yet I tell you he is. Every day he gathers strength, and there is little we can do to lessen it without the assistance of Rome. Make an example of this man, or you will have more false Neros rising, reminding the people of the Emperor they loved, and whose death led to so much misery for Rome.

Send me your orders as quickly as possible. I realize that winter is nearly upon us, and there will be few ships coming here before spring, but it is necessary that we hear from you at the earliest moment. Each day's procrastination is one more day for him to gather men about him. The need is urgent, Vespasianus and Senators. The danger is real.

This by my own hand on the twenty-fourth day of October in the 823rd Year of the City, from the garrison of Mars' Favorites in Amisus.

Hercules Ennius Peregrinian
Tribune

11

THERE WAS scattered applause as Sanct' Germain finished playing and stood back from the tall Egyptian harp. He nodded his acknowledgment to the gathering, right hand touched to his breast in the Egyptian manner. The harp, his manner, his jewelry and clothes, the songs he sang, everything about him was Egyptian tonight.

His host called for more wine to be poured, then called across the dining room to Sanct' Germain, "Wonderful! I've never heard anything like it, not even in Egypt!"

"If you will pardon me, Titus," Sanct' Germain said wryly to the Emperor's older son, "there are many things Romans never hear in Egypt."

"So it would seem." He drank deeply from his golden cup. "Do one more for us, please. We love to hear you." This was not quite an imperial command, but from the look on Titus' handsome face, he did not want to be refused.

Sanct' Germain measured Titus with his eyes, thinking that it would be wrong to indulge him too far. He did not want Vespasianus' heir to think that he could command anything at his convenience. Sanct' Germain had learned long ago that it was foolish to indulge kings and princes too far. "I think," he said lightly, "that rather than bore your guests with more Egyptian songs, I would prefer to sing something Roman, something that will please them and be familiar. There is a song . . . they say that Gaius Valerius Catullus wrote it, but who may be sure of it?"

One of the women in an almost transparent stola looked over her exposed shoulder at Titus. "But he's so *dreary*," she protested. "Always suffer, suffer, suffer. Can't he do something by Ovidius? I like Ovidius."

Titus looked at Sanct' Germain inquiringly as a few of the guests seconded the woman's request. "Well?"

"I think you will find the song isn't dreary," he said with a half-smile. He had no intention of pandering to these seventeen Romans. "Ovidius is delightful, there's no denying it, but he has little left to imagine. After the first theme, it's all said and there is nothing to expand upon, wouldn't you say? With Valerius Catullus, there is more to play with."

Despite the protests around him, Titus waved his hand as he settled back on the couch. "As you wish, Sanct' Germain. Sing us one of those dreary songs of Valerius Catullus."

The other guests took their cue from Titus, and reclined, though the woman who had made the objection began to pout as she held out her cup for more wine.

Sanct' Germain watched them a moment, his fingers touching the harp strings softly, so that there was almost no sound from them. Then he leaned the instrument against his shoulder and began.

> Why, O Lesbia, should tender love torment me?
> What malevolent sweetness works your magic
> That makes travail of a single embrace?
> My love is like a tattered rag in the wind:
> Your promise burns me to the core
> Even as your touch scalds my flesh.

Sanct' Germain began the melody simply, and saw Titus' party grow interested. Gone were the little restive movements and the sharp glances. As he caught their attention, he made more complicated chords with the harp, though he was still keeping to a simple, declamatory style.

> Yet what is freedom worth, compared
> To this delirium of my passions?

What meager pleasure can match this hurt?
What can joy offer richer than this pain?
I desire to be consumed by your love
Though it thrives on its own ashes.

The guests were silent now, and the cup boys stood by the wall, unmoving. Only the sound of Sanct' Germain's voice and the ringing notes of his tall harp were heard in the room. No one spoke. No one moved. No one drank.

His first variation was light and mocking, the high strings making flirtatious countermelody to his voice. He saw the knowing expressions in the eyes of Titus' company, the suggestive, lascivious smiles on those indulged faces. The second variation was angry and dissonant, the harp tolling out accusations against his harsh phrases, bitterness stinging each note. Now the listeners were startled, and one woman seemed more pale than she had been a moment ago. She toyed with her rings as she listened. The third variation was a long, caressing lament, a soaring plea that rose in spiraling cadences, the harp and the voice each drawing the other onward in rhapsodic despair.

When he was finished the room was completely still, as if even breathing was an intolerable interruption to the song. Then Titus thumped the table with his golden cup, roaring his approval. In the next instant, all the others followed his example.

"Thank you, Titus," Sanct' Germain said as he returned the harp to its upright position. There was an enigmatic expression in his dark eyes.

"Splendid! Splendid! I wish more of our Roman musicians could do as well." He had risen from his couch and was picking his way toward the raised platform where Sanct' Germain stood like an archaic statue in a kalasiris of three layers of sheer fluted linen. The Emperor's son stumbled up the step and draped an arm over Sanct' Germain's shoulder. "I wish I could hear that again."

"I will copy out the music if you like, Titus." He moved slightly so that Titus had to drop his arm.

"No, no. There's no artistry in that. I'll have to remember it as best I can. I wish I hadn't had quite so much wine." As he spoke he moved a little nearer Sanct' Germain's harp. "It's quite big, isn't it?"

"It's two handbreadths taller than I am," Sanct' Germain

said quickly. "It's very old and must be handled carefully."

Titus, who was about to try his hand with the instrument, grinned sheepishly. "Then I won't touch it. Amazing the variety of sound that you can get out of it. I heard harps in Egypt, of course, but none of them were like this."

Sanct' Germain smiled. "Mine is unusual. I was given it long before I came to Rome." He did not choose to elaborate on this, but nodded toward the others. "Do you think they might enjoy the tumblers I brought with me tonight? They're most remarkable."

"Tumblers?" Titus said, puzzled. "You mean you brought more?"

"These are slaves of mine, very gifted. I think you would find them entertaining. There are four of them. The other three who usually work with them were arrested with the other arena slaves in June." He said this quite calmly, but was pleased at the rather guilty expression in Titus' eyes.

"I'd like to have them entertain, of course," he said uneasily, not willing to commit himself. "It is late, however . . ."

"They will be here as long as I am," Sanct' Germain assured him. "I don't mean to distress you, but I would like to know precisely what my imprisoned slaves are accused of." He looked away so that the Emperor's son could not see the full power of his dark eyes. "I can't abandon them, Titus. They are mine. I have certain . . . obligations to them."

"Obligations to slaves?" Titus laughed at that, then broke off as he realized that Sanct' Germain had not echoed him, though his other guests, who had not heard what he said, dutifully laughed with him. "How can you have obligations to slaves? They're your property. You may dispose of them as you wish."

"Would you feel that way if you wore the collar, I wonder?" Sanct' Germain asked gently. "Let me send for the tumblers, and you will enjoy them."

Titus nodded his acceptance. "Tumblers. Very good. By all means, have them in."

"They are from Panticapeum at the mouth of Lake Maeotis in Sarmatia. I don't think you have seen the like in Rome before." He knew the Roman love of novelty. "They have performed in the arena only once, and then it was with trained bears, but they have other . . . demonstrations that they do in closer surroundings."

"Excellent," Titus said with false enthusiasm. "Bring them

in, certainly." He got down from the platform. "I'll have my slaves put your harp away. . . ."

"But, Titus," Sanct' Germain reminded him, "it is old and delicate. I will do it."

"As you wish." Titus was feeling uncomfortable now, and his face was beginning to flush. He hated being asked to do things, though it was worse, in this case, not being asked. "I'll see what can be done about your slaves. It's silly, keeping them in prison. It's all nonsense, of course, but we have to take precautions."

Sanct' Germain had picked up his harp, holding it with affectionate care. "Certainly. You need not explain."

This permission made it more difficult for Titus. "There's an investigation, though it's just a formality. It's not as if you're a Roman. The Roman slaves have all been condemned. Your being foreign is what makes it so difficult."

One of the women called to Titus. He turned toward her, annoyed to be interrupted. "What is it, Statillia?"

She read the irritation in his face. "Nothing," she responded quickly. "A small matter."

"I will see to it later." He faced Sanct' Germain once more. "That woman. She thinks if she gets into my bed that I will make her husband governor of Lusitania or something of the sort. Look at her—panting with false lust. It's my father who appoints the governors. She should go pant at him."

"But you," Sanct' Germain pointed out tactfully, "are young and handsome. Can you blame her for preferring to try with you?" This was a calculated remark, but he relied on Titus' vanity to mask its insincerity.

Titus chuckled. "Now, if she had sent her son . . . Have you seen him? Just fourteen, graceful as a dancer, with a face like a young god. Next to Berenice, I can't think of anyone I'd rather have in my bed." He gave Sanct' Germain a friendly pat on the arm. "I don't suppose you understand. So many foreigners don't. They want either boys or women, but not both."

"I understand you, in my way," Sanct' Germain said with an irony that was lost on Titus.

"Do you? That's amazing. I'd expect it of a Roman, but you're . . ."

"Foreign?" Sanct' Germain finished for him, hoping to divert him from questioning him about his meaning. "Let me get the tumblers."

"Good." He motioned to slaves waiting by the doors. "This man has brought tumblers to entertain us. Escort them here."

Sanct' Germain stepped down from the platform. "I must put this in my chariot. I will return shortly."

"Your couch will be ready." He hesitated, then said, "I will do what I can about your slaves, Sanct' Germain. As prefect of the Praetorians, it shouldn't take me long. But you realize, it can't seem like a favor, or my father will forbid it. Give me a few months, and all will be well."

"It has been several months already," he pointed out.

"I know." He frowned and tugged at the folds of his toga. "It's not a simple matter. There are certain questions . . ." He was aware that he should not be saying so much to Sanct' Germain, but he was sufficiently embarrassed to speak further. "I'll tell you what I will do: as soon as the first report is filed, I'll end the investigation, and then you can petition for the release of your slaves." He wished he had never mentioned the matter, but this should end it.

"I would be most grateful," Sanct' Germain said quietly, thinking as he spoke that the months in prison must have been painful for Kosrozd. He had been put in a cell with Tishtry, that much Sanct' Germain had learned, and for this he was grateful, since Tishtry could serve his needs without difficulty. If they had not been together . . . Resolutely Sanct' Germain put that thought from his mind. There was nothing to be gained from such reflections. He made a gesture that might have been a salute, then went swiftly from the elaborate banqueting room.

He found Aumtehoutep waiting in the covered chariot, wax tablets in one hand, a stylus in the other.

"How has it been tonight?" Sanct' Germain asked as he handed the harp up to his slave.

"There are ten men dining with the Emperor, none of them very influential. It seems to be more courtesy than anything else. You know who dines with Titus. I have seen six Praetorians come to the palace, but that's not unusual." He paused and the ghost of a scowl passed over his impassive face. "Domitianus is closeted with Justus Silius."

Sanct' Germain looked up sharply. "Where?"

"I don't know. I tried asking one of the kitchen slaves, and was told it was none of my concern." He tapped the stylus against the wooden frames of the tablets. "Justus Silius has been busy with the Emperor and the younger son. Titus and

Domitianus do not love each other. Justus could be encouraging that alienation."

"It would seem so," Sanct' Germain agreed. "Why? What would he gain from that? He's no relative and is not likely to be an heir. Vespasianus is not about to assign power away from the Flavian House. What does Justus want?" He did not expect an answer to the question, and got none.

"Did you speak to Titus?" Aumtehoutep asked flatly.

"For what good it may have done." He sighed. "He has said he will help, but Titus will promise anything if he thinks it will please the asker. If he will act upon his word, who knows?"

Aumtehoutep wisely said nothing.

"If the matter were to be heard tomorrow, then it might be possible to expect Titus' aid. He will not hurry the investigation, however, which will delay action for some while yet. In that time, Titus can forget a great deal." He leaned against the chariot as he cast a knowing glance at the troubled winter sky. "Rain by morning," he remarked.

"Will you go to the prison?" the Egyptian asked.

"I suppose I will have to. It will cast more suspicion on me, but it can't be helped. After tonight there will be suspicions, anyway." He felt strangely tired, a fatigue that grew out of his frustration.

"Would you prefer that I go?" The question hung between them, for both knew the risk that Aumtehoutep would be taking. "I understand the danger. They might decide to imprison me as well, and it would not make matters any easier for you. But for you to visit slaves in prison would be very suspect." He said nothing more while Sanct' Germain thought.

"You're right, of course," he said heavily. "It would only make things worse if I went to the prison. But I don't want to ask it of you."

"When you took me from the Temple of Thoth," Aumtehoutep said distantly, "I was dead. You restored me to life then, and I have served you ever since. Had you made me like you, perhaps I would have done otherwise. You couldn't do that, but you did all that was possible, and so I have cheated Anubis for years without number. I am not of your blood, but still I am somewhat like you. You have protected me and used me honorably. It would not displease me to do this for you now."

This time Sanct' Germain was silent for a longer time.

"Aumtehoutep. . . ." He stopped. "Why must you be right, old friend? Do as you think best." His small hands closed tightly on the handrail. "But go carefully." It seemed for a moment he would say more, and there was a hardness in his eyes. Then he opened his hands and stepped back. "Keep watch until I return. And if you can find out what Justus Silius is doing with Domitianus . . ."

"You will learn of it," Aumtehoutep assured him.

"I know that. I'm not able to deal with him as I should. I have too much hatred." He made an odd gesture, as if to close off some ruinous thought. "I must get back. Doubtless Titus will want to know more about the tumblers." His mouth widened in what was supposed to have been a smile. "They are very beautiful, the tumblers, young and athletic. Titus is certain to be interested."

"And will you give them to him?" Aumtehoutep kept his voice carefully neutral.

"No. But I don't think I'll tell him that just yet. It may mean a speedier investigation, since I have told him about the others who are in prison. Titus is greedier than his father, and he might find this an incentive." He took a few steps back from the chariot. "Look for me in two hours."

"The chariot will be ready, my master." Since they might now be overheard, Aumtehoutep adopted a more servile tone. "If you will be later, send me word so that I may stable the horses."

"Of course," Sanct' Germain called back through the gathering dusk. He went quickly through the long corridors, toward the sound of cheers and laughter, where Titus sat with his guests, watching the tumblers with blurred, avid eyes.

Text of a letter from Constantinus Modestinus Datus to the prefect of the Praetorian Guard, Titus Flavius Vespasianus.

To the revered prefect of Praetorians, greetings:

I have in hand your inquiry concerning one Ragoczy Sanct' Germain Franciscus in which you ask me if he has ever spoken or behaved in such a way that I thought perhaps he was an enemy of Rome, or working for enemies of Rome.

Good Praetorian, I don't know how to answer you. Not that there is doubt in my mind concerning this worthy foreigner, but because I am baffled by your asking at all. Surely all that the man has done for Rome has shown that his interests are one with ours. He breeds the best mules and sells them to the army more reasonably than do many of our Senators. He has been active in the interests of the Games, owning some of the best charioteers as well as helping to improve the Circus Maximus with the hydraulic organ installed there. He has often supplied various patricians with rare and costly items for a fraction of what it might have cost them to procure such goods. He has helped those in need and his slaves are considered some of the best-treated in the empire. Why, then, do you ask about him? It would benefit us if more Romans showed the same degree of attention and activity on behalf of the empire that Franciscus does.

To be sure, I have personal knowledge of one who was much troubled by this Franciscus. An Armenian scholar, Led Arashnur by name, who visited me about two years ago told a fantastic tale that Franciscus was the same man as a legendary Egyptian physician and had the secret of eternal life, and was not a natural being. He claimed to have had proof of an old man in Egypt, but that in itself is little to go on. You know that Armenians, even the most educated of them, are superstitious fools, easily swayed by their fears and myths. Certainly it would be folly to believe such a man in a matter like this. No doubt this scholar had some reason to dislike Franciscus, for such aversions are common, though none can say why. To assume that it is because Franciscus is an unnatural being, unable to cross water or walk in sunlight—this is patently ridiculous, for all of us have seen him in the day, and if he could not cross water, what would he be doing living so near the Tiber?

There is a question about his slaves, you indicate here,

saying that they are being held with the others suspected of insurrection. Of all slaves in Rome, I can imagine none with less reason to revolt than those owned by Sanct' Germain Franciscus. They are well-fed, well-housed, kindly treated and each is given his chance to excel in his work. There are some who would not be satisfied with purple silk, but most are grateful and value their master as they should. There are no legion deserters in his slaves, no foreign army men, no gladiators at all. Why should anyone suspect them? Were I asked to judge those slaves, I would say that they are wrongfully accused and I would free them immediately with compensation to their master for the loss of their labor and income.

Why does the prefect of the Praetorians seek to antagonize a man who has been tireless in his work and forthright in his business affairs? You say that there have been complaints against this man, signed by no one, and that the complaints have so far proven false. Why do you put faith in such flimsy and contemptible accusations? Is the foreignness of the man such that it blinds you to his excellent qualities? If so, must he forever be under a cloud of questions and suspicions? I confess your questions disquiet me. What must he do that will convince you of his intent?

My own association with the man, though rather slight, has always been the most satisfactory and honest. He has found texts for me that I feared did not exist in the world. He has been glad to assist in learning and teaching when my studies have gone into areas where I am not expert. It is true that he spent much time with Nero, but many of us did. That does not mean that he is disloyal to the Flavian House. He also, as you will recall, was a friend of Titus Petronius Niger, even when the Arbiter fell from favor, and it was said that he was at Cumae when Petronius died. It is true that Rome has not always enjoyed good relations with Dacia, which is Franciscus' homeland, but by his own admission, he is not himself a Daci. What would it profit him to aid them when they are not one of his blood?

If you have other questions, or if my testimony may help in any way, I urge you to send for me and I will gladly put myself at your disposal. It amazes me that these questions need be asked at all, but since it seems that they must, then let us dispose of the matter quickly and apologize to this distinguished man who has done so much to aid us.

Most respectfully by my own hand on the tenth day of December, the 823rd Year of the City,

Constantinus Modestinus Datus

12

HE WAS VERY OLD and softly obese like a white toad, though he had no treasure to squat on, only his position of power which he wielded with the love of authority only a freed slave could have. His name was Alastor, for the Greek demon of vengeance.

"Your complaint will be filed, naturally," he said to Sanct' Germain as he sat in his gloomy office in the Curia where the Senate met.

"I beg your pardon," Sanct' Germain corrected him with a great show of deference, "but this is not a complaint, it's a petition. I have already filed complaints for the illegal seizure and imprisonment of my slaves. It was one thing to arrest my arena slaves with all the others, but it is a different matter entirely when you arrest my slave who visited them in prison on my orders. Or don't you agree?" It was difficult to keep the anger out of his voice, but Sanct' Germain had had much experience with men like these to know that if he once revealed his irritation, he was lost.

"It is somewhat unusual," Alastor allowed, sinking his three chins back against his chest. "There must have been a reason for it. Was the third slave authorized to visit the prison?"

"I authorized him to do so, and I had the assurance of the Emperor's older son that this was permissible."

Again the sage nod. "Yes, of course. But you must realize that Titus has not held his post long and is not entirely familiar with the way such things are done. He should have consulted me first. I have been procurator senior for the Senate since Nero came to the purple. It was Claudius who appointed me." He was proud of this record, and justly so, for he had survived twenty tumultuous years of Roman politics.

"Certainly he should have," Sanct' Germain agreed, his annoyance building afresh. "But it is strange, is it not, that my slave who visited the prison on my orders should be confined? That is not at all like the usual procedure. If there was, or seemed to be, reason for such an arrest, don't you think I should have been notified? The slave belongs to me."

"You weren't notified?" Alastor said, shocked. "You should have been. It's required that owners of detained slaves be notified immediately, or as soon as is possible."

"I live three thousand paces from the Porta Viminalis, good procurator. It was more than three days before the prison officials sent me word." He hoped that this might win Alastor to his side, and for a moment the old freedman seemed to be wavering. "Good procurator, I have been careful to live within the laws of Rome. It appalls me that certain Romans do not show a like respect."

"Truly," Alastor muttered. He looked down at the five sheets of closely written arguments. "It is distressing. Very distressing. It must be looked into. Such arrests are irregular. I was not aware they had occurred." There was a real sense of affront in the old man. "These matters are most complex. You are a foreigner and the slaves in question are foreigners as well." His manner changed abruptly, becoming very bland. "There are other foreign slave owners petitioning the Senate just now. They have problems similar to yours. I'll see that your . . . petition is given every consideration. Someone has abused his authority, that's plain. You may be confident that he will be dealt with."

Sanct' Germain knew that this was intended as a dismissal, but he stood his ground. "Good procurator, I would appreciate being kept informed of your progress. My slaves are valuable. Every day they remain incarcerated is one more day they do not win for me in the arena, and the longer they are inactive, the more time it will require to rebuild their strength. I'm not the only one who is losing money. My charioteer Kosrozd races quite regularly for the Reds and they are displeased. They want to know when he will be available to race again." The Reds, like most of the racing factions, were made up primarily of equestrian- and Senatorial-rank Romans, and this might spur Alastor to work if other considerations could not.

"The Reds. Yes." He gave Sanct' Germain a quick, pointed

look, very unlike the crafty laziness he had affected. "The Emperor has many friends among the Whites." Then his face was calm again and he murmured, "You will hear from me."

This time Sanct' Germain accepted the eviction. He gave a slight bow, which was more than courtesy required, then drew his heavy black cloak around him and stepped out into the rotunda of the Curia. It was cold today, with few Senators about, since the weather was dismal. This was the third day of the first winter rains and almost all Rome was indoors. Not even the swine market had opened that morning.

But there were beggars in the streets, as there were through every winter. They lingered around the fora of Julius and Augustus, along the Vicus Triumphalis; they huddled under the Claudian Aqueduct and in the half-built first-story arches of what would be the Flavian Circus. At the Aventine Hill they gathered in the narrow streets around the Circus Maximus. When it was raining as it was this afternoon, they were more bedraggled than the mongrel curs that yapped in the streets, ribs showing under mangy coats.

Sanct' Germain's light one-horse chariot was mud-splashed and dripping as he pulled away from the Curia. The beggars flocked around him like scavenger birds, crying shrilly for alms. Absentmindedly Sanct' Germain threw them a handful of copper coins before turning down the Vicus Triumphalis. The interview with Alastor had not been encouraging. Sanct' Germain smiled grimly as he thought of the procurator senior and his smug, soft face. He knew it would be useless to approach the Senate again.

One of the beggars, a girl of scarcely more than seven, grabbed for the handrail of the chariot. Her shapeless tunica of rough sacking barely came to her knees, and was torn at the neck. It dripped water like a sodden sponge. "Patrician!" she shouted in a high voice, her grimy face upturned and her sticklike arms stretched out as she clung to the side of his vehicle. "Good noble! I'm a virgin! Guaranteed! Ten sesterces for a virgin, good noble! Ten sesterces! You'll like it!"

He had heard such calls before too many times to be shocked, but this time he was saddened. "Ten sesterces, child?"

"Five!" she yelled, trying with one hand to clutch his thick woolen cape in her filthy fingers. "Five! A noble like you, five! No more!"

Sanct' Germain pulled his horse into a walk. "A virgin for

five sesterces? They charge ten times that in the lupanar for an experienced twelve-year-old."

"Four! Good patrician, four. I like you, maybe. Four will be enough." She sniffed, still reaching for him.

Sanct' Germain opened his money pouch and brought out two silver denari and two copper sesterces, her original price. "Here," he said, offering them to her. "Take them. Buy yourself some food and a place to sleep."

She stared at him, blank-faced. "And you?"

"You don't have to sell yourself to me, child." He tried to smile, but did not quite succeed. "My . . . tastes do not run to children."

"Don't you want me?" she demanded fiercely. "I'm a virgin! It's true! No diseases, no babies!"

His horse was hardly moving. "Child, take the money and be grateful that I will not accept your . . . proposition. You do not need to sell me your body. You would not want to."

Suddenly her face contorted with rage. "Eunuch! Pervert!" She pushed back from the chariot, almost falling on the paving stones as Sanct' Germain's horse lurched into a trot. "Dried-up worm! Fucker of pigs! Dung-licker!" She continued to yell at him, though her fist was closed tightly around the coins he had given her.

The beggars gathered around the huge buildings laughed, pointing to the chariot as it rattled south toward the Circus Maximus. As he drove, Sanct' Germain could hear the laughter over the rain and it stung him. Why had he bothered? he asked himself. What was the use of it, if the only reaction was open derision? His mood darkened with the leaden sky. He glanced to his left, toward the Oppius Hill where the Golden House sat, empty but for one wing where Vespasianus lived while he decided what was to be done with the rambling building. In the rain the walls were drab and the palace looked no more inviting than the worst of the insulae in the poorest quarter of the city.

Near the first upthrustings of the Flavian Circus the streets grew muddy, token of the earth that had been excavated after the lake had been drained. Now the huge foundations were almost complete and it was possible to look into the enormous ring and see the corridors, cages and braces that would run under the sands when the mammoth amphitheatre was finished. There had been many times that Sanct' Germain had stopped to look at the progress that had been made, but he knew he would not do so today. He had yet to see Juvines Acestes, the tribune who acted as warden of the slaves' prison just beyond the Porta Navalis. Two previous visits had been fruitless, as this one would probably be, if Alastor's attitude were any indication of the official posture at the moment. What had gone wrong between Titus and the Senate, Sanct' Germain asked himself, that the foreign slaves had become such an issue? If the senior procurator of the Senate was vying with the prefect of the Praetorian Guard for power, then whatever they chose to be the issue for their battle was certain to be ruined by one side or the other. Fear for Aumtehoutep, Kosrozd and Tishtry bit sharply into him.

So preoccupied was Sanct' Germain that he did not notice the small crowd of twenty or thirty that gathered around a still, supine figure under the nearest arch of the Flavian Circus. Only when his horse shied, skittering on the mud-slicked pavement, did Sanct' Germain glimpse the fallen man and rein in, looking on the group with awakened interest.

There were men and children, ancient women and young, slatternly women, each indelibly stamped with misery, each taking a cruel satisfaction in tormenting someone more wretched than they.

The man at their feet was indeed pitiable. Under the filth that slimed his face, his skin was chalky where it was not bruised and lacerated. There were angry, dark-fleshed, festering wounds on his hands and feet, as if he had been burned with hot irons. He was almost naked—only a short tunica covered him, and it was ragged and stained. Those who milled around him pelted him with offal, laughing and jeering.

Sanct' Germain took his driving lash from the holder in his chariot as he stopped his horse. "You!" he shouted to the little crowd. One or two looked up, indifferent to this well-dressed stranger, their vacuous, malicious faces glazed with excitement. "*You!*" he repeated, this time his voice cracking with the lash as the thing slapped against the wet pavement.

A few more turned at this, and one whooped with delight as he charged the black-cloaked interloper.

Sanct' Germain made no attempt to avoid the rush of the thick-bodied beggar. As the man ran at him, he turned, leaning aside, and the beggar overbalanced and fell, sliding, in the muddy street. He pulled himself to his hands and knees, enraged, and turned on Sanct' Germain once more, this time approaching more cautiously as a few of the crowd moved to watch this more exciting entertainment.

As the beggar approached Sanct' Germain, he feinted a blow at the foreigner's head. Sanct' Germain seized his wrist and pulled it gently, stepping aside as the beggar once again fell.

This time when the beggar got up, he held a large broken brick in his hand, and he rushed Sanct' Germain, cheered on by the others, who had left the unconscious man in the mud.

"Get behind him, Vardos!" the beggar shouted to someone in the crowd, and Sanct' Germain grew wary. It was one thing to fight a single man, but if there were two, or the entire crowd turned on him, his danger would be very great. For an instant he wondered why he had bothered to stop, but a glance at the unconscious man lying like a discarded, broken doll fed his determination to remain.

The beggar who had attacked him first now took swipes at his head with the brick in his hand. Sanct' Germain dodged cautiously, feeling his way on the slick, uncertain footing. He moved quickly, making swift half-turns to protect his back while the beggar came closer.

"Vardos! His arms!" The beggar lunged at him just as Sanct' Germain felt huge arms grip him from behind.

He responded without thought, pivoting to break the hold on his arms even as he reached for the beggar with the brick. He lifted the beggar from his feet and hurled him down on his accomplice Vardos with the full strength of his wrath. Vardos collapsed silently and the beggar who had attacked him howled as he pressed one hand to a deep cut in his face. Sanct' Germain bent and picked up his driving lash. "Get back," he said quietly. "Every one of you."

With a few cuts of the long whip, Sanct' Germain cut himself a path through the denizens of the unfinished building. The beggar stumbled to his feet and lurched away from the place. Vardos lay in the street, groaning.

"If any of you are thinking of taking my chariot," Sanct' Germain remarked conversationally, "the penalty for such theft is crucifixion after the joints in the arms and legs have been broken with an iron bar."

Now the crowd gave way before him, a few cursing him openly for interfering with their sport more than his treatment of the beggar. They muttered among themselves in their almost incomprehensible patois, but did not stay to contest

Sanct' Germain's rights. Any richly dressed stranger who fought as he did would be respected and avoided. In very little time the small crowd had melted away into the shadows and crannies of the tall unfinished arches.

When he was alone with the unconscious man, Sanct' Germain dropped down on one knee, heedless of the mud and ordure that mired his embroidered Persian trousers and woolen cape. As gently as he could, he wiped away the worst of the muck from his face and chest, wincing as this revealed purulent sores. He lifted the battered shoulders so that the man's head lolled against his upraised knee. When Sanct' Germain lifted his eyelids, he saw red-streaked whites with a crescent of blue showing. The man was barely breathing, and even that was shallow and labored, as if a weight had collapsed on his chest. A further examination revealed three broken ribs and a massively swollen ankle that might have been fractured.

Vardos began to drag himself away, moaning steadily.

Sanct' Germain told himself he was being a fool, that there was no way he could help this stranger now, for the man was clearly close to death. But to leave him here was to abandon him to those who had been torturing him. As he accepted this, he lifted the man in his arms and carried him toward his waiting chariot.

His horse snorted and sidled, eyes showing whites as Sanct' Germain attempted to make a place on the floor of the chariot for the unconscious man. It was a difficult task for the chariot was small and light, built to hold one standing driver. Working carefully, Sanct' Germain wedged the man into the front curve of the chariot, bracing the man with his legs as he reached to drive the now-restive horse. With great care he flicked the reins and the chariot moved off through the wet afternoon toward the Porta Navalis and the slaves' prison.

It was an old building, of rough-hewn stone, and it rose in a bend of the Tiber, a grim monument surrounded by mausoleums of many ancient Roman houses. A low barracks on the south side of the prison provided the housing for the soldiers who guarded the place, and though it was technically in the care of the Watch, most of the guards were legionnaires who had been assigned to the prison as punishment.

In the officers' portion of the barracks Sanct' Germain waited half an hour to see the tribune Juvines Acestes, and at the end of that time was denied. He was tempted to challenge the young, badly scarred officer who delivered the message, but contained himself: the warden of this prison and his guards had Aumtehoutep, Tishtry and Kosrozd within the walls, and his outburst of anger could only bring more hardships to them. So, though his temper seethed, he thanked the officer most patiently and went back out into the rain.

The wind was higher now, and it whipped the clouds across the sky, driving the rain in long, slanted sheets toward the ground. Sanct' Germain's clothes were soaked and his horse shivered as the water streamed off his coat. Now Sanct' Germain was truly glad of the earth that lined the heels and soles of his Scythian boots, protecting him from the ghastly weakness he might otherwise have felt. He turned his horse toward the east and began the slow drive toward Villa Ragoczy.

It was almost dark when at last he drew up in his own stableyard. The lamps that hung in the archway were nearly invisible in the torrential rain. Sanct' Germain stepped down from the chariot and came around to his horse's head. "Good boy," he said, giving the animal an affectionate pat. "You did well." Then he turned toward the stable door. "Raides! Domius! Brinie!" he shouted, not sure that the grooms could hear him over the drumming of the rain.

The oldest groom, a grizzled old man from Londinium in Britannia, stumbled out into the rain. "Master?" he called. "We're coming. What a night!"

"And you were not driving in it," Sanct' Germain snapped, at which Raides stared in surprise. Usually his master had a kind word for every service. "Stable him, rub him down, give him warm gruel to eat and be certain that he stays warm," Sanct' Germain went on, patting the horse once more. "He's done more than his share of labor today."

Raides shrugged, then reached for the reins to lead the horse into the stable where he could be unhitched from the chariot out of the force of the storm, but once again Sanct' Germain stopped him.

"There's a man in the chariot. Wait until I get him out." As he spoke he bent over the vehicle and pulled the emaciated, battered figure from it. "What did he do to deserve this?" Sanct' Germain wondered aloud.

Because he knew from experience that not all masters had the same respect for their slaves as Sanct' Germain did,

Raides held his peace, though it was obvious to him that the unconscious man had been harshly used deliberately.

"He does not wear a collar," Sanct' Germain pointed out.

"Collars can be removed," Raides said philosophically as he tugged the reins to pull the horse toward the stables.

"Yes, they can," Sanct' Germain responded enigmatically, then turned away toward his private wing on the north side of the villa.

Three hours later he had bathed the man and examined his wounds. The infections alone were sufficient to kill him; bruising and exposure only hastened the inevitable. Sanct' Germain sat beside the narrow table on which the unknown man lay. He wished that Aumtehoutep were with him. After their centuries together, the Egyptian knew him nearly as well as he knew himself. As he had saved Aumtehoutep once, so he could restore this man now.

The unconscious man took two deep, gurgling breaths, then shuddered and was still.

Sanct' Germain rose. Standing over the man, he could see the waxy stillness of death begin to take hold of his features. Before morning he would be stiff, nothing more than carrion. There was a little time, very little, when it would be possible to regenerate the life in the man. It was a thing that Sanct' Germain had not done for more years than he cared to count. The work was precarious—there was no room for error.

From his inlaid Egyptian chest he took certain herbs and rare spices and resins, and after a last moment of hesitation, as he remembered the three times he had attempted this restoration since he had brought Aumtehoutep back to life, he made the ritual invocations and began to work.

The sun was a golden smear in the eastern sky before the man's chest rose for breath once more. His flesh was still cold to the touch and there was a bluish cast to his hands and feet but life stirred in him again.

Satisfied that the work had been successful, Sanct' Germain let exhaustion take hold of him. He moved the man to a bed, then went to his bath to soak away the tension of the night, and to search his mind for a way to explain to the unknown man, who had been dead the day before, how he came to live again.

Text of a document from the Emperor Titus Flavius Vespasianus.

To the Senate and the People of Rome, greetings:

I have considered the grave matter of the rebellious arena slaves for some time now, and have listened to the advice of those around me. My older son, in his capacity as Praetorian prefect, has pursued the matter most diligently and thoroughly, so that nothing be decided capriciously. My younger son has spoken to many of you, soliciting your thoughts and opinions, and has learned much from you that aids my decision in this difficult matter.

Those of you who have had your Roman-owned arena slaves condemned must surely know with what reluctance that command was given, and now, in the case of the foreign-owned slaves, where the law is less clear, it has required a great deal of thought and reflection to arrive at a decision in the matter. Because this situation is unique in imperial experience, and not precisely like the lamentable revolt of the last century, I am asking the Senate to add their voice to mine in this sentence. I am submitting my decision to the Senate for their vote of concurrence.

It is not an easy matter for me to declare this, as it was not easy to condemn the Roman slaves. And for this reason, among others, the case has dragged on much longer than is advisable or wise. It must be remedied quickly.

Therefore, should the Senate decide with me, the foreign slaves of foreign owners will be sent to the arena at the next imperial Games, and there they will be executed in whatever manner the Master of the Games decides is fitting. The date currently fixed for the next imperial Games is the twentieth day of April, roughly two months hence.

I am aware that there are many petitions before the Senate as regards these foreign slaves of foreign masters, and that each master is naturally anxious that decisions be made in his favor. If each of these petitions were to be considered and judged separately, it would require years and an enormous amount of time and money. Because Roman-owned slaves were not given this benefit, it would be unfair to our Roman citizens to offer to foreigners what we have not provided to our own people. We will therefore declare all such petitions as inadmissible and the owners may, at their convenience, apply to the Senate for full market compensation and reasonable losses, as was provided to Roman masters. It is not our intention to penalize the foreign slave owner, and this seems to be most equitable. Certainly there are slaves who will be condemned who are not in any way guilty of violating the laws of Rome or dishonoring their duty to their owners, but this cannot now be avoided. The matter must be settled quickly if there is to be order, and for that reason we urge the foreign arena-slave owners to accept this edict and try to understand the particular problems that have beset the empire for the last four years.

Upon ratification by the Senate, this decision is to be posted on all notice walls and published in the *Acta Diurna.* Further inquiries into the matter will be suspended for a period of one year. If at that time there is reason to investigate further, an order to that point will be issued.

Caesar Vespasianus
on the eighteenth day of February
in the 824th Year of the City

13

JUSTUS LOOKED UP sharply as Monostades came into his study. "Where have you been?" he demanded as he thrust a letter aside impatiently.

Monostades winced but said in an even tone, "You gave me orders several days ago and I have been attempting to follow them. You indicated you wanted to speak to someone who has knowledge of deadly herbs." He smiled insolently. "You remember, do you not?"

Ordinarily this would have offended Justus and the rods would have been called for, but not now. "You have found such a person?"

"An old woman, master, a very old woman. She lives away from Rome, near Tusculum, in the hills. I heard of her from the body slave of a wealthy young widow. It took ten golden denari to bring her to Rome. That, and a covered chariot."

"Covered? Very wise. Where is this . . . woman?" His tongue flicked over his lips and for a moment he was frightened. The plan, when he had conceived it, seemed to be the most effective he could invent, but now, facing the actual execution . . . He would not call it an execution. He studied Monostades. "Whom did you send to get her?"

"The mute," Monostades replied as if to a child. "I am not stupid enough to send a slave who can speak." He chose one of the cushioned benches and sat, a liberty that Justus knew was an intolerable insult. Monostades waited for the objection that never came. "He will return her, as well, and meet with an accident on his return. Only after he gets to the Via Appia, so that there will be great difficulty in knowing where he has been."

"Excellent," Justus said in a rather distracted tone. He knew he had entrusted too much power to Monostades, and he resolved to change this as soon as the current problem had been settled. There were more important matters at stake, but after, it would please him to chastise Monostades personally, unhurriedly. "When may I see her?"

"She is in the kitchen now. She is eating and investigating your resources. A very able woman, from what I have learned. You can put your faith in her."

Once again Justus faltered. It was a drastic move, he told himself, and though it would rid him of Olivia at last, so that he would be free to ally himself with the Flavian House, it was a drastic course and might go badly. He stared at the far wall where a lavish mural depicted the heavily chained Andromeda being attacked by a sea monster. He had always liked that mural, he thought inconsequently.

"What do you want me to do with the woman, master?"

Monostades asked somewhat later when Justus still had not spoken.

"Bring her in here. Make sure that only the kitchen staff sees her. Be quick about it. I'll have to talk to her, at least." His hands moved nervously and it was an effort to still them. Though Justus hated to admit it, even to himself, he had reservations about this course. It was wise, certainly it was wise, and he would be rid of Olivia at last, he reminded himself.

Monostades left the study, returning shortly with a wizened, monkey-faced woman in fantastic dress. Every conceivable color of cloth was represented among the tunicae, stollae and pallae she wore, one on top of the other, hems at any length, all held together with a series of brooches and fibulae no two of which were alike. She smelled strongly of camphor and cloves.

"Good day, old woman," Justus said without rising, though her great years demanded that respect. He pointed to one of the uncushioned chairs. "You may sit there."

"Generous of you, Senator." She chuckled in a voice as deep as a man's, and vibrant with life. She took the chair and stared at Justus. "Well, what is it to be, Senator? Is there a rival or a lover you want to be rid of? A political enemy? Is one of your unmarried daughters in need of a little lightening?" There was no embarrassment in her, only a rich, sad amusement.

"I haven't got any daughters," Justus said curtly. "My slave there"—he favored Monostades with a contemptuous nod—"tells me that you know something of poisons."

"I thought that was why you sent for me, Senator." She folded her thin arms, adding in her forthright way, "I don't haggle and I don't blackmail. There will be one price. If you think to denounce me, you may find that is difficult. There are those higher than you who will protect me. For their own reasons, of course."

Justus did not respond at once. "Is it possible, old woman, to poison someone so that it is clear he has been poisoned, but have him live?" He had picked up the letter he had been reading and began to fold it.

"Certainly it is possible. But do you want this to happen over a time, or at once? Is this person in good health? If he has shortened breath or pains in the stomach, it is much more difficult." There was a calculating look to her now that her curiosity was aroused.

"No shortness of breath, no stomach pains," Justus said crisply, committed now to his plan.

"How old a man is this? Is he athletic? How much does he drink? What are his habits? Does he often dine in company?" The questions came quickly, incisively, and the little currant eyes sparkled.

"The man," Justus answered with a sigh, "is in his fifties, of regular but not athletic habits, drinks heavily upon occasion, dines in company quite often. He is, in fact, myself." He was pleased with the startled look in the old woman's eyes. "So you see why I am anxious that the poison should not be fatal."

"I fail to see why you should want it at all," she snapped.

"It's a very delicate situation," he began, and then decided that he would tell this old woman what he intended to do. Once she had supplied his needs, it would not be too arduous a task to see that she disappeared from the earth. He gave her his most frank expression. "I am married. She is my third wife. The first I divorced when I learned that she had an unsound mind, though I have continued to support her, the second died when we had been married little more than two years. You would have thought that this was sufficient to teach me, but I married again, about ten years ago. My wife is a much younger woman, and at the moment we are living apart. I want to divorce her because she has shown herself to be given over to harlotry. I can disgrace her in the courts, but that might not effect the ends I most desire. She would still be in Rome, well-connected and in a position to cause trouble in my life. She is the sort of woman who would do that, I assure you. If, however, it was proven that she has acted against me, there would be no question about a divorce, and at the least she would be exiled. That, woman, is why I want poison, enough to hurt but not enough to kill. I plan to dine with my wife in a few days. It is my intention to fall ill after that meal, and after subsequent meals with her and to have it known that poison was the cause. That way my wife will be suspected of the crime. It is known that our marriage is not happy. If my plan is successful, she will be out of my life and I will be free to pursue other—"

"Game?" the old woman suggested nastily. "You're a truly vile creature, aren't you, Senator," she said conversationally.

Justus brought himself up as if slapped. "I will not listen to such—"

"You'll listen to whatever I tell you if you want the poison," the old woman informed him sharply. "I've heard what you had to say, and now you'll hear what I have to say. Otherwise I will return to my hut and you will get nothing from me."

"This is absurd," Justus said at his most condescending.

"Then find your poisons elsewhere." She made a move as if to leave.

"After all, I suppose I must give age its due." Justus sighed as he rolled his eyes upward. "If you find it so necessary, old woman, say your piece." He folded his hands and fixed his eyes on the Andromeda mural.

If this behavior daunted the old woman, she gave no sign of it. Her voice was as deep and firm as it had been the first time she spoke to him. "You want to make sure that your wife is deprived of her rights under the law, and perhaps exiled. What's the matter? Have you spent her dowry? Or do you have some other goal in mind?"

"She was not dowered," Justus said evenly. "Will you provide me the poison or not?"

"Oh, yes. I'll see that you have it. And you need not worry. It will be enough to do as you want and not so much that you die of it, unfortuantely. You will be abominably sick for a day or so, and there will be weakness and flux for five or six days, but nothing that you can't survive."

"Survive and be strong?" Justus asked with a shade more anxiety than he had intended.

"Certainly. That is what you want, isn't it? Then you will be able to accuse your blameless wife of your own perfidy and have no calumny attached to you when you offer for the Emperor's niece." She laughed outright at the dismay on Justus' face. "Why are you surprised? Do you think that because I live in a hut near Tusculum that I don't know you, Cornelius Justus Silius? Do you think that I have not heard the gossip about you, not only from other Senators, but from the gladiators who come to me for the elixirs to keep them strong, and from brutish men wanting to sustain their potency through a secret assignation. Three years ago I would have been foolish enough to blame your wife, since it sounded as if she were a debauched woman. Then there came two men who told me how you helped them with her, and I began to understand."

"They lied," Justus said without a flicker of emotion.

"Did they? So you are no longer pleased with Atta Olivia Clemens, and are going to get rid of her? This is better than murder, I suppose." The little bright eyes grew flinty. She got to her feet and met Justus' furious gaze fearlessly. "You will have your poison, Silius, and it will be as you require. It will make you sick." She turned her head and spat.

"You are impertinent, old woman!" Justus exploded at last, his face turning plum-red.

"I'm honest, you mean," she answered him calmly. "You speak of impertinence, you, who are planning to ruin your wife. Well, the world changes little, and it is all made of dung. In my day, we murdered openly, but that's no longer the fashion."

"In your day," he scoffed in his anger.

"In my day, I stood higher than you, Senator." The small bright eyes held his and there was amusement in them. "I would advise against having me killed. Now or later. They've all tried and I am still alive."

Justus would have liked to know whom she meant. Which of his patrician associates had come to this strange old woman over the years? What had she done for them? Why was she still alive, if she had done so much? He kept these questions to himself, and instead glared at her. "Fine claims and talk are cheap. If the poison you give me is not as promised, a letter will go to the prefect of the Praetorian Guard and another to the Senate. If the poison is precisely as you've said it will be, I will send rewards to you in excess of your price. . . ."

"Keep your gifts!" she cried with unexpected vehemence. "If I wanted luxury, I could have had it. I did have it once and it sickened me!" She went to the study door and looked back at Justus. "I will give the poison to your slave. At my hut. He can return here with it. If there is any attempt to interfere with me, you will regret it." She anticipated his objections. "If I had been unprotected, Silius, I would have been dead years ago. Remember that." She stepped into the open doorway.

"Old woman," Justus called, genuinely curious, "why do you do it?"

The smile she gave him was colder than any Justus had

seen. "Because I hate you all. I should have thought that was obvious." The door closed behind her.

"Follow her," was Justus' terse order to Monostades. "Don't let her wander about the house. Don't let her out of your sight."

Monostades obeyed slowly, a slight, sarcastic grin on his full lips. "She's probably right about the protection, master," he pointed out.

"Probably." He did not want to discuss it with this slave.

"You would not be wise to put it to the test," he went on unpleasantly. "If she informed on you, it would go badly."

Justus regarded Monostades with open hostility. "I am still permitted to discipline my slaves for disobedience, Monostades. No one would question me if I took the skin off you with a flagellum if you continue in this way. I would enjoy doing that." He looked Monostades up and down once as if sizing up an animal for slaughter. "You're not weak. It would be a long time to hurt."

"I'm obedient," Monostades said quickly, rather pale, though whether from fear or rage, it was hard to say.

"Then follow that old woman." He sat still while Monostades bolted from his study.

Once alone, he sat down to draft a letter to Olivia, informing her of his intention to dine with her in four days' time. He selected his phrases with care, wishing to frighten her without causing her to refuse to see him. He worked on a wax tablet so that he could have the underlying threat perfectly expressed when he copied it out.

He was completing this letter when the houseman knocked timidly at his door. "I'm not to be disturbed," he said without looking up from the sheet in front of him.

The knock was renewed. "Master, there is a gentleman . . . He says that you will want to see him."

"I'm not to be disturbed," Justus repeated sharply. He was out of patience with his household today.

"The man insists, master," the houseman whined, waiting on the other side of the door.

"Tell him I cannot see him." He picked up his tablet and set it aside, then reached for his ink.

"He says it is urgent." The voice had risen almost an octave, and hearing it, Justus ground his teeth.

"Very well, then, he may have a few moments. If this is a capricious interruption, I will have him thrown out of my house and beaten." He turned toward the door. "Hurry. I am busy and this is an unwanted interruption." From beyond the door he heard his houseman scurry away.

He did not have long to wait: there were crisp, quick footsteps through the atrium, a knock and then the door to Justus' study was thrown open and a harshly handsome young man dressed in elegant Armenian brocades stepped into the study. "You are Senator Silius?" he asked perfunctorily.

"I am. You may tell me what you want quickly." He was somewhat impressed with his guest.

"My name is Led Arashnur," said the newcomer. "I am an Armenian scholar studying in Rome. I have been investigating the movements of one Ragoczy Sanct' Germain Franciscus, who, among other things, is your wife's lover." He waited for a response.

"My wife's lover," Justus repeated as if to himself. He motioned to the high-backed, silk-cushioned chair on the other side of the room. "Sit down, Arashnur," he said.

Text of a note smuggled from the slaves' prison to Sanct' Germain, written in the symbols of ancient Egypt.

> To my master, from Tishtry, Kosrozd and myself, respectful greetings:
>
> We have learned today of the sentence that has been handed down from Caesar Vespasianus, and we are not surprised. It was that or the galleys, and since we are suspected of planning rebellion, they could hardly put us on warships. So it is to be the arena. It will be a new experience for me, but for Tishtry and Kosrozd it will be familiar. Kosrozd said that he is disappointed.
>
> Many of the Roman slaves who have already been executed were crucified as common felons. That is probably what will happen to us, as well. At least, that is the current rumor.

You will be able, I think, to claim our bodies, which ought to keep us from any awkwardness. Kosrozd even jokes about it, but Tishtry is doubtful since she has yet to make the true change. It has been fortunate that we have been together. We all understand each other so well. Tishtry had chided Kosrozd for his eagerness and says that it will be a very long time before he matches you. It is probably just as well that I am not of your blood as they are. To be bound to you by the life you returned to me is quite enough.

We are prepared for our ordeal and wish to do you credit. Kosrozd is becoming impatient, though I have reminded him that he will have to leave Rome immediately after you claim our bodies. It would not do for him to be seen walking around unfettered after all Rome watches him die in the arena. I have warned him that you will probably forbid him to race chariots anywhere for a few years. There is that estate of yours in Gallia, and we could live very privately there. Whatever your plans for us are, we are ready to do as you wish. In a few years we may return to Rome, when we have been sufficiently forgotten. A century should be enough. It was the last time.

Until our reunion, then, this from our cell in the slaves' prison.

Aumtehoutep
on the twenty-seventh day of March,
the 824th Year of the City

14

SANCT' GERMAIN finished reading the document the young Praetorian tribune had given him. "Thank you," he said quietly as he refolded the fine Egyptian paper. "Thank you. Tell your Prefect Titus for me that I am . . . eternally grateful." Perhaps, he thought, all those days of pestering half the officials of Rome had been worthwhile. It was not the outcome he had hoped for, but was better than he had feared. "I will claim the bodies as soon as they go out through the Gates of Death."

The young tribune gave Sanct' Germain a long, measuring look. "They are slaves. Why is it so important that you have their bodies?"

Sanct' Germain hesitated, then said, "Among my people it is believed that the slaves that predecease you must be buried with you or they will rob and plunder your treasures and your tomb in the afterlife." It was true that he had known those who subscribed to that idea when he had been young.

"Oh," said the tribune, relieved. "It's a matter of religion." He knew that all sorts of outlandish customs were part of religious practices, particularly among foreigners. "The prefect was curious," he explained hastily.

"Rome has her customs, we have ours," Sanct' Germain said calmly, glad for Rome's tolerant attitudes toward foreign religions.

"Of course," the tribune agreed without understanding.

For courtesy's sake, Sanct' Germain asked, "Would you like wine or food to refresh yourself? I will be honored to send for them." He gestured to his blue-and-silver reception room. "You may be served here or in the garden, which is just coming into flower."

The tribune waved his hand politely. "No, no, Franciscus. I can't spare the time, but I appreciate the offer. The prefect said that you're a most obliging man. It's quite true." He gave a stiff nod and turned toward the door. "Impressive villa you've got," he added as an afterthought.

"I hope so," Sanct' Germain said dryly as he followed the tribune to the colonnaded front of Villa Ragoczy, where the tribune's horse was being held by one of Sanct' Germain's grooms. He stood while the young Praetorian vaulted into his saddle, then nodded and turned back to his villa, the official release from Titus still held firmly in his hands. Only when he had heard the Praetorian's horse clatter away from the villa did he hasten to the private north wing of his villa, shouting, "Rogerian! Rogerian!"

The man who answered the summons had almost recovered from the terrible wounds that had been inflicted upon him. He moved as if his bones were brittle and his pleasant middle-aged face was set into somber lines. "Yes, my master?" he asked as he approached. His accent was that of his native Gades.

Sanct' Germain closed the outer door with a bang and

strode rapidly down the inner hall. "We must work quickly. There isn't much time."

"Time for what?" Rogerian asked, keeping up with Sanct' Germain as best he could.

"Titus has finally sent an official release. When the slaves are executed, I will be allowed to claim the bodies of Aumtehoutep, Kosrozd and Tishtry. Then we must move swiftly, to get them away from Rome as quickly as possible." He burst into his library, going at once to his desk. "I will need the reports on my ships. You know where they are. I know I have one docked at Pisae that will be leaving soon for Corsica and Utica. She's getting some minor repairs just now. I will need to notify the captain at once to delay his departure." He sat as he spoke and drew a fine papyrus sheet toward him. "One of the charioteers must leave for the north tonight. I'll give him authorization and money to change horses as often as necessary. I want this message delivered within six days."

Rogerian nodded, and while Sanct' Germain began to write his instructions to his captian, went into the side room where Sanct' Germain kept his commercial records. He could not read the ancient and foreign script in which they were written, so he took the whole stack of fan-folded scrolls and carried them back to the library.

A second sheet lay beside the first now, and Sanct' Germain was writing identical messages on two sheets at once. Rogerian had never seen him do this, and he stopped to watch, amazed.

Sanct' Germain signed both messages, then looked up. "Good. You're back. One of these is for Tishtry, the other is for the person in Utica where I'm sending her. He's an old sorcerer and will be happy to add her to his household. He knows about her . . . requirements and will be able to deal with them." He started to say something more, but changed his mind and pulled another sheet of papyrus forward and began writing, this time in Greek. "Once Tishtry is out of danger," he went on rather remotely, "she need only be sensibly cautious and there will be little to fear. She is not foolish, and Sbratius will be there to guide her."

"Is he like you, this Sbratius?" Rogerian asked, not entirely comfortably.

"Certainly not." Sanct' Germain laughed softly. "He is like *you.*"

Rogerian looked at his master in consternation. "Like me? How many of us are there?"

Sanct' Germain did not answer at once; his attention was on the letter he wrote. Finally he looked up once more. "I personally know of six of you, that is, six who were truly restored. There were many other failures. I have heard that there are others, but I don't know where they are or who they are." He folded the papyrus and sealed it with wax impressed with his signet, the eclipse. "This is for Kosrozd."

But Rogerian was not willing to abandon the matter of Sbratius so casually. "Why was he brought back to life?" He was afraid to ask why he had been.

"Because he had certain special knowledge, and because the priests of Imhotep had said they would try. We succeeded that time." Suddenly he turned the full force of his penetrating dark eyes on Rogerian. "Why don't you ask about yourself? That's what you wish to know, isn't it?"

Numbly Rogerian nodded. "Yes. I want to know," he blurted out as he felt his courage failing.

"If you had seen yourself as I first saw you, you would have done the same thing." He stopped. "No, that isn't the whole of it. I had to do something of worth for somebody, and you . . . You were being systematically excoriated by those vermin. Given enough time, they would have had the skin off you." The depth of his feeling surprised him. "I couldn't leave you there. There may be no reason more than that—I couldn't leave you there."

Rogerian was silent. "When I was still a bondsman in Baetica, I remember how I felt when my son died," he said quietly after some little time. "He had a little wound, a very little, little wound, but it was deadly all the same. He bent like a bow before it was over, and all of us were helpless." He turned to stare out the window. "Shall I have Raides harness a team and select a charioteer to drive north?"

"Yes," Sanct' Germain said crisply. "I'll write out orders for the charioteer, whoever he is, so that none of the legion garrisons along the way can detain him. I will want him to be ready to leave within the hour. Have him carry a change of clothes."

"I'll see to it, and to the purse. It should not take long. Raides knows which of the charioteers are best-suited to work like this." He inclined his head to his master as he left the library.

Sanct' Germain smiled sadly. Kosrozd would be the best for the long, grueling drive north, but that, of course, was not possible. He was reasonably certain that Raides would select one of the charioteers Kosrozd had trained. He took his shipping records and began to read them, looking for other vessels to carry his three slaves away from Rome and Roman garrisons.

By the time Rogerian returned, Sanct' Germain had found the proper ships for Aumtehoutep and Kosrozd. "Here's the *Storm Spray,* due at Sipontum bound for Carthago Novo. The captain is planning to come to Rome to attend his brother's wedding, and it will be a simple matter to have him return to Sipontum with Aumtehoutep. There is a dealer in art and antiquities in Carthago Novo who will be delighted to have Aumtehoutep as his bondman." He saw the sharp, closed look in Rogerian's face. "Not all bond holders abuse their bondsmen, Rogerian. I would not send Aumtehoutep to this man if I thought he would misuse him in any way."

"But you don't know that," Rogerian said in deadly quiet.

"I know that if there is one word of complaint from Aumtehoutep, the man to whom I'm sending Aumtehoutep will find his jewel collection foreclosed. I don't take foolish chances, Rogerian, not even with honorable men. Does that meet with your approval?" He regarded Rogerian sardonically.

"It isn't my place to approve or disapprove," he said, standing as if his back had petrified.

"Indeed." Sanct' Germain pointed to another stack of folded and sealed papyrus sheets. "Those are for Kosrozd. His route is more difficult, but he must get away from the limits of the empire, at least for a time. Not only for his fame here in the arena, but because there have been attempts from some of his former connections in Persia who wish to get their hands on him for their own political purposes." He gave a short sound that might have been a laugh. "I think they would get much more than they anticipate if they seized him now, but we can't safely put that to the test."

"Where will he go?" Rogerian asked, unaware that it was remarkable that he was so much in Sanct' Germain's confidence.

"At Rhegium, he will go on the *Trident* to Pola in Histria, then overland into Pannonia, along the Tisia and into the mountains to Alba Lulia. It's a miserable little outpost, but he will be able to stay there for a time, undisturbed."

"How can you be certain?" Rogerian demanded.

"I was born in those mountains, Rogerian, and though it was a very long time ago, I know that the people there remember those of my blood. We are legends to them, but they respect their legends." His eyes had a distant look. With an effort he brought his attention back to Rogerian. "After a time, if he decides that he misses cities, there are those in Sinope in Bithynia who will welcome him on my behalf." He rose suddenly. "At least I have found a way to save them. For a time I feared . . ." He could not finish the words.

"Is it so necessary that you save them?" Rogerian asked gently, watching his master.

It was almost as if Sanct' Germain had not heard him, for he gave no indication of it, just stood looking down at the three stacks of letters on his desk. "For those of my blood, there is a tie. I cannot entirely forget them. We are bound by the blood."

"And Aumtehoutep?" He wanted to know for himself.

"Aumtehoutep is bound by an oath of the flesh. It is a different matter." He looked at Rogerian, and relented. "Very well. You are not inexorably tied to me. If that were the case, I would have Sbratius here, and would not be able to send Aumtehoutep away. There is a bond, but it is not so strong that it robs you of your will or choice. Should you stay with me, Rogerian, it will be because that is what you wish to do, not because I have compelled you. Whether you stay or go, I will keep my word. Your bond-holder will be punished for his abuse of you."

Rogerian stood quite still. "For a time, then, I will stay."

"Thank you." Sanct' Germain gathered up the letters. "Come with me. I want to see the charioteer Raides has selected and be sure he gets away in good time." He moved with that fluid grace that was deceptively swift. Rogerian hurried after him.

Raides was standing at the head of the chariot calming the four restive horses. "They're fresh," he assured Sanct' Germain as his master came into the stableyard.

"I can see that. Who is driving?" He ran an expert eye over the team. "The bay is sweating."

"It's not a problem. He'd been out in the sun most of the afternoon. He's rested and eager." Raides patted the second horse in the rig. "This fellow is the one I was worried about, but I checked his hooves myself, and he'll be fine."

"I'm counting on it," Sanct' Germain said sternly.

As he spoke, a young Cymric charioteer came striding across the stableyard. He was tall and loose-limbed and there was a confidence in him that reminded Sanct' Germain of Kosrozd. "My master," he called his greeting as he approached. "I'll be in Pisae five days from now or you may throw me to the sharks at Tiberius' villa."

"If you are in Pisae in five days, you may have your freedom and five brood mares," Sanct' Germain said promptly as he watched the Cymric charioteer lash the bundle he carried into place in the chariot.

"Five brood mares and my freedom?" He turned to stare at Sanct' Germain. "For that I'd drive to Britannia, over the ocean." He stepped into the chariot and nodded toward Raides. "I'll take their heads now." He had already begun to gather the reins into his hands. "This new harness of yours, master," he said as he steadied the team, "it's better than the old one. I didn't like it at first, but Kosrozd taught me its tricks. It helps to have so much control of each horse. If you know what you're doing." His grin plainly indicated that he did.

Sanct' Germain put a restraining hand on the rail of the chariot. "You are not to be reckless. What is important is that the message is delivered, in time, intact, and that you do not bring unnecessary attention to yourself. In your authorization from me it says that you are bearing a message from me to my captain and that there is a side wager on your speed. That is all you should need to know. If you are detained on the road, it could go very badly for us all." There was no levity and no mockery in what he said, and some of the jauntiness of the Cymric charioteer was lost.

"I will remember, my master," he said, his young face quite serious.

"Yes. I think you will." Sanct' Germain stood back from the chariot and gave a quick gesture of permission. Raides stood back, the charioteer let the reins run as the horses sprang forward out of the stableyard and toward the road a fair distance down the gentle slope.

"He'll do," Raides assured Sanct' Germain. "He's young and he's eager, but he has sense. He'll let the team shake the fidgets out of their legs and then hold them to a long trot.

That's the best plan, I told him. Horses like that can trot a long way."

"If their hooves hold out," Sanct' Germain reminded him, a crease showing between his fine brows. "That's what concerns me." He shook his head and said in another, more rueful voice, "That's my worry talking, Raides. It's been such a long battle that I can't believe that we've won through."

Raides shrugged. "Well, when your slaves are taken, it's not every master who would care to fight for them as you have. Oh, it's talked about in the quarters, never doubt it." He brushed the sleeve of his tunica and dust puffed around his hand. "We know what's been happening."

"Slaves always know," Sanct' Germain said with amusement.

"We know more than most," Raides informed his master with a great show of dignity. "That's what I wanted to tell you. We know, and we're grateful. If more masters would do half of what you've done for those three, there'd be few runaways turning bandit in the hills." He folded his arms and thrust out his jaw. "That's all."

Sanct' Germain was silent as he thought that his slaves did not fully understand what he had done, and why. Kosrozd, Tishtry and Aumtehoutep were not common slaves to him. If the ones in prison were Raides or the Cymric charioteer who had rushed away to the north, or three of the bestiarii, would he have tried so much? he asked himself. He doubted it. Perhaps if he had known the slaves, it would have been different, and he would have fought for them though there was no deeper tie between them. "Perhaps," he doubted, aloud.

Raides stared at him. "Perhaps?" he repeated.

"Nothing, Raides. More worry." He looked about and saw Rogerian standing nearby. "Come. I have a message packet to prepare. It will go by messenger in the morning." He paced back toward his private wing, Rogerian beside him. His face was closed in thought, his eyes looked inward. As he neared his side entrance and the black guard that waited there, he said to Rogerian in a low voice, "I tell myself that it is a matter of time now, that we are prepared." He stopped walking and looked toward the fountain in the central garden.

"My master?" Rogerian asked. His feelings to his new, foreign master were still confused. Though he felt increasing gratitude for the return of his life, he was distressed at some of the changes he had perceived in himself. It was true that he was not like Sanct' Germain, but he was no longer like other men, either. He responded with circumspection to Sanct' Germain's kindness while his respect grew hourly. At the back of his mind was the feeling that this erudite man was more dangerous than the most brutal overseer he had ever known. Standing beside him in the garden of Villa Ragoczy in the cool violet shadows of late afternoon, he found it difficult to accept all the things Sanct' Germain had told him about himself. That was, he found it difficult until Sanct' Germain turned his dark, compelling eyes on him. Then all the rational doubts vanished before their penetrating brightness.

Sanct' Germain gave an impatient jerk to his head. "I can't convince myself that it's settled." He had had that strange sensation many times before, over the centuries, and always it had been a warning. As he went into the north wing of his villa, the pervading apprehension closed around him, darker and more inexorable than the lengthening shadows in the garden.

Text of a note from the slave Monostades to his master, Cornelius Justus Silius.

Master:

They have met again, at her father's house. He arrived quite late in the night and entered by climbing over the kitchen sheds, onto the roof and then, apparently, going into the atrium. None of the slaves raised a cry against him, so it may be true that he has bribed them. He did not go until the hour before dawn, when he left by the slaves' door in the garden. Everything that the Armenian said would appear to be true. There was no way I could approach her bedroom, and so I did not, in fact, see them in the act itself, but the hour, the locations, the previous circumstances make it obvious that this visit was not one of courtesy.

I have spoken to one of the kitchen slaves (there are only three) and she said that her mistress has been completely alone, that no one has visited her and that no slaves have come with messages to her. However she and Franciscus arrange to meet, I cannot discover who in the household assists her. You have said yourself that your wife is not regarded sympathetically by your staff. It might be wise to examine a few of them and find out if this has changed. You would have little control of her in this house if she has found allies among her slaves.

Let me suggest that you do not confront her yet. You have said that you wish incontrovertible proof that she is adulterous, and that is proof I have yet to obtain. I have asked the slave who does the washing if there has been any evidence of lust on the sheets, but the slave claims that she has seen nothing, and she is very much the sort who would find such spillings if there were any. Perhaps Franciscus is cleverer than we know, and takes your wife on the floor, or puts his clothing over the bed so that we will have nothing to offer in court. Since it is obvious that he does not come to her often, it may take a little time to observe them properly, but with your other plan going forth, if you arrange to have another attack of poisoning after a meal with your wife, and if I have been able to observe her lying with this foreigner, your way will be clear. There will be no defense she can make against your accusations and you will have no blame coming to you. It will be a simple matter to have your divorce, with scandal attaching only to your wife. If there are those who have lain with her before who would be willing to testify in court that they have taken their pleasure of her, it will be so much the better, as she cannot then rely on countertestimony from this Franciscus.

I have decided that of the rewards you've offered me, I would like best to have a tavern and inn at Ostia. I don't know enough about crops and livestock to do well on an estate, even a small one, but a tavern would please me very well. I look forward to my freedom, master. You will always be the most welcome guest at Ostia, and I will be thankful for the rest of my life.

You may be certain, with this reward awaiting me, that I will be diligent in my work, and nothing will stop me from getting the necessary evidence and testimony to condemn your wife.

From my own hand, written and sealed on the morning of the ninth day of April, the 824th Year of the City, with all duty and fidelity,

Monostades

15

When the fourth event of the imperial Games, a cavalry combat, was finished, the sun was directly overhead and the heat in the Circus Maximus was intense. In his imperial box, Vespasianus could be seen drinking iced wine, while in the stands the vendors of juices and other beverages did a far more brisk business than those who sold sausages and meat pies.

On the spina, a large military band was playing popular marching songs, and many of the enormous crowd sang the rousing verses with more enthusiasm than accuracy. Little boys dressed as cherubs with painted wings strapped to their shoulders swung over the spectators on ropes hung from the rigging of the enormous awning. The boys carried baskets of flowers and coins which they tossed to the people below in the stands.

Constantinus Modestinus Datus turned to his guest, holding out a wide fan. "Here, Sanct' Germain. I'm sure you want this."

Sanct' Germain's face was quite dry, unlike that of Modestinus. "It's not necessary," he said as he took the fan and waved it through the stifling air.

"It's a pity about your slaves," Modestinus said as he adjusted the pillows on his marble seat.

"Yes." He hated talking about it, but there was no way he could say so without offending Modestinus.

"I think it's shameful the way Domitianus forced the Emperor to cater to the demands of the crowd. Executions should be according to the law not according to imperial whim," he said disapprovingly.

Sanct' Germain was suddenly very still. He no longer heard the sound of the eighty thousand Romans in the stands, or the cries of the vendors as they passed up and down the tiers. He was only distantly aware of it when the hydraulic organ began to play. "What do you mean?" he asked when he could trust himself to speak.

"What?" Modestinus turned toward him. "Oh, the execution. The foreign-owned slaves are to be torn apart by wild beasts. I thought you knew."

"Torn apart?" Sanct' Germain whispered. "No. I didn't know." He rose, feeling ill. "Pardon me," he said to Modestinus in a voice he could not recognize as his own, "I must . . . I must attend to . . ." He gestured meaninglessly.

"I don't blame you for not wanting to watch," Modestinus called after Sanct' Germain as he stepped into the corridor behind the patrician boxes. "There's no dignity in that kind of death. I share your feeling. It's a discredit to Rome."

"Yes," Sanct' Germain said vaguely as he tried to force his mind to think. It was his body that responded. He moved quickly and purposefully down the corridor toward one of the staircases that led to the passages under the stands. There might still be time, he told himself in desperation, to reach Kosrozd and Aumtehoutep and Tishtry. What he would do, even if he could reach them, he did not know. They were condemned. They would not be crucified. They would be torn apart by wild beasts, and that would be the true death. His jaw tightened and his stride lengthened as he reached the stairs, going down them two at a time. When he reached the foot of them a guard stepped forward, prepared to challenge him. Then he saw Sanct' Germain's face and hastily stepped back into the shadows.

On this side of the Circus the bestiarii were engaged in raising the cages from the level below. Heavy ropes groaned and men tugged, sweating as much from fear as labor, to bring up the ferocious animals that were trained to attack and kill men.

As Sanct' Germain made his way through the passage one cage tilted precariously as it reached this level and a huge shaggy paw with long curved claws swiped out from between the heavy bars at the slaves trying to right the cage. The bear made a low, barking sound as the terrified slaves eluded him.

Sanct' Germain saw a gladiatorial trainer he knew and approached the man. "Where are they holding the condemned slaves?" he demanded without preamble. "Tell me, Tsoudes."

The old trainer looked up. "The other side of the Circus," he answered before he realized who it was. Then he rose, a lopsided grin on his scar-seamed face. "Don't try it, Franciscus," he said kindly. "There's half a century of Praetorians guarding them, and they've already arrested two men who wanted to get near them, just to touch them." He looked at Sanct' Germain rather wistfully. "It is a shame about the Armenian woman. She was a real credit to the Circus, though most of those louts haven't the sense to appreciate it."

"I must try to reach them," Sanct' Germain said with deadly calm. He moved nearer to Tsoudes. "They didn't tell me about the beasts. I thought it would be crucifixion."

Tsoudes sighed. "So did we all," he agreed, falling into step beside Sanct' Germain as they made their way through the dark passageway. "Domitianus was the one who had it changed. He said that it would be more effective, since these were not Roman-owned slaves. He thought it would remind foreigners that they are here on sufferance."

They had to stop as another cage was raised into place. This one held three tigers, each in a fury. Sanct' Germain watched these cats expressionlessly.

"I think it's a mistake," Tsoudes said philosophically. "If they're part of a conspiracy or rebellion, then treat them like rebels, but otherwise, why pretend?"

"You need not follow me, if there are soldiers guarding the condemned slaves," Sanct' Germain said, as if he had not heard Tsoudes comment. "I will find them."

"And when you do, you'll need someone to stop you from making it worse for your slaves; I know." They were almost to the stableyard and the passageway was growing light. "It's bad enough to send them out on the sands to face the beasts, but if you give the Praetorians any trouble, they'll cut your slaves a few times—hamstring them so that they're helpless and bleeding, which means the animals will take them first." He put a huge hand on Sanct' Germain's shoulder, a hand that was missing two fingers. "It's cruel to make it worse for them. Fifty Praetorians, armed with short swords, under orders from the Emperor to guard the slaves and be sure that no one approaches them. What can you do against that?" He meant it kindly, and Sanct' Germain knew that his advice was sound, that he was helpless, but he could not accept it.

"I must see them," he insisted.

Tsoudes sighed. "Listen, Franciscus: if you give me your word that you will not behave stupidly or foolishly, there may be a way I can do that. But if you ever reveal what I show you, it will be the cross for me, and hardship for many others." He squinted as they walked into the sunlight, raising his hand to shade his eyes. "Will you give me your word?"

"Yes," Sanct' Germain said promptly, feeling senseless hope. "I will never speak of it."

Tsoudes watched him a moment, then made up his mind. "Follow me. Be silent and step warily." He started off across the stableyard, limping a little. He motioned Sanct' Germain to come along.

Sanct' Germain did not hesitate. He was no more than half a step behind Tsoudes when they entered the passage on the far side of the stableyard.

This part of the passage was almost deserted, for it had been used for the cavalry battle which had just concluded. It would be more than an hour before there would be much activity in this quarter of the Circus Maximus.

"Here." Tsoudes stopped to face a narrow light well where sunlight lanced down into the gloom. He stepped into the light well and reached up to a bracing bar, then pulled himself up. "Come quickly," he whispered to Sanct' Germain. "Hurry!"

Sanct' Germain for a moment was still, a tall figure in close-fitting black. Then in one deceptively easy motion, he touched the bar and swung upward. Tsoudes was crouched in a narrow opening to the side of the bar.

"Here. Hurry. Someone could see your shadow!" He held out his arm to Sanct' Germain and pulled him into the opening. "From here you must not speak." He put his hand to his lips as emphasis, then darted away into the low tunnel that led away from the light well.

Over the years, Sanct' Germain had heard rumors of these secret passages in the Circus Maximus, though he had given the tales little credence, since there were so many corridors and tunnels in the structure in any case. Yet the rumors had been true. He ducked down and went into the irregular and twisted course through the very walls of the Circus Maximus. The footing was uneven and occasionally the walls narrowed almost to impassability, yet they kept on in silence. It was like climbing through a seashell, Sanct' Germain thought as the sounds from the stands above and the corridors below mixed eerily in the little space.

Suddenly Tsoudes stopped and motioned Sanct' Germain to be still. He had reached a corner, and he looked around it with great care. When he was satisfied, he beckoned to Sanct' Germain to join him at the junction of the corridors.

When Sanct' Germain was beside him, Tsoudes pointed and said to his ear, "That way. A few paces farther along, the right side. There's only room for one. I'll wait for you here." He drew back into the aperture. "Don't be too long. They're about to be sent out."

Sanct' Germain nodded to show he understood, then crept past Tsoudes into the cross-corridor. It was just as Tsoudes had said. It was no more than half a dozen steps to another opening on his right, a shallow niche that looked down into the large holding cell where, at the moment, the foreign-owned slaves were kept. With great care Sanct' Germain slipped into the little space and looked down.

More than eighty people huddled there, most of them with strong bodies. Through the bars of the cell Sanct' Germain was able to see the squad of Praetorians guarding the cell. Once he had assured himself that he could not easily be seen by the soldiers, he turned his attention to those eighty people below him. He recognized many of the slaves. There were a dozen essedarii, their long hair bound in unruly knots at the backs of their necks. There were gladiators and retriarii, secutori, andabantae, bestiarii and charioteers. They were sullen, for the most part, knowing what they were to face. A few were gambling, though there was nothing to gamble for now. Others, watching the gamblers, jeered. One of the women, an andabante, lay in the far corner, inviting those men who wished to have a last taste of joy.

At last Sanct' Germain saw Kosrozd, standing a little apart from the others. Behind him were Tishtry and Aumtehoutep. They were grave and very calm, which worried Sanct' Germain. There was no way he could call out to them without exposing himself and his hiding place to all the slaves in the cell, and to the soldiers beyond. He stared at them with the full weight of his eyes, willing them to look up at him.

It was Aumtehoutep who saw him first, though his recognition was little more than a sharp intake of breath. He bent his head, and apparently spoke softly because Tishtry moved closer to him and plucked at Kosrozd's sleeve. Her eyes flicked toward Sanct' Germain once, then away. Kosrozd stood with his back to his master.

Finally Kosrozd turned from the other two and began what appeared to be an aimless stroll around the confines of the cell. Others were doing the same thing and there was no notice paid to him. After rather slow progress, he paused under the cranny where Sanct' Germain watched. He glanced up swiftly once, and then looked away. "You've heard, then."

"Yes," Sanct' Germain whispered. "There is nothing I can do, except die with you." He spoke calmly, just loud enough for Kosrozd to hear him.

"No," Kosrozd objected quickly with a swift motion of his hand. "That's useless."

"What, then?" Sanct' Germain asked, staring down at the Persian charioteer.

"Avenge us!" Kosrozd hissed, then moved away abruptly.

Sanct' Germain looked after him, fury rising in him with renewed intensity. He did not know yet where to vent his wrath, but there was a new, cold-burning rage lighting his dark eyes.

"All right!" the Master of the Games shouted from outside the cell. "It's time. Out onto the sands. You know where you're going."

A handful of the gladiators attacked the Praetorians as they pushed their way into the cell to drive the slaves out into the arena. The fight was quick, ending in the gladiators' being knocked down and superficially wounded.

"That's what will happen to all of you, if you resist," the Master of the Games said coolly. "You have all fought here before. You know what will be tolerated and what will not be."

"We've never faced beasts with empty hands before!" One of the slaves shouted this objection and many of the others joined in it.

"You may believe me or not, as you wish," the Master of the Games said in a voice that could be heard over the growing resentful murmur. "I asked that you be crucified. I opposed this contest. You deserve better than this." There was an unmistakable sincerity in his tone. "If it were not an imperial order, I would refuse to honor the requirements for your executions."

The last of the Praetorians forced their way into the cell, using their short swords to prod the most reluctant of the fighters toward the sunlight.

Sanct' Germain quitted his hiding place and went back to Tsoudes. "Where can I watch?" he whispered through clenched teeth as he brought Tsoudes to his feet.

"You want to watch?" Tsoudes was aghast.

"No. But I must." He dragged Tsoudes by the elbow. "Show me. Quickly."

Tsoudes obeyed, heading back the way they had come, but turning near another light well along the way. "There's a slot here. You can see most of them." He hung back. "I don't want to stay," he muttered.

"Then go." Sanct' Germain felt a surge of gratitude for the old trainer. "I will not forget what you've done for me, Tsoudes."

"No matter," was the answer as Tsoudes hurried away through the secret corridor.

From the hidden place where he watched, Sanct' Germain could see that most of the slaves were well onto the sand now, and many of them were beginning to form small fighting units, so that they could resist the first rushes of whatever wild animals were being released to kill them. Being arena slaves, they were wise to the behavior of most of the man-killers they were to face, and one of the bestiarii had boasted that if they sent lions against him, he would be safe, for he knew them all and need only give them orders to lie down and he could walk through them unharmed.

But it was not lions that raced around the spina toward them, but Sarmatian wolves, huge, fearless and deadly. Two of the bestiarii who had worked with the wolves cried out in despair, but a few of the others rallied. Sanct' Germain could hear one of the slaves bellow, "Get them apart and break their necks! Stomp on their necks!"

Around the other end of the spina came more than a dozen bears, running with surprising speed, clearly maddened by teasing given them while they waited in their cages.

Sanct' Germain pressed nearer the wall so that he could see more of the arena.

From the Gates of Life, there came a terrifying sound—the rasping squeal of wild boars. These enormous pigs were often twice the weight of a man, and their speed and tusks made wolves and bears avoid them. The barrier was raised and twenty boars, the bristles on their backs singed to make them furious, dashed onto the sands. The nearest wolves faltered, swerving to avoid the rush of the boars.

There was real fear among the slaves now, and one or two of them broke away, trying to run for the empty cages where they might hide. The wolves caught these without trouble. There were screams, thrashing limbs and the sickening sound of splintering bone as the wolves fell on their first victim, and an excited shout went up from the spectators in the stands.

In the imperial box, Vespasianus leaned back in his chair and nodded once to his son Titus.

Now that one of the slaves had been pulled down, the wolves grew bolder, rushing the clusters of men and snapping at their arms and legs, trying to drag the men away from the closed groups.

The bears saw this, and a few of them joined the wolves, rising on their hind legs as they attacked.

More of the slaves were screaming. Four of the boars charged the largest group of slaves, and sent the men scattering, except for those unlucky enough to be trampled and slashed with razor tusks.

The wolves were circling around for another attack now that the way was opened to them. Two of them began to stalk Kosrozd, Aumtehoutep and Tishtry. One of the wolves darted in, snapping. The crowd roared more loudly than the animals. Kosrozd took the wolf at the height of its leap, lifting the wolf as it opened its jaws. Possessing the same unnatural strength as his master, the young Persian forced the wolf's head back until the spine snapped. He dropped the big animal and turned to deal with its partner, yelling over his shoulder to Tishtry. She nodded, and began to decoy the second wolf while Kosrozd moved in on it.

They had killed four more wolves and were beginning to be cheered by the thousands of people watching when more wolves were released into the arena, causing something of a panic among the animals already there.

Many of the slaves were dead or dying, mangled and rent by the wolves, bears and boars that had been trained to kill them. Less than half of the men were still on their feet. A bear with an essedari in his jaws was attacked by one of the wolves, and between them they pulled the body into pieces as they fought over it.

Sanct' Germain closed his eyes in anguish as one of the

boars charged Aumtehoutep, tossing him into the air and slashing him from collarbone to the top of his hip as he fell. The stink of blood and entrails was hanging in the humid air, dense, almost palpable. One of the wolves trotted over to where Aumtehoutep lay and began to tear at his throat.

Kosrozd saw that, and rose from the wolf he and Tishtry had just killed. He began to walk toward the dead Egyptian, fury hot in his eyes.

"No," Sanct' Germain gasped as he saw a bear turn to charge with the speed of a racehorse. *"No!"*

The bear struck Tishtry a glancing blow that flung her into the path of a running boar. With infuriated squeals, the boar began to trample her.

At this sound Kosrozd turned sharply and saw the bear coming down on him. In that instant before the huge curved claws caught him and threw him and broke him, Kosrozd stood as straight and splendid as the prince he was, betraying no fear, accepting no defeat.

Sanct' Germain's arms were crossed over his abdomen and he bent with a pain that was not part of his body. The loss was a raw and open wound in him, and for a moment he wanted to break though the wall into the arena and go down with them. He slumped against the stones, a thin, keening sound in his throat. Sanct' Germain was blind with grief, battered in his soul by the true deaths that he had felt with Tishtry—agony stabbed him again—with Aumtehoutep, with Kosrozd. He drew his knees up to his chin, a tightened knot of suffering.

He never knew how long he lay there. When he came to himself, the bodies—what was left of them—had been dragged out through the Gates of Death and there were mounted Gauls pursuing what was left of the wolves and bears with long spears. He could do no more than glance once out the spy hole, then had to look away, telling himself it was the reek of the sands that affected him. It was an effort to stand. With each motion an unspeakable pain tore at him, keen as the teeth of wolves and bears, as the tusks of boars.

He had managed to stumble most of the length of the secret passage when the sound of voices stopped him. He steadied himself against the wall and listened.

"I took your word for the necessity," said a clipped voice that Sanct' Germain recognized with difficulty as belonging to the Emperor's younger son. "The crowd found it exciting, and that's to the good, but . . ."

The other voice was indistinct, muffled.

"I don't care what he told you. I don't want to discuss it with either of you. It's done. The people were satisfied. My father said it was a welcome change." He was silent while the other voice spoke. When Domitianus answered, the words were louder, more impatient. "I made no promises to either of you. Leave me alone!"

There was a garbled objection and the slap of retreating sandals. Sanct' Germain hugged the entrance to the corridor above the light well and waited for silence. When he could hear nothing but the tidal murmur from the stands above him, he reached for the bar and swung down.

He moved numbly, thinking that he must claim the bodies, what was left of them. Titus had given him a release and it would be peculiar if he refused to present it. He did not think he could bear to see the shattered limbs and ruined bodies. Yet he steeled himself to do it, feeling as if his soul were clad in granite and ice.

Sanct' Germain had almost reached the Gates of Death when he heard a voice behind him, calling his name. He did not want to turn. He did not want to speak.

"Franciscus!" the call was repeated, nearer.

He thought that it must be Necredes, wanting to gloat now that Tishtry and Kosrozd were dead. If he had to face the Master of the Bestiarii, he would tear him apart. He set his expression to a cold mask.

"Franciscus!" The man was right behind him.

"What?" Sanct' Germain spun around and found that it was the Armenian Led Arashnur who had followed him. "You!"

Arashnur gave him an insolent stare. "You should not have scorned my offer," he said with a sharp laugh. "Now neither of us have him. If you'd given in, this could have been avoided." He was relishing the power of his situation now.

"What do you mean, this could have been avoided?" Sanct' Germain asked in a soft, poisonous tone.

"The arrests, the imprisonment, the execution." Arashnur was preening. "A few letters to the right people, and look what can be accomplished. Romans are very touchy about slave rebellions, aren't they?"

"This was your doing?" It was a painful question to ask,

but there was no echo of his hurt in the words. He stood very still, his senses as alert and quivering as the string of a lyre.

"Some of it," he said blithely. "A letter here, a word there, and these foolish Romans did the rest. You should have listened to me. If we'd had a bargain—"

Arashnur never finished his speculation. Sanct' Germain had launched himself at the Persian spy, his small, powerful hands sinking into the muscles of his shoulder, then gripping, gripping, forcing bones and flesh closer together. Over the throbbing in his head and chest, Arashnur could hear the soft, cold voice. "You vile, pernicious butcher. You offal." The hands closed, viselike, as Led Arashnur's face contorted. "You take pride in their deaths, do you? Then join them, Arashnur. Join them." Arashnur shrieked once as his collarbone snapped on both sides, groaning as the jagged ends of the bones were driven downward into his chest.

Sanct' Germain watched Arashnur as the life began to go out of him. He told himself that this was the vengeance that Kosrozd desired, that he wanted for the slaughtered Kosrozd and Tishtry and Aumtehoutep. There was no sensation within him at all. No anger, no hatred, no release; only the stupefying numbness that spread through him like a drug.

Led Arashnur felt another hot eruption in his chest and he coughed as blood welled in his lungs. He looked up into Sanct' Germain's masklike face and tried to laugh, spitting blood in order to speak. "Too late, Franciscus." He choked. "Too late. *He knows.*" There was no more laughter, but a terrible bubbling, and then Led Arashnur fell heavily to his side, blood spreading out of his mouth and nose, a permanent derisive grin on his face.

For a moment Sanct' Germain stood over him. What had he meant—he knows? Who knows? What does he know? Then, as he realized that there was blood on his clothes and a dead man at his feet, Sanct' Germain moved away, slowly at first, and then almost at a run. The torment of his loss grew within him as he went, blotting out the world.

Report of the physician Pollux to Cornelius Justus Silius.

To the distinguished Senator Cornelius Justus Silius, greetings:

It is my most unpleasant duty to inform you, Senator, that your fears were well-founded. Certain procedures have been performed on the material you gave me, and I have the grave duty to inform you that the attacks of which you complained were due, indeed, to poison.

You mentioned that on both occasions these attacks followed an evening spent at the house of your wife's father, where she is currently living. Painful though the thought may be, you must consider the possibility that someone in your wife's family wishes you ill. You say that your relationship with your wife is less cordial than you would like, and that you suspect her of having a secret lover. Should this be the case, she may feel that you should be persuaded to divorce her. Oftentimes poisonings are not meant to kill, but rather to disable in various ways. Women who do not desire to deal with a man sexually have been known to administer mild poisons so that the man will not be capable to perform the act, or disinclined to do it.

Please understand that these are only suspicions. It may be that there is a food to which you have an antipathy of which your wife's cook is unaware. Many persons have such antipathies. The indication gained from the samples you gave us suggests that poison was indeed the factor, but an antipathy might contribute to your problem.

I am honored to have been able to serve you, and I wish that the outcome had been less unfortunate. I shall, should you wish it, be available to testify to my findings, and to that end have made a copy of the report that is included with this letter. It tells what was done, how, and what the results were. Should you have any questions concerning any of this, please inform me of your desires and I will do all that I can to make the matter clear.

Pollux
Physician
on the third day of May,
the 824th Year of the City

The procedures:

Taking the vomitus provided by the Senator, it was added to the food of three large rats. Food that was identical in every way except for the addition of the recovered material was given to three other rats. The three eating of the mixed food died.

The rats were then examined for signs of poisoning, and two were found to have the look of internal burns, with irritation in the mouth and anus.

Other material provided by the Senator was mixed with various herbs and then spread on a small sheet of ivory, which turned indelibly black. Certain poisons have this effect on ivory.

Drying of feces revealed some crystallike formations which may or may not be indicative of irritative substances in the body.

16

THERE WERE NOW two slaves quartered in the room adjoining hers, so Olivia had fled to the garden at night, hoping that Sanct' Germain would come. Each night for the last ten days she had kept her vigil under the fruit trees near the wall, sitting in the deepest shadows concealed by the drooping branches and the dark green palla she wore. Here she had the illusion that she had escaped her guards, and was free of them not just for the hours in the garden, but for her life. The flowers, which had been for so long neglected, now rioted in tangled confusion out of their beds, over the pathways and around the unused fountain. Olivia found the little wilderness a comfort, a way to bolster her self-deception. In this forgotten place, she could believe that she, too, had been forgotten: it was a great consolation.

Her desire for Sanct' Germain intruded into this dream. She missed him as she missed sustenance. Each night she longed for him, and each night she returned to her bed alone. She had sensed in the last several days that there was something very wrong, that he had been badly hurt, that there was a distress in him she had never known before.

Finally he came to her. It was past the middle of the night and the moon was low. The scent of flowers still tinged the air, but elusively now. A slow wind strummed the fruit trees where Olivia waited, half-asleep, on a rough wooden bench.

A rustle that could easily have been caused by the wind, a soft click of heeled boots on the overgrown path, a figure tall, powerful, in black Persian trousers and a short, wide-sleeved dalmatica, the gleam of moonlight in dark, compelling eyes that touched her with ice, a beautiful voice that she knew well and had yearned to hear; Olivia warned herself that it could be a dream even as she sat up and opened her arms.

Instead of gathering her close to him, Sanct' Germain dropped to his knees before her, his eyes meeting hers and then looking away. He did not touch her. "Olivia," he said.

"Sanct' Germain." She knew it would be a mistake to reach for him, though it took the full strength of her will to hold her hands at her sides.

In the shadows of the empty stable, a figure moved, silently approaching the garden.

Olivia wanted to ask him what had happened, where he had been, why he was so strange now, but she knew that she must keep silent. She saw his head bent, hardly more than two handbreadths away, and she wished she could reach out to fondle the dark, neat hair that fell in short, loose curls. He was so different tonight. She held back.

He felt her nearness as if across a chasm. She was a beacon to him, a point of light, of warmth in his newly desolate world. "Tell me, Olivia," he said quietly as his eyes looked into a dreadful emptiness. "When your father and brothers died, how did you feel? Was it as if a limb had been torn off or the heart pulled out of you? Did you hate the sun for rising?"

"Part of the time," she answered, as if she spoke to a curious child. "Part of the time there was nothing left within me but my hatred of Justus. My life was mechanical. I breathed and walked, slept, bathed, ate, as if it were someone else's body that did these things, and I was trapped within it. I, myself, was chained in a dungeon far away, crying aloud at walls of wet stone. I . . ." she faltered as she put a hand to her eyes—"I wondered why I bothered. Each day was like the last, and I thought there was no use in it." She looked away across the garden, blue in the fading moonlight. The breeze felt chilly now, and she shivered as it raced through the apple trees.

"Why didn't you end it?" he asked. There were pebbles under his knees and he knew they should hurt, but all he was aware of was the awkwardness they gave his balance. He saw Olivia shiver and could not tell whether it was from cold or her memories.

"You," she said, making the word a caress. "And my anger. I refused to give Justus the satisfaction. In time the worst was over. Whole hours would pass in which I did not want to die." She attempted to laugh at her foolishness, and almost succeeded.

At that sound, Sanct' Germain's arms went around her waist and he pressed his head into her lap. "Olivia, I killed a man, and felt nothing, no rage, no hate, no remorse, no satisfaction. I thought it was because of what I had just seen . . . their blood, their deaths . . ."

"Whose blood?" she interrupted him as she felt his arms become rigid.

"My slaves who were arrested. They were much more than slaves."

There was a cat in the garden, picking his way through the weeds with finicky determination. His eyes were spangle-bright as he looked toward Sanct' Germain and Olivia, bent together under the trees. He hissed once, then went on toward the stable.

"They were like you?" she whispered, her cheek pressed against his head.

"One was," he told her, wishing the admission affected him in some way, any way. "There was so little time. One would have been . . . I thought it was settled, for crucifixion, not the beasts . . . The third . . ." He stopped, feeling himself endlessly falling from darkness to darkness, and he held her with new strength. "Olivia, make me feel again. If I have any right to ask it of you, please make me feel again."

She had sunk her hands in his hair to turn his face up to her when a sound at the end of the garden caught her attention and she looked up sharply. "Oh," she said shakily. "The cat." Night lay thickly here under the trees, and she had to lean quite close to Sanct' Germain to see his pale face. She kissed his brow and eyes. His lips opened to her, and she was hideously reminded of a drowning man fighting for air. She took his face in her hands and drew him nearer.

Sanct' Germain's dark eyes searched hers. "Olivia," he said, as if recognizing her at last. He rose to his feet, pulling her with him, holding her with a fierceness that was new to both of them. His hands, his mouth roamed over her, demanding passion of her, calling forth the very limits of her ecstasy. "More, Olivia," he whispered, his voice hoarse with fervor. "More." His body was hard against hers, his desire intense, compounded of mourning and lust, of sorrow and ardor.

Monostades crouched in the shadow of the garden wall, his expression unreadable, as he watched his master's wife in Sanct' Germain's embrace. He dared not move closer for fear he would be noticed. The distance was too great for him to hear what they said to each other, and in the shadowed night he saw only the largest movements, but, he told himself cynically, he did not need to see the small ones, not watching them together. In spite of the darkness he could observe how eagerly Sanct' Germain lifted Olivia, catching her up in his arms, arching over her, his head bent to the lovely curve of her neck while she held him, abandoned to her pleasure. He watched while Sanct' Germain lowered her to the bench under the fruit trees and then knelt beside it, leaning above her as she opened her garments to him. Monostades saw the lightness of her skin in the night, and in the next instant this was obscured by Sanct' Germain as he moved over her. Deeply pleased with himself, Monostades made his way back to the stable, anticipating the reward that awaited him.

Sanct' Germain's head rested against Olivia's breasts. There was a tearing pain within him, a hurt that burned and bit with the ferocity of acid; there was also overwhelming gratitude. He moved his hands over her gently, kindly, and felt her tremble. "I have no tears. We don't, when we change." Anguish stifled him, and it was some little time before he spoke again. "If you had refused me . . ."

"Shush," she murmured.

"When they died, each of them, it was like . . . being given to the flames, which are as deadly to me as to you, my cherished one. I feel it now." He moved over her again. "I *feel* it." His lips touched hers.

His kiss sounded her to her depths, and when he drew back, she looked up through the gloom into his dark eyes. "Sanct' Germain," she began a little breathlessly, "will you . . . I want . . ."

"What do you want, Olivia?" He faced her, his hands still as he listened to her.

"I want to be free of . . . myself. I want, just once, to break out of the tyranny of my mind, and my senses, so that my whole being is consumed with loving. Make me free of my flesh, Sanct' Germain." Until she spoke, she had not known how deeply she longed for that freedom, for the rapture on the far side of gratification.

"Ah." His sad smile was compassionate. "Beyond your greatest fear is your greatest desire." He was barely touching her now; he had half-risen and only the feather touch of his fingers was on her. "Imagine," he said, his voice low and musical, "the petals of a flower opening in the heat of the sun, perfuming the air that passes, lingers and passes, like the figures of a dance." He paused, one hand on her shoulder, one at her waist. "Think of warmth, growing like a plant, like tendrils, rising around you, containing you though you are unfettered." He was closer to her. "Be like sunlight, that turns from white to gold to red, a fire, a torch, a blazing comet against the sky."

Olivia never knew how or when her miracle happened, but it was as she had wished, and for that one eternal moment, while her body was wrung with passion, she broke free of herself and knew only the immense force of her love.

There was dew in the garden when Sanct' Germain rose from his place beside Olivia. Though the dawn chorus had not yet begun, a single bird was piping two high, perfect notes. Far to the east the night was rimmed with silver.

"I wish you could stay," Olivia murmured, her fingers laced through his.

Sanct' Germain stood still. "If that's what you wish, I will." He had never consented before, and she had asked him but once.

"Truly?" She sat up on the bench then, reaching for her

discarded palla. Now that Sanct' Germain was not holding her, she felt cold.

"Yes." His dark eyes smoldered down at her.

"Justus . . ." She had no way to describe the things she feared her husband would do should he learn she had a lover, had had him for several years. She could recall the way he looked at her when the men he forced upon her did not treat her as violently as he required. His wrath then was nothing compared to what it would be if he learned of Sanct' Germain. She shuddered. "No, Sanct' Germain. Go. I want you here, but I don't want what would come of it. Justus would . . . he might do anything to me. Or to you." She did not want to think of her husband anymore, not with Sanct' Germain holding her hand and watching her with an expression she could not describe.

"When shall I return?" he asked. "Tonight? Tomorrow? Tell me and I will be here." He let go her fingers, but only to tilt her face up toward him. "I have an obligation to those who are dead, but beyond that, no one can command me but you." He leaned down quickly and kissed her once. "Get me word and I will come to you, anywhere, at any time. You have only to send for me. I have been a secret part of your life, and you of mine. Time is too short for that, even when you have had as much of it as I have." He stood straight, listening as footsteps passed in the street. "If you want me gone before your household wakes, then I must go now. What do those slaves who guard your room think when you pass the night in the garden?"

"They think I am foolish. They can see the walls, and there are others to watch outside. They think I am alone, trying to escape them."

"Well, so you are," Sanct' Germain smiled. Then he sobered. "Do I go?"

Reluctantly she nodded. "If there are people in the streets, it's probably best. My guards will be out of the house shortly, to be here when I wake at dawn." She finished securing her clothes. "I will send you word when it will be safe to come again. If you are here too often, someone might notice, and then . . ."

"Olivia." He held out his small, beautiful hands and lifted her to her feet. "Don't be troubled." He wrapped her in his arms and whispered against her hair, "Olivia, you have given me hope again." Then he stood back from her, turned sharply and went quickly along the garden path without looking back.

When he was gone, Olivia sank back down on the bench, assuring herself that she and Sanct' Germain were safe.

By the time she dozed, Sanct' Germain was at the Porta Viminalis, and Monostades was back at the house of Cornelius Justus Silius, waiting to tell him all that had occurred in the garden.

A petition filed with the procurator senior of the Senate.

Worthy Senators:

On behalf of the bondsman Rogerian of Gades, this petition for compensation and damages is being presented to you so that the bondsman Rogerian may claim his rights under the laws of Rome.

This man's bond was held by one Linus Aeneas Desider, who resides in Rome and Gades. Desider carried the usual contract with this man, and assigned him to overseeing the operation of his estate near Gades, which task the bondsman performed to the satisfaction of Desider and others in authority there.

On his last visit to Gades, Desider told the bondsman Rogerian that he was planning to take Rogerian with him to Rome upon his return there. Rogerian was not eager to make such a change, for though he is a good manager of estates, his experience does not include working in a Roman patrician household. He mentioned this to Desider, who told him it was unimportant.

When he arrived in Rome, the bondsman Rogerian states that he was badly housed and fed, and given nothing to do, either for his bond-holder or for his Roman household. He often asked to be given work, and was told that Desider forbade it. The houseman expressed concern on the bondsman Rogerian's behalf, in such a way that the said Rogerian was filled with doubts and apprehensions. These turned out to be well-founded, for Desider came home one evening, after having drunk a great deal of wine, and accused Rogerian of laziness and poor attention to duty. When Rogerian objected that he had often asked to be assigned work in the household, Desider accused him of impudence as well. Rogerian was then flogged, that day and each of nine succeeding days. Desider was present at each flogging and urged the overseer to be more free with his use of the flagellum.

One of the slaves who was given the task of keeping Rogerian alive told him, during those nine days, that this is a habit with Desider, who brings slaves and bondsmen from his country estates and keeps them for his amusement. He brings foreigners so that the Roman household will not revolt against this cruelty, and so that the victim will be without friends to protect him. Rogerian was thought of sympathetically by the household, but none of them were willing to make complaint, either to their master or to the officials of the city, for fear that their master would do the same thing to them that he had done to Rogerian. None of them told Rogerian that he was entitled to sue Desider for damages in such an instance.

Surely Roman justice means more than this. Surely a man who has been as ill-treated as Rogerian from Gades is entitled to a full remedy under law. He has discharged the conditions of his bond most honorably and has been rewarded with treatment that should have killed him.

I, Ragoczy Sanct' Germain Franciscus, am filing this petition with you so that the great wrongs that have been done to this bondsman may be given the fair hearing to which the law entitles him. I state now that I found this Rogerian grievously wounded and abandoned by the beginning of the Flavian Circus. It was raining. The man had no protection, and was hardly conscious, so had no means to obtain protection. Many of those living in the arches were aware of his plight but disinclined to help him.

The deliberate abuse of slaves and of bondsmen, I remind you good Senators, is a flagrant contempt for Roman law, which specifically states that a slave may not be egregiously hurt by his master. Chastisement is to be conducted with rods for minor infractions and with the flagellum only when there has been a crime committed. There has been a crime committed here, truly, but it was against Rogerian.

I freely reveal that the man Rogerian is acting as houseman at my villa and will remain there. If there can be any question of the term of his bond, I will purchase the remaining years for whatever is reasonable. I have already secured Rogerian's bond to me in the form of one copper Brutus, that being the least-valued coin in my possession. He refused to take more.

Rogerian will be at your disposal, good Senators, and will appear when it is required of him. I am certain you will decide his case on its merits and award him the full measure of restitution that you are empowered to give.

This by my own hand, most respectfully, on the tenth day of June in the 824th Year of the City.

Ragoczy Sanct' Germain Franciscus
at Villa Ragoczy

17

JUSTUS' LANGUOR was deceptive: he was lying back in his bed, supported by five huge pillows, gazing across the room with an expression of patient resignation on his face. His visitor paced back and forth, his red-and-tan-striped toga flapping around his ankles. He glared at the man in bed. "But, Justus, I need you. You said you'd help me."

"I will help you," he assured the young man. "But you see how it is with me."

"It's unfortunate!" his guest snapped. "It couldn't have happened at a worse time. My father has been wavering on his decisions about the Jews. He's forgotten the hard lesson we learned at Jerusalem."

"And your brother sleeps with a Jewish queen." Justus sighed and motioned his visitor to a chair. "Sit down, Domitianus. You're fatiguing me."

Domitianus did as he was told, though he watched Justus

petulantly. "What is the matter with you, anyway? Are you ill?"

"No, my friend," Justus answered with a disquieting smile, "I'm being poisoned. I have a physician's report. Now all I have to do is find the poison in—"

"You're serious!" Domitianus declared, getting to his feet once more. "Poisoned? That's dreadful. What enemies of yours are doing this?"

Justus was delighted to answer him. "My wife, I think. I have had three attacks, each one after spending the evening in her company. We have lived apart awhile, and I thought her rancor had lessened, but I fear, I very much fear, that she and her lover are more interested in my death than I had thought." He gestured to show that his attitude was philosophical. "She's young but her youth is leaving her quickly. I suppose she wants adventure while it is still available to her."

"But to plot your death with her lover! No, Justus, that's beyond the acceptable. It's one thing to tolerate an affair—it is expected—but murder, even the attempt, is not to be taken so calmly. If you do not act against her, she may succeed, and then others may feel that it is their right."

Justus looked away. "I can't help but feel that I brought much of this on myself," he said heavily, knowing that Domitianus would believe the whole preposterous story. "She has been a woman of intense . . . appetites, and I have not always been capable of doing all that she wishes. I thought at first that this was only the excitement of youth and that she would change, given time and affection. I have begun to worry of late that I was wrong and that her desires are not the caprice of juvenile freedom, but a true depravity." He let his voice drop to almost nothing. "You're a young man, Domitianus, and you don't know how, as you grow old, your mind can be so easily swayed by the promise of love. I hope you never have to . . ." He cleared his throat and faced the Emperor's younger son. "I should not have said this to you. I know you will keep this confidential."

"But we're talking about a plot against your life!" Domitianus protested, taking a brisk turn about the room. "You can't lie there and let that woman kill you."

"Perhaps I would wish to die," Justus said, fixing a wistful smile on his sensual mouth. "I never intended to harm her, but it is clear that she thinks that I have not treated her well. That's a great condemnation, Domitianus."

"Do you honestly mean that you're willing to be murdered just so that your wife can be pleased? Justus, you're being a fool. Divorce her, prove her adultery and her attempts on your life. This is no tiff between husband and wife, this is a terrible crime against the home and the state." He slammed his closed fist into his hand, his voice rising. He stopped at the foot of Justus' bed. "Who is the lover? Do you know that?"

"Oh, yes. I know." He folded his hands on the sheet. "I appreciate your concern for me, Domitianus. Truly. But you must let me deal with this as I think best."

"No!" Domitianus shouted. His voice had been rising since he came into the room and now it was enough to bring a worried slave to the door. Domitianus gave a short oath.

"Please do not disturb me again while the Emperor's son is with me," Justus said to the slave, masking his annoyance. He had nearly managed to maneuver Domitianus into demanding to know who Olivia's lover was, and it was quite necessary for his stratagem that Domitianus know this.

Domitianus made an effort to control himself. "We haven't found the murderer of that Armenian scholar you brought to meet me. It's a shame."

"Yes. Probably one of the foreign slaves killed him. There were many who were angry, and it's likely that Led Arashnur did not realize how dangerous his position was there." Secretly, Justus was delighted that Arashnur was dead, for the man had known too much about the plans that Justus had made. If Arashnur had been questioned, or had grown angry and decided to inform against him, it would have been awkward. And although Justus was quite sure that Arashnur had been a Persian spy, it would have been unpleasant to have to prove it. "A pity," he added. "And so young."

"A pity, as you say," he agreed, dismissing the matter. "Your wife is what must concern us now."

"If you insist on discussing something so painful . . ." Justus muttered, letting himself be coaxed and prodded.

"You say you know who her lover is." Domitianus sat once more, leaning forward in his chair, elbows on his knees, hands clasped under his chin. He looked extremely young.

"My library slave, a Greek, has been watching her, on my orders. You must understand that I have seen nothing of this myself. I have only his reports to go on, and he has observed them together but twice." He rubbed his face, fussed with the sheet. "It is difficult. Her lover is well-respected, with powerful friends."

"As powerful as yours?" Domitianus asked, with obvious reference to himself. "What is he, one of my brother's cronies?"

"He does know your brother," Justus admitted, knowing that the life-long rivalry between Titus and Domitianus would be useful in this situation. "I recall that they have had some association, and I have heard your brother speak highly of this man."

"Naturally," Domitianus scoffed. "A Roman who stoops to live with a Jewish queen would not balk at condoning adultery among Romans."

"The man is not a Roman," Justus said very quietly, watching Domitianus covertly, his face averted.

"Not a Roman? Who is it? What foreigner would dare . . . ? How could she stoop . . . ?"

Before Domitianus grew too excited again, Justus said, "The man is Ragoczy Sanct' Germain Franciscus."

"Franciscus?" Domitianus was on his feet again. "Franciscus? But there's never been any talk at all . . . never a hint . . . And you say that he is your wife's lover?" Bewildered, he stopped. "He has dealt with Titus occasionally. Titus likes him." This was sure condemnation in Domitianus' eyes. He spun toward Justus. "How did your wife meet him? When?"

Justus took his time answering. "They met for the first time at a banquet given by Titus Petronius Niger. He's been dead for years, but he was in favor once. Franciscus was there. He brought some slaves from Hind who danced for us. It was really most remarkable."

"Do you mean," Domitianus demanded, his voice raising again, "that your wife has lain with this man for—what is it?—seven years?"

"I don't know," Justus said, his mouth tightening at the thought that had infuriated him since he had learned of Olivia's deceit, the thought that she might have been intimate with him since that night when Sanct' Germain had first come to her bed and dared to give her pleasure. "I don't see how she could have," he added, more for his own assurance than for Domitianus'.

Something occurred to the Emperor's son. He stopped his restless pacing and came to sit on the foot of Justus' bed. "Did you know that there were investigations begun against him that were dropped? One of them was in connection with the rebellious arena slaves, of course, but there was a question about smuggling. He owns ships, you know, and I remember that one of the captains was found to be carrying illegal grain. There was a report in the Praetorian records about it. I remember looking at it while *I* was prefect." He grinned at Justus. "The investigations might be reopened. They were never concluded. If my father should decide that foreigners like Franciscus, who owns rebellious slaves and whose captains smuggle goods, should be given something more than a cursory check every three years, well, it could be that part of your trouble with your wife may be removed." He fairly beamed. "If he were out of the way, she is sure to think twice about harming you, particularly since the interference will not come from you, but from the Senate itself."

It would not do to give in too easily, Justus reminded himself. "That might not be a good idea. Wouldn't she be suspicious? I would hate to do this and have it be for nothing."

"Justus, Justus," Domitianus said with great sincerity, "the woman is your wife. You have your rights with her and she is using you shamefully. You could divorce her. It might be wise if you did. My father has said that he is well-inclined on your behalf, and would be willing to do what he could for the advancement of your house with ours."

"I have considered divorce," Justus said slowly. "I think I mentioned it once to your father. This is very difficult for me. No man wishes to think ill of his wife . . ." He leaned back against the pillows. "Very well, Domitianus. You are most persuasive. See if the Praetorian Guard know anything more about this foreigner, and if there is cause, remove him from my wife's company. I would not like to disgrace her with him. She might be willing to deal more kindly with me."

"You're fooling yourself, Justus," Domitianus insisted in a kindly way. "Be rid of her lover and of her. Consider what it has been like for her—she has had the excitement of this foreigner, and perhaps others. Offer her a quiet settlement and be rid of her." He made an effort to sound as logical as possible, not allowing his rather strident voice to rise.

Justus wanted to laugh. When he rid himself of Olivia, she would be sentenced to death. He had no intention of leaving another live wife about where she might start spreading tales about him. He had the physician's report, the report that Monostades had written and the testimony of the slaves who guarded Olivia at her father's house. These would be enough, when he was ready, to establish her guilt beyond question. "I'll consider it, Domitianus, but you must understand that when a man is my age and has been married to a beautiful young woman, he has reasons to forgive . . . many things."

Domitianus gave an uncomprehending nod. "There is such a thing as too much forgiveness, Justus, and it can only breed contempt in those who receive it. Consider that, as well." He came and stood by the head of the bed. "You've been very helpful to me, Justus, and it would upset me if anything were to happen to you. If you were to be ill again, for example. I might then insist that your wife be questioned as persuasively as possible. You say you admire her beauty. Wouldn't it be better to divorce her and leave her as she is than to give her to the questioners to practice with, and deprive her of both her looks and health?" He patted Justus' shoulder, then turned and left the room.

"Young fool!" Justus erupted when Domitianus was gone. "He's going too fast. If he forces me to act before I'm ready . . ." He threw back the sheet and climbed out of bed. "I'll have to keep him distracted a little longer. If he makes up his mind to go after Franciscus . . ." He sounded a gong and a few moments later a slave opened the door.

"Master. What do you wish?" The slave stood in the arch of the door, away from Justus' arm.

"Send Monostades to me. At once. I will require wine in an hour. See to it." As he waited for Monostades, he threw off his bed robe and dragged a long-skirted tunica over his head, belting it with links of gold.

"Master?" Monostades said as he came through the door. There was an air of derision about him, a barely disguised repugnance in his aloof features that made Justus more irascible than ever.

"Smug slaves get whipped in this house," Justus said conversationally. "Remember that, Monostades."

Monostades' face was wooden. "What do you require, Master?" If he had used less inflection, he could not have spoken at all.

"You have all your reports on Sanct' Germain, don't you? Not just his nights with my wife, but other material?"

"Yes," Monostades said carefully. "As much as I could find out easily. There are records of ownership for land and slaves and ships; those are simply come by. There is other information, more obscure, that is a matter of report and rumor. You may read those records as well, if you wish." It was an effort not to unmask Justus as the hypocrite he was, but that was dangerous work for a slave. He had promised himself that when he was free, he would denounce Cornelius Justus Silius, and knew, secretly, that he would never do it.

"I want to know the worst of those rumors. Prepare them for me and bring them when they are ready." He did not bother to look at Monostades. "I will then have a message I want you to deliver to . . . an important person. No one is to know where you are going. Is that understood?"

"I understand. You want the worst gossip about Sanct' Germain Franciscus, and then I am to deliver a message clandestinely." He recited the instructions tonelessly while fixing his gaze on the rumpled sheets of the bed.

"See that it goes properly. That's all until you bring the report." He stood with his back to the door until he heard it close. As he moved to a low writing table, he tried to recall what he had heard about Sanct' Germain from one of the gladiators. There had been a ridiculous rumor that he had a special skill that made it impossible to wound him. After his Persian charioteer had walked away from that accident and returned to racing with only a few scars, there had been a great deal of speculation, most of it more envy than fact, which certainly was disproved when the charioteer was pulled to pieces in the arena. Still, he ruminated, such things could be useful. A man who can convince others he is invincible is a very dangerous man.

Justus rose from the desk and went to the window, looking out at Rome. His smile was greedy. The Emperor, he told himself, was older than he, and it had not been considered unlikely that he would rise to the purple when he was so old. Caesar himself had not begun his career until quite late in life. Why, then, for himself, many things were possible. If he could marry into the Flavian House, it would be simple to convince Domitianus to make Justus' children—for there must be children—his heir, and then, if Domitianus did not live to rule, Justus would have to guide his infant Caesars. Vespasianus, he was certain, would not last more than five years, and Titus would not prove himself capable for any length of time. Domitianus, on the other hand, was tenacious and bitter enough to take risks that his handsome older brother would not consider. Domitianus would have to be the rung that lifted Justus to supreme power. He chuckled, knowing that Domitianus thought he was using Justus, and not the other way around. Seven years, at the most, he thought, seven years and he would be Caesar in all but actual name and honors. The lust for power gave him new potency, and he wished that Olivia had not fled to her father's house, for at moments like this, he longed most to see her writhe under the assault of a muscular provincial. He forced his mind to other matters.

At the desk he pulled a sheet of vellum from its drawer and began to write out his authorization to the prefect of the main prison. Occasionally he whistled as he wrote.

When Monostades returned, the vellum sheet was folded and sealed. Justus took the papyrus pages from his slave and gave him the vellum.

"This is to the prefect of the Mamertinus Prison. You are to take it to him personally and remain until he has read it. Do you understand?" He held out the sealed letter.

"Yes. Certainly." Monostades took the note. "I will make sure the prefect reads it. Shall I wait for a message in return?"

Justus hesitated. "No. I doubt that will be necessary." He folded his hands. "Don't linger on my account, Monostades."

The Greek slave paled, bowed slightly and went quickly out of the room, and for that reason did not see the malicious smirk that Justus wore when he left. As it was, Monostades went directly to the prison, bearing in his own hands the note that instructed the prefect of the Mamertinus Prison to seize the slave that brought the note, geld him, cut out his tongue, and send him to labor with the rebellious Jews building the Flavian Circus. The slave, according to Justus' note, had forced the Senator's wife to lie with him, and because of her sense of disgrace, she had removed herself from her husband's house. The slave had then attempted to blackmail his master, and for that reason Senator Silius would be glad, he wrote to the prefect, if the business were kept as quiet as possible.

In the first hour after sunset, a slave came to the house of Cornelius Justus Silius, carrying a small bloodstained bag from the prefect of the Mamertinus.

Text of a warrant given to the Praetorian Guard.

To the prefect, the tribunes, the centurians and men of the Praetorian Guard, from the Emperor, his greetings:

This will empower you to take in charge the foreigner Ragoczy Sanct' Germain Franciscus, who lives at an extensive villa and estate three thousand paces to the east of Rome. You are hereby given authority to hold this foreigner for five days while the full investigation of his activities is concluded. You may question him, you may starve him, but you may not torture him, as there are no formal accusations filed against him yet.

Since the Praetorian Guard has done some preliminary investigations of this foreigner before now, it is requested that any and all information in the files of the Guard be made available to the procurator senior of the Senate and to myself, should I require them.

This Franciscus has shown himself to be kindly disposed to Rome, and for that reason a degree of circumspection in his treatment is advisable, until it is determined that he has truly violated the laws of the state.

Do this with as much secrecy as possible. It is necessary that great caution be exercised; this man is well-respected. Keep watch on him by day and night and be certain that everything he says is accurately recorded. I will decide how best to act when I have examined the evidence.

Caesar Vespasianus
on the second day of August,
the 824th Year of the City

18

AN OLD hunchbacked fruit vendor had been crying his apples and grapes outside Olivia's garden for most of the morning before she said to one of the slaves who guarded her, "I'm going to go buy whatever he's selling. I don't want to have to listen to that bagpipe voice any longer."

"Have him beaten with whips," the guard suggested laconically. "That way he won't come back."

"No," she said quickly. "If I pay what he asks, and then remark that there is more traffic two streets farther down, I think we'll be left alone." She looked at the slave who guarded her. "I am not going to run off. You may watch me, if you like." Her disdain was genuine, and might have shamed him, but the slave knew his master, and said, "I will watch you from the door, Domita, and will do what I must."

"Mother Isis!" she exclaimed, giving him a quelling stare. "Do watch me, then." She had lifted her stola, which had been flung casually around her neck, and pulled a portion of the fabric over her head, as befitted a woman of her years and station. There were five gold denari in her desk drawer, and a few coppers in the kitchen for the cook, and that was all the money she was allowed. Allowed! That still rankled with her, for she knew that there were three estates that were hers and her sister's, though she had never seen them and did not know what they earned. She took one gold denarius from the desk. It would be enough to buy the hunchback's fruit ten times over, but she was willing to pay that to be rid of the monotonous call of "Apples, grapes, fresh this morning, apples, grapes, fresh this morning, apples, grapes . . ." Clutching the coin, she stepped out of the house onto the narrow street.

The hunchback was seated on a box, with another box filled with fruit beside him. He was middle-aged, with a saturnine cast to his features. As Olivia approached, he fell silent, holding up grapes. "The very finest," he announced, then dropped his voice to a whisper, "from Villa Ragoczy."

Olivia had to restrain the urge to jump, or shout, or demand of this strange man what had become of Sanct' Germain. Instead, she took the grapes, saying, "Fresh this morning?"

"Very fresh, Domita. You cannot find better." He bent to his box to pull out more fruit, saying in a low voice, "The Praetorians came ten days ago and arrested him. There was no explanation. He is not in the Mamertinus Prison. He is not in the slaves' prison. I've looked."

"Let me see the apples, instead," Olivia said loudly enough for the slave standing in the doorway to hear. "Who are you?"

"Rogerian. I suppose I am his houseman now." He brought three apples out of the box and held them up so she could see them. "Very fresh. Unblemished. No worms."

Olivia took the apples. "Why was he arrested?"

"I don't know," Rogerian confessed softly. "He was not informed. They were supposed to take him before the Emperor five days ago, but I have heard nothing of it."

"Is he condemned?" she asked, frightened, then raised her voice. "They are fine quality, hunchback." She looked at him closely. "Are you really hunchbacked?"

"No," he admitted quietly. "I can bring more tomorrow, Domita, if these are what you like."

"Excellent, but I will want to inspect what you bring. There are times when vendors will show fine goods to the mistress and shoddy goods to the cook. Here is money for all that you have; tomorrow I will give you half the amount." She took the box he handed to her as he rose. "Thank you."

"Tomorrow, Domita," Rogerian said respectfully. "The wares will be good."

"I hope so." With the box held against her hip with one arm, she went back into the house. She paid no notice to the slave standing in the door, but went directly to the kitchen, holding out the contents of the box to her cook. "Well, here is some very good, unblemished fresh fruit. Do you think you can use it?"

The cook eyed the box suspiciously. "It might be going bad. Lots of vendors do that."

"I have inspected the fruit myself. It's satisfactory. I think I would like to have chicken cooked with grapes today. If you are willing to do it, of course." There was an extra glitter in Olivia's eyes that would not brook opposition.

"Chicken with grapes. Of course, Domita," said the cook

as she took the box and set it to the side of the enormous open hearth.

Through midday, Olivia sat in the atrium, pretending to read from one of the rare stitched books her father had prized. Some of the paragraphs she read four and five times without comprehending a word of them. Where was Sanct' Germain? Had he been condemned? She did not know whom she could ask, or how she could act without Justus learning of it. She looked down at the account of the war with Lars Porsena by Titus Livius. What did she care about the Etruscans? she asked herself as she got up from the chair. She had needlework to finish, and had considered doing something to put the garden in order, but those things could not hold her attention for very long: her thoughts returned to Sanct' Germain as she paced through the corridors of her father's house.

She had just risen from her midday meal—which she had praised heavily for the chicken with grapes, though to her it had tasted like straw—when one of her guards announced that her husband had come to speak with her.

"Indeed I have, Olivia," Justus said, strolling in behind the slave and looking around at the shabbiness of the house. "It's a shame to see these old houses in disrepair, however . . ." He shrugged.

"Perhaps," said Olivia as she lifted her chin, "if I had the money from my family's estates, the house would not be neglected."

Justus laughed. "Still ready to take up cudgels, are you, Olivia? It would have been better for you if you had lost a little of that pride of yours."

"Better for whom, Justus?"

The question went unanswered. Justus walked across the little dining room, his hands locked behind his back. When he was at the window, he turned to face her. "Your lover is going to die," he said quite calmly.

For an instant Olivia felt as if she had been felled by an ax. She swayed on her feet, then straightened. "My lover?" she asked in a cool voice.

"The man who has been lying in your bed since you chose to live here," Justus said, an edge in his voice.

"I did not choose to live here, Justus; you sent me here so that you would be free to pursue your political ambitions." She crossed her arms and gripped her elbows, as if holding herself erect this way. It pleased her that Justus did not know how long her affair with Sanct' Germain had lasted. That, at least, was one victory.

"You agreed, Domita." He watched her from under strong brows.

"What else could I do?" Suddenly she sank onto one of the five couches. "Justus, what do you want now? Why are you here?"

He opened his hands in innocence. "May not a man visit his wife when it suits him? Must there be a reason beyond that?"

"Isn't there?" she countered, tired of his game.

"Well," he conceded, "if you had a lover there would be. I wanted you to know that Ragoczy Sanct' Germain Franciscus—you may remember him: he's the one who wore black when he came to you, though among so many . . . Be that as it may, this Ragoczy Sanct' Germain Franciscus has been detained on very serious charges, very serious. Domitianus himself told me about it. Since this man is not your lover, you say, then there is no need for me to go into it." He had picked up a small cup of blue glass. "What a very common thing," he said, and dropped it so that it broke at his feet.

"Justus! Tell me what you have to say and leave me!" Her breath was shaky when she drew it and she wanted desperately to weep, though she knew she must not.

"Say what I have come to say," he repeated thoughtfully. "Then leave you. I suppose that's what you're hoping for. All right, Olivia. I'll tell you why I am here." He put one hand on his hip. "I'm going to be married. To Flavia Lesbia Fabulens Marco. There's nothing official yet, but the Emperor has said he'd approve the match. He's encouraging it. There is, naturally, a problem."

"I'm the problem," Olivia said flatly. "I agree to divorce you. You may say what you want of me. I will divorce you and not ask a single pea in settlement." She knew she spoke too eagerly, that it could not be this simple, that Justus would use this as another way to torment her.

"But I have been divorced before, and to do it twice, even with such a flagrantly unfaithful wife as you . . ." He grinned at her gasp. "Oh, yes, I have a sad record of your infidelities. Such low tastes you have—gladiators and other ruffians. The Senate would be shocked to hear how you have behaved."

Olivia's voice dropped very low. "Justus, say what you like. Tell any lies that please you, but let me go. I know that my mother has no interest in me, but let me go to the estate near Brixellum. I don't care if it's the meanest you own . . ."

"My poor, misled Olivia," Justus said sweetly, "it is my sad duty to tell you that you can't go to your mother. She's dead, Olivia."

There was horror in Olivia's face now. "Dead? Dead? But that's not possible . . ."

"She died some time ago, I fear, a year ago, perhaps two. I'm afraid I don't remember." He flicked his fingers at the back of the chair, as if rubbing away dust.

"One year ago? Perhaps two?" Olivia got to her feet, white with rage. "I have let myself be abused, manipulated and bullied because you told me you would have my mother killed if I disobeyed you. I have consented to be treated like a bondswoman rather than a wife because I wanted to spare my mother any more hurt from you, Justus." She had come closer to him. For the first time she felt no fear of him whatever. He could not hurt her again, even if he killed her. "You have made me worse than a slave." She threw herself at him, her hands tearing, her teeth bared. Fury strengthened her, made her glad to hear the sound of ripping cloth as Justus toppled to the floor.

Then there were hands pulling her off her husband, dragging her to the other side of the room, holding her roughly while Justus got slowly to his feet.

"Keep hold of her," Justus said to his slaves. "Did you see what she did? Not content with poisoning me, she's now flying at my throat."

"Poisoning you?" Olivia asked. "What insanity is this?"

"No insanity, Domita," Justus said as he approached her. "I have evidence from a physician that proves you have tried to poison me. I have had three attacks, each after spending the evening here with you. The physician is willing to testify for me, as are others. I have a report on your adulteries. It's quite a simple matter." He grabbed her jaw in his hand. "There will have to be a trial, of course."

"I will deny it! I will answer every lie with the truth, and I will bring evidence as to how you have used me." Her head was twisted by his hand. She spat in his face.

His open-handed blow jarred her out of her guard's hold and she almost fell.

"You're an insolent child!" Justus hissed as he wiped his face. "For that, it will be worse for you. I will bring men into court who will say all that they did with you and to you. I will shame you, Olivia, so that no one in Rome will dare to look at you. That I promise."

Olivia thought that she had never seen him so angry, and as she watched him, some of her fear returned. "I wish I had killed you," she said in a voice as tight as her fists. "I wish I had given you poison. I wish I had stabbed you. I wish I had smashed your brains out."

Justus gave the guard who held her a cynical smile. "You heard what she said, didn't you?"

"I heard," said the slave.

"Though you can't give testimony, you can make a report." He gave an offhanded frown toward Olivia. "Women like this one are dangerous."

"Shall I report to Monostades?" the slave asked.

"Monostades? No. I will send another. Monostades is . . . away for a time." With a negligent finger he toyed with the fibula on Olivia's shoulder. "If I had the time, Domita, I would have this clothing off you and I would use you on the floor like the murderous slut you are." He began to tear the fine cloth of her palla. "You don't deserve better. I should make a present of you to one of the legions. You could serve a cohort, couldn't you? What's six hundred men to you?" The rip extended beyond her waist. "Skin like this would be a treat to the legionnaires, wouldn't you say? You might not keep it long, but for a time, it would please them." The cloth was torn almost as far as her knees. "There's a gladiatorial school that keeps women for their fighters. It's a hard life. Should I send you to Capua?"

Olivia twisted in the slave's expert hold, but could not break free of him. "You have no authority over me. You have no rights at all. If you send me to Capua, I will denounce you. If you try to give me to a legion, I will have you flogged!" She knew he was lying to her. It was too much of a gamble. He had to keep her under control.

The palla was torn in half now, and the cloth fell away, revealing her body. The slave's hands tightened.

"Actually," Justus continued as he looked her over critically, "I won't need to do any of that. You'll be condemned for attempting to murder me, and it will simply be a matter of choosing the most appropriate death. How would immurement suit you?" He saw Olivia shudder. "Walled up. In a tomb, perhaps, to save later expense. They frown on impaling women these days, but they might make an exception for you." He turned to the slave. "You'll have to watch her very closely now. She's very clever, and you saw for yourself that she will not stop at violence." He moved away from her. "It will be soon, Olivia. There are a few questions that must be settled before everything is ready, but when that happens, you will know."

"Justus," Olivia said, and her voice was surprisingly calm, "why? Why can't you simply divorce me? People get divorces all the time."

"It would not be enough," he said shortly.

"But why? The Emperor won't mind if there are two former wives of yours in the world, if you will keep your bargains with your fourth wife." She was intent now, for this was something she wanted very much to understand, since he thought it was important enough to require her death.

He had wandered back toward the window, but at that question he rounded on her, his face darkening. "Three times—three times my family has been *that* close to wearing the purple." He held up his hand, finger and thumb almost touching. "Each time it was snatched away from us by stupidity and malice. We are an old house, a noble house. We have the right. I have the right. My cousin could not get the power. My father tried and failed, but I tell you now, Olivia, that I will not fail. I need so little now to have it happen."

"So little?" she asked in a low, chiding tone. "My death is that to you?"

Justus stepped back, saying nothing. He kicked at the bits of broken glass, then said to the slave, "You will be certain that she is watched at every moment. She must be in plain sight at all times. Otherwise . . ."—his glance twitched toward her, then back—"she might find a way to escape, and that must not happen. If she is gone, every one of you in this house will be given thirty lashes with the plumbatae."

The slave turned a shade lighter. Such punishment was a death sentence.

"See that the others know," Justus said quietly, then looked one last time at Olivia. "If you had given me children, this might not have been necessary."

She smiled at him, her eyes fever-bright. "No, Justus, it was you who did not give me children. And you will fail with your fourth wife, as you failed with the others." She stood very straight as she saw that dart strike home.

Justus regarded her with open hatred. "You will pay for that, dear wife. I promise you, you will pay." Then he was gone from the room and Olivia felt the strength that had grown within her begin to fail. She coughed once to keep from sobbing. "You will release me," she said to the slave, and waited until he had obeyed.

"I can't leave you alone, Domita," he said almost apologetically. "The plumbatae . . ."

"Yes," she said with a dryness not unlike Sanct' Germain's. "I want to go into the garden for a while," she told him with a control that startled her. "I must . . . be out-of-doors . . . You may watch from the doors or the windows. I don't care." She had broken away from him, and then, quite to her astonishment, she was running down the corridor toward the back garden, her ruined palla flapping about her, her face contorted with tears. As she ran, there was one ember of hope: tomorrow morning Rogerian would come again, and through him, somehow, there would be Sanct' Germain.

Text of an interim report from Titus Flavius Vespasianus, prefect of the Praetorian Guard, to his younger brother, Titus Flavius Domitianus.

To Titus Flavius Domitianus, brotherly greetings:

Domi, I've reviewed the material you sent on Ragoczy Sanct' Germain Franciscus, and it would be fairly conclusive stuff if there were any way to prove one word of it. The trouble is that these suppositions and rumors are nothing more than that, and not even the most credulous Senator will believe half of the things that are said about him. It may be true that he owns more ships than we know, but as long as they operate within the law and trade honestly, it is no concern of ours. It may be true that he practices sorcery in his private wing of his villa, and if it is true, it is a dangerous thing, but there is no confirmation that he has such skills, or if he has them, that he uses them for evil purposes. It may be that he is unnaturally strong, but it is more likely that he is an experienced and accomplished fighter who does not often lose. It may even be that he drinks blood when lying with a woman. I have heard of stranger things happening in bed. But so long as none of his partners complain, what does it matter if he gives his companion a nip or two? Haven't you ever used your teeth in love play?

Your note suggests that you think I don't want to act against Sanct' Germain. You're right. I like the man, and I don't think any good will come of killing him. You're pushing things that needn't be pushed. If Sanct' Germain has done anything truly criminal (which I must say I doubt) then the Senate can bring full and formal proceedings against him. This rushed condemnation is not what I think of as being admirable in Rome. Neither you nor I rule Rome yet, Domi, and it is well that we both remember that fact. If, when you are Caesar, you want to murder half the city, that will be your affair. What is done by imperial edict is now our father's affair, and if either of us is to wear the purple, it will be because Rome likes him, not because we are any more promising than half the young patricians in the streets.

If you honestly believe that Romans will not pay attention to the treatment of a foreigner like Franciscus, you're deluding yourself, brother. Sanct' Germain, as you yourself have pointed out, has a great many powerful friends, and is himself a very rich man. No Emperor can afford to despise wealth, Domi. You must recall our days in Egypt, when we had very little. It was quite a change from the fun of Claudius' palace. You're too young to remember that, but you know what it is to be poor. Think of the goodwill that a man of Sanct' Germain's wealth can generate for Rome. Is it worth killing him out of spite when he could enrich the country?

If you still feel that you must have this man dead, I will side with you, because there have been fights enough in this family. But it is sad that you had to insist on this man. You told me that Cornelius Justus Silius was the one who alerted you to the duplicity of this foreigner. While I hold Senator Silius in as high esteem as anyone, I think that he might be mistaken about Sanct' Germain. There are those we cannot agree with, and this might be such a case. Think about that before you accept his statements as incontrovertible facts.

May I have your response by tomorrow? I want to spend a few days at the beach, and I'd like to leave in two days. You might want to join us. It will be a very lively group, good music, wine, dancing, privacy when you want it, with whom you want it. We'd be happy to have you along.

By my hand, the eighth day of September, the 824th Year of the City.

Titus.
Prefect, Praetorian Guard

19

WHAT LITTLE LIGHT there was reached the underground cell through the foot of a light well. Those who lived under the stands of the Circus Maximus often used it to dump garbage and other, less attractive things. On this humid afternoon, the stench from the light well was miasmic.

In the center of the little cell there were two pillars placed close together. Between these pillars Sanct' Germain hung from the fetters that bound his wrists. He had been there twelve days.

"Still breathing?" the Master of the Bestiarii mocked from the door. He had made a point of coming each day to jeer at the prisoner. "They're going to kill you, foreigner."

"Go away, Necredes," Sanct' Germain said wearily through bruised and torn lips.

"You can't give orders here, Franciscus: This is my kingdom, and I give the orders. I can order them to whip you again," he said as if this were a delightful new idea instead of the one he had had each day. "Another twenty lashes, Franciscus, what do you say?"

Sanct' Germain was silent. They would bring the flagellum whether he spoke or not. His shoulders were raw from the previous beatings; his black dalmatica was in tatters. He closed his eyes and waited for Necredes to say the rest.

"I told you that this day would come, but you, so fine and foreign, you wouldn't believe me." He relished this moment of vindication. "Now you know that you should not have defied me. Your slave deserved whipping, and you'll take the strokes for her now." He pressed against the bars. "I'm going to count each blow, Franciscus. I want to hear you scream."

"Have you yet?" Sanct' Germain asked ironically. His refusal to cry out was infuriating the Master of the Bestiarii. "If I indulge you, will you whip me less?" He stood straighter and flexed his fingers, feeling lightheaded. He had had no nourishment since he had been seized. The food they brought him he refused. He doubted it was possible for him to starve, but it might be that his hunger—his special hunger—would madden him. Twice before he had been imprisoned for long periods and each time he had become senselessly ravenous. He did not want to remember those times, or repeat them.

"Answer me!" Necredes demanded, and Sanct' Germain realized that he had not been listening.

"Why?" It was a safe response, one that did not admit his attention had wandered.

"Crocodiles don't frighten you, then?" Necredes was incredulous. "These are the big ones; three times your height, nearly four times. Those jaws can go through logs as if they were loaves of bread. Think what they will do to you."

Sanct' Germain did not move. Crocodiles. Water, running water. Vampire limbs did not grow back. Vampires torn in pieces died as true a death as anyone. Water. Sunlight. If they removed his earth-lined boots, he would have no protection, and he was already weak. If his hunger were great enough by then, it might give him a desperation that would serve as strength for a time. After that, he would be at the mercy of the crocodiles and the water and the sun.

There was a sound as the bolt was drawn and Necredes came into the little cell, carrying a metal-tipped flagellum. When he had come up beside Sanct' Germain, he pressed the base of the whip against his face to look at the dried blood on it. "No scars yet," he said, disappointed.

"There won't be any. I've told you." He knew that Necredes did not believe him, yet he said it as he had before. "Get on with it."

Necredes laughed slowly, savoring the moment. He took

three steps back, so that there would be room for a good swing, and brought down the parchment lashes with the full force of his arm.

Sanct' Germain caught his breath as the whip struck, grateful for once for the fetters that held him upright. He did not want to fall before Necredes. The pain went through him like living fire, narrowing his world down to his flesh, where the parchment and metal claws tore at him. With the pain came a terrible fatigue, a lassitude that he knew was dangerous.

"Tomorrow, Franciscus," Necredes promised when he had finished. His face was flushed from effort and there was a slight glazing to his eyes. "That will be the last. The day after, you go on the sands." He took a handful of Sanct' Germain's hair and pulled his head up. "I'm going to watch you die, Franciscus. I'll enjoy it." Still holding the bloodied whip in his hand, he went to the cell door, letting himself out with insulting slowness.

To forget the hurt that raged in his body, Sanct' Germain let his mind wander. His memories spanned very nearly two thousand years, and now, with an aquatic venation two days away, those years did not seem enough to him.

A sliver of sunlight angled its way across the floor, preternaturally bright in these dim surroundings. Sanct' Germain watched it avidly, giving it his whole attention as it marked the passage of the sun. It climbed a section of wall, faded, and was gone. The light well was now a soft amber color, and this once Sanct' Germain did not mind the stench. His arms were almost entirely without sensation and his eyes felt as if they had been burned into his head. When they took him down, the day after tomorrow, he thought he might fall, and he did not want to do that. He stiffened his legs, held himself erect until his thighs shook. It was easier, easier and less painful, to hang in the fetters. Night had begun to close in on the city, lightly shrouding the Seven Hills, lending the Tiber its darkness and stars.

There was a noise near at hand and Sanct' Germain winced as he remembered the huge rats that had scurried through his cell on the previous nights. One of the rats had been attracted by the blood caking his shoulder, and had climbed his trousers and dalmatica to stand on his shoulder, on the raw flesh, and nibble at what he found. He considered his revulsion ironically. It was strange that he, of all men, should be upset by the rat with a taste for blood, but so it was. He steeled himself to endure the rats.

Another sound, sharper and more metallic, brought him out of his thoughts. He tried to turn his head to see what had made it, but the pain in his lacerated shoulders flared as he moved, and he held himself still, waiting for what would be next. He had not been flogged twice in the same day before, but he was not surprised to find that it could happen. Was it Necredes? he asked himself, wishing he knew who had come into the cell on this quiet, oppressive, beautiful night.

"Sanct' Germain?" The hand on his arm was light, long-fingered, kindly.

He dragged his mind away from the despairing fears that had taken hold of it. "Olivia?" he breathed.

She touched his face, her eyes filled with tears. "Oh, Sanct' Germain. What's become of you?"

"Olivia?" he repeated, his exhausted eyes on her, so it seemed she brightened and fluttered, like a torch in the wind. There was the light touch of her mouth on his, her trembling hands on his fettered arms. "How? . . ."

"Rogerian found you," she said quickly. "He asked a few of the children who live under the stands, and an old trainer, who said he knew you and had heard the Master of the Bestiarii talk about you. We've been looking for days." The whispered words stopped. "I have left my father's house. I have left Justus. My mother is dead. She's been dead for some time." Her lips compressed to a tight line.

"I'm sorry," Sanct' Germain said, feeling useless. He wanted to take her in his arms, to draw her close to him so that the pain and the dark would be shut away from him. There was one other thing he wanted of her, wanted so desperately that he dared hardly think of it. He forced his mind away from it.

"He said things . . . They were like the things he did to me . . ." She looked around suddenly as a rat dashed across the earthen floor. "How can you bear it here?" she asked, stifling the hysteria she felt in herself.

"I don't have much choice in the matter," he replied with a degree of sardonic humor.

"But here . . . a dungeon!" She glanced upward once at his wrists.

"A dungeon is a dungeon, whether in Nineveh, or Rome, or Lo Yang. I've been in dungeons in all three places, and there's little difference. Once you are in a cell, it becomes the world, Olivia, and it matters little if those outside are Romans or Parthians or Hyperborean barbarians." He pushed himself far enough forward to be able to brush her face with his lips. "I'm glad you've come. I've thought of you a great deal."

"We wanted to find you sooner," she said. "Sanct' Germain, does it give you much pain?"

He was startled at the intensity in her face. "I've known worse," he answered noncommittally.

"Do they take care of you?" She knew the question was inane.

"As you see." Olivia started to reach for the fetters at his wrists. "Olivia, don't do that," he said quietly.

"But your arms—" she began.

"First," he said harshly, "I would rather remain standing, and this is the only way I can. Second, the fetters are burred on the inside. If you move my hands, the fetters cut me."

She drew back as if the metal were white-hot. "Burred—that's unspeakable!"

"Then let's not mention it again." He did not want to talk about what had happened to him since his imprisonment, so he asked her with genuine curiosity, "How did you get here?"

Olivia met his eyes with difficulty. "One of the gladiators who . . . used me once"—her voice sank to a whisper—"was willing to show me where you were. He'd heard about the prisoner being held in the second-level cell. He took me down the nearest stairs, and pointed the way."

"Was there a price for this?" he inquired gently, searching her face. He wanted to hold her pressed against him, to blot out the dim, fetid cell with passion and need.

She closed her eyes a moment. "No. There was no price."

He sighed, relieved.

"Would it have mattered?" she asked in a small voice. "You know what my life has been. How could one more make any difference to you."

He stared at her incredulously. "It would be different because you had to suffer that on my account. By Charon, Olivia, what else would I mean? Roman virtues are very unimportant to me." He attempted to laugh. "Why should they be otherwise? A woman leaves my embrace exactly as chaste as she came to it, if penetration is your standard for chastity." He looked down at her, feeling an overwhelming sorrow. "Olivia, I will miss you as much as I have missed anything in the world." He regretted his words the moment he said them, for her face went blank with anguish.

"No," she said from the depths of her soul. "You won't die." There was a kind of madness in her eyes.

"It is not what I would wish to do, either," he said, trying again to ease her hurt. "Rogerian is new to me, but he is good-hearted and learns quickly. You will do well to keep him near you. There are precautions you must learn, for later. There is not enough time to tell you all that you must know." How many hazards she would face, he thought, and how much she would have to accomplish in very little time. "Have one of your gardeners fill a couple of chests with your native earth, and be certain that it is always near at hand. You will need it when you travel. You must travel. Once we change, we age very little, and there are many who notice such things. Give yourself ten, at the most, twenty years in a place, and then move elsewhere. You may always return to the first place later. I have a great number of shipping and importing businesses, and it is a good way to make money, and gives you escape should you ever need it. Don't interrupt," he said sharply. "Be careful where you live. You will do better in cities than in villages."

"Don't talk like that!" she said wildly. "If I must know these things, I will ask you then."

"But I may not still be with you," he said. There was a grave tenderness in his dark eyes. "Olivia, this grows difficult. I have no wish to hurt you, but you must hear these things from me, and forget your pain, truly you must. Otherwise I will have failed you more terribly than I failed Kosrozd and Tishtry and Aumtehoutep."

Some of the frenzy left her eyes. "I will listen, Sanct' Germain."

The night breeze had sprung up and wafted the charnel smell of the Gates of Death to them. Olivia hated the sweetly rotten odor, and tried to ignore it, to concentrate on the haunted expression in Sanct' Germain's dark eyes, to listen to his worn, beautiful voice give her instructions.

"When you come into my life," he said some while later, "you will be tempted to set aside your humanity. It is easy to do. I did it, for a time. That's an emptiness that leads nowhere but to the true death. Loneliness is better than abuse; you must know that, my Olivia. It is never easy to resist the seductive lure of cynicism, but cynicism is its own little death. Guard yourself against it. Our kind cannot afford to be uncompassionate. You will find it a formidable task at times, when the ignorant and zealous despise you and those you care for shrink from you. It *will* happen, Olivia. When it does, try not to feel contumely. Intimacy like ours is frightening to those who have never known it. Olivia," he said in another, deeper tone, "I had meant to be with you when you woke, but it may not be possible. If I am not there—"

"Sanct' Germain . . ." she said quickly, wanting to stop what he would say next.

"If I am not there, remember that there is no shame in your desires. And remember that the blood is so much chaff if there is nothing more than blood."

She could not keep her misery out of her voice. "The only lover I want is you." She knew there were tears on her face and smudged them away with grimy fingers.

"You will want others," he said with a wise, sad smile. "It is our nature."

"But now?" She knew his mouth was torn, but she kissed it as deeply as she knew. "Don't you want this?"

"Infinitely," he said wryly. "I have had no . . . nourishment since our last night in your garden." He smiled at her shock. "I want that strength from you, I admit it. But more, I want your love." He swung his arms, grimacing at the pain it gave him. "I can't take you in my arms. I can't caress you. If that is repugnant to you, kiss me again, and then go. I don't think I can stand to have you so near and not hunger for you."

Olivia looked at him, her face possessing a new serenity that she had never had before. "Love me, then." She stepped next to him and loosened her paenula. The long cape fell to the floor and left her dressed only in a light sapparum, as if she were going to enter in a race or other sporting contest. She saw his brows lift quizzically and glowered at him. "I had to get in here unnoticed," she said severely. "I thought I'd dress as if I belonged here."

"Very wise," he agreed. "It becomes you."

Her chin went up, though there were tears in her eyes. "What now?" she asked.

"Come closer, so you can lean against me." His voice had deepened and some of his private grandeur had returned.

"Lean against you?" she whispered. "But your wrists . . . I can't, Sanct' Germain."

"My wrists will not trouble me," he lied. "It's because of them that I'm not likely to fall." He set his jaw and moved his arms in proof of this. He could feel the chafing of his wrists and the hot wetness as the burrs scraped.

She took one more step, and her body touched his. "I want to hold you," she confessed softly. "But your shoulders . . ."

"Put your arms around my waist," he told her, his lips against her hair. She turned her head and their mouths met, this time with fire and reckless abandon. It seemed he had breathed his very soul into her with that kiss, enfolding her in the whole glory of his desire as surely as if he clasped her in his bleeding arms.

Text of an order from the Senate authorizing the seizure and detainment of Atta Olivia Clemens, Domita Silius.

> To the Watch and the Praetorian Guard, greetings:
>
> You are hereby authorized and mandated to find and hold Atta Olivia Clemens, Domita Silius. The woman has left the house of her husband and the house of her father and her present location is not known to us.
>
> There are grave charges laid against this woman, that will be heard in court as soon as she is found and can appear to speak for herself. Of the nature of the charges we are not at liberty to reveal except to inform you that the crimes are capital. For this reason we ask that you treat this woman with great circumspection.
>
> Upon the finding and seizing of this woman, the Senate is to be notified at once, and there will be proper provision for her made at once. If you fail to treat this woman with the honor and respect due to her station

and lineage, you will be punished for such actions to the full limit of the law.

For the Senate, by hand and messenger,

Alastor
Procurator Senior

20

WHILE THE THOUSANDS of Romans jammed into the Circus Maximus paused for an hour, the Master of the Games and many of his slaves were busy putting the last of the tarred beams into place so that the arena could be flooded. The Master of the Games had had a difficult day, what with a disastrous chariot race where three of the four chariots had ended up tangled together, horses screaming, men moaning, while the fourth chariot made all seven circles of the spina. The battle between pygmies and ostriches had gone well, but had not been long enough, which had annoyed the people watching. Three women condemned for murdering their children were staked spread-eagled on the sands and raped by carefully trained leopards. Now there was little more than an hour to get the arena ready for the aquatic venation. He sighed deeply and turned to shout orders at his assistants.

In the imperial box, musicians were playing to the Emperor and his family while they ate a light meal of pork ribs cooked with honey and spices, fruit, and scallops broiled with bacon. Titus and Domitianus sat as far away from each other as they possibly could, saying little.

"You're not being wise, my sons," Vespasianus said as he licked his fingers. "Rome watches you here, and if they see behavior like this, word will have it by tomorrow that there are plots being laid against both of you. Rome does not like civil wars." He poured himself a generous amount of wine diluted with pomegranate juice.

"It's awkward, being here today," Titus said to no one in particular. Sun had browned his body and bleached his hair so that in the softened light under the Circus awning, he seemed to be made of gold, an illusion he chose to enhance by wearing a short sleeveless tunica of brass-colored silk. "Franciscus has been something of a friend to me."

"Clever of him," Domitianus said with an insinuating smile.

"Because he didn't befriend you—" Titus snapped back, turning on his brother.

"Stop it, both of you," Vespasianus interrupted them patiently. "The man is a foreigner and there is reason to believe that he could be a danger to Rome—"

"But most of those allegations are unsupported," Titus protested with a vehemence unusual in him. "If he's guilty, let's find out and settle it quickly, otherwise we're executing him on Domi's whim."

"That's it, isn't it," Domitianus said, flushing slightly. "It's that I want it done, because I think he's dangerous. If our father had decided that Franciscus was a threat to Rome, you would have gone along with it, but when your younger brother is the one to bring the charge . . ."

Titus was glaring now. "No matter what he's done, throwing him to the crocodiles is unnecessary. He's not a slave."

"I wish," the Emperor said plaintively, "that you would find something else to argue about. You're both being fools. Titus, I know that Franciscus did a few favors for you, and I know you don't like it when Domi intrudes into your jurisdiction, but you must admit that the man is suspicious."

"Not suspicious enough to execute this way," he insisted petulantly. He stared around the Circus, then at the musicians, and he gestured to them as if to prove a point. "Who do you think found these for us? That was Sanct' Germain. You can't execute a man with his imperial gifts watching."

Vespasianus chuckled. "It's happened before, my son."

Behind them there was a flurry of activity and a moment later Cornelius Justus Silius stepped into the box. "You sent for me, Caesar?" he said to Vespasianus, nodding to Titus and Domitianus.

"This trouble with your wife is lamentable," Vespasianus said with a raising of his brows.

"She still hasn't been found. I've set a dozen of my slaves to looking for her. I fear . . . I fear that she has done something desperate. I have sent messengers downriver in case they should find her."

"Suicide?" Vespasianus said, mildly surprised. "I didn't think that a member of the Clementine House would behave so. If she wanted to die, she would have done it properly, with witnesses, instead of leaving things so uncertain." He was very definite now. "A noblewoman doesn't throw herself in the Tiber like a common whore. The search must continue. But I warn you, Justus, this must be resolved soon. Lesbia wants a husband this year. It's nothing to me if your wife wants to kill herself rather than be executed by the state, but it must be conclusive." He tapped the marble arm of his chair. "Submit your complaint to the Senate tomorrow and they will grant you a provisional divorce, and authorize the prosecution of your wife when she's found. That I will approve."

Justus made a sour attempt at a smile. Once again he was being forced to submit to new demands. He gave a quick, covert glance at Domitianus. "I have the documents prepared. All I need do is have them delivered to the Curia."

"Do that," Vespasianus said cordially, but there was no attempt to make this other than an order.

"Excellent, excellent," Justus said, trying to make it seem that he was anxious to obey.

"When we find her," Vespasianus went on, his bright, shrewd eyes meeting Justus' light brown ones, "I hope that she is well. It is awkward for a man to have two demented wives. It makes others think poorly of his judgment." The warning was plain, and Justus knew it would be folly to ignore it.

Domitianus came to his rescue. "A woman who has lived the way that Domita Silius has appeared to live must be demented, Father. A woman who lies with slaves and gladiators and refuses her husband, who tries to poison him, what can we think of such a creature, but that she is mad?"

Justus decided to say nothing. He stared at his crossed arms.

"That's for the Senate to consider," Vespasianus said. "Make sure the documents are sent tomorrow." This was clearly his dismissal.

"I'm honored that you concern yourself with my welfare," Justus said slowly.

"That's what you want, isn't it?" Now the shrewd eyes were narrowing, measuring Justus.

"Of course, but as you must know, Caesar, many seek your notice and few achieve it." Then, in another tone, he added, "I know that much of my good fortune comes through your son, who has been most . . . kind to me." The smile he gave Domitianus was as wide as it was insincere.

The need to respond to this cloying sycophancy was eliminated when trumpeters appeared on the spina and raised their instruments to their lips, sounding a fanfare as a way to quiet the enormous crowd and to alert those who had left the stands to return to them.

"Ah." Vespasianus settled himself more comfortably in the chair, punching at one of the cushions he sat on. "The aquatic venation. Those crocodiles were brought from near the second cataract. I've never seen them capture one of the brutes. I wish I had: I'd like to know how they do it."

"I must return to my box," Justus said ungratefully when no invitation to join the Emperor's party had been given.

"Fine, fine," Vespasianus said, watching the Gates of Life, where barges appeared. "I look forward to seeing your complaint."

With ill-concealed irritation, Justus turned and left the imperial box.

"Domi, how you can stand that toad confounds me," Titus said with disgust.

"He's a fine, respectable man," Domitianus shot back, ready to take up cudgels with his brother again.

"The venation is beginning," Vespasianus said, and motioned his musicians to silence.

Trumpets brayed out a second fanfare, then played a fast, rhythmic version of the currently popular song *Don't Be Sad When I'm Gone.*

Titus whistled the tune through his teeth and Domitianus said to the air, "I'm getting sick of that thing."

At last four barges floated onto the flooded arena, each drawn by two small boats with five rowers in each. On two of the barges stood tall, black Numidians with wicker shields and long spears. On the other two were light-haired northerners from Lugdunum Batavorum, with double-pronged fishing tridents and crude brazen breastplates.

"They'll fight first," Necredes said maliciously to Sanct' Germain, who stood with six other men on one end of the spina. "When that's almost over, the crocodiles will be released to clean up the remains, and then you'll go in to clean up the crocodiles while we drain the water off. We'll do that slowly. You'll have almost an hour to battle the crocodiles. Do you think that will be enough?" He shook his head in mock concern over the condition of Sanct' Germain's back and shoulders. "That might be a problem, having your back cut up that way. The blood brings the crocodiles, you know, Franciscus."

"There will be blood enough in the water by then," Sanct' Germain said, squinting down into the arena, feeling slightly sick. The sun was painful as nettles on his skin, the water made him dizzy. He wished fervently and uselessly for his earth-lined boots. He had not willingly stood in the open sunlight unshod for more than a thousand years. His only garment now was a loincloth, his only protection one small knife.

"When those lizards get their teeth in you," Necredes muttered with satisfaction, "you'll shriek like a woman in childbed."

Sanct' Germain did not answer; he stood watching the four barges as they lined up for battle.

At the other end of the spina, the trumpeters fell silent.

There was a quick flurry of activity as the rowers cast off from the barges, and then the first weapon, a Numidian spear, was thrown.

Lacking their boats to pull them, the barges began to drift with the movement of the water. The Numidians hurled spears again, this time in a coordinated effort, and all but two found marks in the blond northmen. This was what the crowd wanted to see, and they shouted encouragement to the barges.

On the second northmen's barge, there was a brief conference going on, and at the end of it three men set down their double-pronged tridents and took up positions on the back of the barge, where they paddled with their arms. Some of the spectators applauded. The Numidians immediately appointed paddlers, and the battle of the barges was joined in earnest.

Sanct' Germain watched with sad detachment. So much skill, he thought, going to amuse bored citizens with ceremony and death. He gazed at the stands, where people sweltered under the great awning. There were men screaming, their faces filled with lust and anger. There were women panting, eyes glittering. He watched lovers fondle each other as the men on the barges bled and died. All the time the sunlight hammered at him, and the water glinted.

There were half a dozen bodies in the water when the signal was given to release the crocodiles. The long, lethal shapes slid out of their cages at the sides of the arena, and the Numidians cried out in horror as they saw the size of the beasts. The northmen, unfamiliar with crocodiles, since they had been brought to Rome only two weeks before, exchanged dismayed looks as the first of the huge reptiles reached a body and opened its jaws.

Almost at once the battle between the barges stopped and a rout to escape the crocodiles began. But there was no place for the men on the barges to go. The water was more than twelve arm-lengths deep, the first row of seats was almost that high above them. The Gates of Life were closed, and even the Gates of Death were barred until the arena was drained of water.

Finally a crocodile rammed one of the barges, upsetting it and throwing the northmen on it into the water, where open jaws waited for them. Almost directly below where he stood on the spina, Sanct' Germain saw two crocodiles seize a Numidian, one holding the black man's foot, the other his upper arm, and, oblivious of his struggles, pull him under the water, where each huge animal turned over in opposite directions, literally twisting the Numidian apart.

"You've got that to look forward to, Franciscus," Necredes said in his ear. "It won't be long now."

Sanct' Germain took one last look at the stands, hoping to see a familiar face, Olivia's face, but among so many, he knew he would never find her, if she were there. He glanced at the other men who were condemned to the crocodiles with him. "Why do we wait?" he asked, and before anyone realized what he was doing, he had walked to the edge of the spina and dived neatly into the water. As he rose to the surface, he pulled his knife from where it had been tucked in his loincloth, then began, very clumsily, to swim toward one of the rafts.

The northmen looked about in confusion as this unknown man climbed onto the barge, but they were too busy fending off the nearest crocodile to challenge this stranger.

Sanct' Germain got to his feet slowly. Having wood under him was not quite so bad as being in water, but he still felt somnambulistic. He bent to pick up two of the pronged tridents that lay abandoned by his feet. Speaking in the language of the Suevi, Sanct' Germain said to the few remaining defenders on the barge, "It does no good to pierce their hide. They feel very little pain, and their hide is thick. You must take them in the mouth, and get the points as far back as you can."

The northmen stared at him. "Are you one of us?" the oldest of them asked in his native tongue. "You don't look like us." He motioned toward the other Suevi on the barge.

A crocodile was nudging the barge as if testing it, little eyes fixed on the men on the barge.

"Never mind," Sanct' Germain rapped out. "Here." He thrust one of the tridents into the oldest man's hands. "When he opens his mouth, press that in as far as you can. Let go at once, or he'll pull you in with him."

The Suevus did not hesitate. He took his stance at the edge of the barge, and as the crocodile approached, jaws gaping, he plunged forward, the trident extended, forcing it deeply into the gullet of the animal. The crocodile made a grunting sound, whipped his body about, and sank back in the water, thrashing in an attempt to dislodge the trident. The northman looked at Sanct' Germain. "It worked," he said.

"The crocodile isn't dead yet," Sanct' Germain pointed out. He was pulling a mangled body over the edge of the barge.

"Get that off!" the oldest man shouted. "It's unholy."

"Would you rather the crocodile bit off your arm? If another comes near, let him attack this instead of you."

Slightly mollified, the Suevus nodded once to the others. "Do as he tells you."

The crocodile beside the barge closed his mouth suddenly, splintering the shaft of the trident that was in his throat. The northmen watched soberly.

"How many of these monsters were let out?" one of the men said softly.

"Ten or twelve," Sanct' Germain told him. "Too many."

The oldest man was awed. "Twelve?"

"They will try to ram this barge, as they did the other. When that happens, we must be ready."

Another of the crocodiles swam nearer and this time the northmen waited until the reptile had come quite close before trying to kill it.

"The mouth and the eyes!" Sanct' Germain called to them all. "The mouth and the eyes! Anything else is useless!" As he shouted he took a broken trident shaft and ground it into the crocodile's eye as it came alongside the barge. The animal croaked in fury and drew off, body twisting in irritation.

"Watch him," Sanct' Germain said, pointing to the half-blinded crocodile. "He's maddened now."

The Suevi accepted this, and waited for the next assault.

One of the Numidians' barges was breaking apart as a huge crocodile battered at it with snout and tail. As the men fell into the water, the crocodiles converged on them, churning the water as they sped to the attack. The horrible sounds of the Numidians was drowned in a cry of delight from the stands as thousands of Romans rose to their feet to have a better view of the carnage.

"Move closer," Sanct' Germain shouted.

"Closer?" the old Suevus repeated, horrified.

"While they're like that, we can kill a few more. Otherwise, they'll start hunting us again." His head ached from the intensity of the sun and he had to fight to keep his concentration. He felt abominably weak, sick, old.

The remaining Numidians saw what the northmen were doing, and joined with them. A seventh crocodile had been killed when the northmen's barge was upset, throwing everyone on it into the water. As Sanct' Germain fell, he dropped the trident he carried, but grimly hung on to his knife.

A long, leathery snout grazed by his arm. Sanct' Germain pushed back from it, resisting the crazed fear that had flickered through him. The crocodile opened its jaws lazily and they closed on the hip of the old Suevus, who shrieked once, then fell silent.

The Numidians' barge passed over his head and Sanct' Germain tried to reach it. As he broke the surface of the water, he saw two crocodiles bearing down on the Numidians, so he swam off a little way, looking about him for pieces of the men who had already been killed by the reptiles. He had part of an arm and a whole leg in his grasp when one of the crocodiles turned on him, putting on a burst of speed as it closed the distance between them. Sanct' Germain barely had time to force the torn leg into the open maw as the crocodile slammed into him. Sanct' Germain slipped under the water, and as the crocodile passed over his head, he raised his knife and plunged it into the belly of the animal, jerking the knife sharply to pull it free. In the next instant the monstrous tail smashed his shoulders, flinging him back through the water. He was nearly blind with weakness and pain, but for the moment he was away from the slaughter. As he paddled to stay afloat, he looked at the spina, wondering whether he could risk swimming to it. The other condemned men stood there no longer, but in the frothing, bloody water there was no way for Sanct' Germain to tell what had become of them. Then he noticed that there was a wide stripe of wetness on the wall above the water. Slowly, very slowly, the Circus Maximus was being drained. He wanted to laugh at the preposterous hope that leaped in him at that sight.

Some of the men had clambered onto the broken bits of the barges that floated on the water, and from there they fended off the crocodiles with the systematic courage of the doomed. There were nine crocodiles dead now—nine crocodiles and thirty-eight men.

Low in the rust-colored water, Sanct' Germain caught a sudden movement. Another crocodile was stalking him. He moved farther away from the ruined barges, seeking more distance between himself and the reptile. The crocodile came after him. A patch of shade from the awning high overhead lay across the water, a little wing of shadow. Desperately Sanct' Germain swam toward it, his arms aching, the welts on his shoulders becoming more unbearable with each movement. That shade, he thought, was his one hope, for there at least he would be out of the direct sunlight and could husband what little strength remained to him.

A ripple against his neck warned him an instant before the crocodile struck. He sheered off through the water, coming at last into the shadow by the wall. He knew enough not to expect a sudden return of energy, and the minor respite the shade gave him was so small that he very nearly lost heart. The crocodile had turned and was coming in again, drifting lazily, jaws still shut. Watching the huge reptile, Sanct' Germain remembered days centuries before when he had watched the priests feed the crocodiles at the Temple of the Second Cataract, singing the praises of their charges, some which grew to twice the length of those now in the arena. The priests of the temple would occasionally lure a crocodile onto the land, and prove their power over the animal by holding his terrible jaws closed. One of the priests had told Sanct' Germain that it was much simpler to hold the jaws closed than to hold them open, and that the real might of the animal was in the bite. Sanct' Germain began to unwind his loincloth. As he did, he revealed massive, age-whitened scars, running deep across his abdomen.

The crocodile was somewhat startled when, as it neared

Sanct' Germain, he sank under the water, trailing something strange behind him. The crocodile, curious, nosed the end of the cloth.

It was the moment Sanct' Germain had hoped for. He rose at once, wrapping the cloth around the crocodile's snout three, then four times. The knot was awkward but it held as the crocodile began to writhe.

With the last of his strength, Sanct' Germain took hold of the cloth knotted around the crocodile's jaws and pulled the head back while the reptile floundered, his tail churning the water in a vain attempt to break Sanct' Germain's hold.

The water had dropped even more. The crowd was starting to cheer for the few survivors of the barges who were being dragged out of the arena by the same boats that had pulled the barges onto the water.

Dizziness threatened to overcome Sanct' Germain and he strove to master it: if he faltered for an instant now, the crocodile would turn on him. He could not survive another attack, he knew, and as the water level dropped, he focused his whole attention on that knotted cloth.

The crocodile gave a jolt as its back feet touched the sand. Then it tried to scrabble away from the man holding it captive, but Sanct' Germain pulled at the cloth, bending the head even farther. With a last shattering effort, Sanct' Germain forced the huge head back. The crocodile gave one tremendous convulsion, then twitched and lay limp in the water.

Sanct' Germain let his legs sink and was surprised to find that the water was now little more than waist-deep. He took his knife and placed it low on the side of the crocodile's neck, slamming it into the beast with such force that he staggered and would have fallen had not one of the boats nudged up behind him then. Ghastly pale, hideously weak, Sanct' Germain nevertheless motioned the boat away. The imperial box was a little farther down the wall, and Sanct' Germain began to slog his way toward it.

The sudden gasp of the crowd brought his head around a moment too late. Four razor teeth gouged his side and he fell back, nearly unconscious. The crocodile was turning, getting ready for the final rush, when another one of the boats came gliding down the now-shallow water, iron spikes held at the ready. Before the crocodile could charge again, one of the sharp spikes was driven home through its back. It jerked violently, upsetting the boat, drifted away and died.

Blood ran through his fingers pressed against his side as Sanct' Germain took uncertain steps toward the imperial box. In a small part of his mind, he mocked himself for this gesture, but it had become a point of honor for him. The water was no higher than his calves as he stopped under the imperial box, taking his hand away from the wounds in his side as he raised his arm in a Roman salute. "Hail, Caesar," he croaked up at Vespasianus. "Though I did not die."

Vespasianus leaned forward. "The odds were against you, however." His bright eyes were amused. "A fine gesture, Franciscus."

"Do I appeal to you or the Vestal Virgins?" Sanct' Germain asked weakly.

"To me. I think you must have paid for anything you might have done. By the look of those scars, you've paid a greater price before. It would be convenient for me, however, if you would leave Rome for a time after this. You might require an extended recuperation." He patted his older son on the shoulder. "Titus has a pleasant estate in Egypt you might enjoy."

"I might join you there," Titus said quickly with a too-wide smile that was directed more at Domitianus than at Sanct' Germain.

"Thank you. I can fend for myself." Sanct' Germain never knew exactly when he sank to his knees. He was aware that the Emperor was speaking to him and that the crowd was cheering. The world spun in his head and his eyes felt hot and cloudy. Someone who might have been the Master of the Games had waded out to him and stood beside him to place a wreath on his dripping, blood-matted hair. All at once it was deliciously funny to be standing before the Emperor and more than eighty thousand Romans, naked, with only a laurel wreath on his brow. Laughter threatened to overcome him.

The Master of the Games had given a signal and a moment later a red caracalla was thrown over Sanct' Germain's shoulders. He was pleased that it did not hurt. There was just enough sense left to him to be alarmed. The world wobbled around him.

"Get my boots," he muttered before he fainted.

Excerpts from the complaint of Cornelius Justus Silius against his wife, Atta Olivia Clemens.

> . . . Though no man wishes to think ill of his wife, I have had to learn to distrust this woman and regard her as a subtle enemy. You have already seen the report from the physician, revealing that I have three times been poisoned. Those occasions always followed evenings spent in the company of my wife. It could be that I have an unknown enemy who has ingratiated himself with my wife, or it might be that she is being used without her knowledge, and that it is her cook who has been dragged into a plot. I realize that this possibility is somewhat remote, but I would prefer to believe that than to believe that Atta Olivia Clemens could have been so unhappy or ambitious that she felt she must be rid of me entirely rather than divorce me. I will not believe that such a noble and refined woman could be so perverse.
>
> There is testimony with these documents that shows that my wife had a desire to take her sexual pleasures with gladiators and other rough men, that she was most pleased when the act was accomplished violently. I understand that such was her conduct from the time of our marriage, but, as you can see by these papers enclosed, I did not know of it until we had been married for more than five years. It is often true that older men are not adequate lovers for their young wives, and this may have been the case with my wife, for her wants did often exceed my abilities, and if she has erred, it may be that her passions were greater than even I knew and that because she was a woman of honor and good family, she could not dishonor me with my associates and sought those who were removed from me. It would make me

happy to think that this is the case. No man, I suppose, likes to think of his wife in the lascivious embraces of another, and Roman wives have made a virtue of chastity that is of great credit to them. Is it to be held against me that I chose to think that my wife behaved as Roman women of her station were trained to behave? Certainly I thought that if she took a lover, it would be one worthy of her, not some ignorant barbarian who would treat her cruelly because that was what she most desired.

A few of you have been unkind enough to mention the execution of her father and brothers, and it is true that her family was dishonored, but that was in the reign of Nero, when it was not quite so reprehensible to oppose the purple as it is now. Atta Olivia Clemens was greatly distressed at the death and condemnation of her male relatives, as were a great many other patricians who shared my shock at their treason. But to suggest that she is somehow tainted by her family, and that she must therefore be incapable of good conduct, is more for the theatre than for our lives here. There is nothing in that woman that would reveal her to be of a traitorous nature. Let those who died be enough.

. . . The testimony of my former library slave, Monostades, tells what he learned of the clandestine meetings of my wife with the foreigner Ragoczy Sanct' Germain Franciscus. Their meetings took place after she went to the house of her father to live, and from what Monostades learned, they did not meet often. My slaves there, who had much of my interests at heart, did mention that her conduct there was strange, but I did not then suspect that there was any reason more than our separation. Also, the testimony of the Armenian scholar Led Arashnur, written in Greek, enclosed, tells of his seeing them together, but not often. Those who have said that my wife had anything to do with the Armenian's still-unsolved murder are being spiteful, I am sure, for there is no indication that she knew he had been following her lover. If you insist on pursuing her unlikely complicity in Arashnur's death, I will most certainly object to such an investigation.

. . . Much of what is included in this collection of documents would demand the death penalty for my wife. I would not like to have that happen, but I will not stand in the way of the laws of Rome, for the law is the strength of the empire. Rather, let me request that if it is found that my wife has committed those crimes which will require the ultimate penalty, that there will be some dignity left to her, and that she will not be humiliated by a public execution, where the most disgusting inhabitants of the city may watch her suffering. Let any punishment be private and respectful. As I am the man she has most wronged, let me have some say in her death, if that is what you will demand of her. . . .

It is true that her flight puts all she may have done in the most negative aspect, but there could have been extenuating circumstances. She may have felt a deep remorse and decided to leave rather than face what she feared must be the end of her. I beseech you good men of the Senate not to be too severe in your judgment of her. There was so much confusion in her then, that her actions ought not to be thought of as a tacit admission of guilt. Though it is true it would be difficult for you not to believe the worst of her, make allowances for her troubles.

Apparently she has told a few people that it was I who abused her and I who ruined her family. Since she so obviously hates me, I can understand why she might come to think this of me. When you hear her testimony, I hope you will not forget that she does not say this out of an innate tendency to lie but because she has come to believe this about me most sincerely. You will have to show your compassion for her. She has suffered a great deal through her family's dishonor and her own appetites, and this has preyed much upon her mind. Like chastity, charity is a Roman virtue, and I feel I must importune you to keep that in mind when you question my wife. . . .

The documents are clear in their intent, but remember that the documents are not the whole of the case, and withhold your judgment until you have heard her speak in her own behalf. There may be extenuations of which you and I know nothing.

. . . Remember that Atta Olivia Clemens thinks she is unfortunate. What woman, believing that, would be satisfied with her life, no matter how fine, how luxurious?

In that, she is like her father, for he was not pleased with the sad deterioration of his fortunes. That is an unfortunate comparison. Be assured that she is not very much like her father despite this similarity. Children almost always retain some quality of their parents.

In honesty I must say that our marriage was not happy and that my wife feels, perhaps with some justification, that much of it was my fault.

. . . In order to avoid further hostilities between us, I trust that you good Senators will decide this matter quickly, and whatever decision you make regarding my wife's punishment will be carried out swiftly and mercifully. Let this whole disgraceful and sordid case be concluded as rapidly as the law allows. Why prolong my wife's suffering? Why subject her to greater indignities than she has experienced already?

I most respectfully urge you to listen to what she tells you with patience and indulgence. Do not condemn her out of hand. When she rails at you, remember that it is her disappointment speaking, not a lack of appreciation of any of you. If she accuses me, let her say what is in her heart. She has had much to distress her, and she can do me no worse harm than she has already.

Cornelius Justus Silius

21

SANCT' GERMAIN had left Villa Ragoczy flanked by soldiers and now he returned there with an escort of forty Praetorians. All along the road to his villa, slaves were waiting for their master's return.

The laurel wreath was still on his hair, but the short, loose curls were now clean and shining. The caracalla that had been draped around his shoulders in the Circus Maximus was there now, but under it he wore a knee-length tunica of rare brocaded black silk. His red Scythian boots were on his feet. Pale, haggard, with a weary and ironic smile creasing his face, Sanct' Germain turned to the men accompanying him. "Thank you, tribune. I'm quite . . . honored."

The tribune was properly stiff, standing at rigid attention as he reached the colonnade of Villa Ragoczy. "Very kind, sir," he barked, and ordered his troops to salute as Sanct' Germain walked toward his garden.

A door in the northern wing opened and Rogerian stepped out. "I'm glad you're back," he said in an unperturbed way.

Sanct' Germain nodded his approval. "I'm not alone, as you see. Is there anything ready that they can eat?"

Rogerian blinked in confusion. "I don't know. We were so worried, I don't think the cooks have fixed meals today or yesterday. But I'm certain," he said, making a smooth recovery, "that given the greater part of an hour, there can be quite a satisfactory meal."

"The greater part of an hour?" Sanct' Germain inquired, one brow elevating. He knew well the consternation such orders caused in the kitchen. "If you can persuade the cooks to do that, you will have my everlasting gratitude." He had come up the three shallow steps, back onto his property, in the building that was constructed over a foundation laid with his native earth. Some of the fatigue that had possessed him began to vanish.

"The arena . . ." Rogerian began uneasily. "Yesterday when you fought, we were deeply concerned."

"So was I," Sanct' Germain said as lightly as he could; then he swung around to the forty Praetorians. "You're welcome, Praetorians. There will be a meal for you spread shortly. In the meantime, you might like the chance of examining my stables and the various pens and cages here. I am certain Raides will be pleased to escort you." He beckoned to Rogerian and said to him quietly, "Go to the stables and tell Raides that I'm sending these soldiers out to him. He's to answer any questions they have, of course, and if they want to try out any of the horses, unless they're one of my personal mounts, let them."

Rogerian nodded and hurried away through the garden as Sanct' Germain bowed the Praetorians toward the south wing of Villa Ragoczy. He took them not to the silver-and-blue reception room but to the largest dining room in the wing. "Good tribune," he said to their leader, "I'm going to the kitchen to issue orders for wine to be brought. In the time I've been gone, it seems that there has been a shocking lapse on the part of my staff."

"Slaves are like that," the tribune agreed sagely, not hearing the sarcasm in Sanct' Germain's voice.

In the kitchen Sanct' Germain issued a number of orders to the cooks. "And if there is any suckling pig, fill it with onions and raisins. That's nine dishes. What else can you do in an hour?"

The chief cook patted his girth at its widest part. "May I suggest geese on a spit? That will make ten dishes, and with fruits and breads, that should be enough, even for soldiers. If it's good enough for charioteers, it's good enough for soldiers," the chief cook maintained, then saw the unhappiness in his master's face. He rushed on, "These are Praetorians, though, and it probably wouldn't hurt to make them something fancy as well. While they are eating the main part of the meal, I will think of a special sweet for the end of the feast."

"I thank you," Sanct' Germain said to the cook, knowing that the man had misunderstood his expression. But there was no way he could tell the large, good-natured man that his words had reminded him of Kosrozd, and Tishtry, his charioteers for whom he still mourned, and Aumtehoutep, who had been with him for the greater part of a millennium. He forced cheer into his face. "It's unforgivable of me to give you such a task with so little notice, and it would be no more than I deserve if you refused to do more than bake a currant pudding for them. I'm most grateful."

The cook beamed over all of his wide face. "My master, excellency, it is my pleasure to do this for you." He was much too proud of himself to remind Sanct' Germain that he had never tasted his food.

Assured that the Praetorians would eat well, Sanct' Germain crossed the garden and entered his private wing. The peace and strength of the place took hold of him at once and he let his exhaustion claim him. He reached his bed, his narrow, hard bed that lay over an open chest filled with his native earth. Without bothering to undress, he pulled the red soldier's cape more tightly around him, lay back, and slept.

Night was far advanced when he woke again. His side ached with a dull persistence under the bandages the arena physician had wrapped around him after he had been carried to him. He moved, testing his weakness, bending gingerly, rising slowly. It was reassuring that his weariness was not greater than it had been. His native earth had restored him somewhat, and his face, had there been a mirror that would reflect him, had lost the deeply cut lines of utter fatigue that had marked him earlier.

In his study there were three lamps burning, and Sanct' Germain went toward their gentle light.

Rogerian was seated in one of the padded chairs, a stack of vellum sheets on a little table beside him. At the sharp sound of Sanct' Germain's heeled boots, he looked up. "Good evening, my master."

"Surely it's later than evening," Sanct' Germain said as he came across the floor. "What are you reading?"

He patted the closely written pages of vellum. "I am reading about Roman law."

"As pertains to bond-holders?" Sanct' Germain inquired politely.

"As pertains to divorce and adulterous wives." His cool eyes met Sanct' Germain's. "The complaint was filed against Atta Olivia Clemens yesterday. Her husband delivered all his 'evidence' to the Senate. It's alleged that she tried to poison him."

"That's ridiculous," Sanct' Germain said, very annoyed. "Does Silius honestly think that the Senate will listen to him?"

"He has a physician's report as part of his evidence. It says that he had been eating poison." Rogerian said this gravely.

"He did not get it from Olivia." He folded his arms over his chest and the gouges in his side radiated pain through him for this. Sanct' Germain's face paled but he did not flinch.

"No. That is not what the Senate believes, however." Rogerian put one of the sheets aside. "It will be most difficult for her to convince them that Justus is lying."

"For her to convince them, they must first find her." He knew she had been missing the day before, from the gossip he had overheard from the Master of the Games.

"They did find her. Yesterday." He watched Sanct' Germain closely.

"But they couldn't have found her," Sanct' Germain protested. "Her hiding place was completely secure."

"She let herself be found."

Sanct' Germain's eyes went flinty and he fixed them on Rogerian. "What do you mean? Why didn't you stop her?"

"Stop Atta Olivia Clemens, when she is determined on a course of action?" Rogerian asked incredulously. "I pointed out that you had survived and that it would be very little time before you could leave Rome in peace. She said she refused to go with such charges hanging over her that might catch up with her at any time. She said she wanted it over with. They will hear her case in three days and pass sentence in two more. The Emperor favors a quick decision."

"Where did they take her, do you know?" Sanct' Germain demanded. "There must be a way we can get her out before she appears at the Senate?"

"She wouldn't go. She told me you would want to spirit her away, and that she would refuse to go with you until this is settled." Rogerian sighed. "I told her that her husband would want to see her condemned for attempted murder, but she was convinced that if she appeared before the Senate and told them all that her husband had done to her—how he betrayed her father and brothers, how he had abused her over the years—then she could have some vengeance for all she has endured." His voice had dropped and he looked at one of his long hands. "She said very little about what was done to her, but it was enough to let me understand why she might want to be revenged."

"It won't work," Sanct' Germain said with certainty. "It can't work. Justus is not a stupid man. He won't allow Olivia to best him in this. He wants to marry into the Flavian House, so Titus told me, and that means he knows without doubt that Olivia will be condemned." He stared at the wall where a rare picture of a golden Buddha hung, though he did not see the picture at all. "Vespasianus wants a quick decision? That means he's encouraging Justus' pretensions. The Senate will do as the Emperor wishes."

"How can you be sure?" Rogerian asked, not just to calm his master. "The Senate is not the toy of the Emperor."

"Or so they say," Sanct' Germain agreed. "It is mere coincidence that their decisions are always those that Vespasianus requires." His lips set into a grim line and he paced the length of the room. "I won't let them execute her. I won't lose her, Rogerian."

"But what can you do?" Rogerian asked after a moment. "If she is determined, and if, as you say, her husband will work to have her condemned . . ." He turned over the vellum sheet he held. "There can be an execution."

Sanct' Germain rubbed his face with his hands, wishing that he were more rested. "What nature of execution?"

Rogerian consulted the sheets, and after paging through them, found what he sought. "Here. The wife can sue for the right to die by her own hand, in which case witnesses are required. She may be beheaded for infanticide, at the discretion of the Senate. She may be entombed alive. She may be flogged to death if she succeeds in killing her husband. There are other options, but those are the main ones."

"Beheading is out of the question," Sanct' Germain said darkly, fearing again that Olivia might die the true death and not change to his life. "Flogging is possible, but there are risks, if one of those heavy whips damages the spine. If she dies by her own hand, witnesses or not, we might find a way to help her. Entombing is frightening. She would not die—she would live, growing weaker, alone in that terrible dark." He stopped. It would be like Justus, he thought, to give her more torment, though he could not know how much. Sanct' Germain shuddered. His Olivia, entombed in a wall or a foundation or the arch of a bridge. He had heard of criminals being immured in all those places, and others less appealing. What would happen to Olivia when she woke to his life in a place she could not leave? The images flickered through his mind, each more dire than the one before: Olivia in the dark, her hands torn and bloodied as she exhausted herself attempting to find a loose stone to pry away; Olivia shuddering in the corner of the tomb, plucking at her hair, singing wisps of song; Olivia licking her lacerated fingers; Olivia, shrunken, mad, husbanding her strength to be able to dash her head against the stones of the tomb and crack open her skull, ending her misery.

"My master . . ." Rogerian said tentatively, and Sanct' Germain saw his own appalled expression reflected in Rogerian's eyes.

"Forgive me," he said as he dragged a chair across the marble-inlaid floor. "I'm not quite myself yet. I think we must see if there is a way we can speak to Olivia. If there is not . . ."

Rogerian put the sheets neatly back on the pile at his elbow. "I understand that her husband has forbidden her to have any visitors until she appears before the Senate. He's afraid that someone will come to harm her." Rogerian added the last in a contemptuous tone. "He intends to be certain that she is dealt with as he wishes. Domitianus has arranged for her guards." He hesitated, looking for a tactful way to say the next.

"You can't offend me. What were you going to say?" Sanct' Germain broke into his thoughts.

"As you wish," Rogerian said, unperturbed. "You are named in the complaint as her lover. Any attempt you make to see her will only make her appear as her husband describes her. If you inquire too closely, you will confirm the suspicions about her."

Sanct' Germain's teeth were tightly set. "I see," he mused, twisting in his chair. "He's always been crafty, but I didn't think . . ." Inwardly he chided himself. No, he did not think. He had acted too impetuously, and now Olivia would have to pay for it. Resolutely he turned his mind away from his fears. "Rogerian, how much can you learn from the slaves of Senators?"

"It would depend, of course, on the slaves," he said after a moment of deliberation. "There are some slaves who are very reliable, and who like to pass on bits of information. But they know I am your bondsman, and might not speak of this case. There are other slaves, however, who do not know me and might tell me a bit if I bought them a cup of wine. I would have to be careful."

"I respect your judgment enough. Do as you think wisest," Sanct' Germain said.

"I've made myself a disguise. I wore it to see Olivia. I might be able to get near her in it." He sounded tentative. "I made myself a hump for my back and little bits of leather for my face, like warts, and then I took fruit to sell and cried my wares outside her door. Eventually she came and spoke to me. I might be able to do that again. Her guards saw me, the slaves that her husband put at the house. They would recognize me and I could say that I wanted to do the unfortunate lady a kindness, because she gave me so much money for my fruit." He had been building on the ideas as they occurred to him, but at the end of this, he was prepared to believe it might be possible. He looked at his master and saw admiration in Sanct' Germain's eyes.

"My compliments," Sanct' Germain said with quiet sincerity. "It's enough. We have time to refine the plan, but if we can find out what they intend to do with her and where and when they will do it, we might be able to reach her, so it will be no worse for her than it must." His face hardened.

"Vespasianus wants me to leave Rome. If I had more time, I would make Justus howl for each minute of unhappiness and cruelty he gave her."

"In time, perhaps—" Rogerian began.

"Oh, come, Rogerian," Sanct' Germain cut him off. "When you have lived as long as I, you will have seen that wish fail too often. Men like Justus survive and profit, leaving the wreckage of others' lives behind them. They are called wise by the envious and worthy by the ambitious. Justus is ruthless, and determined to be part of the Flavian House. He longs for the purple, and if he does not achieve it, it won't be because he neglected opportunity. There were men like him in Egypt, and they brought the country to ruin. There were men like that in Athens, and Damascus, and Eridu." He rose slowly and stared down at Rogerian. "It's likely to be hazardous."

"It was hazardous to take me away from the Flavian Circus, but you did." He gave Sanct' Germain a steady look.

Sanct' Germain capitulated. "We'll try it, then." He started across the room. "We must be prepared to leave as soon as we have her safe. We'll need chariots, chests with the proper earth in them, clothing, money . . ." He ran his fingers through his hair. "There will have to be arrangements made for changes of horses between here and whatever port we decide upon. Check my records and find out where we can leave quickly on one of my boats." For the first time since he had wakened, he smiled. "I'm afraid that sailing is a wretched way for those of my blood to travel, but if it can be arranged, Olivia and I will spend most of our time sleeping."

"I'll see to it," Rogerian said with a great deal of reserve.

"You'll also need to find someone to take over your duties here. I don't know whom to ask." His side was beginning to hurt again and he touched the bandages through his tunica.

"You want me to come with you?" Rogerian asked as if afraid of the answer.

"Well, of course," Sanct' Germain answered, surprised. "You will find that I am a man of rather set habits, and I don't like having to find a new body servant every few years. You said that you would consider staying with me. I thought—or rather, I hoped—that it was settled." He did not let his apprehension sound in his voice.

Rogerian had got to his feet. "I will see that arrangements

are made for three," he said with dignity as he began to put the protective cover around the vellum sheets.

Text of a letter from the Christian slave Jaddeus to a fellow Christian, the freedman clerk Lysander.

To my brother in Christ, Lysander, Jaddeus sends greetings:

I pray that this reaches you safely, for the matter which I am to disclose to you is of very grave importance, and I rely upon you to act in such a way that earthly justice is done, for though my hopes are all for heaven, there are still remedies of this world, and what I have learned, since it does not affect those who are called to Jesus, cries out for the stern tribunals of Rome.

There is a new slave here, not a Jew or Christian, who arrived in chains very late one night. The man was not well, and had been treated most brutally by those who had held him. He had had his right hand smashed, his testicles docked and his tongue cut out. I am ashamed to say that I, along with most of the others here, at first shunned this unfortunate man. But he heard me reading from our texts one night, in Greek, and he approached me, this pitiful creature, and gave me to understand, by signs, that there was something he wanted to import to me. I thought he might be Greek (and so he has turned out to be, though I understand now that he came to me because I am literate), and I spoke to him in that language, at which he made gobbling sounds and dragged his finger in the dirt. May Our Lord forgive me, but I wanted to send the wretch away. But he pulled my arm so that I was near the floor, and to my amazement, there were crudely drawn Greek letters there.

The slave is named Monostades and he was owned by

the Senator Cornelius Justus Silius. The reason that this slave was mutilated and sent to labor among us after his mutilation, he says, is because he helped his master create a fraudulent case against his wife, wherein it was made to seem his master was dying of poison that the wife gave him, which, in fact, he took himself after he had been with her, so it would appear that he was taking harm from her rather than inflicting it upon himself. He has also said that this poor woman was abused by her husband, who insisted she take the most degraded men to her bed so that he could watch her being ravished. He also believes that it was his master who betrayed his wife's father and brothers to the government when Nero was Caesar.

All this is very distressing to learn, and this Monostades has begged me to write down what he scribbles in the earth and see if there is a way for the information to reach the authorities.

I realize that we have had little contact, but surely our love of the Lord is such that our interests must march together in this matter. I have copied out all he has said on the back of the teachings of our faith. You, being a clerk, have access to the Senate. It would be possible for you to lay this letter and the transcription before someone in power, would it not? Please, in the name of the Mercy of Christ, do this thing, for the peace of this man Monostades' soul. He is ill now, and may soon die. Before he leaves this dreadful world, he desires above all things to show how his master used his wife. He has said also, in moments of despair, that he wants to bring his master down to lower than he has been brought, but this is the petulance of an instant, and he has begun to listen to what I tell him. He is pleased to know that at Judgment Day we will all stand equal in the Sight of God and all that we have done and all that we have not done will be revealed and each of us will stand answerable for our lives.

Monostades has sworn by the Living God and the gods of Rome that what he has said is true and accurate, that at no time has he said one thing which is exaggerated or untrue. He further says he will declare the same truth in any place required.

Do reflect on the plight of this unfortunate man, Lysander, and help him to make restitution for the great wrong he has done this blameless lady, and aid him in his attempt to reveal to the world the great evil her husband has inflicted on her and other helpless souls. For as long as men like this woman's husband have power and honor on the earth, the Kingdom of Christ is far off for all of us. This is surely the work that Our Lord bade us do, or nothing is.

Labor goes on here, as anyone can see if they choose to look, but in spite of the rumors that are circulating in Rome, I tell you the Flavian Circus will not be ready this year, or the next, or the year after that. The structure is enormous now, and will be much larger before it is done. The building of it would wear out all beasts of burden but man in the course of a summer.

We must pray for the Christian who followed the misled teachings of Paul, for he has gone from the earth. A pillar of marble was upset and it fell on him. He suffered greatly, but with fortitude. I knelt and prayed with him, keeping with him until his soul returned to God and Christ. His austerity was sad to behold, but he was strong in his faith and never wavered. He worshiped with the brotherhood that meets at the Fisherman's Cove Inn on the north side of the city. It would be charitable to let them know of the man's death so that they can pray for the joy of his soul.

I rely on you to put the enclosed testimony before the Senate, and I thank you and Christ that it was given to me to help bring a terrible wrong to an end. I pray for you all, and long for the day that Christ calls me, and my earthly travail will end. There is no sweeter promise than that of resurrection and eternal life. Think of the love that Christ had, that bestows everlasting life on those who accept Him, think of His Holy Blood that saves us, think how he bade us love one another as He loves us.

In the Name of the Risen Christ, my blessing for all that you will do for Monostades, who will praise you on that Day which will come upon us before any of us are aware of it.

By the Fish, the Cross and the Dove,
Jaddeus

22

BETWEEN THE Tiber and the Via Appia was a long row of tombs, stretching from the city walls to a wide bend in the river, some two thousand paces farther south. There were large mausoleums looking like small temples; there were low tombs like stone cushions; there were tombs with crenellated towers and battlements as if the dead expected to have to defend themselves against the living; there were tombs in the shape of pyramids, and boxes, and beehives, and cylinders.

The moon was bright, four days short of full, and it lit the high curdled clouds with a soft light that made them glow. It was a beautiful and silent night, as no Roman liked to be among the tombs after sunset, for fear of the ghosts that lingered around their earthly remains.

Mounted on his blue roan, Sanct' Germain came along the Via Appia, his dark eyes piercing the night with intensity. Among these thousands of tombs, there was one he sought, the one where Olivia waited for him.

Three days before, on orders of the Senate, she had been entombed alive, and a guard of two soldiers set to watch her. At sunset the guards had at last been dismissed from their duty. Now there was no one to hamper Sanct' Germain's work, and he felt profoundly relieved, for after three days Olivia would be very frightened, for three days walled into a tomb, as he had learned, was a prolonged and unique torture.

There were three tombs for the Silius family, two of which were large and handsome, containing urns of the most distinguished ashes of their family. Eighteen generations were represented on the plaques and inscriptions, from a minor tribune in the Republic to the high-ranking members of the staff of Divus Julius, to the Gaius Silius who had been foolish enough to love Claudius' wife, Messalina.

Somewhat behind the first two was a third mausoleum, this one little more than a large stone box, with the name of Silius appearing over the entrance, an entrance that was now bricked up. This was where the disgraced Silii were sent to lie after death, where they could be forgotten by the more illustrious members of the family. Four days ago there had been an iron door to the tomb. The closely laid bricks were new. No laudatory verses were pasted to the wall of the tomb, no flowers or fruit lay on the threshold of the bricked-up door.

Sanct' Germain dismounted and led his blue roan behind the elaborate tomb of the Marco family, tethering the horse and taking a long iron pry-bar from the lashings that held it to the saddle before pulling the saddle off the roan and concealing it. He had wanted to bring an iron mallet, also, but he had not wanted to carry too many articles with him that might arouse suspicion in an officer of the Watch. With a pry-bar he could claim he was going to lever a chariot out of a ditch, but with a mallet as well, other possibilities arose.

The grass was high around the tomb except where the guards had trampled it. There was a cold, neglected air about it, and the little stone building seemed aware of this disapprobation, for it kept to the shadows behind the grander, more acceptable tombs. Sanct' Germain approached it, touching the bricks with his outstretched hand, fingering the mortar in the hope it might be damp enough to make his job easier. Roman workmen mixed their mortar with whole crushed eggs and the stuff that resulted was the most tenacious mortar Sanct' Germain had ever encountered. He wanted to call out to Olivia, but knew that she could not hear him, and that his voice might bring soldiers to investigate. Not far from him, the bulk of the slaves' prison rose up, and Sanct' Germain could see the occasional smudges of brightness that revealed that the guards there were still awake.

He reached under his woolen dalmatica and found the bandages around his side. He untied and unwound these, fingering the deep grooves that remained along his ribs. The grooves would be there forever, he knew. There would be grooves, but no scar.

The bandage was made of close-woven linen, a strong, rather thick cloth that could take rough treatment. Sanct' Germain bent down to grab handfuls of dry grass, which he tied to the end of his pry-bar with the linen. This would muffle the sound of his work. He tapped the bricks with the bound end of the bar and was rewarded with a sound less noisy than horses' hooves on sand. Somewhat reassured, he began to test the bricks, going systematically from the top of the doorway to the bottom, pressing each one to see if it was loose. None of them were. The tomb was sealed tight.

Though Sanct' Germain was not surprised, he had been hoping that he might find such a brick, so that his task would be quicker and easier.

Rogerian was waiting even now at an inn seven thousand paces to the south. A traveling chariot was waiting, four strong matched horses to pull it, their route set from Rome to Terracina, where one of Sanct' Germain's merchant ships, the *Capricorn,* was waiting, bound for Crete, Ephesus and Byzantium.

He chose one of the bricks and began to work on it, tapping and scraping with the unmuffled end of the pry-bar, tapping and scraping, working patiently and persistently, resolutely determined not to notice the too-rapid passage of the moon through the night sky.

The clouds were growing denser, blotting out the moonlight. It was early for rain, but perhaps, though Sanct' Germain as he paused in his work, the autumn would come early to Rome this year. He leaned on the pry-bar, inspecting the linen and straw to be sure the metal had not yet poked through.

A little while later, Sanct' Germain heard the sound of approaching horses, and he dropped back into the shadows by the tomb, keeping very still, his eyes alert in the darkness.

The hoofbeats drew nearer, and then three riders swung into view, one of them carrying a lantern that caught the molten colors of the capes and loricae worn by the soldiers. One of them carried a short brass baton with a Roman eagle mounted on it, a sign that designated them imperial messengers.

They had almost gone past the Silius tombs when Sanct' Germain's blue roan whinnied.

The soldiers faltered, one of them drawing up sharply.

"Don't bother about that. It's probably lovers. They like their privacy," called the one with the lantern.

"It might be someone wishing to intercept this message. Those are the Silii tombs there," the one who had reined in objected.

"You don't think that any man would wait near his wife's tomb at night, do you?" scoffed the third. "If he was going to stop us, he wouldn't let his horse give us warning."

The first officer had ridden his mount closer to where Sanct' Germain was hidden in the shadows. "If you're going to attack us," he called out, "do it now!"

Sanct' Germain was still.

"Brutus, I've been in the saddle for most of today. I'm tired, I'm sore and I haven't had a decent meal since sunup. Come on," protested the one with the lantern.

Brutus rode between the two big tombs and squinted at the third one. "Looks all right," he said suspiciously.

"When we get back to the barracks, you can tell the tribune to send troops out to check it, if you think there's any real danger that someone might be desecrating the place," the third said, and yawned. "By Venus' tits, I'm tired."

"You don't suppose," said the one with the lantern, "that she's still alive, do you?"

"After three days? No food, no water, no air?" the other mocked. "She's dead; no doubt of it."

Brutus pulled his horse back. "Let's go on. But someone should come back and have a look at this. Silius could be attempting to deceive us again. . . ."

"Brutus," complained the one with the lantern. "Tell the tribune. Come on."

"All right." He wheeled his horse about and rejoined the messengers on the road. "The tribune better get men back here before dawn, or whatever is going on will be over." He kicked his horse into a run, and the three were soon gone into the night toward the walls of Rome.

Sanct' Germain leaned against the wall of the tomb, his arms quite suddenly tired. He had thought there would be more time, but he was very much afraid that Brutus' report would bring soldiers to the tomb before first light. Grimly he picked up the pry-bar and set to work on the brick again.

It was more than an hour later that he was able to knock the brick through the wall into the tomb. It made an eerie, drumlike echo as it fell. Immediately Sanct' Germain spoke into the small opening. "Olivia!"

There was a sound, soft and scraping, and Sanct' Germain feared that perhaps she had been chained within the tomb, or mutilated in some way, so that she could not come to the hole. He raised his voice a little. "Olivia!"

This was met with strange silence, and then he heard a few faltering steps. "Sanct' Germain?" Olivia said, as if afraid of the answer.

"Yes. Are you all right?" It was a foolish question, he knew. She had been entombed three days.

"I think so. Yesterday . . . was it yesterday? I felt very

faint, and I think I must have been delirious, or unconscious, or sick, but I'm all right now." Her voice grew stronger. "I am all right, Sanct' Germain."

"Good." There was just room enough for him to stretch his hand through, and he felt her fingers close on his own. They were strong and vital. "Listen to me, Olivia," he said when he had withdrawn his hand again. "It's very late, and there are some soldiers coming here at first light. We will have to work very quickly, or we will be discovered. Neither Justus nor Vespasianus would be pleased to find us here." Something one of the soldiers had said claimed his attention then. Something about Silius deceiving them. For a moment he wondered what the messengers had meant by that, but then the more urgent matter was on his mind. "We can't make too much noise, but we've got to be quick. As soon as we have a big enough hole for you to climb through, we'll be fine. I'm going to put the end of the pry-bar in this hole, and I want you to push it against the bricks from your side while I do the same on mine. When I tell you, push." As he spoke, he carefully put the end of the pry-bar through the hole. "Can you see that?"

There was a tug on the end of the pry-bar. "Yes," she said, sounding quite confident.

"We've got to be as quiet as possible," he reminded her, working with his end of the pry-bar to get it into position.

"I'll remember," she whispered through the hole left by the missing brick.

The first time he lined the tool up and gave his command to press on it, nothing happened. The metal thrummed against the brick, there was a steady grating noise as the pry-bar scraped on the bricks, but nothing else occurred.

"What now?" Olivia asked, not letting her disappointment be heard in her voice.

"We try again," Sanct Germain informed her grimly. He realigned the pry-bar and tested it once. "Good. Now, push!" He leaned against the iron bar with all his strength, and this time they were rewarded by a popping sound from the bricks. "Good!" Sanct' Germain called out. "Very good. Olivia, are you holding the bar at the very end?"

"No," she said. "Should I?"

"Yes. And put all your weight behind it." He was careful with the pry-bar, placing it with care. "Now!"

Two more bricks broke under the impact and Sanct' Germain began to feel encouraged.

"There's another brick loose, I think," Olivia called from inside the tomb. "To your left. There's mortar scattering around it." She sounded very pleased.

"Fine. Good." This time he took his stance so that he could swing more of his weight against the bricks. At the end of this attempt, two more bricks had been dislodged. "Olivia," he called to her softly, "I'm going to change the angle of the bar. I know it will be awkward for you to reach it, but do what you can. If I don't do it this way, the bricks might fall inside the tomb rather than outside. I don't want you to get hurt."

"But if it would be easier another way—" she began.

"I have much more room out here," he said, cutting her objections short. "Do what you can." This time, his end of the pry-bar was pointing downward and it was an easy thing to put all his weight on it, pressing down on the bar until the metal seemed to hum with his effort.

"There're a few bricks loosening," Olivia cried, by way of encouragement. "I can see the mortar starting to crumble."

Sanct' Germain redoubled his efforts. This time the masonry groaned as the pry-bar began to bend. He refused to let up.

A breeze had sprung up at moonset and there were the first gentle rustlings that were the precursors of dawn. The soldiers would be back soon, Sanct' Germain thought, prepared to investigate the disturbance that the messenger Brutus had observed. That could mean imprisonment for them both. Sanct' Germain bore down on the pry-bar with all his might, and the iron bent.

"How are the bricks?" he asked, disheartened.

"Holding," she said unhappily.

"Turn the pry-bar around, so that the part that's curving down is curving into the bricks." It was a last chance, he knew, for he could not dare to remain here at the Silius tomb much longer. He had to get Olivia out. He took the bar in both hands, lifted it, then came down on it with all his might.

There was a strange sound, like distant thunder or the tearing of thick silk. Bricks fell around him, one knocking him on the shoulder as the top part of the bricked-up tomb gave way.

Sanct' Germain moved quickly, reaching in through the

gaping hole. He felt Olivia's hands slip into his own. "Climb!" he whispered fiercely. "Hurry!"

In the distance he could hear a bird singing in the sky, and the rustlings in the long grass around the tombs got louder as the nocturnal animals sought their nests and dens and hiding places. There was a distant sound of trumpets, the changing of guards at the slaves' prison. In very little time there would be people on the Via Appia, coming to Rome for market and pleasure.

"It's awfully high," Olivia said, disquieted. "I don't know if I can—"

"Climb!" The word was quiet, but there was no mistaking the order. He held out his hands to her, and a moment later she took them.

Though it took her no more than a quarter of an hour to struggle out of the tomb, to Sanct' Germain it seemed as if days had passed and that this was the culmination of the effort of months of work.

Olivia's face was scraped, her funereal garments were soiled and her hair hung about her face in lank strings. As she pulled herself through the gaping and ragged hole in the bricks, Sanct' Germain opened his arms to her and caught her as she fell.

Their embrace was long and tender. He held her tightly until she had stopped shaking.

"I thought you weren't coming," she said shamefacedly.

"What? Didn't you know I wouldn't desert you?" He shook her by the shoulders in kindly ire. "When I cherish you so, you can believe that?"

"I know," she said, putting her hands on his shoulders. "But after my trial, when there was no word from you . . ."

"No word?" he repeated, incredulous. "Rogerian left you a basket of fruit. There was a small scrap of paper in the bottom of the basket, and there was a message on it. I was sure that . . . What is it?" he asked, breaking off.

"I was never given the basket of fruit. I was told that no one had left anything for me." She nuzzled her head into the curve of his neck. "Oh, Sanct' Germain, I was frightened. All that time alone in the dark, with the air more and more foul and the walls closing in. It was like being dead."

"Was it?" he asked ironically.

There were more bird calls now, and a second trumpet call sounded from the slaves' prison.

Sanct' Germain broke away from Olivia. "Come. It's nearly morning, and we must be gone. Rogerian is waiting, and there is a ship ready to take us away from here." His hand closed around one of Olivia's. "Did you truly believe I would abandon you?"

She shook her head. "You said you wouldn't. But alone in the dark like that . . ." Her voice almost broke. Her free hand came up to her eyes. "It was so long, and I was frightened," she said, by way of apology.

He kissed her brow. "Well, never mind. You're free now. That's all that counts." He stepped back, tugging at her hand. "You must come with me. There are soldiers not far away, and by the time they arrive, we must be gone."

She accepted this, following him through the tall dry grass toward the Marco tomb, where he had tethered the blue roan.

"Can you ride?" he asked as he steadied the horse.

"I haven't before, but I can learn." She looked at the roan with some apprehension.

"There's no saddle. I've hidden it—it won't seat two, so . . . ," he pointed out. "You'll have to sit astride behind me and hang on. Are you willing?" He had no idea how he would get her away if she said no.

"Of course." The answer was brisk, almost amused. She stood back while Sanct' Germain gathered the reins at the base of the neck and vaulted onto the horse. The roan minced eagerly as Sanct' Germain got his seat. Then he steadied the horse and reached down his hand. "Here. Come up behind me and put your arms around my waist. We have a way to go."

Without a word she took his hand and came up behind him. Her arms went around his waist, her legs dangled behind his. He touched the roan with his booted heels and the horse sprang away toward the Via Appia.

As they reached the first crest of the southward hill, Sanct' Germain glanced back once to see the first pale light catch the bright articulated loricae of a line of mounted soldiers riding out from the Praetorian camp on the east side of Rome. He watched them a moment, checking the roan. Then the horse lengthened his stride and the ridge cut off the sight. Olivia's arms tightened around him as he turned his face toward the south and the inn where Rogerian waited.

Text of authorization from Ragoczy Sanct' Germain Franciscus.

To the Senate and the procurator of the Praetorian Guard:

It has pleased the Emperor to lift the sentence against me and to remove any and all claims against me. He has also asked that I absent myself from Rome, and this I am very willing to do. I have arranged passage for myself, my body slave and a companion, and will depart with haste.

Because there is little time to make formal arrangements, I cannot make full provision for my property. I therefore place my estate under the administration of Constantinus Modestinus Datus, and give him full rights and powers to be exercised at his discretion. A copy of his annual accounting will suffice me and his decisions are to be regarded as my own. I will provide this man with a record of my whereabouts in the unlikely event that my formal agreement is needed in any matter concerning my estate.

I have three requests to make of the state and Constantinus Modestinus Datus. First, that those slaves who have been in my household for more than ten years, upon their request, be given their freedom and be provided with land plots of their own. Deeds to such plots on my own holdings are to be found in my records and C. M. Datus is at liberty to award them as he chooses. At the time of freeing, the slave is to be given two mules and three pigs and the sum of one hundred sesterces. Second, that my private wing of Villa Ragoczy be sealed until such time as I or one bearing my authorization endorsed by my sigil, the eclipse, return to occupy it.

Third, that my ships be regularly inspected and maintained at the highest possible level, and that the captains be given a portion of all moneys in trade, not to exceed fifteen percent of the profit they bring me. All reasonable requests for improvements upon a ship should be granted.

Until such time as I set foot in Rome again, I commend myself to the justice and the wisdom of the Emperor and the Senate.

By my own hand, under seal, in the trust of the Emperor's messenger.

Ragoczy Sanct' Germain Franciscus

23

IT WAS a very select gathering that evening. The Emperor had invited only the most respected Senators and patricians. There were sixteen of them, and for once women had been excluded.

"I don't want them adding more intrigues to our business," Vespasianus had explained when questioned about his decision. "Women do very well, but they wield too much power already. There are some things a man must keep among men."

"Very wise," Cornelius Justus Silius had applauded him that afternoon, and now, in the torchlit dining room, he repeated his praise more lavishly. "Women are as necessary to men as air, and who of us would willingly bar them from every aspect of our lives. Yet what Caesar says is true. Women thrive on intrigue and it is a wise man who does not share his secrets with them."

"You're bitter, Justus." Domitianus laughed nastily.

Justus lowered his head and cursed the Emperor's younger son in his mind. That rough-tongued young cur would ruin everything! When he knew he could present a proper face, he looked up again. "I probably am," he said heavily. "I have tried not to be. Olivia was perverse and her demands such that no man, not the most stalwart man alive, could meet all her desires. She came from a family whose honor was stained, and I should not have let myself believe that the taint had not touched her." He raised his golden cup. "To your wisdom, Caesar." In the next instant he had recklessly drunk all the wine.

Vespasianus nodded, his bright, shrewd eyes studying his effusive guest. "To justice," he responded, chuckling at his own pun.

"To justice," he answered promptly, and drank, to show that he did not believe he deserved the praise the Emperor had implied.

"You've met Lesbia?" Vespasianus asked as he motioned to the slaves to serve the next course.

"Twice now. A lovely, delightful girl, intelligent, charming, a winsome way about her. She is a most pleasant change from . . ." He stopped suddenly, as if embarrassed. "I didn't mean to compare them, Caesar."

"Certainly not," Vespasianus agreed, his mouth strangely stern.

"It was an unwitting offense," Justus added, determined to be conciliating. "If the memory were not so fresh, I would not have said . . ."

"The memory . . ." Vespasianus said in an odd voice as he broke off a piece of bread to scoop up chunks of pork cooked with dates and raisins in gravy from the platter that had just been set before him. He chewed a moment, then added, "Lesbia wanted me to ask you a few questions, since you desire to marry her. That is what you desire, isn't it?"

Domitianus started to speak but was quelled by a look from his father. He turned to Justus and gestured helplessly. Two of the Senators reclining on the silk-covered couches snickered.

"Certainly I desire to marry her, if she and her family are willing." Justus could feel color mounting in his cheeks and he breathed a little faster.

"Would you feel that way if she weren't my niece?" Vespasianus asked without looking at Justus. He dropped a section of bread into the gravy to sop it up. "Well?"

At that moment Justus wanted to attack the Emperor for this abuse. He wanted to see that common face turn purple and black, the tongue protruding as the life was squeezed out of him. It was an effort to keep his tone respectful. "Certainly I would want her. A girl like that is always desirable. But marriage is another matter. I might prefer to have an understanding with her if an important marriage were offered me." He knew that this candor was risky, but at the moment he had no choice. A lie now, a single question from the Emperor, and there would be endless difficulties later. "I'm an ambitious man, I admit. I've never sought to hide that. My three marriages were made largely for political reasons. As were the marriages of all the men here, I wager." He glanced over the couches and chose a Senator younger than himself. "Arminius Aloisius Vulpius Solis there"—he gave the man an understanding nod—"is known to have made a marriage for the advantage of all his family. Who among us has not? Is Vulpius questioned because of this? Certainly not. He is considered a responsible and practical man. He and his wife do not enjoy each other's society, which is unfortunate but not unusual. He makes few demands upon her and she is free to live her life as she sees fit. The law supports the wisdom of this, and all around us there is evidence that such decisions are wise. I can appreciate your concern, Caesar, knowing what you have learned about Atta Olivia Clemens."

"I would not like Lesbia to meet with a similar fate," Vespasianus said quietly as he held out his wine cup to be refilled.

Justus achieved what he hoped was a heroic smile, the smile of a man who has had to endure much. "If she does not have a taste for gladiators and other low-life—"

The Emperor interrupted him. "She tells me that you are attentive and respectful, Justus. She said she would not mind having you for a husband, in a year or so, when the scandal about your wife has died down."

A year? Justus wanted to shout a challenge to this. A year could be too long. He could lose his influence with Vespasianus and his sons in a year. There were other men, as ambitious as he, who would be eager to wed any of the Emperor's nieces. "I . . ." He stopped while he gained control of his voice. "I am not a young man, Caesar. It is hard to wait so long."

"No doubt. Well, perhaps if the talk is stopped, she might change her mind. You are free to persuade her, if you can." He picked up the gravy-soaked bread and popped it into his mouth.

Justus refused to be trapped by this. "What would you suggest, Caesar? I don't want to act in any way contrary to your wishes."

There was a moment of silence while Vespasianus swirled the wine in his cup. "I leave the matter to you, Justus."

"Would you object, then," Justus said through clenched teeth, "if I tried to change her mind. I confess that I am eager to wed her, for reasons as much personal as they are political. What man here," he asked with a nod to the others, "in my position would feel otherwise?" He was relieved when Livianus Septimus Oralen came to his rescue.

"Pay no attention to the scandal, Caesar," said the sixty-eight-year-old Senator in a wheezing voice. "Rome thrives on it. If it is not Justus they speak of, it would be one of us, or you. Gossip is the breath of Rome and scandal her bread. If you listen to half of what you hear, every one of us should be condemned as degenerate criminals."

Vespasianus nodded. "That's true, Septimus. It's lamentably true."

"And if Lesbia likes him . . ." Domitianus began, then said in another voice, "Well, she *does* like him as much as she likes any of them. Why shouldn't she?"

If only he could get Vespasianus to encourage him, Justus thought. Here, in front of these select and powerful men, to have the Emperor acknowledge him as part of his imperial line, a contributor to the dynasty . . . He kept the impatience out of his voice. "I'm glad to hear that. I can understand why she might have reservations about me, especially with the tales my wife told at her trial."

"Ah, yes," Vespasianus said, lingering over the words. "The tales she told."

"Quite incredible," Justus murmured.

"Quite incredible," Vespasianus echoed. "I'm surprised that she did not divorce you."

Justus looked up, startled. "Divorce me?" What was Vespasianus getting at now? he wondered.

"If she thought so ill of you and had the passions you describe," Vespasianus said blandly.

Prefacing his words with a discreet cough, Justus said, "As to that, Caesar, her family was nearly destitute, her one surviving sister lives in Gallia, and there was no one she could turn to."

"Not even to Franciscus? According to what was said, he was her lover." Vespasianus was playing with his wine cup again. The room had fallen silent and for the first time Justus noticed that the slaves had been dismissed. The Emperor reached for the amphora and began slowly to pour.

"He and half of the men at the Circus Maximus," Justus

scoffed. He had not seen the slaves leave, and now he could sense the eyes of his powerful, cynical colleagues upon him.

"Still," Vespasianus said conversationally as if he were wholly unaware of the tension in the room, "I would have thought that in a like situation, with so little advantage to be gained from the alliance, you might have arrived at a settlement with your late wife some time ago."

Justus straightened himself. "There is honor, Caesar. Not many care for it now, but it is real nonetheless. Vicious and ruthless men use the word to mask their evil, but the virtue remains, and proves its worth by its very abuse."

One of the Senators laughed.

"She didn't divorce you, and that puzzled me," Vespasianus remarked, as if they were discussing crops in Lusitania. "I will allow that most marriages are made for political convenience or for inheritance, but in your case, with disgraced in-laws and a sluttish wife whom you admit you could not satisfy . . . It seemed odd."

This time Justus had to clear his throat before he spoke. "I had given her father my word that Olivia would be cared for. You must excuse me, Caesar, but it's painful for me to discuss this. May we speak of other things?"

"I think not," Vespasianus said quietly.

"But . . ." Justus objected before he could stop himself.

"But what, Senator Silius? Surely you want to convince me that the rumors I have heard are nothing more than rumors. People will talk, and I can't stop that. But I can stop my family from suffering further humiliation." He put his wine cup aside and leaned back, propping himself on his elbow.

"I don't know why I should be subjected to this," Justus protested with as much good humor as he could summon up. "If you are truly anxious to avoid gossip, perhaps a more private occasion . . ."

"If you wish to marry into my family," Vespasianus said bluntly, over the shocked objection of his younger son, "you will answer these and any other questions I may put to you now, or in the future. Why didn't Atta Olivia Clemens divorce you?"

Justus swallowed. "I imagine it was advantageous to be married to me."

"Why did she claim that she had asked you to divorce her and you refused, threatening to ruin her reputation if she took you into court?" The questions rattled out like wheels over cobblestones.

"I don't know. I suppose she wanted it to seem that I would not be coerced into supporting her and her lusts." He folded his thick arms and glared at the Emperor.

"Is that what you suppose?" Vespasianus chuckled unpleasantly. "Are you sure it was not because you had threatened to treat her family, and then, when her father and brothers were dead, her mother, with harshness?"

Justus gasped. How had the Emperor come to learn that, or was it only a parroting of Olivia's testimony? "That's ridiculous," he said, and there was a tremor in his voice.

"Was it you who betrayed her father and brothers? Did she make that up as well?" Vespasianus' eyes were glittering now, and the easygoing bonhomie was gone. "Answer me, Cornelius Justus Silius."

"These accusations," Justus said, and made an unsuccessful attempt to laugh them away. "They're distressing, of course. I thought this had been settled." He looked to the other guests for support and found none. "How can you suppose that I would behave as Olivia charged? It's . . . it's absurd; a man of my standing, with so much to lose . . ."

"And so much to gain," said a voice behind him.

It took almost all his will for Justus to control his rage. But his fury was what his enemies wanted, so that he would be discredited and all that he had worked for would be gone. His light brown eyes grew shiny as glass. "It's no secret that I began my action against my late wife after I had spoken to you, Caesar, about the possibility of marrying into your house. Until that time I was reluctant to shame Olivia, as I knew I must if I brought her conduct to public attention. I don't know what I might have done otherwise. I might have kept on in the marriage out of, well, habit as much as anything. I might have sent her away if there had been more gossip than there was. It's difficult to know, since my circumstances were altered. It's true that I welcomed the opportunity that you presented to me. I don't deny it." He tried to read the expression in the Emperor's eyes and failed. "It gave me the necessary impetus to leave a marriage that was not . . . successful."

"Truly?" Vespasianus said sarcastically.

Domitianus hurried to his friend's defense. "We discussed this very point, Father. We agreed that if the rumors about

Domita Silius were true, it would not be wrong for Justus to divorce her and marry Lesbia. You said that the Senate was certain to approve the divorce."

"And they did," Vespasianus agreed. "They'd heard the rumors, too, and read the bill of indictment against her. You're a subtle man, Justus."

"Caesar?" The Emperor's tone had changed again and Justus felt a new apprehension.

"I have a slave," Vespasianus commented to the gathering, "a most unfortunate one. He has lost a hand and his tongue and his manhood, yet there is spirit enough in him that he can still tell a most interesting story." There was a small gong set beside his couch and the Emperor struck it negligently.

Justus was suddenly cold. "What has that slave to do with me?"

"A great deal, it seems." The Emperor lay back on his couch, looking up at the ceiling.

The fear that had gripped Justus still held him, but he told himself that it was foolish. There was no way that Vespasianus could learn of what he had done. Only he knew it, and Sibinus, and Monostades. Sibinus was dead and Monostades was . . . His face froze into the travesty of a smile. Monostades had been emasculated, and his tongue cut out and hand struck off.

Beyond the carved and inlaid door to the banquet hall there were the sounds of feet. The sixteen guests turned toward the door as it was flung open and six Praetorians escorted a ragged, emaciated figure into the room.

There was none of the hauteur that Monostades had displayed before. His body now was bent, his arms and legs like jointed twigs. His hair a year ago had been abundant, glossy, a shining mass of curls. Now it was almost white, with no more shine than chalk. It seemed impossible that a man so maimed, so tortured, could still be alive, for the body was a fleshly catalog of abuses. Only his eyes were vital, sunk deeply and blackly into his face, hot as banked embers.

"Do you recognize this slave?" Vespasianus asked Justus as he got to his feet.

Under the force of the slave's stare, Justus faltered an instant. "N . . . no."

"Perhaps I should not have said 'recognize,' since he is much changed. Do you know who this man is?" Vespasianus sauntered down from the dais and approached the Praetorians. "He can't speak. You would think he could not write. It is amazing the fortitude hate gives us." He turned toward Monostades. "Hold up your left hand if this man was your master." He pointed to Justus.

Monostades' arm shot up with such power that he staggered.

"He's intelligent and determined," Vespasianus informed the gathering. "Deprived of his right hand, he learned to use his left and he found another slave who could read and write who was willing to copy the letters he scratched in the dust. That slave was courageous enough to smuggle that record to freedmen, who saw that it was handed over to the proper authorities. If all the men around me were as honorable as that Jewish slave and this Greek, I would not have to fear for the safety of myself and my heirs."

Justus shook his head slowly. It was not possible that this could happen, not to him, not now, not when he had done so much and come so close. *"No!"* he screamed, and rushed forward, whether toward the Emperor or the slave standing hunched beside him, even Justus did not know.

There was a flurry of movement as two of the Praetorians sprang forward to catch Justus and hold him while he shrieked.

On the dais both Domitianus and Titus were standing, the latter with his lips drawn in a wide tight smile, the former wide-eyed and pale. The Senators and patricians were goggling, whispers passing between them like a sudden rushing wind.

Vespasianus had stepped back. His face had reddened a bit and his breath was quickened. He turned to the centurion. "The Mamertinus Prison. You have your instructions."

The centurion nodded and gave a terse order. It required four of the men to carry Cornelius Justus Silius from the dining hall. His screams and imprecations could be heard until the soldiers dragged him from the palace.

Vespasianus turned to Monostades. "Do you still want to help them obtain his confession?"

The Greek slave made a terrible gargling sound and his left arm shot into the air.

"Very well," Vespasianus said. "You will have your vengeance." He had to turn away from the lambent ferocity that lit those hot, dead eyes.

Text of an order of execution given by the Emperor Titus Flavius Vespasianus.

To the commander and prefect of the Praetorian Guard and the tribune senior of the Mamertinus Prison, greetings:

Regarding the matter of the Senator Cornelius Justus Silius:

The testimony of the slave Monostades has been examined for error and found to be without falsehood, guile or fabrication. The testimony of the gladiators Frontux and Celedes has been examined and been determined to be truthful. The testimony of the slaves of said Senator Cornelius Justus Silius has been examined in all points and has been found to be, in the main, honest and exact.

It is the opinion of the Praetorian procurator that Silius is also responsible for the death of the Armenian Led Arashnur, but there is no way to prove this one way or the other, for the incident was without witnesses and the Senator has adamantly refused to confess to this, as he has refused to confess to his other heinous and criminal acts. The slave Monostades, when questioned, wrote that he believed it was to Silius' advantage that Arashnur died, but has no knowledge himself that the Senator participated in the Armenian's death.

On the suggestion of Monostades, a search was made of the records of said Silius and it appears that the evidence that convicted his father-in-law and brothers-in-law was, at least in part, manufactured by Silius himself for his own benefit, and that their deaths, instead of banishment, were advised by Silius to the Senate and Emperor at that time. Though his motives for this action are still uncertain, it is plain to the throne and the Praetorian Guard that this man used his in-laws in a shameful and degrading way, causing them public disgrace that they, in fact, did not deserve.

The testimony regarding his conduct with his wife is sufficiently barbaric and disgusting that it will not be detailed here. Let it suffice to say that what Atta Olivia Clemens told the Senate was a kindly interpretation of what she had to suffer at the hands of her husband. Her continued and systematic humiliation at the hands of her husband and the men he insisted lie with her is a shame to all of us.

We have yet to determine why Senator Silius broke into the tomb of his wife and removed her body, though it is the opinion of the procurator of the Praetorians that Silius had it in mind to commit further indignities on the body, and that he may have done so before he was detained by the Watch.

From what we can learn of this man, he has taken every opportunity to be of harm to those who trusted him, to betray those he had sworn to protect and to abuse those to whom he owed the greatest respect. Judging from the things we have learned, Silius intended to ingratiate himself with the members of this House, and then use them in the same reprehensible way that he has used so many others before now.

Therefore, regarding the matter of his execution: it would ordinarily be recommended that he be beheaded in privacy, or be allowed to fall on his sword, whichever he felt was more acceptable. But since he was not willing to let others make that choice in his life, we will not grant him that right, either. He will die publicly, with most of Rome looking on, and with the entire enormity of his crimes made public.

The Master of the Bestiarii, a man called Necredes, has informed me that he has recently made the addition to the Circus menagerie of an eagle that has been trained to duplicate the torment of Prometheus, in that he will attack a man in chains until the man's liver be torn out of his body. I have decided that this will be the fate that Cornelius Justus Silius will meet. He will be taken to the Circus Maximus and there he will hang in chains from the spina, where the eagle may tear at his flesh until he is dead. Then his body will be cut into sections, and each buried in a different place, with no marking and no ceremony. His estates will be given to the sister of his wife, who at present resides in Gallia Belgica. This will be to repay in part the great wrong Silius did to his wife's family.

When the remains of Atta Olivia Clemens are found, if they are found, they are to be cremated and put in the mausoleum of her own family, and until the time her urn stands there, a plaque, telling the whole of her suffering, will be placed there.

This from my own hand and with all the weight of my will, on the fourth day of October in the 824th Year of the City.

Caesar Vespasianus

Epilogue

Text of a letter from Atta Olivia Clemens in Rome to Ragoczy Sanct' Germain Franciscus in Panticapaeum on the Palus Maeotis.

To my dearest Sanct' Germain, greetings:

As you can see, I am once again in Rome. How little and yet how much has changed! The Flavian Circus is quite complete, and puts the Circus Maximus to shame. They have much worse crowding in the Flavian Circus. There are Games held much oftener than when you lived here, and the costs are simply tremendous. There's not the skill there used to be; butchery is what is wanted and what is given. The gladiators, if you can call them that, are worse than anything you have ever seen. I was aghast to see how sloppily they fight now, though it is hardly worth the investment to train them to fight any better. The bestiarii are the new heroes, if they can train their animals to be clever in their killing. There is one man with four killer elephants, and they all have learned to impale the men they fight on their tusks. The people love it, but I found it disgusting.

Your lands are in good heart, and I will take advantage of your offer to live at Villa Ragoczy while I remain here. It has been kept very well, though some of the rarer plants in the garden have died because they lacked the proper care. Otherwise, there is a fourth slaves' barracks by the exercise ring, very nicely made, just as you would like.

I had occasion to see my nephew the other day. Imagine, he is a stolid man of almost fifty years. He was gallant enough to say that he was reminded of his mother when he saw me. How strange it felt to look at this man who is my sister's son, and know that he saw me as much younger than he. As you promised me, it is a disquieting experience.

The Emperor, Marcus Ulpius Traianus, is on a building spree. He is determined to leave his mark in Rome if he has to rebuild the city to do it. He would seem to be fairly well-liked, and except for this building mania is as sensible an Emperor as most are. He has been using what little is left of Nero's Golden House to build baths and arches from one end of the city to the other. Oh, Sanct' Germain, do you remember that night long ago when we met in Nero's gardens? Where the lake was, the Flavian Circus now stands, and all that is left of the Golden House is part of the transitoria and the vestibule. How sad that extravagant dream is gone.

There are times when I walk Roman streets that I cannot believe I have been gone for thirty years. The swine market is the same, the vendors are as aggressive as ever, the prices for housing are ridiculous, as they have always been. At those moments it seems I have never left. Then I come to a new building or I hear the music they're playing today, and I know that Rome is not quite the city I was born in. One of the changes that most astounds me is the increase in Nazarene Jews, the ones who call themselves Christians. Half the freedmen clerks you meet are members of that faith. You'd think they were trying to conquer the empire by taking over the bureaucracy.

I have found two young men and a lovely and accomplished young woman to share my bed upon occasion. It pleases me very much to give them love and pleasure. You were right, I think, when you told me I had been gone from Rome too long.

But I miss you, Sanct' Germain. I miss your thoughts and your kindness and your wisdom and your love. One day we shall be together again, and you can tell me of all your journeys through the world. Does the travel help? I wonder. Or does it make your loneliness worse? Yes, I know how much you want to find someone to come to you freely and willingly, without reservation or qualification. Who does not want that kind of love? Yet, if you had insisted that you have only that sort of love, you and I would never have met, and I would have died of despair more than forty years ago. Your generosity saved me then, as it has aided me these last thirty years. I would be less than honest, less than grateful if I did not value above all other things the great gift you gave me when you made me like yourself.

Oh, this may amuse you: there is a new book that's very popular in Rome just now, that the author hints is based on actual circumstances, about a very corrupt and malicious Senator who disgraced his own wife, plotted against the Senate, made fraudulent complaints against others, forced his slaves to manufacture evidence, and was driven to suicide. It's set in Republican days, but the older Senators are shaking their heads and muttering about the story, and a few of them have said the publisher ought to apologize, though no one knows to whom. Justus would be furious if he knew what had been made of him. There, you see? I can write his name and hear him spoken of now without fury or hatred or fear. No, I haven't forgot what he did and possibly never will, but never, as you have told me before, is a long time and it may happen in a century or two that he will be like the names on the tombs of the Via Appia, simple curiosities with a slightly unwholesome reputation.

I visited my tomb, by the way, the one you pulled me out of so many years ago. It has not been repaired and there are thistles growing around it. Quite a number of the people living on the south side of the city have insisted that the place is haunted and that the ghost of the tomb appears there, trailing a bloody shroud and cursing the husband who betrayed her. Splendid stuff, I promise you. I wanted to laugh, in a way, but also I felt a kind of vertigo, as if I stood at the top of a high promontory and saw below in the distance one little speck of light glowing.

Rogerian has been good enough to send me a record of where you plan to be for the next several years. I did not know you had so many estates in Persia. Are you taking that religious dancer with you, or are you hoping to find other interests in Persia? I've grown too used to living with you, and I must remind myself that I can't walk across the courtyard when I want to talk with you. Knowing where you will be is helpful, though Isis only knows how long the letters will take to reach you. Or how long yours will take to reach me. And that, my dearest, dearest friend, is an order. I will have letters from you or I will pack a few chests full of good Roman earth and set out over the world to find you.

The one thing I regret about coming to your life is that the change put an end to our physical intimacy. How sad that we are not able to take sustenance from our own kind. To this moment I can remember the last time you gave me that special rapture—in that horrible cell under the Circus Maximus. It did not seem possible that there would be enough love from those times to last for as long as there is your life in me, but it is true. And, as you have said, there are compensations.

I must leave. There is a state funeral this afternoon and the entire world goes to it. The honored dead was once Master of the Bestiarii at the Circus Maximus. He became a crony of Titus Flavius Domitianus when he was Caesar, was given three estates, took to raising horses and died surrounded by his family. Domitianus married him to one of his cousins, so old Necredes did very well for himself in his seventy-one years. To hear the gossip, Necredes single-handedly contained a gladiatorial rebellion more than thirty years ago, and if he hadn't, Rome would have been sacked by arena slaves. I promise you I will not laugh too loudly.

By my own hand on the seventeenth day of April in the 855th Year of the City, though it hardly seems possible.

Olivia